A CHRISTMAS QUESTION

"Daed didn't believe in coddling us, and he didn't want us to cry. You're so good for Maleah." She ducked her head and peeped up at him shyly from beneath her lashes. "You're good for all of us."

Was this the opening he'd been waiting for?

"And all of you have been good for me too." He hesitated a moment, then added softly, "Especially you."

A slow smile spread across her face, and she stared up at him, starry-eyed.

All the words he'd rehearsed fled. All he wanted to do was sweep her into his arms, but he restrained himself. "I have something to ask you," he stammered.

"The answer is *jah*."

"You don't know the question."

Her expression softened. "I'll always say *jah* to you . . ."

Books by Rachel J. Good

HIS UNEXPECTED AMISH TWINS

HIS PRETEND AMISH BRIDE

HIS ACCIDENTAL AMISH FAMILY

AN UNEXPECTED AMISH PROPOSAL

AN UNEXPECTED AMISH COURTSHIP

AN UNEXPECTED AMISH CHRISTMAS

Published by Kensington Publishing Corp.

An
UNEXPECTED
AMISH
CHRISTMAS

RACHEL J. GOOD

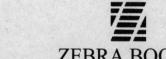

ZEBRA BOOKS
KENSINGTON PUBLISHING CORP.
www.kensingtonbooks.com

Chapter One

Jeremiah Zook gritted his teeth and shifted in his wheelchair. Pain shot through him as he angled his body to make it easier to write. Then, each movement an agony, he forced his fingers around the thick cushioning on the pen. He had to do this. He just had to. Not only for himself, but for her.

Every day, he fought a new battle—a battle for control of his body. And control of his life.

Until he could do basic physical tasks and take care of himself, they wouldn't discharge him from rehab. And he desperately wanted to escape the torture of therapy and the daily reminder of his loss. He longed to be in his own home. To be independent.

Lord, please give me the strength and patience to face this day.

He wanted to pray for the pain to be taken away—not only the physical pain, but the deeper heartache. Nothing could ease his loss but time . . . and concentrating on others rather than himself.

He bent his head over the sheet of paper. Wrestling his hand into position, he formed one laborious letter at a time. The words came out crooked and jagged across the page, but he poured his heart into every sentence.

> *Dear Keturah,*
>
>   *Last week in* Die Botschaft, *I read about the loss of your parents, and I'm praying for you and your sisters.*

Ever since he'd read the story about the four orphaned sisters, they'd been on his mind. The writer had indicated Keturah, age twenty-two, now had custody of her three younger sisters. Jeremiah's own struggles seemed minimal compared with this older sister who'd taken on such a heavy responsibility.

He hesitated. Should he share his own tragedy? Would it help her to know he, too, had suffered?

After a moment, he decided against it. He should focus on comforting her.

> *We're taught to accept everything as God's will and never question Him, but sometimes, you may wonder why. Especially on long, sleepless nights when you lie awake staring at the ceiling and nothing makes sense and your grief feels unbearable.*

Jeremiah had many such nights. He prayed Keturah's would be fewer and less intense than his.

> *You may feel guilty questioning Him, but God understands our pain. Confess your doubts and fears to Him. Ask Him to show you His purpose.*

*And most of all, ask for His comfort. He'll wrap
His arms around you.*

Even when you're racked with guilt and feeling un-
worthy of being alive. Even when you're blaming yourself
for the tragedy. Even when . . .

Once again, Jeremiah pulled himself back to the letter.
He needed to focus on Keturah rather than himself.

*When sorrow overwhelms you, lean on the
Lord. He has promised to wipe every tear from our
eyes. And He is faithful to His promises.*

Jeremiah sent up another prayer for God to ease Keturah's pain. Then he began the laborious task of writing
several Scripture verses that spoke of God's comfort and
healing.

Following another break to rest his cramped fingers,
he wrote a few lines about things that had helped him
cope. What else could he say? Bending his head, he added
one more paragraph.

*In addition to prayer and staying busy, helping
others can take your mind off your grief.
Sometimes it isn't easy to think of anything other
than the loved ones you've lost, but reaching out
and putting your focus on someone else may help
to dull the sharp ache of your loss.*

Jeremiah paused to wriggle his hand. While immersed
in the letter, his own grief had receded. Temporarily.
He'd even forgotten his physical pain. Now it came back
full force.

His muscles refused to cooperate. He'd have to finish this letter another time.

Just before bed, he headed to the desk and penned a few more words.

> *We don't always know God's purpose in sending tragedy our way, but cling to Him during these dark times. He will see you through.*
>
> *I'll be praying for you every day. And I'm sure many around you are doing the same.*

Jeremiah agonized over the closing. *Sincerely* sounded too businesslike, but he couldn't write *Love*. *Many blessings* seemed a bit jarring after a death. Maybe he should just sign his name.

If he did that, she might feel obligated to reply. Better to remain anonymous. But not signing the letter seemed cold and impersonal. Words for the rest of the letter had flowed, despite his aching hands and messy handwriting, but the signature eluded him.

Please, Lord, give me inspiration.

He finally settled on *A Friend Who Cares*.

With a loud sigh, he set down his pen and *rutsched* around to ease the pressure points from sitting so long in one position. Then he reread the letter and corrected a few mistakes. Tomorrow he'd mail it.

But as he set the sealed envelope on his desk, one niggling question remained: Had he written this letter to help Keturah or to ease his own guilt?

Keturah Esch breathed a sigh of relief. She had the house to herself for a few hours. While her aunt took her three sisters to a Stop & Shop after school, Keturah had opted to stay home. She needed some time alone. But her footfalls echoed in the silent house, emphasizing its emptiness. And her loneliness and loss.

She'd held herself together the past few weeks for her sisters' sakes, but she could let her guard down while they were gone. First, though, she needed to pay several bills before the postman collected the mail.

Grimacing at the balance in the checkbook, Keturah wrote out the amounts due and carefully subtracted each one, leaving her with a much lower total. Thank heavens, she'd be going back to work at their family pretzel stand tomorrow. Mrs. Vandenberg, who used to own the Green Valley Farmer's Market and still liked to oversee things, even though she'd turned the management over to Gideon Hartzler, had found staff to fill in for Keturah and her sisters temporarily.

Keturah would be glad for the distraction of making and selling pretzels four days a week. On market days, they stayed so busy, she'd barely have time to think . . . or grieve. But this time, they'd work there without Mamm and Daed.

With a hard shove, Keturah pushed back her chair, along with the tears threatening to overwhelm her. She picked up the bills, shrugged into a jacket, and carried the envelopes to the mailbox. A freezing wind whisked the last of the brown, brittle leaves from the trees. The weather had gotten chillier much earlier than usual this year. Keturah pulled her jacket closer around her.

When she opened the black metal mailbox, it was stuffed so tightly she could barely pull out the mail. And, unfortunately, she'd missed the carrier. After dislodging the thick stack of envelopes, she set the bills inside and raised the red flag to alert the mailman to collect them tomorrow.

She riffled through the pile in her hands. More cards. For some reason, the cards that had consoled her the first few weeks now only stirred sadness. Perhaps because during the early days, she'd moved by rote, but as each day passed, the haze of disbelief cushioning her from the truth slowly dissipated, exposing harsh reality.

Each card she read now shot a sharp arrow of reminder through her heart. Never again would she sit at the table across from Mamm. Never again would the whole family gather while Daed read Scripture. Never again would she and her sisters swelter in the kitchen helping Mamm can vegetables.

Although Keturah tried not to let her thoughts wander too far ahead, she couldn't keep her mind from the upcoming holidays. Thanksgiving dinner without her parents, without Mamm's pumpkin pie. Christmas without Mamm's special presents. Presents that always touched their hearts.

She needed to fill in for her mother and come up with the perfect gift for each of her sisters. But she didn't have her *mamm*'s talent for giving. That was one more area where she'd fail her sisters.

Keturah sat at the table again and lowered her head into her hands. So much responsibility. Her relatives would help, but how would she ever take her mother's place? How could she do her father's job of running the market stand and handling the finances? And how could she be both a parent and a sister to her siblings?

Shaking off her gloom, she opened the cards, trying to distance herself from the pain they brought to the surface by thanking God for the sender. Then she set each card on the mantel.

Next, she turned her attention to the letter. Unfamiliar handwriting scrawled across the envelope. The jagged, spidery script indicated it might have come from one of her youngest sister's second-grade friends, but *neh*, the letter bore Keturah's name and no return address.

Curious, Keturah slit open the envelope and unfolded the yellow paper inside. She traced her finger down the page to the signature, *A Friend Who Cares*.

She crinkled her brow trying to make out the almost illegible words.

Dear Keturah,

The writer seemed to know her. The next lines contradicted that. *Neh*, he—or she—had read of her parents' passing in *Die Botschaft*. Keturah didn't even know the accident had been mentioned, but she hadn't had the time, or the energy, to read the newspaper the past few weeks.

Her eyes followed the crooked trail of letters across the page. She read through the next paragraphs with amazement.

She had no idea if this letter had been sent by a man or a woman, old or young. For some reason, the writing appeared more masculine. But whoever had sent it had intimate knowledge of her grief. The anonymous letter writer understood her burdens, offered support, and lifted her spirits.

She reached the end of the page and ran a finger over the signature again.

How did this person know her so well? As if the letter

writer had stepped off the page and peeked into her mind, the words reflected all of her feelings and doubts. A few tears trickled down her cheeks. Of all the condolences she'd received, this one had reached deep inside and touched her heart.

A knock on the door interrupted her second read-through of the letter. She tucked the page in her pocket to keep it close all day. Swiping at her cheeks with her sleeve, she rose and rushed to the front door.

"Mrs. Vandenberg?"

The elderly woman stood on the stoop, wobbling on her cane. The wind was strong enough to blow her over.

"Come in, come in." Keturah stepped aside so Mrs. Vandenberg could totter across the threshold.

"I'm sure you're busy, dear," the elderly woman said, "but this won't take long. I'm only dropping off the check."

"Check?"

"The money the stand took in over the past few weeks."

Keturah waved it away. "That belongs to the people who worked there while we were . . . um . . ."

Mrs. Vandenberg shook her head. "They've all been paid. The profit belongs to you."

"Are you sure?"

"Absolutely."

Still, Keturah hesitated to take it. When she did, she gasped. "This can't be right."

"Well, people added donations for you girls too, but if it's not enough to tide you over, please let me know. I'd be happy to help out."

"Not enough? It's too much. The church will help if we need it." Keturah tried to hand it back.

Mrs. Vandenberg waved it away. "I'm sure God had a reason for sending this money. Why don't you pray and ask Him what He wants you to use it for?"

"I—I will." Dazed, Keturah slid the check into her pocket next to the letter. Two unexpected blessings in one day.

"I have a favor to ask. Olivia Hoover, one of the Mennonite girls who helped at your stand, is working her way through community college. The market days of Tuesday, Thursday, and Friday fit her Monday and Wednesday class schedule perfectly. She can't work most Saturdays, but your younger sisters will be available then."

Keturah did need someone to help during the day while her two youngest sisters were in school. Maybe that's how God wanted her to use the check. She tried not to think about Olivia replacing Mamm.

"I'll pay Olivia," Mrs. Vandenberg said, "so you won't need to worry about that."

"You don't need to do that."

"She'll only be working three days a week, but I want her to earn enough to cover her tuition. I can't ask you to pay that much. My charity will handle it."

Keturah couldn't believe it. A paid worker to help on the days she and her sister Lilliane needed help. That made three unexpected blessings today. Or was it four?

By the time Mrs. Vandenberg left, Keturah had only enough time to straighten the house and start supper. She pasted on her best imitation of a smile and prepared to meet her sisters' needs.

The paper crinkled in her pocket, and she rested a hand there as if to draw comfort from the words.

A Friend Who Cares. How she needed a friend like that.

Jah, she had relatives and neighbors and her buddy bunch and the Amish community, but Keturah didn't want to burden anyone with her pain.

This letter writer understood the rawness of her misery and had come alongside her to lift her burdens. With no return address, she'd never be able to thank the letter writer. She did the only thing she could.

Lord, please reach out and bless my "friend" with as much comfort as I've received and many times more.

Although she dreaded facing the dark days ahead, she thanked God for Mrs. Vandenberg, the new worker, the check, and the letter—all special signs of His care and comfort.

Chapter Two

After her sisters had gone to bed, Keturah lay awake dreading tomorrow. Her father had always checked the inventory, packed the needed supplies, and taken charge of the finances. She'd been too busy with her own responsibilities to pay attention to how he'd handled everything. Now she had to keep up with that as well as Mamm's jobs, plus serve customers.

How would she do it all?

The paper she'd tucked under her pillow crinkled. Maybe it was foolish to gain so much reassurance from a letter, but she slipped her hand under the pillowcase. She'd read the page so often she'd memorized the words. Touching the folded paper brought back the message.

The sentences floated through her mind, along with one of the verses. She repeated the words of John 14:18, "*I will not leave you comfortless: I will come to you,*" over and over until she drifted off asleep.

When she woke the next morning, the verse stayed with her as she packed everything for the market and helped her younger sisters get ready to go to school. Mamm had always done Maleah's hair, and Maleah bawled while Keturah worked.

"I want Mamm," her little sister choked out.

"I know, *liebchen*." A lump rose in Keturah's throat after she said the endearment Mamm always used. But she remained stoic. Her sister depended on her, so she needed to be strong. But Keturah longed for Mamm too.

"I don't want to go to school today. Let me come to the market with you," Maleah begged.

"I wish you could." Keturah wanted to keep all four of them together, but Maleah and Rose couldn't miss school. "What would Teacher Emily say if you didn't come in?"

"I don't know."

"I do." Rose gave a perfect imitation of Teacher Emily's voice. "Where were you yesterday, Maleah?"

Maleah giggled. "You sound just like her."

Rose put an arm around Maleah. "Besides, I don't want to stay here at the house alone after Keturah and Lilliane leave."

The word *alone* vibrated with a different meaning than it had when both their parents were alive. And Keturah regretted she couldn't take Rose and Maleah with her.

She'll be all right, Rose mouthed over Maleah's head. *I'll take care of her.*

Keturah's heart overflowed with gratitude for Rose, who led Maleah to the kitchen to wash and dry the breakfast dishes. Keturah and Lilliane had to leave, and now, while Maleah was occupied, would be good.

Praying she'd remembered everything they needed, Keturah hustled out to the buggy. This first day back would be the worst. If they made it through, things would only get easier. At least she hoped they would.

When they arrived at the market, Keturah faced another problem. Normally, everyone helped unload supplies, but Daed carried the heaviest containers. She'd have to do it, but she couldn't lift these herself.

"Lilliane," Keturah called, "can you help me?"

A sober expression on her face, sixteen-year-old Lilliane left the smaller items and came over to assist. "Daed always did this." She swallowed hard.

"I know. We'll have to do it from now on."

Her sister blinked back tears. "I miss him."

Keturah's eyes clouded for her sister's pain. Of all the girls, Lilliane had been closest to their *daed*.

Once they'd unloaded everything, she and her sister fell into their regular routine, but without Mamm, their timing was off. Mamm had kept everything moving smoothly. Missing her mother more than ever, Keturah assisted Lilliane in preparing the first few batches of pretzels. By the time they came out of the oven, Olivia had arrived. She washed her hands and hung the pretzels in the warmer.

"*Danke* for helping us, Olivia."

The girl, who at nineteen was three years younger than Keturah and wore a peach dress with a tiny floral print and a lace doily over her bun, gave her a wide smile. "I should be thanking you. Finding a job to fit around my class schedule seemed impossible. But God always provides what we need, doesn't He?"

Keturah nodded and slipped her hand into her pocket to touch the comforting letter. She'd been drawing strength from the verses and the letter writer's encouragement this morning as she faced handling Mamm's and Daed's tasks as well as her own.

Now someone else needed to take over one of Mamm's jobs. "Olivia, could you keep an eye on the pretzel warmer and let Lilliane know what kinds of pretzels are getting low?"

Lilliane, who had her back to the warmer, drew in a sharp breath. "I could switch places with Olivia."

Keturah understood Lilliane didn't want a stranger doing Mamm's job, but it didn't make sense for her sister to move. "How will you get to the water bath?"

"I—I could . . ." Lilliane hung her head. "I couldn't." She picked up a few pretzels and, averting her face, dipped them into the boiling water and baking soda.

"I'm sorry," Keturah whispered.

"It's not your fault," Lilliane mumbled.

Then why does it weigh so heavily on me? Keturah disliked making decisions that added to her sister's heartache. She headed for the counter and faced the long line that streamed in when Gideon opened the market doors.

Many of their regular customers stared sadly at her and offered their condolences. Although Keturah appreciated their kindness, each expression of sympathy pierced her and reminded her of what she so desperately wanted to forget. The line grew longer, and Keturah rushed to fill the orders. Olivia joined her once or twice to help, but then headed back to make more pretzels.

Keturah made her best attempt at a smile as the next customer stared up at the sign. The *Englisch* woman, a stranger, didn't say anything about the deaths, and Keturah sighed in relief.

"I'll take your half-dozen special." She scanned the

sign. "Make it two regular, two cinnamon sugar, and two raisin."

Keturah reached for the tongs, opened the warmer, and stopped. They were all out of raisin. She turned toward her sister. "Are the raisin almost ready?"

Olivia clapped a hand over her lips and glanced at Lilliane.

Lilliane looked stricken. "We just put batches of regular in all the ovens. I'm so sorry," she said to the customer. "It'll be at least twenty minutes until we have raisin ready."

"I can't wait that long." The *Englischer* huffed. "Fine. Give me three plain and three cinnamon sugar."

Ach, they had only two cinnamon sugar, and no plain pretzels they could coat with cinnamon sugar.

Keturah motioned to Olivia and whispered, "Can you take the salt off this pretzel as best you can and roll it in cinnamon sugar?" She took the pretzel from the warmer and set it on a prep tray.

Olivia nodded and turned her back so the customer couldn't see her fixing the pretzel.

Keturah lifted the plain pretzels off the metal rack and slipped them into a bag. "It'll just be a minute for the cinnamon sugar." She took the payment.

The woman sniffed and said to the lady behind her, "I don't understand why so many of the Amish let their children work in their businesses. The adults should at least be here supervising."

Nick, from the candy stand in the market, stood several places behind her in line. He frowned. "These girls just lost their parents. Maybe you should think before you speak."

Spots of red blossomed on the woman's cheeks, and with downcast eyes, she muttered *Sorry.*

Nick had provided a temporary distraction, which gave Olivia time to coat the pretzel in cinnamon sugar. Keturah slid the three pretzels into another bag, handed it to the *Englischer*, and turned her attention to the next customer.

"I heard you don't have raisin, right?" The lady smiled sympathetically. "I'll take two regulars."

Keturah said in a low voice, "Tell Lilliane we're out of unsalted pretzels."

Olivia rushed back with the message while Keturah filled the next few orders. By the time Nick reached the counter, Olivia was loading the warmer with plain and salted pretzels. A trayful of pretzels waited to be rolled in cinnamon sugar, and Lilliane was shaping raisin dough.

"Nick, I'm sorry, but we don't have any raisin pretzels." After Nick had been so kind, she regretted not being able to fill his usual order. "They'll be ready in about fifteen minutes."

"Don't worry about it. I'll take two salted ones for Gideon and Fern. Nettie, Caroline, and Aidan all want cinnamon sugar. I guess I'll have that too."

Keturah couldn't believe Nick was buying a pretzel for his son. For years, Aidan and Nick had made no secret of their disdain for each other. Things must be going better between them. That was a blessing. She'd learned the hard way not to let things come between you and others— especially family members.

As she handed Nick the bag, he lowered his head and

muttered in a gruff voice, "So sorry about your parents. They were good people."

That, too, was out of character for Nick. He usually avoided sentiment of any kind. His shuffling feet revealed his discomfort.

"*Danke* for that and for helping with the *Englischer*." Keturah wouldn't have added Nick's final sentence to the lady, but for him, that had been only a mild reprimand. Nick seemed to be softening.

"Nick, wait!" Gina Rossi, the owner of Plant Paradise, the stand next to the pretzel stand, waved a stack of papers. "I can talk to both of you at once."

She handed a flyer to each of them and gave an apologetic smile to the *Englischer* behind Nick. "All of you might be interested in this. Pass it on." Gina handed a small stack of pages to the lady.

Keturah glanced down at hers. *Christmas Extravaganza: A Raffle to Feed the Homeless*. The word *Christmas* pierced her. The last thing she wanted was to be reminded of the upcoming holidays without her parents.

"Christmas?" Nick practically screeched. "Back in my day, we didn't start talking about it until after Thanksgiving. Now it starts at Halloween."

"I know it's early," Gina soothed, "but I wanted to give all of you stand owners a chance to decorate your stands."

"We don't decorate." Lilliane's flat comment came from behind Keturah.

"Oh." Gina's face fell, but only for a second. "Could you come up with something? It's for charity. People will vote for their favorite decorations."

"I'm not into decorations either." Nick headed off.

"Please, Nick?" Gina called after him. When he didn't answer, she turned to Keturah. "You'll try, won't you?"

Keturah hated to disappoint her. "I'll try." Behind her, Lilliane huffed, and Keturah knew exactly what her sister was thinking: *Daed would never agree to do this.*

She folded the flyer and slid it under the cash box. But she couldn't get away from the Christmas Extravaganza. All the stand owners in line chattered about the upcoming event.

The day proved to be unusually busy. Keturah suspected people were making an excuse to pay a sympathy call and perhaps to help support her and her sisters by buying pretzels. The increase in customers, though, made it impossible to keep up.

Several times, they completely ran out of pretzels, and people had to wait while they mixed up dough, shaped, and baked the pretzels. They lost some customers, mainly new buyers who didn't want to wait that long.

During a rare five-minute break, Keturah headed back to talk to her sister. "Lilliane, I know it won't be easy"—Keturah kept her voice low so Olivia couldn't overhear—"but can you keep an eye on the pretzel warmer to be sure we don't run out?"

"I'll try. I never had to do that before. Mamm always—" Lilliane bit her lip.

"I know." Keturah squeezed her eyes shut to get her own feelings under control. Mamm had anticipated what they needed before they ran low. She'd study the lines to gauge what people wanted, and she remembered all the regular customers and prepared for them before they arrived. Lilliane had her back to the warmer, so she'd never had to pay attention to that.

Olivia moved closer. "I'm sorry we ran out of pretzels. It was my fault."

She looked so guilty, Keturah wanted to reassure her. "It takes time to learn what regular customers order and plan ahead. And we've had so many more customers than usual."

"I noticed that." Olivia looked over and checked the warmer. "I'll try harder."

Stocking the warmer took more than noticing what pretzels were running low. One customer could wipe out almost full racks if they ordered half a dozen or a dozen. Knowing who might request that many and spotting them ahead of time helped to avoid long waits or lost customers.

Lilliane took a tray of pretzels from the oven, and Olivia hurried over to roll them in butter and then dip them in cinnamon sugar.

"Keep a few plain ones out," Lilliane called to Olivia before lowering her voice. "She's a nice girl, but she's so slow with shaping the pretzels, and she doesn't know how to plan ahead."

Keturah took a deep breath. "I hope she'll catch on. But running the stand won't be easy, because Mamm did so much." She met her sister's teary eyes. "We need to do all of her jobs. And Daed's too."

But one of Daed's roles Keturah refused to fill. Keeping track of everyone's mistakes and scolding them.

One of the cheerful Mennonite volunteers tapped on the doorjamb before entering Jeremiah's room. "Here's your copy of *Die Botschaft*." She anchored the newspaper to the book holder on his desk to keep it in place. "And I brought new stationery and more stamps."

"*Danke.*"

The rehab center had a small gift shop that sold essential items and snacks. Jeremiah had requested the paper and stamps for his daily project—sending sympathy letters to people mentioned in *Die Botschaft* who'd lost loved ones. He could have purchased cards, but he felt led to write letters. When he mentioned his idea to the physical therapist, Bert had been overjoyed and brought Jeremiah paper and a special pen he could grip. They'd also installed the page turner on his desk.

He'd already used up all the paper the therapist had given him, so he'd ordered more packs of stationery with envelopes and postage from the gift shop.

As the volunteer bustled away, Jeremiah rolled over to the desk and read the front page of the newspaper. Then he slid his hand into the loop of the page turner and brushed the bumpy rubber tip across the lower part of the page. He blew out a frustrated breath as he struggled to slide the right-hand page of the thick newspaper inch by inch to the other side to reveal the next two-page spread. Even turning the pages of the newspaper served as therapy.

A month ago, he would have flipped through *Die Botschaft* searching for letters and news that interested him. Now, because it took so long to turn each page, he read every paragraph.

Jeremiah tried not to complain. He had nothing better to do with his time. Going from an active life on a dairy farm to being wheelchair bound left him with pent-up energy and no way to use it. Before, he'd always delighted in helping others. Now he needed help with everyday tasks. Writing letters kept his mind occupied and let him practice his muscle movements.

A letter in the paper caught his eye. It was signed *Keturah Esch*. Eagerly, he bent over the desk to devour every word.

To: A Friend Who Cares

Your letter touched me and eased my grief. You seem to know all the struggles I've been going through. I have a few questions I want to ask you. If you don't mind, I'd like to send you a message. Could you reply with your address if you're willing to exchange letters?

Thank you for your kindness,
Keturah Esch

Jeremiah smiled. She'd addressed it to *A Friend Who Cares*. Although he hadn't wanted to make her feel obligated to reply, his heart leapt that she'd taken the time to respond. And she'd asked to send him a letter.

Eagerly, he reached for his stationery and strapped on the thick, cushioned pen.

Dear Keturah,

I'm so glad my letter helped. I felt God calling me to send a message to you.

He'd written to many others who had suffered losses, but for some reason, she'd stayed on his mind.

I'd be glad to exchange letters.

But . . .

Jeremiah dropped his pen. He didn't want to give her the address of the rehab center. If she saw that, she might pity him. He already had enough people who felt sorry for him. It would be nice to communicate with someone who didn't know about his accident.

Zeke Lantz should be here soon to discuss finalizing the sale of the farm. Maybe he'd be willing to collect and deliver Keturah's letter. If she replied again. Jeremiah hoped she would. Maybe she'd write more than once.

"Hey, Jeremiah." Zeke startled Jeremiah.

He'd been so engrossed in his thoughts, he hadn't heard Zeke entering. Jeremiah slid the letter under the newspaper. He wasn't sure why he did that.

Jeremiah wheeled around to face his friend. "Hi, Zeke. Good to see you."

Zeke motioned toward the desk. "You reading the newspaper?"

"*Jah*, not much else to do in here besides exercises."

"I'm sorry."

The last thing Jeremiah wanted was pity. "I'm sure God has a reason for this. So, you ready to take over the farm?"

"I am." Zeke held out a paper. "Daed and I came up with some figures for the repayment. Will this work for you?"

When Jeremiah didn't immediately reach out for the proposal, Zeke apologized again and set it on the desk. Jeremiah gritted his teeth. He wasn't helpless. Sometimes it took a while for his intentions to reach his muscles. But he let it go. His friend was only trying to be kind.

Jeremiah turned toward the desk and skimmed over the numbers. He planned to accept whatever Zeke proposed. Zeke's family didn't have a lot of money, and Jeremiah had more than enough to take care of his own needs. He'd received a huge payment for his mother's wrongful death from the drunk driver's father—a wealthy and prominent politician covering up his son's indiscretions. The politician had not only paid off the newspapers to keep them from printing the story, he'd also paid all of Jeremiah's medical and rehab bills. Jeremiah assumed the man had done the same for the other Amish families whose relatives had died or been hurt in the van crash.

He hadn't been in any condition to protest the payment after the accident. And when the pain and fuzziness in his brain finally subsided, he didn't understand why the politician insisted on paying a wrongful death benefit, because Amish families accepted accidents as God's will. They'd never sue the man or talk to the newspaper about his son. And no amount of money could ever replace Mamm. But Jeremiah planned to use it to help Zeke.

"This looks fine." He nodded in Zeke's direction. "Let's go with it."

Zeke's eyes lit up. "You sure it's enough money every month?"

"*Jah*. It's more than enough." Jeremiah had already had plenty in the bank with what he'd earned running the dairy farm. The politician's payments had only added to that. Zeke's monthly installments would easily cover Jeremiah's bills even once he finished rehab, and they would allow Zeke to make a decent profit too.

"*Danke*." Zeke's shoulders straightened as if a huge boulder had rolled off them. "I appreciate you letting me take over the farm like this."

The joy and relief shining in Zeke's eyes more than repaid Jeremiah for the loss of his dairy farm. His voice husky, Jeremiah thanked Zeke for what he'd done. "You deserve the business after the way you stepped in and took care of everything following my accident. I know the farm is in good hands."

"I only did what any neighbor would do." Zeke started toward the door but then stopped. "By the way, Snickers, the puppy my brother Isaac raised, is now in training to become a service dog. Isaac thinks Snickers would be perfect for you because she's learning to pick up objects and pull wheelchairs and things like that."

"*Hmm.* I hadn't thought about having a service dog." Before the accident, Jeremiah had seen Snickers at church and youth activities because, while Isaac was raising the puppy, he took Snickers everywhere he went. "Maybe I can talk to him about that."

"*Gut.* Isaac would love it if Snickers came to church on Sundays again."

Jeremiah had no idea how long it'd be before he'd be out of here and ready for a service dog, but he nodded. "Isaac and Snickers spent so much time together. I'm sure he must miss his puppy."

"He does. But he still has the kennel, and he'll raise another service dog when he has more time."

Once Jeremiah got out of here, he might enjoy having some companionship. He'd have long, lonely hours to fill.

Zeke glanced up at the large clock on the wall. "I'd better go, but if there's anything else I can do for you, just ask."

"Actually, there is. I may have a letter coming. Could I have it sent to the farm?"

"Of course. I'll bring it over here when it arrives."

"Would it be all right if it's addressed to you?" Jeremiah wanted to keep his identity a secret.

Zeke stared at him, confused. "Me?"

"The mailman knows I don't live there anymore. And I, um, wrote to someone—this girl—who lost her parents. I read about the funeral in *Die Botschaft*. She wants to write back to ask me some questions. I thought maybe . . ." Jeremiah trailed off. This seemed underhanded.

"I'm fine with you using the address. You still own the farm until I've paid it off. But is it right to give her the wrong name?"

"I don't want to give her the rehab address. What if she feels sorry for me and tries to visit? And I don't want her to pity me."

A guilty expression on his face, Zeke shuffled his feet. "I see. But what if she looks me up instead?"

"You did say you wanted to find someone to date." Jeremiah couldn't help teasing.

For years, Zeke had lamented that the girls at church he wanted to date always found other boyfriends because he was too shy to ask any of them out. Zeke had become even more downcast since his two younger brothers had both fallen in love.

"Look at it this way," Jeremiah pointed out, "you won't even have to approach her. She'll come to you."

Zeke shot him a quelling glance. "I didn't tell you about my troubles so you could throw them back at me."

"Sorry."

"It's all right." Zeke sighed. "I'm glad you're getting your old spirit back. For a while there, I worried if—"

"That's all over now." Jeremiah cut Zeke off before he started describing his concerns about Jeremiah's concussion and temporary amnesia. Thank the Lord, he'd come out of that.

Zeke cleared his throat and gave Jeremiah a suspicious glance. "How old is she, anyway? Do you even know?"

"Twenty-two. The perfect age for you."

"And you."

Pinching his lips together, Jeremiah tried not to let the pain show on his face, but he wasn't sure he'd succeeded. What girl would want to be with him? *Neh*, he'd never marry. The accident had taken that possibility from him. He couldn't burden a wife with caring for all his needs.

As if sensing his comment had been hurtful, Zeke laid a hand on Jeremiah's shoulder. "You never know. You might find a girlfriend before I do."

Jeremiah snorted. "I doubt it."

"God can work miracles."

"For both of us." Jeremiah's snappy comeback covered up his doubts. "Oh, and if the girl does look you up, you should know she has three younger sisters to care for. I felt sorry for her. That's what made me write in the first place."

"Poor girl."

"And don't worry, Zeke, I'll have her address the letter to *The Lantzes* but make it clear that's not my last name." With a twinkle in his eye, Jeremiah added, "Unless you want her to address it to you."

Zeke laughed as he headed for the door. "Well, if she's twenty-two, I might not mind meeting her." Then he sobered. "Actually, I couldn't support this girl and her sisters. I have enough to handle with buying the farm and helping my family. I guess God knows I'm not ready for marriage yet."

As the door clicked shut behind Zeke, Jeremiah squeezed his eyes shut. *And God knows I'm not ready for marriage either. And most likely never will be.*

Chapter Three

"Hey, Jeremiah!" The cheery Mennonite woman who served as program coordinator for the rehab center stuck her head into Jeremiah's partially open door soon after Zeke left. "Feel like going out after lunch?"

He released a long, slow sigh. He'd been turning down Arlene's requests since he'd arrived here, but she never stopped trying to include him in the group outings.

After years of hard work as a dairy farmer, he'd been proud of his strength and stamina. Now, confined to a wheelchair, he disliked being dependent on others. Perhaps once he could walk—if he ever walked again—he'd brave the outside world. At the moment, he'd rather hide.

"We're headed to the Green Valley Farmer's Market and Auction for a few hours. You could get some treats, maybe buy something at the auction."

"I don't think so, *danke*."

"If you change your mind, we're meeting in the lobby at twelve thirty. It would do you good to practice getting around in some real-life situations."

As Arlene walked away, Jeremiah shook his head. Not now. Not for a long while.

He headed back to his desk. Letter writing took his mind off his troubles. So did reading that sweet note in the newspaper from Keturah. He skimmed it several times. Every time he reread the heading, *To A Friend Who Cares*, his heart leapt a little.

When he'd sent his letter, he'd had no idea he'd make an impact on anyone's life. Or that she'd want to ask him questions. Something about being needed made his heart swell with gratitude.

Now he had an address, so he could finish his reply.

> *I'm in the process of selling my dairy farm,*
> *but if you address your letter to "The Lantzes,"*
> *they'll see that I get it.*

He added Zeke's address. Once again, he signed the letter the way he had before.

As Jeremiah addressed the envelope, he paused. *Green Valley Farmer's Market*. Keturah Esch worked there. The newspaper article about the family's loss had mentioned that the girls worked at the pretzel stand their parents had owned.

Maybe he could meet Keturah and introduce himself as the letter writer. Or maybe not. What was the point of not telling her he was at rehab if he arrived in a wheelchair? As he'd told Zeke, the last thing Jeremiah wanted was for Keturah to pity him. But he could meet her without telling her who he was.

Long before twelve thirty, Jeremiah wheeled himself into the lobby. He didn't want to miss the van. He turned his letter over to the young lady at the desk.

"I'll see that it goes out with the afternoon mail," she promised.

Jeremiah wished he could hand the envelope to Keturah, but it would arrive in her mailbox soon enough, and he had her reply to look forward to. Even more exciting, he'd get to see her today. It would be fun to put a face with the name and to picture her as he answered her questions.

"I'm so glad you're coming, Jeremiah." Arlene beamed as if she'd won a huge prize. "What made you change your mind?"

He shrugged. If he shared his real reason, she'd pester him for details.

Jeremiah supposed activity coordinators needed to be enthusiastic and outgoing, and Arlene certainly fit that profile. Unfortunately, he'd also learned she loved to chatter about everyone's news, so he wanted to keep his goal of meeting Keturah secret.

Now that he'd decided to visit the market, he chafed at the delay as Arlene made sure they had enough spaces in the vans to accommodate everyone. Finally, they set off, and for the first time in a long time, Jeremiah's spirits lifted.

When Keturah and her sisters arrived on Saturday morning, Christmas carols played through the overhead speakers, and glittery stars and snowflakes hung from the ceiling in every aisle.

Maleah stared at the decorations. "It looks so pretty."

"I agree with Nick about not decorating for this early." Lilliane moved closer to Keturah. "People forget the real meaning behind Christmas. And I hope you didn't mean it when you told Gina we'd participate."

"I'm sure Mamm wouldn't have minded us draping pine garlands around the counter."

"I don't think that's what Gina has in mind."

Maybe not, but she'd have to accept that most Amish stands wouldn't do much decorating.

The morning flew by with no time for breaks, and by early afternoon, the lines hadn't slowed.

Keturah reached into the warmer for an unsalted pretzel, and an empty rack stared back at her. *Not again!*

She'd hoped with it being Saturday and with all four of her sisters here, they'd do a better job of keeping things stocked. But this was the fifth time they'd run out. Keeping her back to the customers, she sighed. "Lilliane, how long until the next batch comes out?"

Her sister stared at her with an *I'm-so-sorry* expression before she glanced at the timer on the top oven. "About five minutes for this top batch."

"I'm so sorry," Keturah said to the Amish man in the wheelchair. "The plain pretzels won't be ready for about five minutes."

"That's no problem. I can wait." He moved his chair to one side and seemed to be studying her closely as she waited on the next two customers.

"Maleah," Keturah called, "can you move the pretzels up to the top rack so the next batch can go in?"

Mamm had always watched to be sure the older pretzels hung on the top racks and the newly baked ones went on the lower rods. That way none of them remained in the warmer too long and went stale.

Speaking of stale, Keturah plucked out a cinnamon

sugar one that seemed a bit too firm. Maleah edged in beside her, took the tongs, and lifted the few remaining pretzels to the highest row.

Once her sister had finished, Keturah pulled out the drawer holding the water container. She lifted the metal panel covering it, removed the basin inside, and handed it to Maleah. "Fill this with water, please, and put it back in the warmer."

One more thing Mamm had overseen.

Keturah turned to get the next customer's order and collided with Maleah, who'd raced back with the basin. Water splashed everywhere. Most of it puddled on the floor or soaked into Keturah's dress and work apron.

"*Ach!*" Maleah's eyes welled with tears. "I didn't mean to do that." Her whole body shook, and she peeked over her shoulder as if to gauge Daed's reaction.

"He's not here," Keturah reminded her. Maleah had always been exuberant and accident-prone, so Daed had scolded her multiple times every day for carelessness.

Like Maleah, Keturah glanced toward the back of the stand, where Daed usually stood, watching them with eagle eyes for the slightest infractions. She'd just re-minded her sister their father wasn't here, yet her whole body stiffened, waiting for his criticism.

Keturah could feel Daed's eyes boring into her back. His constant admonition rang in her ears: *Never neglect the customers.* "I have to get back to the counter. Refill the water basin again and set it in the warmer. Carefully this time. Then mop up the water so nobody slips."

Her chin quivering, Maleah nodded and headed back to the sink.

"May I help you?" Keturah asked the *Englischer* who'd been waiting. Behind him, a line of people stared at her.

"Is everything okay?" The *Englischer*'s brows scrunched together as he examined her and Maleah.

How did Keturah answer that? If she said, *Of course*, it would be a fib. Nothing was all right. Their entire world had been turned upside down, and she had no idea if they'd ever be able to flip it right-side-up.

She didn't want to ignore him. Even saying *We'll be fine* seemed like a lie. Keturah had no idea if things would ever be normal again.

The young man in the wheelchair sent her a sympathetic smile. He seemed to see straight into her soul, and his eyes flashed a message: *You'll get through this.*

She wished she could believe it, but she did draw some strength from his reassurance.

As her sister clattered the panel back into place over the basin and slid the drawer shut, Keturah tried to focus on the *Englischer*. "I'm sorry. What kind of pretzel did you want?"

"I didn't order yet," he said, "but I'm not in a hurry. If you need to clean up a bit, I can wait."

Do I look that bad? Keturah had gotten little sleep last night, and she'd been rushing around all morning handling one minor crisis after another.

His nod toward the spill made it clear he meant the floor and not her. How kind he was to think of that. Maleah hurried over with the mop and pushed it back and forth over the wet floor.

"*Danke*," Keturah told him, "but my sister will take care of it."

"I think—" His eyebrows rose.

"Watch out!" the man in the wheelchair called.

Crash!

Keturah spun around. The end of the mop had upended the metal tray of pretzels Lilliane had just taken from the oven. The tray hit the floor, and pretzels flew everywhere.

"*Ach*, Maleah." Lilliane bit down on her lip as if holding back tears.

Maleah hung her head. "I'm sorry."

Setting a hand on Maleah's shoulder, Keturah gave it a gentle squeeze. "It was an accident. The customers who are waiting for these pretzels can wait until the next batch finishes baking. That'll only be a few more minutes, won't it?"

Lilliane's distressed eyes met Keturah's. "The only batches we have in the oven now are raisin. They'll be done in eight minutes. Rose is making more regulars, but she just started shaping them."

Keturah pressed her fingertips to her forehead, where a sharp pain kept shooting from one temple to the other. Eight minutes for raisin, plus ten more to bake. "Twenty minutes for all kinds except raisin." And the poor man in the wheelchair had to wait all this time for the third batch.

"I heard that, and it's all right," he assured her. "Take care of the other customers first. I can wait for the batch after that."

She vowed not to delay his order that long. Her cheeks burning, she turned and apologized to the *Englischer*.

"What kinds do you have now?" he asked, his eyes filled with sympathy.

"Three salted, one cinnamon sugar."

"I'll wait for a raisin one, if you don't mind. Eight minutes, right?" When she nodded, he stepped aside so the woman behind him could reach the counter.

One Amish man sat on her left, and one *Englisch* man stood on the right, both acting as if they didn't mind the time it might take to fill their orders. Gratitude filled Keturah at their kindness.

The next two customers in line took the last of the pretzels in the warmer. They seemed to be trying to make life easier for Keturah by choosing pretzels she already had. She whispered a prayer of thanks. Often when they ran out of pretzels, customers sighed or got testy. Then Daed's lips thinned, and Keturah waited for the explosion.

For once, that didn't happen. It took a moment for the silence to register. The only thing filling the air were strains of "White Christmas." Daed was not about to pounce. He wasn't here and never would be. Still, Keturah couldn't let go of her edginess. Then a wave of sadness swept over her, along with fear at the heavy yoke of responsibility she had to shoulder—the full weight of the business and caring for her sisters.

She rubbed her forehead again. The headache that had started earlier shot new sparks of pain behind her eyes. How would she get through the rest of the day?

She had no time to analyze her problems now, but tonight after the market closed, they'd have to figure out how to keep the right flavors and amounts of pretzels stocked. Lilliane worked frantically to mix up more dough to pass to Rose, who twisted it into the praying-hands shapes. Maleah kept her head bowed as she gathered soggy pretzels and dropped them in the trash. The hem of her dress dragged in the puddle she still hadn't finished mopping.

Since they were out of pretzels, Keturah returned to the

line in front of the stand. "It'll be a short wait for raisin pretzels. Or about ten minutes for other kinds."

Some people grumbled and walked away, but most people, especially other owners of market stands, stayed in place. Once Maleah hung the raisin pretzels in the warmer, the crowd waved for those who wanted raisin to move to the head of the line, and everyone else plodded forward slowly as Keturah gave those customers their orders.

She appreciated their patience. If only she didn't have to deal with everyone's sympathy. They only meant to show how much they cared, but each mention of her parents jolted Keturah from her cocoon of forgetfulness into the reality of her loss.

Ten minutes ago, Jeremiah had wheeled himself into the line that snaked around the Esches' stand and down the aisle, although he was more interested in Keturah than in the pretzels. The four girls with strawberry blonde hair looked enough alike that he could tell they were sisters. He'd picked out Keturah as the oldest one immediately. Dressed in black, which emphasized her lovely porcelain complexion, she seemed to be rushing everywhere at once.

The closer he got, though, the more he sensed the heaviness of her sorrow. Despite the cheery Christmas music blasting around her, her whirlwind activity, and her cheery greetings to each customer, he read the sadness in her eyes. But the set of her jaw revealed a determination to hold herself together.

After he gave his order and her cheeks reddened when she realized they were all out of plain, Jeremiah regretted not choosing one of the other pretzels from the warmer instead of embarrassing her. But having to wait gave him a chance to observe all four girls as they worked.

While he'd sat watching, he'd spotted the impending accident. He cried out, but not in time to stop the collision of the mop and the tray that sent pretzels cascading everywhere. That mishap, along with running out of pretzels, had added to Keturah's frantic motion. She rushed back to help her little sister dip the pretzels in butter, sprinkle salt, or add cinnamon sugar.

The peaceful notes of "Silent Night" drifted around them. Jeremiah prayed God would touch Keturah with the calm and beauty of the song.

When she headed back to the counter, she spotted him and clapped a hand over her mouth. Her cheeks flushed an attractive shade of pink. "*Ach*, I forgot to keep a plain pretzel out for you."

"I have nowhere to go." Now his face flamed. "I mean we won't be leaving yet, so I can sit here until another batch is ready. I really don't mind." That was true. He'd been engrossed in watching her work.

"*Neh*, I can't ask you to do that."

"You didn't ask me. I offered. It's no trouble at all." What could he say to ease her mind? "I enjoy watching how you make pretzels."

Her face turned a deeper shade of red—almost the color of cranberries. "I'm sure we gave you quite a comedy show. We aren't normally this disorganized."

"I understand, and I'm sorry for your loss."

Her startled eyes met his, and he drowned in their velvety green depths. But they also questioned how a stranger knew about her parents. By speaking the words weighing heavily on his heart, he'd given himself away.

To cover up how much he knew, he motioned to her and her sister's black dresses and her two younger sisters' gray ones. "You're in mourning."

"*Jah*, we lost both of our parents a few weeks ago."

"You're doing quite well under the circumstances. In addition to dealing with sadness, you have to fill in for your missing parents."

Teardrops trembled on the tips of her lashes as she nodded, making him want to sweep her into his arms. He scolded himself. Whatever had caused that odd thought to flit through his mind?

"Mamm kept things running smoothly," she said in a broken voice. "She kept track of all the details. I don't have her skills."

"But how can you do her job when you're so busy with customers?" He gestured toward the line, and it dawned on him that he'd been holding her up. "Can I help with anything?"

The words popped out of his mouth before he realized his question sounded foolish. He'd always been the first to help neighbors and friends, but that had been before the accident.

Keturah stared at him, surprise written all over her face. "I, um, don't think so. *Danke* for offering."

The pain in her eyes lessened a little, but Jeremiah's face heated again as she scrutinized him. Why had he called attention to himself? He squirmed. No doubt she wondered what he could possibly do.

At that moment, a tiny spark inside him burst into flames. He had to get out of this wheelchair and walk again. He had to regain the use of his fingers. Whatever it took, he'd never stop working until he accomplished that. He wanted to reclaim his freedom, his ability to do all the things he used to do.

Please, Lord, give me the strength to reach these goals.

A still, small voice spoke to his heart. *I have put you here, and this is where I want you. You don't need to be able to walk to assist others.*

More than anything, Jeremiah wanted to help Keturah. But how?

Chapter Four

Keturah fought back tears at his thoughtful offer. "That's kind of you." She hoped she hadn't hurt his feelings by saying *neh*. She added an excuse she hoped might explain her hesitancy. "We're still trying to figure out what needs to be done without our parents here to help."

"I understand. I'm sure it's not easy."

"That's true. Nobody can replace our *mamm*."

"You seem to be doing a *gut* job of filling in for her."

Keturah shook her head. "*Neh*, I made so many mistakes today."

Maybe she shouldn't have mentioned that or talked about her parents. Because this young man wore Amish clothes and had such kind eyes, Keturah had made a major blunder by confiding in a customer. Good thing Daed wasn't around to hear. After all his lectures on keeping family business private, he'd have been upset.

Admiration shone in the man's eyes. "I've only been here for a short while, but you've made few mistakes with all you have to do."

Though his words soothed her dented pride, Daed had

warned her so often about *hochmut* that guilt squeezed all the pleasure from the young man's flattery.

Flustered, Keturah turned to the line of people who'd been waiting for the pretzels she'd put in the warmer. She filled order after order while her mind remained on the man waiting for his plain pretzel.

"Maleah," Keturah whispered to her sister, who was helping Rose form pretzels, "as soon as the next batch comes out, bring me two plain ones right away." She'd make sure the poor gentleman, sitting patiently in his wheelchair, would get his pretzels first.

"Here they are," Maleah called twelve minutes later.

Keturah spun around as her sister rushed from the back table, holding two fresh pretzels in her tongs. Just before Maleah reached the counter, she hit the still-damp floor and slid, her arms pinwheeling in the air.

"*Ach!*" Keturah reached out and grabbed her sister's arms to steady her. They couldn't lose these pretzels too.

Maleah fought for her balance, but she managed to keep her grip on the pretzels. The force of the impact pushed Keturah into the counter. She'd have a bruise on her back, but at least she'd saved her sister from a fall. And she'd rescued the pretzels.

Well, almost . . . They'd been squished by the tongs.

The man in the wheelchair laughed as Keturah took the tongs from her sister and examined the now-mangled pretzels. "It's all right," he called to them. "I'll buy both of those."

"*Neh*, I'll get you fresh ones." Keturah couldn't do that to him. Not after he'd waited all this time.

"I'm serious about taking those pretzels. They're fine."

"Absolutely not." She held the tongs out to Maleah.

"Let's break these into pieces and turn them into samples."
Usually, they set out a small container with sample flavors.
Another thing Keturah had forgotten to do this morning.

But Maleah didn't reach for the tongs. She didn't even
lift her head to look at Keturah. "I messed up everything
today," Maleah choked out.

"It's all right," Keturah tried to reassure her, but her
sister only shook her head.

Maleah had always been accident-prone, but today
she'd tripled her usual quota. Perhaps her eyes were as
blurry with unshed tears as Keturah's. Or maybe in her
grief, Maleah was more careless.

Either way, Keturah wanted to calm her sister, who'd
covered her face with her hands. Putting a hand on
Maleah's shoulder, Keturah whispered, "Why don't you
go to the restroom for a bit?" Maybe having a good cry
would help.

"You don't want me around to mess things up."

Heedless of the line waiting behind her, Keturah drew
Maleah into her arms. "You know that's not true. I thought
you might want some time alone without everyone watching."

Maleah's head snapped up, and she stared at the customers. "They're all looking at me," she wailed. Then she
whirled around and fled from the stand.

Keturah wanted to yell after her sister to be careful, but
that might only embarrass her more. Turning back to face
the counter, Keturah rubbed her back and tried to banish
pictures of Daed scolding both of them for making such
a commotion in front of the customers. She put on a neutral expression and prayed her cheeks didn't appear as
hot as they felt. Tugging the corner of her lips up slightly,

Keturah managed a semi-welcoming smile. The hand clasping the tongs dangled at her side.

"I'll be right with everyone." *As soon as I can calm my racing mind and think straight.* "And you'll be first," she promised the man who waited off to the side.

His brow wrinkled in concern. "Do you need to go after your sister?"

Keturah glanced toward the aisle where Maleah had dashed off. Keturah desperately wanted to chase after her sister and comfort her. But Daed had always trained them to hide their feelings and pay attention to the customers' needs first.

"I—I . . ."

His eyes bored into her as if he could see into her soul. "You do."

How perceptive he was!

He smiled at her with compassion. "Go ahead. If you trust me, I can help in the stand while you're gone."

She wouldn't be gone long, but could she trust this stranger?

Keturah glanced at him and then in the direction where her sister had disappeared. He could sense her distress. She seemed torn. And fearful of turning the stand over to someone she didn't know.

"Don't worry. I've sold things before." He tipped his head toward the aisle her sister had darted down. "Besides, your sister needs you."

"I can't—" She looked where he'd indicated. "I don't even know your name."

"I'm Jeremiah. Jeremiah Zook."

She looked as if she was weakening, so he headed around the end of the stand to the waist-high, swinging wooden door.

After a rapid glance at her two sisters and then toward the restrooms partway down the aisle, she gave in. "I won't be gone long. It'll only take me a few minutes to bring Maleah back. Lilliane, can you help Jeremiah keep an eye on things?"

Lilliane's eyes widened as Keturah held the door open wide enough for Jeremiah to wheel through.

"Help yourself to as many pretzels as you want," Keturah called over her shoulder as she jogged toward the restroom.

As Jeremiah awkwardly maneuvered to the counter, it struck him that he might not be able to hold or riffle through dollar bills to count out change. Could he even squeeze the tongs to lift pretzels off the racks?

As soon as he saw Keturah's distressed face, though, he had to do something, anything to help her. He'd forgotten about his fingers. For a few moments, he'd even forgotten about the wheelchair.

Now, all his limitations overwhelmed him. He struggled to fit through the narrow spaces. Although he was tall, he could barely see over the counter. And he'd need to roll backward to open the pretzel warmer, which had been placed for a standing person.

Lord, please help me to do what needs to be done.

He opened his eyes and smiled at the people in line. Then he focused his attention on the first customer. "How can I help you?"

"I'll take two raisin pretzels." The Amish man examined

Jeremiah before glancing toward Keturah's retreating figure. "That was kind of you."

"I'm not so sure about that. I doubt I'll be a good substitute for her."

"Just do your best."

The words rang in Jeremiah's ears as an answer to his prayer. He'd do whatever he could. The thought gave him courage until he tried to wrestle the warmer door open.

Then his clumsy fingers refused to close around the tongs. He needed to pick them up in two hands and use the strength of his palms to squeeze the tips shut. That didn't give him the finesse to grasp pretzels without squashing them. Instead, he managed to maneuver one end of the tongs through a pretzel loop and lift the pretzel enough so it slid down that side of the tongs.

One hurdle overcome. He glowed with accomplishment. Except that led to another difficulty. Without his page turner, he had no way to pick up a paper bag. Using the back of his hand, he rubbed the top bag, hoping to separate it from the pile. Once he did, though, he had no idea how he'd hold it and get it open.

As he struggled to move the bag, two hands reached over the counter, picked up the whole stack, and set it on the counter. "Let us help."

The Amish man turned to the crowd behind him. "Everyone, hold out your own bags." He demonstrated by taking the top bag, shaking it open, and thrusting it under the two pretzels Jeremiah had carried over.

Jeremiah's triumph soon turned to frustration. Getting the pretzels out had been easy compared to flipping the tongs upside down and wriggling them until the pretzels slid into the narrow opening.

Once again, the Amish man came to his rescue. "I'm guessing it isn't easy to make change." He turned around and announced, "Exact change if you have it."

Jeremiah breathed a sigh of relief. That would make things easier. *Thank You, Lord.*

The man rooted through his wallet and sighed. "I don't have exact change. I'm sorry." Then he brightened and pulled out a ten-dollar bill. "Tell you what. Keep the change for the girls."

Jeremiah's hands might be clumsy, but his brain was nimble. "I can total up the amount of donations in my head. That's no problem."

With a smile, the man handed over the money. "I'd need to jot it down. Keeping track of numbers in my head isn't one of my skills, but God has blessed you if you can do it."

Jeremiah found it hard to believe that anyone would have trouble adding numbers. He suspected the man was only trying to make him feel better about all his blunders. "*Danke* for all your help."

"No problem." The man turned to face the people behind him. "If you don't have exact change, you could always leave the rest as a donation for the girls."

"Good idea," several people murmured.

Because Jeremiah worked so slowly, the line grew longer and snaked around the corner into another aisle. If only he could move faster. But he muddled through each step in the process. By the time Keturah returned, she'd have twice as many customers as she'd had when she left.

He hoped she wouldn't think he hadn't waited on anyone while she was gone. It sure looked like he hadn't.

Keturah left the stand and hurried along the aisle to the restrooms. She couldn't believe she'd let a stranger take her place in the stand, but something about Jeremiah's eyes—the calmness, the surety, the caring—reassured her he could be trusted.

She had little choice. She needed to get Maleah back as quickly as possible. When Keturah pushed open the door, the scents of pine and peppermint overwhelmed her. Blinking lights pulsed on the walls. A miniature Christmas tree had been squeezed into a back corner. Evergreen garlands had been draped over all the mirrors. Gina really wanted to immerse customers in the Christmas experience.

But Keturah's eyes went to Maleah. She'd buried her face in a wad of paper towels. Sobs shook her whole body.

"*Ach*, Maleah." Keturah drew her close. "It's all right. We all make mistakes."

"You don't." The paper towels muffled her sister's words.

"*Jah*, I do. Didn't you see how I forgot that man's pretzel order three times?"

Maleah peeked one eye out from the brown wad. "You did?"

"And I forgot to watch the warmer, so we ran out of pretzels."

"That was Lilliane's job," Maleah pointed out.

"We both should have been watching."

"Mamm"—Maleah swallowed hard—"never let us run

out." She drew in a shuddery breath. "If Daed saw me today, he'd be upset."

Many times during the morning, Keturah had had that same thought. Their father wanted everything to go perfectly. He believed not paying attention led to mistakes. And today, they'd proved him right.

"I—I shouldn't say that about him."

Keturah had experienced the same guilt. "Daed wanted us to do our best."

"I know. And I never did what he wanted."

"You tried."

"I thought mean and angry thoughts about Daed that night when . . . when . . ." Maleah sobbed so hard she could barely get out the words. "I spilled my milk."

Keturah knew exactly what her sister meant. She shared her sister's pain. No one wanted to have their final memories of a parent be negative ones. Keturah pushed down her own remorse to concentrate on comforting her sister.

Another sob broke free from Maleah's chest. "It's all my fault they died."

"*Neh*, Maleah, *neh*." Keturah hugged her little sister. "It's not your fault. What happened was God's will."

Maleah tossed her head back and forth, denying Keturah's words. "Before Daed left, he said"—Maleah broke into another spate of weeping—"he'd deal with me later. That night, I—I wished I'd never have to see him again."

"*Ach, liebchen.*" Wrapping her arms more tightly about her sister, Keturah swallowed back her tears and her guilt. "Don't blame yourself. Are you more powerful than God?"

Her sister stared at her, openmouthed.

"Only God has the power to take someone's life. You do not."

"But I was bad."

"When we think or do things we shouldn't, we ask forgiveness."

"I can't," Maleah wailed. "Daed's not here." She buried her face in Keturah's apron, and her voice came out muffled. "I—I didn't even want to. Not then."

Once again, Keturah could sympathize with Maleah's pain. She had her own struggles with guilt and forgiveness. "You can ask the Lord to give you a forgiving spirit. And confess your anger to Him, and ask Him to forgive you." Keturah spoke as much to herself as to her sister.

The restroom door creaked open, and a woman peeked in. She took one look at Maleah's tearstained face and scurried away.

The stand. Keturah straightened up, still cuddling her sister close. She'd forgotten all about the stand, about the long lines of customers, about leaving Jeremiah alone to handle her responsibilities.

She squatted so she'd be at eye level with Maleah. Then she tilted her sister's chin up until their gazes met. "We need to get back to work. I left a stranger in the stand to take my place."

The shame on Maleah's face turned to curiosity. "A stranger?" She sniffled. Then she stared at Keturah. "A stranger is selling our pretzels? Why did you do that?"

"Because we're not there working." She didn't want to heap additional guilt on her sister. Keturah only wanted to remind her of their duty.

Maleah swiped her sleeve across her eyes and pulled her shoulders up. "We should go back."

Keturah's heart swelled with pride. Maleah had been orphaned at only seven years old, and she'd been fighting a huge spiritual battle. Despite that, she soldiered on, willing to do what needed to be done.

After a quick side-hug, Keturah took her sister's hand, and they rushed toward the stand to the thumping rhythm of "Feliz Navidad."

Chapter Five

When Keturah and her little sister reached the pretzel stand, Jeremiah turned relieved eyes in their direction. "Thank the Lord you're back."

Earlier, when he'd sat outside the stand, Jeremiah had admired Keturah's smooth, rapid movements as she'd gone from one job to the next, but now that he'd had a chance to sit behind the counter, he had a whole new appreciation for her work.

He pantomimed wiping the back of his hand across his forehead, although he had to admit, it wasn't all for show. Spending a few minutes in charge had exhausted him. "I don't know how you keep up with all this."

"It's not always easy, and I'm sure it was even harder for you."

Was she referring to his wheelchair? Jeremiah bristled. He disliked being pitied.

She must have read the irritation in his expression, because she quickly added, "I mean because you aren't used to the job."

"There is a lot to learn." Even more so for him. He didn't mention his struggles with lifting out pretzels and aiming them into the bags the customers held out. Or his inability to count money. That had actually turned out to be a blessing in disguise. He'd collected some money for the family.

Keturah gazed at the long line.

"I know it doesn't look like it, but I did wait on customers. I'm just not as skilled at it as you are."

She laughed. "You'd be faster if you'd been doing it for fifteen years the way I have. I started working at the counter when I was my little sister's age."

Jeremiah nodded. He'd read in *Die Botschaft* that the youngest, Maleah, was seven. Lilliane, the other sister dressed in black, was sixteen, and Rose, who was a foot shorter and wore a gray dress, was twelve. Facts like that stuck in his memory. Or maybe his concern for Keturah had made all the information more important.

Keturah startled him from his musing. "*Danke* for your help. It was so kind of you."

"I'm glad I could help. Is M—" Jeremiah stopped abruptly. Keturah might wonder how he knew Maleah's name. He didn't want her to think he'd been stalking her. Even if he sort of had. "Um, is your little sister all right?"

"She's much better. This has been hard on her. Maleah's too young to be an orphan." Keturah bit her lip and stared off into the distance. "I guess we all are."

"It isn't easy to lose both parents when you're so young." At age six, he'd lost his *daed*. That had left a gaping hole, but he'd still had Mamm. Poor Maleah had to deal with missing both of her parents at once. So did Keturah and her other sisters.

Jeremiah understood that pain. He was an orphan too.

Keturah's eyes glazed over with sorrow. Jeremiah regretted reminding her of the harsh reality. "I'll get out of your way now." He moved to one side so she could reach the counter.

The space was tight, and she brushed against him as she slid by. His pulse accelerated. The laundry-fresh scent of her dress, the softness of her skin against his cheek, the rustle of her skirt as she passed. Jeremiah closed his eyes and swallowed.

How he longed to entwine his fingers with a woman's, to stare into her love-filled eyes. All around him, the aroma of baking dough and the sweet scent of sugar added to his daydreams—sitting beside his wife at the supper table, eating her delicious cooking, sharing about their days.

He crashed back to reality with a thud. The impossibility of that fantasy made his body and soul ache.

"Are you all right?" Keturah stared at him in alarm as she passed, holding a white bakery bag.

Her nearness was intoxicating. "I-I'm fine. I didn't mean to worry you. I was just enjoying the smell of pretzels baking."

"Did you get yours?" Her searching glance demanded the truth.

"*Neh*, but I'm not hungry for pretzels anymore." Right now, he was hungry for something totally different. Something he could never have. A wife. A home. A family.

She turned her back for a minute as she handed the bag to her customer and made change with ease. So unlike his fumbling.

He needed to leave. She must be wondering why he remained sitting here. His only answer would be that she mesmerized him with her graceful movements. Reluctantly, he pivoted his chair and headed for the low swinging door.

As he reached the exit, she called, "Wait, Jeremiah."

His name on her lips strummed a chord deep inside him that matched the soaring notes of "O Holy Night." He turned his head to see what she wanted.

She held up a finger to the next customer. "I'll be right with you." Then she headed to the pretzel warmer.

Before he could stop her, she slid three plain pretzels into a bag and darted over to hand them to him. She'd done it all in one fluid motion.

Holding the bag out to him, Keturah gave him a heart-stopping smile. Not the *I'm-attracted-to-you* smile he dreamed of, but an *I'm-so-grateful-to-you* smile. It didn't matter. He'd take whatever kind she gave him. Any smile from her felt like a gift.

He'd been so busy analyzing her smile, he hadn't reached for the bag. She must have decided he couldn't lift his arms. She lowered the bag gently into his lap.

"Anytime you're in the market, come by for a pretzel."

Jeremiah eagerly accepted that invitation. He'd have Arlene put him on her list for the weekly farmer's market visits. "I will."

"And they'll always be free."

He didn't respond, but he had no intention of accepting charity. She'd more than repaid him with her smile and her generosity.

Keturah wished she could do more to thank Jeremiah. He'd been so kind to help out. He had no idea how much it had allayed her anxiety to be able to go after Maleah.

As if she sensed Keturah's thoughts, Maleah gave her a watery smile before going back to rolling pretzels in butter and sprinkling them with salt.

The two of them would need to talk more tonight, but Keturah hoped she'd calmed some of her sister's fears. Maybe all four sisters should discuss their feelings. Daed had always discouraged that, but he was no longer around, and Keturah didn't want any of them laboring under heavy loads of guilt. Losing both parents had been hard enough.

The verses from the letter she'd received went through her mind, comforting her. Perhaps she could read part of the letter to her sisters. They should all keep God's promises in mind.

Keturah took six pretzels from Maleah's tray to take to a customer who'd ordered a dozen. "Maleah, tell Rose we need more plain pretzels. I'll be taking most of these."

As Keturah turned toward the counter, Jeremiah caught her eye. He sat just outside the swinging door, watching her. That made her nervous. Maybe she'd made a mistake in letting him into the stand.

She shook her head. *Neh*, he seemed nice and thoughtful. But one of her *daed*'s warnings flitted through her head: *Even killers can look harmless. You never know what's in someone's heart.*

He'd often cautioned her about being too softhearted and trusting, especially with people she didn't know. Keturah always expected the best of others. Daed usually had to know someone well before he decided whether or not to consider the person reliable and honorable.

"I'm sorry," Jeremiah said. "I didn't mean to interrupt you."

He appeared nervous. She'd drawn her brows together,

trying to decide if she should follow Daed's advice. Maybe he assumed she'd been frowning at him.

"I forgot to tell you. Some people left donations. Sixty-two dollars and twenty-six cents of the money in the cash drawer is for you and your sisters."

Keturah shook her head. "People don't have to donate money to us. We'll be all right." At least, she assumed they would. They could count on the church to take care of them if they needed it. And several of their relatives would help out, not to mention the generous check from Mrs. Vandenberg.

He lowered his head and stared at his hands resting on the pretzel bag in his lap. "They may have done it to help me out."

"What?" She furrowed her brow. Did he mean they tried to pay him for his time? "I'm happy to give you money for working here."

"*Neh*, that's not what I meant. It's just that"—his voice dropped almost to a whisper—"they felt sorry for me because my hands don't work well." Red crept up his neck and splashed across his face. "I had trouble making change, and they said to keep it for you and your sisters."

She hadn't meant to embarrass him. "Well, then, I have two things to thank you for—taking over the stand and collecting donations. I should have given you more pretzels and a salary."

"The pretzels were more than enough. You don't owe me anything. I'm sure you don't expect people to pay when you help them out."

Keturah sighed inwardly. Now she'd insulted him. Why couldn't she get things right around him? She'd hurt his feelings, embarrassed him, and even worried he might be untrustworthy. "You're right. I don't expect to get paid for helping people. I just wanted to give you something to let you know how much I appreciate what you did."

"It was such a little thing. I doubt I was here for twenty minutes."

"But it means a lot to me. And to Maleah."

"Glad I could help. I'll let you go. I can see you're busy."

"*Danke* again, and stop by any time. Only next time, not to work." She flashed him a grateful smile and hurried over to wait on her customers.

Usually, they had several lulls every day when they could snatch time for a lunch break or to catch up, but today they hadn't had a single rest. Most stand owners and many friends from church or the neighborhood had stopped by.

Although she probably shouldn't wish for a slowdown in business, it would be nice to have an occasional break. Jeremiah had given her a brief opportunity today. Keturah thanked God she hadn't followed Daed's advice about being friendly to strangers. Maleah might still be crying in the bathroom, and Keturah would have been frantic with worry. Jeremiah's help had been heaven-sent.

He seemed so nice. She hoped he'd take her up on the invitation to visit them again. It would be nice if he came when they weren't this busy so they could have a chance to chat and get to know each other. His understanding and giving spirit had drawn her in. And she could surely use a friend like that right now.

That made her smile. She had other friends, but Jeremiah seemed to sense what she was going through without her saying a word. Like her other new friend. *A Friend*

Who Cares. It would be special to have two friends like that.

Shortly before the market closed at four, Jeremiah went out to the parking lot to meet the vans. Originally, he'd planned to talk to Isaac Lantz about getting Snickers as a service dog and had only planned to take a quick peek at Keturah before going outside to the auction building to find Isaac. Instead, he'd gotten caught up in her life. And he longed to be even more involved.

Now that he'd met her, he might be able to better answer her questions, if she replied to the letter he'd mailed today. He couldn't wait to receive her response. Just thinking about it made him smile.

"Well, you sure look cheerful." Arlene interrupted the reruns of his time with Keturah and his future imaginings. "What did you do?" Without waiting for an answer, she pointed to the bag he cradled on his lap.

Most of the heat had seeped out as he'd sat outside in the chilly weather. He hadn't even noticed.

"Well, I can see you bought some pretzels. I love their pretzels, don't you?" She threw back her head and laughed. "That was a silly question. I'm sure you wouldn't have bought a bagful if you didn't."

Jeremiah should offer a pretzel to Arlene. Ordinarily, he wouldn't hesitate, but because Keturah had given them to him, he wanted to keep them for himself. As he ate them, he could relive being in the stand with her.

He mentally shook himself. He didn't need a pretzel to remind himself of the way she'd brushed past him. The way she practically danced as she moved. The way her smile lit a fire inside him.

Arlene snapped her fingers in front of his face. "You planning to get in the van?"

Jeremiah started. While he'd been woolgathering, other people from the center had already gotten in, and the van driver had lowered the platform. They'd all fixed their eyes on him as he sat, lost in a world where he was alone with Keturah.

For what must have been the tenth time that afternoon, his cheeks flamed. And not from the blaze Keturah had kindled.

"*Ach*, sorry." He ducked his head and pretended to re-arrange the bag he held. Then he positioned himself on the platform, and Arlene secured the chair.

Just before the van door slid closed, Jeremiah used a napkin to pull out a pretzel. He handed it to Arlene. "I hope you like plain."

"Why, thank you." The broad smile she bestowed on him made it seem as if he'd given her a box of priceless jewels. "Any of their pretzels are delicious. I'll enjoy this one."

Others in the van eyed Arlene's treat with hungry looks. Jeremiah couldn't hoard two more pretzels. Not when others wanted a taste.

As much as he wanted to keep them for himself, he couldn't be that selfish. "Would anyone like to share part of a pretzel?"

Four people indicated they wanted some, so he tore the remaining napkins in half and broke each pretzel in two. Once they'd been distributed, he only had a tiny piece that had fallen into the bag. He nibbled on that to make it last as long as he could. His stomach rumbled for more, and Jeremiah vowed he'd go back the following week. And this time, he hoped to get more than a scrap. But as much as he tried to convince himself differently, pretzels weren't the real reason he planned to return.

Keturah sank into her chair at the supper table. What a day! Running out of pretzels . . . accidents . . . Maleah's breakdown . . . and a perfect stranger coming to her rescue. If she hadn't been flooded with customers, she'd have tried to find out more about him. And she'd have thanked him properly.

She bowed her head for the silent prayer and tacked on an extra *danke*.

Lord, I didn't get to find out who he is or why he was there, but thank You for sending him to help us. He arrived at the perfect time.

When she lifted her head, she took several bites of ham and bean soup to calm her growling stomach. She'd missed lunch today, and so had her sisters. "You all worked so hard today, but we need to figure out how to keep up with all the extra business and have the right flavors of pretzels ready before we need them."

Lilliane's eyes filled with tears. "I'm sorry. I tried to remember to check, but . . ."

Although her words trailed off, they all knew what she'd been about to say: *But it's so hard without Mamm.*

"I understand. I'm not blaming you." Keturah hadn't meant to sound accusing. "It's a lot to keep track of when we were so busy." And Lilliane had her back to the warmer.

Rose gave Lilliane a sympathetic glance. "I think we

had three or four times more sales today than we've ever had before. You really didn't have time to pay attention to anything else."

"*Jah*, that's true." Keturah smiled at Rose. "That's the point I wanted to bring up. If we stay this busy, we'll need to make some changes to how we do things."

Lilliane sighed. "I don't see how we can keep up with everything Mamm did"—she gulped—"and serve four times as many customers. I wish . . ." Her cheeks colored. "Well, that man, Jeremiah, who helped today made me wish we had someone else to work in the stand. Olivia is a help on the weekdays, but it's not enough."

Keturah hadn't thought about hiring anyone else. She'd been thinking about ways to streamline their process. But Jeremiah had been a godsend. He'd arrived at their moment of need.

"He was really nice." Rose's lips twisted in sympathy. "I felt so sorry for him, though."

Lilliane nodded. "Watching him struggling to lift the pretzels made me so sad. I wanted to rush over and offer to help."

"Me too," Rose agreed. "But he found a clever way to do it."

"What do you mean?" Keturah looked from Rose to Lilliane.

"He must not have much control over his fingers," Lilliane explained. "He couldn't squeeze the tongs closed."

"But he didn't let that stop him," Rose chimed in. "He put one side of the tongs into a pretzel loop and lifted it so the pretzel slid down that side of the tongs. I wanted to cheer when he did that."

"*Jah*. I never would have thought of it." Lilliane smiled

at the memory. "Then he rolled over to the counter with the tongs held high, like he'd won a prize."

"He should have gotten a prize." Rose sounded indignant.

"I agree." Lilliane set down her spoon and leaned forward. "He deserved many prizes. He had so many problems to overcome."

Rose nodded. "Remember how he scrabbled so hard to get a bag? He almost managed it using the back of his hand." She pressed a fist against her mouth as if she were watching Jeremiah.

"I'm glad he had Gideon from Hartzler's Chicken Barbecue as a customer. Gideon came up with a solution."

"Gideon picked up the stack of bags, set it on the counter, and told people to open and hold out their own bags." Rose giggled. "Even that grumpy old lady did it. I thought she was going to fuss, but she didn't."

Lilliane's lips curved up. "That was funny. She didn't lose her sour expression, though."

"*Neh*, she never does." Rose hung her head. "I'm sorry. I shouldn't have said that."

"*Jah*, you should have." Her eyes fierce, Maleah looked up for the first time since the meal started. "It's the truth. And you should always tell the truth."

Rose made a little face. "But I shouldn't judge people."

Maleah sighed. "Did you judge me?"

Leaning over, Rose put an arm around Maleah's shoulders. "Of course not. We're all sad about—" She bit her lip.

"And we all have accidents." Keturah wanted to relieve her sister's guilt. Daed's impatience with Maleah's many accidents had made her so tense and nervous, she made even more mistakes.

"Remember when I dropped the bowl of pudding on the floor," Rose said with her arm still around Maleah, "and the glass shattered? It took hours to clean up the chocolate splatters."

Maleah's half-hearted giggle reminded them of Rose's punishment. They all sobered.

Lilliane changed the subject. "Neither of you got to see Gideon's solution to Jeremiah's money problems."

"Money problems?" Keturah echoed faintly. She'd left a stranger in charge of the money. Jeremiah could have robbed them blind. *Neh*, it appeared her sisters had kept a close eye on him.

Rose's eyebrows shot up at Keturah's tone. "He didn't steal money or anything like that."

Lilliane cut in to explain. "You know how we said he couldn't separate the bags? He couldn't lift out the dollar bills."

What? Jeremiah had mentioned his hands when she'd returned, but Keturah had no idea he'd struggled so much. What had she been thinking to agree to him working in the stand? And what had he been thinking to volunteer?

"I'm sorry. I didn't know."

"It worked out fine." Lilliane lifted her spoon to her lips.

Rose stopped spreading butter on her bread and waved her knife in the air as if pointing.

"Careful," Keturah cautioned. "You don't want to cut Maleah." They'd had enough accidents for one day.

"Sorry." Rose set down her knife and gestured with her buttered bread. "Gideon suggested people pay with exact change or donate the extra so Jeremiah wouldn't have to make change."

Keturah wished she'd been there to put a stop to it. She hoped people didn't think she'd suggested it.

Red-faced, Lilliane squirmed in her chair. "I was going to ask them not to do that, but I didn't want to embarrass Jeremiah. Or Gideon. He was the one who suggested it."

"Jeremiah was trying so hard," Rose said with her mouth full. "It wouldn't have been nice to hurt his feelings. Besides, it all worked out in the end."

Jah, it had. Keturah had been able to calm Maleah. And customers got waited on while she was gone. But now that she'd heard about Jeremiah's efforts, she wished she'd given him more than three pretzels. He'd refused pay, but she hoped he'd come to the market again so she could thank him properly.

Chapter Six

Keturah rose early on Sunday morning, grateful they'd have the day off from the market. After church, she needed to finish her conversation with her sisters. And she needed to discuss how to participate in the Christmas Extravaganza. Last night at supper, they'd gotten sidetracked talking about Jeremiah.

He'd been quite a hit with Lilliane and Maleah. For someone who'd worked for such a short time, he'd made a big impression. Keturah, too, had appreciated him. But she wondered why he'd offered to help when he'd struggled to do most of the jobs. Either he hadn't known what he was getting into or he was very courageous.

Lord, please help me to figure out some solutions to make the business easier to handle. And help me to find a way to satisfy Gina's request without Englisch *Christmas decorations.*

She had one idea for the stand to run by her sisters. Keturah dressed and headed downstairs to fix breakfast. An ache started deep in her chest, as it did every morning when she entered the kitchen before dawn. Each time she neared the stove, she pictured Mamm standing there. All the girls helped with meals, but Mamm formed the center pin they revolved around.

Now they'd lost their cog, and their world had spun out of control.

"What do you need help with?" The lost look in Lilliane's eyes showed that she, too, missed Mamm's usual presence in the kitchen.

"I planned to make a breakfast casserole." On market days, they had a hurried breakfast so they could get to the stand by six to make the pretzels, but they had more time today, because church didn't start until eight.

"Good idea. I'll fry the bacon and onion."

Maleah stumbled into the kitchen, still in her nightgown and with her hair tangled.

"Breakfast won't be ready for almost an hour." Keturah set aside the baking pan she'd been greasing. "Why don't you go up and get dressed? Then I'll comb you while the casserole cooks."

Maleah sniffled. "By myself?"

Rose entered the kitchen. "I'll help you dress." She took Maleah's hand and led her upstairs.

Maleah could certainly dress herself, but she'd started acting helpless since . . . Daed would have insisted on Maleah standing on her own two feet, but he wasn't here now. Keturah couldn't decide if Daed was right or if they should coddle Maleah for now. Something inside Keturah nudged her to wait awhile before pushing her sister to be independent. Maybe after a few weeks, she'd encourage Maleah to do more for herself. But Keturah and her other sisters had taken on many other responsibilities by the time they were seven.

Lord, please show me what to do.

When they were all seated around the table, Maleah's face scrubbed and shiny, her hair pulled back into a neat bob, Keturah announced, "After we pray, we need to talk about the business. I meant to do that last night at supper."

Lilliane shot her an apologetic look. "I guess we sidetracked you by talking about Jeremiah, didn't we?"

"That's all right. I needed to know more about him. I learned my lesson. Always ask strangers who offer to help if they know how to do the job."

Maleah snorted. She turned it into a snicker and then a belly laugh.

Rose and Lilliane soon joined her. Keturah hadn't meant to be funny, but the laughter became contagious. They all needed to release some pent-up feelings. When tears started, Keturah edged into the discussion she'd meant to have last night.

With a quick swipe at her eyes, she set her fork on her plate. "I thought maybe we could make a lot of the dough tomorrow and refrigerate it for Tuesday or even freeze some for the rest of the week."

Lilliane gasped. "But Daed . . ." She choked off the rest of her comment.

"*Jah*, Daed said we should make the dough in front of the customers so they'd know it was fresh. But—"

Rose finished Keturah's sentence. "If we made the dough ahead, Lilliane would have more time to keep an eye on the warmer."

Lilliane turned to Keturah. "Do you think people will notice and go elsewhere for pretzels?"

"I don't know about that. But I do know we lost quite a few customers because we didn't have the right kinds of pretzels in the warmer."

Elbows planted on the table, Rose rested her chin in her hands and appeared lost in thought. "Don't you think people would want to have their favorite flavors ready right away, instead of waiting for us to make fresh ones?"

"I don't know." Lilliane hesitated. "I'd feel guilty. Daed wouldn't want us to use refrigerated dough."

The truth of that statement added to Keturah's uncertainty.

"Besides," Lilliane added, "it doesn't take that long to mix up batches of dough. Only five or ten minutes each."

"If we continue to have as many customers as we did yesterday, you'd need to mix up four times as many batches as you usually do. I don't see how you can make any more dough. And on the weekdays, you'll only have Olivia to help. She can't shape pretzels as fast as Rose."

"And we didn't get to eat lunch," Maleah pointed out.

"I don't know." Lilliane squeezed her eyes shut. "Children should honor their parents. Even though Daed isn't here, I'd feel like I'm disobeying."

Keturah tapped her lower lip. She hadn't counted on Lilliane's rejection. The last thing she wanted to do was make her sister go against her conscience. It did feel a bit like they'd be betraying Daed. But what alternatives did they have?

Rose, ever the peacemaker, looked from Keturah to Lilliane and back again. "What about trying it tomorrow? We could see how it works and see if we get any complaints."

Lilliane looked about to burst into tears.

"One day, Lilliane?" Rose pleaded. "Just for one day?"

"You'll still make dough too." Keturah disliked her wheedling tone. "That way, we'd be making fresh pretzels.

We could keep the refrigerated dough for backup if we need it."

"I-I'm not sure." Lilliane jumped up from the table. "I'll be back later to do the dishes." She raced from the room.

"Pray about it," Keturah called after her. She wished she hadn't started this discussion before church. They had less than an hour before they had to leave. And she wasn't about to bring up Christmas decorations for the stand. Lilliane would probably fight any ideas for those.

Maleah and Rose offered to do the dishes because they hadn't helped with breakfast. Well, actually, Rose did the volunteering and included Maleah in her suggestion. To Keturah's relief, Maleah agreed without protest. And amazingly enough, her sister dropped no dishes or food. Maybe waiting for her to adjust might work out well after all.

But what of Lilliane and the objections she'd raised? Would it be wrong to go against Daed's rules when he wasn't here?

Jeremiah woke on Monday morning with a smile on his face. Since Saturday at the market, he'd been filled with hope. It had been a long time since he'd been able to help someone else. His help may not have been perfect. In fact, he cringed when he thought of his mishaps with the bakery bags and money. He appreciated the Amish man who'd come to his aid, and in the end, Jeremiah had collected money for the sisters.

At least he'd given Keturah a chance to help her sister, and that's what counted.

"Wow, you look cheerful today," Bert, his occupational therapist, said. "You in love or something?"

Huh? Where did that come from? Jeremiah squinted at him.

"Arlene told me you took her up on the trip this Saturday. I'm glad you're finally getting out. Did you enjoy it?"

"*Jah.*" Jeremiah tried to sound noncommittal. And his smile soon faded as Bert had him begin the hand exercises.

As he usually did, Bert carried on a conversation to take Jeremiah's mind off the difficulty of the work. "So, what did you do at the market? Go to the auction?"

Jeremiah shook his head. He didn't want to share his experience.

"Have anything good to eat?"

"Not really." One bite of pretzel didn't really count, did it?

"Buy anything?"

"*Neh.*"

"You didn't go to the auction, eat anything, or buy anything?" Bert's brow furrowed. "But you had fun?"

When Bert put it that way, it did sound odd. Jeremiah nodded.

Bert changed to the next exercise. "Why don't you tell me what you enjoyed about it?"

If only Bert would change the subject. Jeremiah didn't want to talk about Keturah. But Bert cocked his head, waiting for an answer.

"They're already starting to decorate for Christmas. I looked around and listened to Christmas carols."

"Wow, it doesn't take much to make you happy, does it?"

"I guess not."

"Come on. Glancing around at stands didn't put that secretive smile on your face. Did you meet a girl?" Bert waggled his eyebrows.

He wouldn't drop the subject until he got an answer. Jeremiah decided to satisfy the therapist's curiosity without giving away too much information.

"I did, but not in the way you mean."

"How do you know what I meant?" Bert's sly look revealed he expected a confession.

"The girl I met needed some help. Her younger sister was crying. I offered to work in their stand so she could care for her sister."

Bert's eyes widened. "You worked in a market stand? What did you do?"

Why did I start this? Jeremiah had hoped to end Bert's questioning. Instead, he'd only increased his interest.

With a sigh, Jeremiah described how he'd managed to get pretzels from the warmer and how the customers had assisted him.

Bert sat back in his chair, a thoughtful expression on his face. "It took a lot of guts to do that. You're really resourceful, Jeremiah. I wonder if we should schedule a meeting with the vocational rehabilitation specialist."

When Jeremiah didn't respond, Bert asked, "You're still writing letters, right?"

Jeremiah nodded.

"And you're using the page turner to read the newspaper?"

"*Jah.*"

"You know, with some adaptations, you could use something like that page turner to move the bags and bills. Do you think the pretzel shop might let you do some part-time work?"

What? Did Bert read my mind? Jeremiah had considered going back and offering to help. But he hadn't counted on Bert taking over—or interfering with—his plans.

"Once we're done with your session, I'm going to call Tina to set up an appointment. Do you know the name of the pretzel place?"

"It's Esch's, but I don't think they'd want me."

"Why? Did you do something to upset or offend them?"

"Of course not. It's just that they have a fast-paced business. I doubt they'd want me there slowing things down."

"Don't worry about that. Most people are happy for volunteer labor."

Although Jeremiah would love to be a part of the business, he didn't have much of value to offer. "I don't think—"

Bert held up a hand. "What do I say about thinking positive? Stop the second-guessing. Let's talk to Tina to see if she thinks this is a viable option."

Jeremiah stayed silent the rest of the session, his mind whirling with possibilities.

On Monday morning, Lilliane entered the kitchen, looking subdued. "I'll do whatever you decide is best."

"We don't have to do this if you don't feel right about it." Keturah could try to find another way.

"It's all right. I prayed about it, and God seemed to be

telling me you've taken Daed's and Mamm's place in our lives."

Keturah's stomach twisted. *Neh.* Although she'd accepted the burden of parenting that had been laid on her shoulders, she didn't want her sisters to put her in Mamm and Daed's place. "I want us all to decide together."

"We don't want to lose customers by making them wait. And I can help you wait on customers."

"*Danke*, Lilliane. Maybe we could just keep the dough for emergencies."

Eyes wet with tears, Lilliane nodded. "I didn't mean to be a problem."

Rose rushed over and threw her arms around Lilliane. "You're never a problem. You always try to do the right thing."

That was true. Daed had never needed to discipline Lilliane. She always obeyed. That made Keturah wonder if she should follow Lilliane's guidance.

But Rose had already pulled Lilliane across the kitchen and taken out the largest mixing bowls she could find.

Keturah made a mental note to buy industrial-sized mixing bowls like the ones they had in the stand. And they'd have to buy flour in bulk to keep here at the house too. She'd also need another refrigerator here and at the stand, although she had no idea how she'd fit it into the small space there. The extra money from Jeremiah and Mrs. Vandenberg would come in handy for these purchases.

As she joined her sisters at the counter, Lilliane's reservations about doing this bothered Keturah. Maybe she was wrong to go against Daed's wishes. Although she'd never been as obedient as Lilliane, Keturah had always tried to be good. Most of the time, anyway.

Was this really wrong? The sign that hung over the stand said, *Baked Fresh Daily*. If they baked the dough in the stand every day, wouldn't they be fulfilling what the sign promised? Or was that cheating?

Chapter Seven

Two hours later, Bert knocked on Jeremiah's doorjamb and stepped into the room. "Tina can meet with us in half an hour. We'll go to her office."

"All right. I'll be ready."

"Working on another letter?"

"*Jah.*" Jeremiah slid out of the pen loop that encircled the back of his hand and wriggled his fingers. He'd taken more than an hour's break following therapy that morning because of the pain and tiredness he always experienced afterward, but then he'd forced himself to begin writing again. Now his fingers ached.

He tried to send at least three letters a week, though none of the other stories had touched him as much as Keturah's plight. And now that he'd met her in person, he wanted to help her more than ever.

"I need to speak with someone else, but I'll stop back to get you." Bert waved and headed off.

Jeremiah struggled to slide his hand back into the elastic bands that held his pen in place. He shouldn't have taken it off. His hand missed and bumped the pen loop off the desk. It landed on the floor, flipped a few times, and ended up under the desk.

Grrr. Jeremiah pushed himself back from the desk, ducked his head, and stretched his arm as far as he could. No way could he reach it without tumbling from his chair.

Did he have anything he could use to pick it up? A long stick or bar with a hook on the end would work. Surely some stores that sold assistive devices must have gadgets to do this. Most likely, they'd have something like that here at the rehab center. He'd ask Bert, but until the therapist arrived, Jeremiah couldn't work on his letter.

Before this, he'd never thanked God for being able to bend, move, pick up dropped objects, or write with a pen when he'd worked at his dairy farm. He'd taken all that for granted.

He'd risen before dawn every morning, dressed himself without assistance, eaten breakfast without thinking about how to hold utensils or lift food to his mouth. He strode down barn aisles, dragged heavy hay bales, cleaned stalls, squatted to check cows' udders, hooked up milk machines, stood for hours. Never once had he expressed his gratitude to God for any of those abilities.

He'd give anything to have some of that mobility back. Now he couldn't walk anywhere. He needed help and training to do simple tasks. He couldn't even pick up a fallen object.

All he wanted was to reach down and get the pen loop. *Neh*, that wasn't all he wanted. He wanted to get out of this chair and walk down the hall and out of this building. He wanted to go back to his barn and milk his cows. But he couldn't do that. He'd sold his beloved business. Even if he hadn't, he couldn't do any of those things.

Why, God, why? I have so many things I dream of doing. When he'd offered to help Keturah, he couldn't handle simple things like picking up a bag, shaking it open, and dropping in a pretzel. He couldn't make change.

Jeremiah had always tried to look on the bright side. But today, he strained to find a bright side. Tired of trying, he slumped over until his forehead rested on the desk and let discouragement wash over him in waves.

Then God spoke to him in a still, small voice, deep in his soul. *You didn't appreciate what you had before. You took it all for granted. You're doing the same thing now.*

At first, the message didn't sink in, but when it did, Jeremiah cried out in his heart. *I'm sorry, Father. Danke for all the years I had full use of my arms and legs. And* danke *for what I can do now.*

Jeremiah had railed about his limitations and prayed for healing, but he'd never focused on all the blessings he had right here. He had a roof over his head and therapists who were working with him to help him restore as much mobility as possible. His pain lessened every day. He had special equipment to help him.

Like that pen holder under the desk.

And that reminded him he might have a service dog soon. Snickers could pick up the pen loop and bring it to him once the Labrador retriever had been fully trained. He had—

A yelp came from the doorway. "Jeremiah!" Bert rushed across the room. "Are you all right?"

Startled by the alarm in Bert's voice, Jeremiah jumped and lifted his head. "I'm fine. Just having what my *mamm* would call a pity party."

He had no business feeling sorry for himself. He had

so much to be grateful for. And right now, he and Bert would meet with Tina to see about a job at Green Valley Farmer's Market. Maybe even with Keturah.

"Why?" Bert asked. "You've been doing really well. Look at how far you've come since you arrived. We can't promise, but if you keep moving ahead this fast, you might make a full recovery. Many people who come in here don't have that hope."

Hope. Jeremiah clung to that word. Along with *faith.* The doctors had told him the first six months were crucial, and the therapists pushed him to exercise so he'd regain as much mobility as he could. Since coming here, Jeremiah had leaned on the promise of Hebrews 11:1. *Now faith is the substance of things hoped for, the evidence of things not seen.*

No matter what happened, he needed to keep believing in the unseen. He tried to view this accident as God's will and believe the Lord had a purpose for everything that had happened.

Thank you, God, for all I had in the past, all I have now, and all You have planned for my future.

Bert patted his chest and exhaled a long, relieved sigh. "When I saw you there like that— Whew! Glad you're all right."

"I dropped my pen, and I couldn't pick it up." Jeremiah didn't explain he'd gotten so frustrated, he'd given up. Or that he'd been at the right distance to bang his forehead on the desk. Except he'd only pressed his forehead on it.

"You should get one of those telescoping tools with a magnet on the end. We have one you can practice with."

"I figured there'd be something like that."

"Sorry, I should have suggested it. It folds up so you

can set it beside you in the chair. Might come in handy to have one if you plan to keep throwing things on the floor," Bert teased.

"If you get me the information, I'll order one. Next time I have a tantrum, I'll use that instead of banging my head on the desk."

Bert's eyes widened. "Was that what you were doing when I came in?"

Jeremiah laughed. "*Neh*, I didn't hit my head." He turned so Bert could examine his forehead. "See? No lumps." He tried not to let his disappointment and frustration seep into his words. "I just gave up."

"You forgot what I always tell you? 'Never give up.'"

But Jeremiah had forgotten a lot of things, including to be grateful and to have hope.

In one fluid motion that Jeremiah envied, Bert bent down and scooped up the pen holder. He set it on the desk.

"Wish I could do that," Jeremiah said wistfully.

"Keep working hard. Maybe you will." Bert glanced at the clock on Jeremiah's wall. "We'd better go. Looks like we're already a little late."

Together they headed down the hall to Tina's office. Bert motioned for Jeremiah to go in first. An elderly woman sat in a chair near Tina's desk, her cane propped against the chair arm.

Jeremiah stopped on the threshold. Had he barged in on another appointment?

"Come in." Tina's voice exuded cheer. "This is Mrs. Vandenberg. She offered to join us today. She's the owner of Green Valley Farmer's Market."

Mrs. Vandenberg waved an arm as if brushing away

what Tina had said. "I used to be the owner. Not anymore. I sold the market to Gideon Hartzler."

Tina laughed. "You can't fool me. You may have sold the market, but you're still the unofficial owner. You keep an eye on everything that happens there."

"Well," Mrs. Vandenberg admitted with a twinkle in her eye, "can I help it if I'm a nosy old woman?"

"You're more than a busybody. You do so much good for everyone there and in the community."

"Oh, hush." Mrs. Vandenberg turned from Tina to study Jeremiah. "So, this is the young man who wants to work in the market?" Her eagle-eyed scrutiny was thorough, but not unkind.

"Yes, it is," Tina answered for him.

"Tina said you worked at Esch's pretzel stand on Tuesday. How did that go?"

With Mrs. Vandenberg's gaze boring into him, Jeremiah couldn't pass off the question with a platitude like *fine*. He had to tell the truth. Not that he had planned to lie. He needed to be honest about his skills—or lack thereof.

Jeremiah started to tell her about his inability to use the tongs, open the bags, and make change, but Bert interrupted.

"But what he's not telling you about is his ingenious solution." Bert described how Jeremiah had figured out how to lift the pretzels and about how he had, with a customer's help, filled the orders and earned extra money for the girls at the stand.

"Gideon told me some of that." Mrs. Vandenberg beamed. *Gideon? The owner of the market had seen his mistakes?*

"Don't look so distressed," she told Jeremiah. "As

usual, Gideon downplayed his part in the story. I assume he suggested collecting the change for Keturah and her sisters."

Jeremiah's heart stuttered at Keturah's name, and the rest of the sentence barely registered. When he realized Mrs. Vandenberg was staring at him, waiting for an answer, he frantically tried to recall her words. She'd said something about the owner suggesting . . .

"That was the owner?" Jeremiah blurted out.

"You didn't know?"

He shook his head. If he had, he'd have been even more embarrassed than he already was. His cheeks heated at the memory.

If anyone knew all about his incompetence, it would be Gideon. He'd observed every detail, from Jeremiah's failure with handling the tongs to the bag fiasco to the problem making change. Surely Gideon had recounted every one of Jeremiah's mishaps. Why had Mrs. Vandenberg asked him about them?

Her gaze rested on him with gentleness and caring. "How much money did you raise?" When Jeremiah told her, she smiled. "I'm so glad. I worry those girls might need the money. Keturah would never tell me if they did."

That troubled Jeremiah. What if they needed financial help? He'd be glad to donate.

Tina's brows pinched together, and she directed her question to Jeremiah. "Doesn't the Amish church help them financially? I've always heard that."

"*Jah*, they do. I'm sure the girls are fine." But he could give money to the church fund. He'd do that right away.

Mrs. Vandenberg's face melted into sadness. "I'm so

concerned about all four of those girls. Recently, both of their parents were killed in an accident."

"I know," Jeremiah said.

Her eyebrows rose. "Keturah told you?"

"*Neh.* I knew about it before I went to the market."

He wasn't about to admit that he'd written to her and then gone to the market to meet her in person.

"Oh, yes. News does get around fast in the Amish community."

Jeremiah didn't answer, but he squirmed inside at allowing Mrs. Vandenberg to believe an untruth.

Tina cleared her throat. "I know you're busy, Mrs. Vandenberg. Shall we tell Jeremiah what we discussed?"

What a tactful way to get the elderly woman back on topic. Jeremiah smiled his thanks not only for Tina bringing up the market but also because she'd broken into the conversation and changed the subject—although it made him uncomfortable to know they'd been talking about him.

Mrs. Vandenberg took her cue. "Tina suggested you might be able to volunteer at the pretzel stand. While I like the idea, I'm not sure it's practical."

Neh, it wasn't. Jeremiah hadn't been much help. Maybe it had been too soon to consider this.

"The girls badly need help, according to Gideon, but—"

Jeremiah cut her off. He'd already guessed what she planned to say. "But they need someone other than me. Someone who can really help them."

Mrs. Vandenberg stared at him in surprise. "You don't think you can do it?"

"Didn't I already prove that?"

She tapped a finger on her lip thoughtfully. "You seem quite resourceful, and with the proper tools, you might be able to handle various duties, but—"

When she'd started the sentence, Jeremiah's spirits had soared. Now they plunged. He'd gotten his hopes up, only to have her dash them with different and unexpected objections.

He schooled his face into a neutral expression. He didn't want her to sense his disappointment.

"I have to admit, I'm torn. I think you might be an upbeat presence for them, Jeremiah. Keturah needs encouragement, perhaps even more than actual help, but—"

If he heard that word *but* one more time, he'd explode. Why didn't she just admit the reason for her hesitation instead of complimenting and then deflating him?

"I'm concerned about the wheelchair." She frowned and stared off into the distance.

So was he. He'd found it hard to get around yesterday. If anyone else worked the counter with him—someone like Keturah, for example—they'd bump into each other while they rushed around. His pulse quickened remembering their closeness.

Not that'd he'd mind bumping into her, but his response to her nearness might distract him from doing his job. And he'd be an obstacle to Keturah doing hers.

Swamped by gloom, he didn't pay close attention to the rest of Mrs. Vandenberg's musings. No doubt she was listing all the negatives.

"Don't you think, Jeremiah?" she asked.

His head shot up. "Excuse me?" He hadn't caught the sentence before her question.

"I said it'd be hard for you to move around inside the stand and impossible for you to reach the back of the stand, where they have the pretzel tables and the oven."

"*Jah.*" He had to be honest. "I also worry about them getting around me when they're waiting on customers."

"Right."

He'd been hoping she'd contradict him and say the tight squeeze would be manageable. Instead, she'd added to his dejection. "I guess this was a bad idea."

All three of them turned startled eyes in his direction.

A puzzled frown on her face, Tina studied him. "You don't want to do this?"

"It sounds like I'd only be in the way. The last thing I want to do is cause more problems for Keturah." He sighed, then added hastily, "And her sisters."

"That's not what I asked." Tina looked a bit annoyed. "I went to a lot of trouble to set up this meeting, and Mrs. Vandenberg spent time making plans."

"Yesterday you seemed excited about doing this." Even Bert acted exasperated.

Mrs. Vandenberg held up a hand. "Wait a minute. I think what you're saying is that you don't want to do anything to upset the girls. Am I right?"

Jeremiah nodded, hoping his glumness didn't show on his face.

"You're worried that expanding the stand will disrupt their business?"

Expanding the stand? He'd missed that. What had she said while he'd been tuned out?

"Won't it?" He wished he'd paid more attention.

"That's up to Keturah to decide. I haven't approached her about the idea yet."

"It's a lot to ask. You think she'd want to do it?" *Please say* jah*!*

"I won't know until I ask, but here are the adaptations Tina and I sketched out." She held out a paper with a hand-drawn sketch.

Jeremiah recognized the layout of the stand from yesterday. Everything seemed to be in the same place—the pretzel warmer to the left of the customer counter, the table behind that where her sisters rolled pretzels in butter and toppings, the narrow ovens stacked one on top of the other, and the table across from there where Lilliane mixed dough and Rose shaped pretzels. He hadn't looked closely at the back of the stand, but Mrs. Vandenberg's labels included a refrigerator, storage shelves, and other cabinets. It didn't look any different, except the counter seemed much longer than he'd remembered it, and the whole stand looked much wider.

Mrs. Vandenberg set a blueprint on the desk near Jeremiah and leaned over to point. "Here's the stand." She tapped a finger in the far corner of the paper. "We left an extra wide passageway here when we first built the market."

Jeremiah bobbed his head up and down, but he was still confused.

"My husband had planned that as a doorway for future expansion." Mrs. Vandenberg's eyes grew sad. "He didn't live long enough to complete his plans."

"I'm sorry." Jeremiah had his own unfinished plans, but at least he was alive and could accomplish them. Or at least some of them. Others had to be put on hold for when—or if—he recovered.

"Before I turned the market over to Gideon, he came

up with plans for expansion elsewhere that will work even better. So he'll be going ahead with the building in the spring." She glanced over at Jeremiah to check if he understood.

"I see."

"That means the pretzel stand could be widened. We have enough room. What do you think?"

"It looks wonderful. But the real question is what will Keturah think?"

"We'll cross that bridge when we come to it." Mrs. Vandenberg rubbed her hands together. "I wanted you to look over the plans to see if you notice any other adaptations that might be needed."

"Me?" Why should he have a say in Keturah's expansion?

"Yes, you. We'd like you and Bert to point out any problems or changes."

Bert stepped closer. "What are the counter heights? And will the tables be able to accommodate a wheelchair?"

"I should have noted that on the sketch." She pulled out a pen and jotted down numbers. "This counter will be higher for the girls. The part to the right will be lower. Hmm." She turned to Bert and Tina. "Maybe we should add a warmer over here so Jeremiah doesn't have to travel across the floor to get pretzels."

"Makes sense." Bert smiled at her, then, as he studied the sketch, he frowned. "You also marked a cash register over here, but Jeremiah isn't able to make change."

"You know how some stores and supermarkets have self-serve machines that dispense change? We'll set it up to allow customers to insert credit cards or cash."

Bert raised his eyebrows at Jeremiah. "Pretty impressive, eh? All you have to do is learn to pick up and open bags. I have some thoughts on that."

Jeremiah hesitated. "Nobody asked Keturah. What if she doesn't want these changes? Or what if she doesn't want me working there?"

Mrs. Vandenberg waved away his concerns. "If Keturah would rather not do this, Tina and I identified three other stands that have enough room to adapt."

Jeremiah's chest tightened. He didn't really want to work at another stand.

"Actually, I may suggest this to Gideon and ask him to work on getting stand owners who are willing to adapt so we can hire several people from the rehab center."

Tina's eyes shone. "That would be wonderful. Finding places for our rehabbers to work can be a challenge. This would expand their options."

"You'd be the first person to do this at the market, so I hope you'll be willing to teach the next person when you're ready to move on." Mrs. Vandenberg trained a questioning eye on Jeremiah.

He swallowed back a *neh*. He didn't want to train someone else to work with Keturah. But it looked like he might not have any choice. If she even agreed to all this.

Mrs. Vandenberg collected her papers and slid them into a leather folder. "I should be going." She stood on shaky feet.

Jeremiah longed to reach out and offer her his arm, but what help would he be?

She leaned on her cane and hobbled to the door. "Oh, I almost forgot. When you're ninety-two, memory failures are to be expected."

Tina pretended to roll her eyes. "Go on with you, Mrs. V. Your mind is sharper than many people my age or younger."

"Don't flatter me." She pinned Jeremiah with her piercing gaze. "We need to talk to Keturah before the market opens tomorrow."

"We?"

"Obviously, I'll need you there."

Jeremiah sat there, stunned. What had just happened? This morning, Bert had mentioned the possibility of working at the market. A few hours later, they'd all been steamrolled by an old lady who could barely stand, let alone walk.

Tomorrow, with her energy and ability to take charge, Mrs. Vandenberg might push Keturah into agreeing. But what if Keturah later regretted it?

Chapter Eight

Keturah stretched the kinks from her arms as they finished the final batch of dough. She'd estimated the number of batches they should prepare. When they didn't have any more refrigerator room, they had to stop.

Lilliane knitted her brow as she squeezed the plastic-wrapped dough into the only available space in their refrigerator. "I may not even use this. I'll make more tomorrow. I'm sorry we lost customers because I couldn't keep up."

"That only happened a few times," Rose pointed out. "And we had many times more customers than we usually do."

"Rose, you're sweet to try to make me feel better, but I did make mistakes."

"That's because"—Rose bit her lip—"Mamm wasn't there to watch the warmers and keep an eye on the customers."

"Keturah asked me to do that." Lilliane blinked back tears.

"I shouldn't have." Keturah pressed her lips together

and sent her sister an apologetic glance. "I had so many customers, I felt overwhelmed. But I didn't stop to think you were doing as much extra work as I was."

"I should have helped more." A guilty expression crossed Rose's face.

Lilliane shook her head. "You have to shape all the extra pretzels. When would you have time?"

Maleah's lower lip quivered. "All I did was make mistakes and mess things up."

Keturah squatted and wrapped her arms around her little sister. "Everyone makes mistakes. And—"

"That's not what Daed says . . . said." Although Maleah's eyes held sorrow at the word change, her tone held a touch of bitterness. "He said mistakes come from carelessness."

"Not always." Keturah felt guilty about contradicting her father, but she'd found the more Maleah worried about making mistakes, the more she made. "You were trying to help."

"But I should have remembered the tray of pretzels behind me when I mopped."

"That was my fault." Rose set her hand on Maleah's shoulder. "I was rushing and didn't slide that tray all the way onto the table. If I hadn't left the baking sheet hanging over the edge, the mop handle wouldn't have caught on it."

Maleah looked up, an incredulous expression on her face. "You made a mistake?"

Rose laughed. "I make plenty."

"You do?"

"Of course. You make it sound like I never do anything wrong."

"I didn't think you ever did." Maleah gazed at Rose with suspicion.

"When I was your age, I had plenty of accidents. Ask Keturah and Lilliane. They'll tell you."

"We all still do." Lilliane turned from the refrigerator. "Why did we have to make all this dough today?" Without waiting for an answer, she continued, "Because I couldn't keep up with my job yesterday. By not watching the warmers the way Keturah asked, I lost us many customers."

"Please don't blame yourself." Keturah hugged Maleah and stood. "We all should have been watching, but we were busy."

"*Jah*," Rose said to Lilliane. "It's not your fault."

Facing all her sisters, Keturah waited until she had everyone's attention. "Let's change the way we look at things."

A pang shot through her. Maybe it was wrong to go against what Daed had taught them, but if they spent all their time focusing on everything that went wrong, they'd end up being negative. That hadn't been Daed's intent. He'd been trying to teach them to take responsibility and own up to their mistakes and sins. Would she be teaching them to avoid accountability?

Her sisters stared at her expectantly.

As much as it made Keturah ache inside not to have her parents here for guidance, she needed to take charge. For Maleah's sake, Keturah believed they needed to concentrate on the positive.

Lord, if I'm doing wrong, please show me.

Keturah waited a few moments with her head bowed. A deep inner peace convinced her she was choosing the right path. She lifted her head and met her sisters' eyes.

Then, taking a deep breath, she explained what was on her heart. "First of all, I want us to look at everything on Friday and Saturday as God's will. He brought us exactly the customers he wanted us to have."

Lilliane expelled a small sigh. "You're right." The worry lines on her face smoothed out.

Gut. It appeared Lilliane had let go of some of her self-blame.

Maleah looked puzzled. "God wanted me to spill the water and knock over the pretzels?"

"Perhaps God allowed that to happen to teach us a lesson." Keturah hoped that she'd given the right explanation. After all, how could she know God's mind?

"*Jah*, I should be more careful. That's what Daed always said."

"And I should make sure the baking sheets are all the way on the table," Rose added.

Maleah looked at Rose with gratitude.

Keturah smiled at her sisters. "I learned a lesson too. I need to find ways to change how we run the stand so we can serve customers more quickly."

"We already did that." Maleah pointed to the refrigerator. "We made lots and lots of dough."

Although Keturah nodded, her mind whirled with other ideas she wasn't quite ready to share with her sisters yet. Getting Lilliane to agree on making dough in advance had been enough of a challenge.

But sometime soon, she wanted them to shape the pretzels ahead of time too. She'd have to research special refrigerators to hold rows of baking sheets. The only problem with that was space. Where would they put any new equipment?

Keturah whispered another brief prayer, asking God for the answer to that question.

They ate a quick supper in silence and headed up to bed. They'd need to leave for work even earlier than usual tomorrow so they could transport the dough.

Long after her sisters had fallen asleep, Keturah lay awake. She had so much on her mind. And not only about the business. Had she done the right thing in going against Daed's directives?

But hadn't reminding her sisters to see everything as God's will been true? Daed had always emphasized that too. Keturah tried to tell herself she hadn't contradicted Daed but had only drawn attention to another important truth.

Surprisingly enough, her sisters hadn't asked the question burning in Keturah's heart. Why had it been God's will for her parents to die? She was glad they hadn't brought it up, because she had no answer.

After a restless night, Keturah tiptoed downstairs long before dawn, carrying the letter with her. She rolled the propane lamp into the kitchen, turned it on, and sat at the table. Smoothing out the letter, she bent her head to skim it again.

Each time she read it, the words brought her comfort and peace. She hadn't heard back from *A Friend Who Cares*, but he might not have seen her letter in the newspaper yet. Maybe she should write a letter anyway. The newspaper would know his address, and she could ask them to pass it on to him.

Even if she never sent it, writing out some of the questions that troubled her might help. She took a pen and a sheet of pink paper from the drawer that housed the checkbook. Then she poured out her heart.

First she thanked the writer for caring.

> *I hope you don't mind me writing back, but you seemed to know exactly what I needed to hear.*

A thought occurred to her. The spindly handwriting might be from an elderly person. The advice had come from someone wise, someone who understood how it feels to lose someone you loved. Why had she assumed it had been written by someone close to her own age? Would it be rude to ask more about the writer?

> *You know so much about me. I'd like to know more about you if you don't mind. It will help me picture you as I write. I also wonder how you know so much about the experience of grief. I hope you haven't been through a tragedy of your own. But if you have, I'll pray for you too.*

Then Keturah wrote down all the questions and heartaches that woke her in the middle of the night, including questions about raising her sisters and her struggle to understand why God had taken her parents and how it could be His will. She'd penned so many personal things, she wasn't sure she'd ever send this letter, although sending it to someone anonymous would make it a little easier.

She added a paragraph explaining about running out of pretzels and her decision to make the dough yesterday.

> *I'm not sure if I've done the right thing about making the pretzels ahead. Our sign advertises Baked Fresh Daily, but is that dishonest if we make the dough ahead? I also worry about going against what Daed wanted. I know we should honor our parents. Do I need to follow that commandment when Daed's no longer here?*
>
> *If so, I've broken it several times. I carry so much guilt inside about that. And it's worse because there's no way to make it right.*

Her letter had turned into a litany of complaints and unanswerable questions. Keturah didn't want to add to her "friend's" burdens. She needed to close with some positives.

> *I've been trying to do as you suggested and look for God's blessings in the small things, so I'll tell you about a kindness that brightened my day on Saturday.*

She explained about Maleah's accidents and that her sister had run off crying and how worried she'd been.

> *Then this stranger who was waiting for a pretzel offered to wait on customers so I could go after Maleah. I was so grateful.*

Keturah debated telling about Jeremiah's struggles, but it didn't feel right to bring up anything negative about someone who'd been so kind. And she'd started this story to change the downbeat mood. Plus, Jeremiah had figured out some clever ways to get around his difficulties. She admired him for that, and so did her sisters.

Keturah moved on to the main reason she'd wanted to reply to the letter. She laid a hand on the page she'd read over and over.

> *But the greatest blessing this past week has been your letter. I've carried it with me and pulled it out to read when grief overwhelms me. Each time one of the verses comforts me, and your words make me feel like someone understands what I'm going through. It's almost as if you're walking beside me and showing me the way. I've thanked God many times that you took the time to care.*

How should she end it?

"Keturah?" Lilliane entered the kitchen, a concerned look in her eyes. "What are you doing up so early?"

Before her sister could see what she'd written, Keturah folded her stationery and her "friend's" message. "I—I was replying to a letter."

She rose from the table and removed an envelope from the drawer. She slid her letter inside and, with her back turned to her sister, hid both letters in her pocket.

"Who was it from?"

"A stranger who read about the accident in the newspaper."

"Oh." Lilliane asked no more questions.

"Why don't we start breakfast?" Keturah wanted to distract her sister. "We should leave soon."

"All right. Should we have cereal?"

"We usually do on market days. Besides, I don't think we have a choice. The eggs and bacon got shoved to the back of the refrigerator." She hoped her rueful expression would make Lilliane laugh.

Instead, her sister asked in a small voice, "Did we do the right thing?"

"I don't know." Keturah had to be honest, but she wanted to reassure Lilliane. "We need to keep up with the orders."

"I guess." Lilliane headed for the pantry and carried several boxes of cereal to the table.

Keturah opened the refrigerator. Thank heavens, the milk was in the door. All the dough stuffed onto the shelves gave her a feeling of relief, but added to her guilt. What would *A Friend Who Cares* say? She could use some of that wisdom and counsel now.

Jeremiah tossed and turned much of the night. Not because of his usual aches and pains, which grew worse at night, but because of anticipation and anxiety. If Keturah said *jah*, he'd be thrilled. He'd have a job and get to spend time around her. If she said *neh*, it would squash his spirits.

He finally dozed off, only to wake well before dawn, groggy and exhausted, his stomach churning with anticipation and uncertainty. Mrs. Vandenberg planned to meet him at the farmer's market before it opened. He'd need to get ready soon. As he did every morning, he wished he could dress himself and take care of all his needs, but he had to wait until an aide came to help him.

He decided to use the time to pray.

Lord, please help me to accept whatever happens today

*as Your will. If Keturah doesn't want to do this, please give
her the courage to say* neh. *Wrap Your arms around her
and her sisters, Heavenly Father, and comfort them.*

Their loss reminded him of his own. All the planning
yesterday had kept him from dwelling on his own grief,
but as he lay in the gray light before sunrise, it flooded
over him.

*Dear Lord, I don't understand why You took Mamm and
spared me, but help me to trust Your wisdom and Your
plans.*

Was it right to ask God to open Keturah's heart to Mrs.
Vandenberg's plans? Or would that be selfish?

Jeremiah decided against it. He'd already asked for
God's will to be done. And he'd determined to accept it.

A light knock on the door startled him. He called for
the aide to come in.

"Good morning, Jeremiah." Darryl flicked on the overhead light. "Bert said you have an appointment this morning."

Jeremiah winced at the sudden blast of light. He still
had trouble adjusting to that much brightness at dawn. "I
do. *Danke* for coming in so early. Sorry to get you out of
bed this time of day."

Darryl's usual grin lifted his lips. "Any time's a good
time to be up. It's always a blessing to see another day."

"You're right. I was just thinking yesterday that I took
it for granted when I could roll out of bed in the morning,
dress myself, and go out to milk the cows. Now I realize
how thankful I should have been."

"Yeah, you often don't realize how good you have it
until it's taken away."

Darryl's words hit Jeremiah with double force. Was that

the answer to the question he'd asked yesterday? Had God wanted him to appreciate all he had? Like Job, who lost everything, only to have it restored?

After that, Job surely thanked God daily for what he had. Jeremiah had not been grateful. He'd spent more time dwelling on the negative. God seemed to be bringing his attitude to his attention.

Darryl's cheerfulness in the face of even the most humbling tasks provided a good example. Why had he never noticed that before?

"Your happiness always lifts my spirits, Darryl." After the aide left each morning, Jeremiah usually felt more upbeat.

"I'm glad. I try to do everything for God's glory. Hard to be unhappy when you're serving Him."

"I need to remember to do the same. I'm sure your family appreciates your attitude."

"Oh, I don't have any family. Well, I have my church family, of course."

"How old are you?"

"Nineteen. I started working here at sixteen. One of the men in my church owns this place. He offered me a job, and I was glad to take it."

Jeremiah wanted to ask more questions, but Darryl changed the subject.

"So where are you off to so early this morning?"

As Darryl helped with shaving and dressing, Jeremiah explained about the farmer's market.

"Sounds like a good deal. That Mrs. Vandenberg helps a lot of people. She goes to my church. If it weren't for her, I might not be here."

"Really?" Jeremiah wanted to hear more.

"Yeah. I'll tell you sometime, but you need to get in the van to make your appointment on time."

Jeremiah definitely wanted to be at the market when he'd promised.

With a twinkle in his eye, Darryl said, "Lots of buggies on the road this time of morning heading to the market. You know how that can back up traffic."

With a chuckle, Jeremiah situated himself in the wheelchair. "*Jah*, they do crawl along."

"That's better. You looked kinda serious. Laughter makes the day brighter. It's also healing. The Bible says so."

"You're right." Maybe Jeremiah should add more humor to his day. He might heal faster. He'd try to remember that *a merry heart doeth good like a medicine.*

He still had a smile on his face when the van arrived at the market. Pink edged the gray sky along the horizon, signaling that the sun would soon rise. Floodlights made small circles of brightness on the asphalt near the entrance. But the most shocking sight was a string of lit-up icicles dangling from the edge of the roof. Underneath, alternating red and green lights spelled out *Christmas Extravaganza*. That hadn't been here a few days ago.

Buggies and pickup trucks filled the parking lot, and people were unloading and carting vegetables, baked goods, and craft items to the doors. Without asking, the van driver headed for a fancy car idling under a light.

"I assume that Bentley's waiting for you?" the van driver asked.

Jeremiah had no idea. "I guess so."

As they approached, the Bentley driver hopped out and came around to open the car door. He assisted Mrs. Vandenberg to her feet and handed her a cane.

"Thank you." She smiled at her driver. "We'll probably be here about forty-five minutes." She looked toward Jeremiah's driver. "Is that okay with you?"

He nodded. "I'll get some coffee and a donut. I'll be waiting here whenever you're ready. We don't have any morning runs until nine today, so take your time."

"Speaking of time"—Mrs. Vandenberg checked her watch and smiled at Jeremiah—"you're punctual. I like that in people I do business with. It says a lot about character."

Although he should correct her and explain that Darryl and the van driver deserved the credit, this elderly woman, who looked so fragile a slight gust of wind might blow her over, awed him with her inner fire and drive. She made him almost tongue-tied.

She tottered a few steps and stopped. "When you get to your nineties, you might find you're a bit creaky in the morning." She laughed. "Or even all day long."

Jeremiah didn't laugh along with her. At twenty-five, he'd be thrilled to hobble along at any pace.

She must have read the resentment in his expression, because she limped closer and patted his arm. "Have faith, my boy. Jesus made the lame walk. I have every confidence He'll heal you."

Easy for her to say. She wasn't confined to a wheelchair.

"I know what it's like to be in one of these." She patted the arm of his wheelchair.

What was it with this woman? She seemed to know his thoughts.

"I used a wheelchair for a while after my hip surgery until I got a power scooter."

For some reason, that made Jeremiah smile. He pictured her terrorizing people as she zipped down hallways or store aisles.

"Yes, the nurses called me a holy terror."

"Can you read minds?"

"No, but I read faces and postures. When you've lived as long as I have, you develop an instinct for what others are thinking and feeling. When I'm with people, I tune in to their reactions. It's a handy skill to have."

Jeremiah imagined it would be. But that made him more cautious. He didn't want to give away his inner thoughts.

"Oh, relax." This time she patted his arm. "I'm not going to pry into your deepest secrets. And if I accidentally figure them out, they're safe with me. I'd never do anything to harm you or anyone else. God gave me an ability to help others, and He often nudges me in a certain direction."

If God was in control, Jeremiah had nothing to fear. But he still couldn't relax. Having to guard his thoughts and meet Keturah to ask this huge favor added to his nervousness.

Mrs. Vandenberg took a jerky step forward, and Jeremiah leaned forward, wondering if he'd need to catch her. If he even could. Once again, he railed at the wheelchair that kept him captive.

She wobbled as she switched her cane to her other hand. "If you don't mind, I'll hold the arm of your wheelchair.

I don't see well, so if I trip on the uneven blacktop, you'll hold me up."

Whether she'd sensed his worries for her safety or she truly needed help, Jeremiah appreciated the opportunity to prevent a fall. Although it wouldn't be him holding her up, but his wheelchair.

Mrs. Vandenberg tilted her head toward the left. "If we go in the back way, it's flat. Most of the other doors have stairs. This'll be easier for both of us."

One of the men pushing a dolly with cartons marked *Organic Chicken* held the door for them.

"Thank you, Gideon." She smiled at the tall man. "You've met Jeremiah, haven't you?"

Even with the roof overhang shadowing the man's face, Jeremiah recognized him as the man who'd helped him with the bags.

"Of course." Gideon nodded at Jeremiah. "I'd offer to shake, but after lifting these cartons, I'd better wait until I wash my hands. Good to see you, though."

"*Danke* for your help the other day."

"No problem. You looked like you had it mostly under control."

Jeremiah wanted to protest, but Gideon didn't give him a chance.

"Welcome to the market. I understand you'll be working here. I need to get this chicken rinsed and ready to go, but I hope Keturah likes the plans as much as the rest of us do."

"Yes, we should be going." Mrs. Vandenberg started through the door. "We don't want to distract Keturah from her work for too long."

Because they couldn't both fit, Jeremiah waited for her.

He studied Gideon from the corner of his eye. This man owned the market? Why was he carting around boxes of chicken?

"By the way, if you're hungry later, stop by our stand," Gideon said.

Mrs. Vandenberg turned in a shaky circle to face the two men. "Gideon runs Hartzler's Chicken Barbecue, the best in the area. We won't be staying that long today, but once Jeremiah starts working here, I'm sure he'll visit your stand often."

"I hope so." Gideon smiled at both of them. "See you later."

"Come, Jeremiah. We don't want to be late."

He followed her through the door.

"The Esches' stand is at the other end of the market." Mrs. Vandenberg once again placed a hand on his chair. "But you already know that, don't you? You've been here before."

He certainly had. And he looked forward to seeing Keturah again. He only hoped she'd be open to Mrs. Vandenberg's proposal.

Chapter Nine

Keturah and Lilliane had carried in all the supplies, including the dough. But when Keturah opened the refrigerator, she sighed. She'd underestimated the space they'd have.

She'd forgotten she'd asked Lilliane to stock up on supplies last Monday. Keturah blew out an exasperated breath.

"Is everything all right?"

Keturah whirled around. "Mrs. Vandenberg, what are you doing here this early?" A shape moved in the shadows behind the elderly woman, and a man's face became visible. "Jeremiah?"

He nodded a greeting but looked to Mrs. Vandenberg to answer Keturah's question.

"Jeremiah and I have something to talk to you about, but first, you look rather distressed. Is there anything we can help you with?"

Keturah's laugh came out sharp and sardonic. "Not unless you can make our refrigerator larger. I misjudged how much room we'd have."

"You don't have enough space? What did you need to put in it?"

"I, well, I came up with the idea of making dough ahead of time, because we ran out several times on Friday and Saturday." Keturah gestured in Jeremiah's direction. "You'd know. You had to wait. More than once."

"Good idea." Mrs. Vandenberg smiled.

"That's what I thought, but . . ." Keturah nibbled her lip.

"But what, dear?"

"We have no more room in the refrigerator. Maybe this is God's way of showing me I was wrong."

Mrs. Vandenberg studied her closely. "Wrong about what?"

"Lilliane didn't want to go against Daed's wishes. He always insisted we make the dough in front of the customers so they'd know it was fresh."

"So it's more than a too-small refrigerator dragging you down. Space issues are easy to handle."

How? Keturah could take out some of the butter they'd use that day. It wouldn't hurt it to soften before they melted it. But that still wouldn't make enough room.

"I can see you're wondering what I mean. Bo Ridley has that huge walk-in refrigerator for his organic meats. I'm sure he wouldn't mind you storing some of your dough there."

Keturah shivered. That *Englisch* seller gave her the creeps the way he stared at her. "I don't know . . ."

Jeremiah studied her with concern. "Would it help if I asked him and carried the dough there for you?"

Did he sense the underlying reason for her reluctance? His protective glance seemed to show he did.

Mrs. Vandenberg beamed. "What a wonderful idea, Jeremiah. Perhaps you could stay here and run back and forth today to keep them supplied with dough."

"*Ach*, I couldn't ask you to do that." Keturah hated to impose on people, and the last thing she wanted to do was make repeated trips to Ridley's Organic Meats.

"I don't mind at all. I'd be happy to do it."

"Of course he would. And that's a great lead-in to what we want to talk to you about. We shouldn't leave the dough sitting out, though."

"I can take it now if you'll put it in my lap."

It troubled Keturah to make him run her errands, but Mrs. Vandenberg called to Lilliane, and she hurried over with a large plastic container of dough.

"Hi, Jeremiah," her sister chirped. "What are you doing here? Are you coming to help us again today?"

"I guess I am." His broad smile seemed to indicate he'd be delighted to help.

"Well, if you do," Keturah said, "you deserve more pay than three pretzels."

"I don't need money. I'm glad to help however I can. You'd be doing me a favor. It's hard feeling so useless."

"Useless?" Lilliane looked shocked. "You aren't useless. You helped a lot the other day."

"She's right. If you hadn't waited on customers, I couldn't have gone after Maleah."

Mrs. Vandenberg's eyes sparkled. "Well, Jeremiah, it seems you've made yourself quite useful here. You've given me the perfect segue into what I wanted to ask you, Keturah."

That was the second time Mrs. Vandenberg had alluded to a request she wanted to make. After all the elderly woman had done for their family, Keturah would agree to anything. "I'd be happy to do whatever you want."

"You should hear my plans before you say yes. I'll wait until Jeremiah gets back to discuss it, though." Mrs. Vandenberg pointed to the other end of the market. "Ridley's is right by the front door. You can't miss it." She winced. "It takes up the whole front wall."

"I'm sure I can find it."

"Tell Bo I sent you. He has a good heart. He'll be happy to assist you."

He has a good heart? Mrs. Vandenberg must have seen a side of Bo that Keturah hadn't. Of course, Bo wouldn't leer at Mrs. Vandenberg the way he did at younger women.

First, Mrs. Vandenberg had winced and then frowned as she'd told Jeremiah where to find Ridley's stand. He couldn't tell if she was worried he'd have trouble with the directions or if something else had made her face darken. And Keturah's response to Bo Ridley's name concerned him.

Jeremiah could see Ridley's Organic Meats & Produce long before he reached it. Multicolored Christmas lights lit up the stand name. Santa Claus in a sleigh flew back and forth on wire overhead, guided by a reindeer with a blinking red nose.

After Keturah's reaction, Jeremiah dreaded meeting Bo himself. But when he reached the stand, he warmed to Bo's friendliness.

"Sure, sure." Bo answered Jeremiah's question about storage with a quick wave toward the large silver doors at the end of the stand. "Plenty of room in there. Be sure to put the dough far away from the meats. Don't want it to get contaminated or pick up any smells."

"Thanks. We appreciate it. I'll be bringing several loads." Jeremiah headed in the direction Bo had indicated.

Jeremiah had to scoot around an eight-foot-tall Christmas tree dripping with ornaments, tinsel, and tiny twinkling lights.

"No problem. If you need help getting those doors open, just ask one of the guys down there. They can hold them for you."

Jeremiah shook his head. He couldn't understand why had Keturah recoiled. Bo seemed nice enough, but even Mrs. Vandenberg, who'd said Bo had a good heart, had had a troubled expression. Perhaps if Jeremiah came to work at the market, he'd discover the answer to that mystery.

Right now, he had a job to do, and he wanted to prove he'd be a worthwhile employee. His heart singing, Jeremiah hurried back as fast as he could for the next load, passing several stands whose decorations outshone Bo's. It looked like the market went all out for the holidays.

After Jeremiah put the final batches of dough in the refrigerator, he made a point of thanking Bo again.

"No problem, man. Will you be the errand boy, or will one of the sisters come for their dough?" Bo waggled his eyebrows in a suggestive manner.

Jeremiah steamed up. No wonder Keturah had flinched. He wanted to tell the man to wipe that sick smirk off his face. But Keturah needed Bo's refrigerator.

Tamping down his disgust, Jeremiah answered as evenly as he could, "I expect I'll probably fetch the dough." *Neh*, he'd make absolutely sure he was the only one who ran this errand.

"Too bad." Bo twisted his lips into a disappointed pout. Then his sunny salesman's smile reappeared. "No offense. I'll be glad to see you, but you know how it is. A pretty woman always brightens our days."

Jeremiah didn't bother to respond to that comment. Although he supposed he was as guilty as Bo. Jeremiah had to admit seeing Keturah lightened his spirits. In fact, he couldn't wipe the grin off his face as he rushed back to her stand.

She and Mrs. Vandenberg were chatting when he returned. Keturah, Lilliane, and a Mennonite girl had formed an assembly line. Keturah shaped pretzels, Lilliane dipped them in the boiling water bath, and the Mennonite girl slid the filled trays into the ovens. The pretzels moved smoothly from one station to another.

Keturah's pretty hands flashing in and out drew Jeremiah's attention. Her graceful fingers curved the center of the long dough rope into a horseshoe shape. Then she twisted the ends over each other twice and flipped them over to rest on the lower curve of the horseshoe, making what Mamm had always called praying hands. She'd often used his pretzel snack to remind him to pray and thank God for his treats.

Jeremiah's eyes blurred until Keturah's hands became Mamm's gnarled ones. Mamm's floury hands rested on his shoulder, or she wiped off her hands to brush his bangs from his eyes. He'd sit at the kitchen table, swinging his legs impatiently, waiting for the pretzels to bake. The fragrance of the dough filled the kitchen, and Jeremiah gulped in the warm, cozy smell.

He took a deep breath, and the memory faded. His

heart still ached, but some of his sadness lessened as he concentrated on Keturah's movements.

Mrs. Vandenberg examined his face. Her half smile made him wonder if she'd read his thoughts again.

"I'm remembering Mamm making pretzels," he mumbled.

The gleam in her eyes revealed she'd read more into his fascination with Keturah than he'd intended.

"Perhaps while those pretzels are baking, you could join us over here, Keturah," Mrs. Vandenberg called.

"Of course." Keturah wiped the flour from her lovely fingers.

Jeremiah kept his attention fixed on her hands, because if he looked into her eyes, she might read the same message Mrs. Vandenberg had. Maybe working in the stand and being around her every day wasn't a good idea.

But Mrs. Vandenberg had pulled out her papers and set them on the ledge. It was too late to back out now. Maybe Keturah would say *neh* and save him from humiliation.

When his friends had developed crushes and later had fallen in love and married, Jeremiah had never understood the intensity of their feelings. He'd observed from a safe distance. No particular girl had ever interested him. He liked them all as friends, but he'd never experienced this all-consuming pull—one he couldn't break.

Of all the times to have a schoolboy crush. Now, when he couldn't date the girl who interested him, he understood his friends' absorption. Too late to do anything about it.

Although it pained him to know he'd never wed, Jeremiah was glad God had kept him from falling for a woman before this. Suppose he'd been married . . . his wife might have died in the crash. Or she'd be living with an invalid.

"Right, Jeremiah?" Mrs. Vandenberg tilted her head in that knowing way.

Heat swept all the way up from Jeremiah's chest. Had they guessed what he'd been thinking?

"Um, sorry. I was thinking about something else."

"I know." Mrs. Vandenberg's half smile made it clear she had no doubt why Jeremiah was distracted.

A quick sideways glance reassured him that Keturah was absorbed in studying the sketch. She ran a finger over the right side, then pointed to the spot outside the stand occupied by Jeremiah and Mrs. Vandenberg. "You mean I could expand from where you are to there?"

"Exactly." Mrs. Vandenberg turned, took several wobbling steps, and tapped her cane far in front of her. "As long as we leave a passageway wide enough to exit your stand, you're free to use all this space."

Keturah's gaze swept the area and back, her eyes shining in wonder. "You don't know how wonderful that would be."

"I think I have a good idea," Mrs. Vandenberg said dryly.

Anyone looking at Keturah's dazzling smile could tell she was thrilled. But that was only part of the plan. How would she react when she learned he would be included in the bargain?

Keturah couldn't believe it. She wanted to wrap her arms around herself and dance with joy. Only the tiny, enclosed space with no room to move kept her still.

"This is such an answer to prayer." She couldn't stop gushing. "Last night, I thought I'd like to have a refrigerated case to hold trays of pretzels and a larger refrigerator with enough room to hold the dough. But I had nowhere to put them."

"God is good, isn't He?" Mrs. Vandenberg's face reflected some of Keturah's joy.

"I could put them back here." Keturah tapped her finger along the back wall of the diagram.

"Perfect." Mrs. Vandenberg took out a pen and drew box shapes on the sketch. "I hadn't thought about what would go along that wall, but I figured you'd want some additional storage space."

"*Jah*, we could use more metal cabinets for sugar and flour and other supplies. I can't believe it. *Danke, danke.*" If Mrs. Vandenberg were closer, Keturah might have thrown her arms around the old woman and given her a hug.

"You're quite welcome. I'm glad it makes you so happy. I did have—"

Keturah's spirits, which had been soaring like a balloon, lost their buoyancy. As if all the air had been let out, her excitement sputtered and fizzled. "I don't know about paying for it, though."

She'd received that large check from Mrs. Vandenberg the other day, but Keturah had no idea when the household bills would be coming, or what the stand rental cost, or how big their mortgage payment might be. She also didn't know what their bill was at the bulk foods store. They'd need to replenish all their flour and sugar soon. And the refrigerators she wanted would be costly, not to mention paying contractors and buying the materials.

"*Danke* for the idea. Would it be all right if I took some time to save up for it?"

Mrs. Vandenberg shook her head, and Keturah's joy nose-dived even farther.

"I'd be happy to pay for it," Jeremiah volunteered. "You could pay me back as you could afford it."

Keturah stared at him. He'd offer to help a perfect stranger? Why was she surprised? Hadn't he done that on Saturday? What a giving heart this man had!

"*Danke* for offering, but I couldn't accept. I really appreciate your kindness."

If she wasn't mistaken, a look of disappointment crossed his face.

"That's very generous of you, Jeremiah, but"—Mrs. Vandenberg set a wrinkled hand on the paper—"this is my project. I plan to pay for it if Keturah is willing to agree to my terms."

Even if it strapped her, Keturah determined to agree to whatever Mrs. Vandenberg asked.

"Did you notice this part of the expansion?" One knobby finger slid across the front counter on the sketch. "I want to help the rehab center, so this side of the counter would be lower. Wheelchair accessible."

"You mean . . . ?" Keturah turned to Jeremiah, then looked back at Mrs. Vandenberg for confirmation. "For Jeremiah?"

"At first." Mrs. Vandenberg stared straight into Keturah's eyes. "This might be a lot to ask of you, so you don't need to answer right away. Once Jeremiah has recovered enough to get a full-time job, I'd like to bring in another rehab worker. It might mean you'd have a frequent turnover of staff, depending on how quickly they heal and/or develop skills that will allow them to get another job."

Keturah wasn't sure she understood. There had to be more to it that she was missing. "You'll provide staff to help me if I agree to help them with their rehab?"

"Exactly."

"But who would say *neh* to that? With the extra help, I'm sure I could afford their salaries." Even if it made money a little tight, it would be worth it to have more people.

Last night, during the few hours she'd slept, she'd dreamed of hiring an extra person. No one could replace Mamm, but it would give them an extra pair of hands.

Mrs. Vandenberg stared at Keturah with a puzzled frown. "You misunderstood me, dear."

Of course she had. It all seemed too good to be true.

"I intend to pay the workers—well, my charity will. It's my gift to the rehab center."

"I can't agree to that."

Both Jeremiah and Mrs. Vandenberg stared at Keturah with crestfallen expressions.

"I understand." Mrs. Vandenberg picked up the papers. "It is a lot to ask you to disrupt your business."

"*Neh*, it's not. I'm happy to have anyone from the rehab center working here, but I should at least pay them myself. Especially if you're paying for the expansion."

"Please, Keturah, give me some pleasure in my old age. I can barely get around or do much anymore. Projects like this are my only chance to stay active and involved in life. Will you let me do this?"

Keturah suspected Mrs. Vandenberg's plea was part of a con. But how could she turn her down?

* * *

Jeremiah turned away to hide a smile. This old lady playing helpless? After he'd watched her sketch out those plans, make all those arrangements with Bert and Tina, and talk Keturah into the stand expansion? She was a ninety-something dynamo with a huge heart and twenty-something energy, stamina, and ideas.

But he'd also turned his head to keep either of them from seeing his joy and excitement. He'd be working here. Coming to a real job, even if he didn't have all the skills he needed yet, would make him feel worthwhile. And, even better, he'd get to spend time with Keturah.

Mrs. Vandenberg touched his arm. "The market will be opening soon. I should go so Keturah can finish getting ready. Can you tell her the rest of the plans?"

"The rest of the plans?" Keturah echoed, looking faint.

"Calm down." Mrs. Vandenberg made a slow chopping motion with her hand in the air as if signaling Keturah to lower her anxiety. "It's only additions to the stand to accommodate your workers from rehab."

"I see," she said faintly.

Jeremiah would give her a little time to absorb all of Mrs. Vandenberg's ideas before he told her about the self-service terminal, additional warmer, and other improvements. Right now, he needed to go out to the parking lot to tell the van driver he'd be staying and make arrangements to be picked up when the market closed.

He couldn't believe he'd actually be working here from now on.

"I'll walk you to the door," he told Mrs. Vandenberg.

Ach, he couldn't walk anyone anywhere. Why had he said that?

Her expression didn't show that she noticed he'd misspoken. With a sly smile, she gripped his chair. "It would be nice to have a steady arm to lean on."

He laughed. Nothing got by her.

"You're so polite and thoughtful, Jeremiah. Any girl would be lucky to have you." She slanted a glance in Keturah's direction and raised her eyebrows as if asking for agreement.

Luckily, Keturah ducked her head and busied herself with lifting the tongs to pick up the next batch of pretzels. Maybe she hadn't caught Mrs. Vandenberg's broad hint.

If only what she'd said were true. Jeremiah would like nothing more than to have an opportunity to court Keturah, but that was impossible. He did intend to make himself indispensable to her, though, so she wouldn't regret having him around.

Chapter Ten

Keturah walked around in a daze. Maybe she was still sleeping and she'd wake from the dream. If it was real, she'd be getting an enlarged stand for free, extra room for the refrigerators she wanted, another worker, and even money to pay for his salary.

Danke, *Lord, for all You've given me.*

Before Jeremiah returned, she helped Lilliane and Olivia make more pretzels while she filled her sister in on Mrs. Vandenberg's plans—what she knew of them, anyway. Evidently, Jeremiah had more to tell her when he returned. She didn't know if she could take in anything else when her heart was filled to bursting.

Or at least it would be, if she didn't have a deep hole inside from missing Mamm.

Lilliane smiled to hear Jeremiah would be working there today and in the future. "He's so nice." She set a tray of steaming pretzels on the final prep work space so Olivia could coat them with butter.

Then Lilliane returned to the baking table and slid the pretzels she and Keturah had shaped into the boiling water bath, one by one. "He's such a hard worker. Maybe we could find jobs that are easier for him to do."

"I have some ideas about that." Keturah moved around Lilliane to wash her hands. "I'll see what he thinks about it when he gets back."

She headed to the cash drawer to count the money. The market would open soon, so she hoped Jeremiah would arrive in time to do a few practice runs. Then she'd find out more about Mrs. Vandenberg's other ideas.

"Hey, Keturah." Gina Rossi waved from her stand on the opposite side of the extra wide walkway where Mrs. Vandenberg planned to build the extension. "Have you thought about your decorations yet? I'm so excited about this Christmas Extravaganza."

"Not yet."

"Look what I've done so far." Gina gestured toward two life-sized Nutcracker figures. "I haven't plugged them in yet, but they lift their arms and open their mouths."

All the hanging plants in Gina's Plant Palace had been adorned with gold bows, and she had a Christmas tree flocked with white and festooned with peppermint-striped bows and cardinals sitting in the aisle.

"I thought I'd put the tree back there." Gina pointed to the back wall between their stands. "I'm going to put down a green carpet and have Mrs. Santa Claus story times on Saturday afternoons before we close at four."

Should Keturah tell her about the expansion?

Lilliane beat her to it. "Mrs. Vandenberg is expanding our stand into that space."

Gina's crestfallen face made Keturah want to soften the blow. "We'll still have a passageway there you can use."

"It might be too narrow for a crowd of children, though," Lilliane warned.

"That's okay." Gina's exuberant spirits returned. "We'll

make do." She carted her tree to the end of the passageway. Then, at the aisle end, she set up a striped barber pole with a globe light on top. A sign saying *North Pole* pointed toward the tree.

As Gina wrestled what looked like a gold throne into place beside the tree, Jeremiah returned. Keturah flashed him a huge smile. They'd have a little time to talk.

Jeremiah's eyebrows rose, and he slowed down as if startled. Then a broad grin brightened his face, and his eyes shone. He hurried toward the stand.

Ach, had she given him the wrong impression? In her relief at seeing him returning, had she smiled too broadly? She needed to remember to act like an employer rather than a friend, even if it went against her natural inclinations.

"I'm glad you're back." She tried to keep her tone brisk and businesslike.

Some of the sparkle faded from Jeremiah's eyes, and his grin slid into the sort of semi-welcoming smile you'd use with an acquaintance. Keturah silently berated herself. She hadn't meant to quash his friendliness.

"I'd like to talk about your duties." Her attempt to act like an employer made her sound stilted and cold. She gave up on it. "I'm glad you're willing to help us. I appreciate what you did on Tuesday."

Jeremiah thawed too, and his smile returned, but he didn't meet her eyes. "Glad I could help."

"One of the problems we've had is keeping the warmer filled and having the right kinds of pretzels. That job . . ." Keturah faltered. She swallowed hard. "Well, Mamm always handled it."

Sympathy blossomed in his eyes. "I know it's hard."

"It is." Keturah pinched her lips together for a moment.

She stared down at her hands bunching her apron and willed them to stay still. Once she'd composed herself, she started again. "The job may not seem like much, but it's essential."

When she kept her head bowed, Jeremiah asked softly, "Is that what you'd like me to do?"

Grateful not to have to speak around the lump in her throat, she nodded. She had other things she wanted to ask him to handle, but she couldn't speak. Her chest ached with unshed tears. The idea of putting a stranger in Mamm's place hurt more than the emptiness of having her missing.

"Where would you like me to stay so I'm out of the way?"

Keturah pointed to the spot on the right where Mamm had stood to supervise. Her mother rarely stayed there long. She usually bounced around from worktable to worktable to help wherever needed. Jeremiah headed toward the place she'd indicated.

"Wait," Keturah called after him. "I, um, have a better idea."

It'd be too painful to see someone else when she glanced over to check, forgetting Mamm was no longer there. Breaking that habit would take a while. Besides, Jeremiah could actually do two jobs at once. It might make him feel like he was contributing more to the business.

He sat there staring at her and waiting for her directive.

"Why don't you help me with the pretzel warmer?"

His eyes widened. "You sure about that?"

"Very sure." Now that she'd made the decision, Keturah's instincts told her she'd chosen well. "My sisters said you can lift the pretzels from the rack. What if you do that as soon as you hear the customers' orders? I'll get the bags ready for you to drop them in."

"I can do that." Jeremiah's whole face lit up. "If it'll help, that is. I'm pretty slow."

"But if you do it as soon as the customers order, you'll be saving me time. I won't have to step back here to get the pretzels, and you can be taking them out while I shake open the bags. I couldn't open bags and get the pretzels at the same time."

"It'll actually be faster?" Jeremiah turned hopeful eyes toward her as if begging for confirmation.

"Of course it will." The more she thought about this, the more Keturah liked it. "And you can keep an eye on the pretzels and the water in the warmer."

Relief flooded his face. "You're not just making up jobs to keep me busy?"

"*Neh*. This will help everything flow better. Maybe we won't lose any customers today."

Keturah flashed him another one of those joyful smiles that had stopped his heart earlier. The one whose meaning he'd mistaken. This time he tried to slow the rapid pitter-pattering of his pulse. She was only expressing happiness. Nothing else.

"You should know the problems we had last time. Look how long you had to wait for your pretzel."

"I didn't mind." He'd enjoyed observing her and her sisters. "I learned a lot about how pretzels are made."

"*Jah*, I'm sure you did." Her voice had a sarcastic edge to it, as if she didn't believe him.

"I'm serious," he said. "I found the whole process"— *and you*—"fascinating."

"Riiight."

She sounded so much like the *Englisch* teens in the

rehab center, he laughed. "So don't believe me, but I did. Seeing R—" He stopped himself before he said Rose's name. "Seeing your, um, your sister flip the dough ends into praying hands reminded me of . . ."

"Are you all right?" Her eyes filled with concern.

Jeremiah shook his head and forced his constricted throat to finish. "My *mamm*," he managed to say without a quaver, "always reminded me to *pray without ceasing* whenever we had pretzels for a snack."

"Our *mamm* did too, when we were small." Keturah gazed off into the distance. "She also taught us to pray for each customer who'd eat the pretzels while we shaped the dough. I need to remember that more often."

"I'll try to do it as I take each pretzel off the rack."

"How lovely. I should too."

"Maybe we could remind each other." To blunt his reaction to Keturah's sunny smile, Jeremiah tried to lighten the mood. "Of course, I'll only be doing it after I pray for help lifting each pretzel off without smushing it."

"I'm sure you'll do fine." Keturah turned to glance at the clock hanging high above a stand several aisles away. "Eight more minutes. I'll introduce you to Olivia. You already met my sister on Saturday." She beckoned them over.

Jeremiah still hadn't decided whether or not to tell Keturah he'd written that letter. He'd already figured out which sister was which, but if he showed how much he knew about the family, he might seem like a creeper.

He smiled and greeted Lilliane and Olivia. Their enthusiastic hellos made him feel like they were welcoming him as part of the team.

"I'm putting Jeremiah in charge of the warmer," Keturah

told them. "He'll get out the pretzels and drop them into the bags. I think that'll speed up the process."

Lilliane's lower lip trembled, and she appeared to be holding back tears.

"Is something wrong?" The last thing Jeremiah wanted to do was upset her.

"*Neh*." She waved a hand to dismiss his concerns. "Those are good jobs for you. And Olivia and I haven't been able to keep up with it. It's just that . . ." She turned her back, and her shoulders shook.

Keturah hurried over, put a hand on Lilliane's shoulder, and squeezed. Her sister gave a brief nod and hurried back to the baking table.

"Don't mind Lilliane," she whispered. "Change is hard for her. Our *mamm* always watched the warmer."

Jeremiah had seen Keturah wince after she'd directed him to that spot on the other side of the stand. Perhaps that had been her mother's place. "I don't want to remind everyone of your losses."

"Mamm stood over there"—she waved to the place Jeremiah had guessed—"when she wasn't running around helping everyone. We need someone to do her jobs, but it isn't easy."

"I understand." If he'd been in the farmhouse bumping up against Mamm's memories every day, he'd have found it much harder. Perhaps that gave him another reason to be thankful to be at the rehab center.

"We're glad to have you." Keturah cast troubled eyes in Lilliane's direction. "And I hope you can give my sister some time to adjust."

"Of course. Everybody grieves in their own time."

Keturah gave him a strange look, and he changed the subject. "Is there anything I should know?"

After she explained about moving pretzels up in the warmer and adding water, she sighed. "The hardest part about warmer watching is predicting what customers will order. Mamm did it for years, so she knew what all the regulars wanted."

Jeremiah wished he'd be here long enough to get proficient at that. For now, he'd notify Lilliane and Olivia when any flavors ran low. "I'll do my best to keep an eye on things," he assured Keturah.

She nodded. "Gideon's heading this way to unlock the doors, so we need to get ready to work now."

But they had one more problem to solve. Once Jeremiah moved into place, Olivia couldn't use the worktable Maleah had used on Saturday.

"Lilliane, can you help me move this?" Keturah grabbed one side of the heavy wooden table.

If he could make tight fists, Jeremiah would have pounded them on his chair arms. He should be the one moving that worktable. How long would it be until he could do things like that again? He might not ever regain his mobility. His hands might fully recover. But what about his legs?

Lilliane rushed over and tried to lift the other side, but she couldn't. With pushing and shoving and Olivia's help, they slid the worktable a few feet closer to the ovens. Then Keturah patted the shorter end of the table. "You can work here, Olivia." Keturah slid the baking tray around. "*Jah*, it fits."

Jeremiah disliked that his being here interfered with the setup of their stand, but this arrangement would only be temporary. Once Mrs. Vandenberg expanded the stand, he'd be on the right taking orders, with a machine that could make change. He'd forgotten to tell Keturah about those plans. And about Mrs. Vandenberg's offer to pick up Rose and Maleah after school to bring them here. She'd told him that as she'd wobbled her way to the Bentley.

Loud squeals came from overhead, and then "Silver Bells" blasted from the speakers. Someone muted it to background-music level.

No time to talk to Keturah now. Gideon had opened the doors, and people poured into the market. Soon a crush of customers had lined up.

The day flew by, and they barely had time to breathe or take a break before the girls arrived after school.

"What are you doing here?" Keturah stepped back, startled, as Maleah and Rose rushed into the stand after school.

"Mrs. Vandenberg's driver picked us up at school." Rose beamed.

"In a fancy car," Maleah added.

At Keturah's puzzled expression, Jeremiah explained, "I'm sorry. Mrs. Vandenberg asked me to tell you she'd be picking the girls up here in the mornings and dropping them off in the afternoons. She thought you could use the extra help."

Keturah frowned. "I can, but I don't want her to do that." She motioned her sisters to the sink at the back of the stand. "Go and wash up."

After the girls left, Jeremiah added, "Mrs. Vandenberg was also worried about your sisters being alone in the mornings and afternoons."

"But they always were before."

"She thought maybe with your, um, with the way things have changed, your sisters might prefer to be with you."

"Maleah definitely would. But Mrs. Vandenberg can't pick them up every day. I'll have to talk to her about that."

Jeremiah smiled to himself. *Good luck with that.* He guessed who'd win that argument.

Maleah skipped over to her usual work space. "Somebody moved my table, and I can't fit."

"Use that end." Lilliane pointed to the narrow side of the table. "And don't be rude to Jeremiah."

Looking contrite, Maleah turned to him. "I didn't mean to hurt your feelings."

"It's all right. I know I take up a lot of room."

"*Neh*, you don't. I'm glad you're here."

"Maleah," Keturah said as she hurried over to take orders, "since you don't have pretzels to fix at the moment, why don't you help Jeremiah check the water?"

Actually, he already knew how to do that. Keturah had demonstrated it earlier, and Olivia or Lilliane fetched the water when needed. But Jeremiah suspected Keturah wanted to distract her sister, so he listened intently to Maleah's explanation.

"Can you fill it?" he asked after she said the water was low.

"Me? I mess things up."

"I'm sure you'll do a better job than me."

Her eyes wide, Maleah stared at him. "I don't think so. You didn't see what happened on Saturday. I spilled water and—"

He interrupted her. "We learn from our mistakes, so today is always better."

"It is?" Maleah studied him as if assessing whether or not he spoke the truth.

"Of course. Mistakes show we're learning what doesn't work. Then next time, we don't do that again, right?" He turned the question back to her.

A smile blossomed on her face. "*Jah*, it's true." Then she sighed. "I wish it didn't take me so many tries to get it right."

"The more tries, the better you get."

"Then I must be getting very, very good."

He smiled. "I'm sure you are."

Maleah filled the water pan and inserted it perfectly. Then, glowing from his thanks and praise, she practically strutted back to the worktable.

Ever since Saturday, he'd wanted to lift her mood. She'd seemed so discouraged after she'd had those accidents so close together. Jeremiah hoped she'd look at her mishaps in a new light from now on.

He'd been so busy talking to Maleah, he'd forgotten about listening to Keturah's customers.

She turned, an open bag in her hand.

"I'm sorry. I wasn't paying attention."

"I'll get this one, then." Keturah leaned past him, opened the warmer, and selected three pretzels.

Jeremiah regretted not doing his job. He positioned himself so he could see and hear the customers, which also allowed him to watch Keturah. He had to force himself to concentrate on the buyers.

"Two regular," the man said.

Determined to do the job right this time, he opened the door and slid the tongs into a loop so he could lift the pretzels. So far, so good. He relaxed a little as both pretzels slid down the one arm of the tongs. Then he turned to find Keturah waiting with the white bag extended.

He hadn't expected her to be so close. She must have thought she'd need to reach into the warmer again. He had to drop the pretzels into the bag, but her soft, delicate hands holding the top of the bag distracted him.

"Oops." He missed the opening, and Keturah grabbed for the pretzels before they landed on the floor. She caught one cleanly, but mangled the other.

After they'd successfully bagged two fresh pretzels and Maleah had broken up the squashed pretzel to put in the sampler dish, she came back to talk to Jeremiah.

She giggled. "You're learning, aren't you?"

"I am. I wish I could say I won't make that mistake again, but I have a feeling I might miss a second time." *And maybe a third and a fourth and . . .*

"*Neh*, you won't." Maleah's statement came out with a confidence Jeremiah wished he had.

He needed to be brave and confident for her sake. "You're right. If I make another mistake, I'll be learning something different." He only hoped so.

With a proud smile, she went back to coating pretzels in butter. He'd been so busy talking and watching her, he hadn't heard the customer's order. Once again, Keturah turned with a bag, waiting expectantly.

"I wasn't paying attention."

"Two plain. Two cinnamon sugar." Keturah waited patiently for him to lift the pretzels with shaking hands. This time, he managed to get them into the bags she held out.

"I promise to stop talking to Maleah and pay attention from now on."

Keturah smiled. "I'm glad the two of you are getting along. And you seem to be catching on."

If you could call two out of three recent successes catching on. He'd had several misses that morning, but he'd gotten much more skillful in lifting the pretzels up and out. And over the next hour, dropping the pretzels into the bags became smoother and faster.

Still, the lines of customers grew. As they waited on one person, two more got in line. He'd never seen any market stand this busy. Keturah called Olivia up to help her wait on people, but Jeremiah held things up. Now he had to listen to two orders and keep them straight.

With two people waiting on customers, the crowds thinned out much more quickly, but they ran out of pretzels faster. Jeremiah kept an eye on the supply and alerted Lilliane before the racks ran too low.

She hurried back to the refrigerator for more dough. "Keturah, we're almost out of flour. Maybe we should get the containers we stored at Ridley's."

No way would Jeremiah let any of the girls go to Ridley's. "If you need that dough, I'll go and get it."

Keturah turned grateful eyes in his direction. "Would you mind?"

"Not at all."

She rewarded him with a relieved smile. "*Danke.* I'll miss having your help getting the pretzels, but I'd rather not send Lilliane."

"I understand that." He called to Lilliane, "I'll get the dough. How much do you want?"

"Maybe three containers."

That would mean three separate trips, but they might appreciate having him out from underfoot. At times, he worried he was an impediment rather than a help. He headed to the other end of the market.

Rather than barging into the stand, he stopped in front of Bo. "All right if I get some containers from your fridge?"

"Sure, sure. No need to ask." The corners of Bo's mouth turned down. "Are you really the one who'll be getting it each time?" He heaved a loud, put-upon sigh.

"Most likely." Jeremiah wanted to say *definitely*, but he didn't know Keturah's plans. Judging from her expression, though, she'd prefer to stay far away from Ridley's. Besides, the containers weighed quite a bit. Jeremiah should be the one hauling them.

"I thought I'd at least get paid back for my trouble," Bo grumbled, "by seeing the girls once in a while."

"If you want payment, I'll bring money tomorrow." If Bo wanted to be compensated for his refrigerator space, Jeremiah would take care of that. "How much do you think is fair?"

"Don't be ridiculous. You don't owe me anything. Just send the girls down here sometimes."

"I think those containers are too heavy for Maleah and Rose."

"Those are the two little ones?" When Jeremiah nodded, Bo's eyes narrowed. "Are you kidding me? I'm no perv."

Jeremiah wasn't so sure he agreed with that, but he breathed a little easier to hear Bo dismiss the two younger girls. Jeremiah didn't have to worry about protecting them from Bo. But Keturah and Lilliane?

Bo shot Jeremiah a hard look. "You know exactly which two girls I'm talking about. I know you Amish try to act all holy and stuff, but you can't tell me you haven't noticed the two older ones are real lookers."

His insinuations riled Jeremiah. And made him even more convinced to keep Keturah and Lilliane from this end of the market. And Olivia too, for that matter.

"Tell me"—Bo leaned over the counter with a conspiratorial look—"are Amish girls good kissers?"

"I have no idea," Jeremiah said icily. "I'm not married yet."

"Not married yet? Ha-ha, that's a good one." Bo burst into peals of laughter. "You really think I believe that?"

Laugh all you want, but I intend to follow the Ordnung. *The only woman I'll ever kiss is my wife.*

"I should go. I'm sure everyone's wondering where I am. Thank you for letting us use the refrigerator." Jeremiah hurried to the far end of the long counter.

Once again, one of the employees held the door for him, and Jeremiah wrestled one of the containers off the shelf and onto his lap, mainly using his palms and forearms, which were stronger and worked better than his fingers.

"I'll be back for two more," he told the man.

Bo overheard. "Why don't you bring one of the girls with you so you don't have to make so many trips?"

"I'm not sure they can leave the stand. We're pretty busy." And even if they had no customers, Jeremiah would never let any of them accompany him.

The market had gotten crowded with people who'd gotten off work, and weaving around shoppers with a heavy container in his lap proved challenging. It took him much longer to return than he'd expected.

"There you are." Keturah sounded relieved. "I was worried you might have gotten lost."

"*Neh.* I just spent a little time talking to Bo."

Her nose wrinkled. "About what?" She must not have wanted an answer, because she took the next customer's order and began filling it.

Jeremiah needed to hurry. He couldn't spend hours lugging the containers from one end of the market to the other.

"Lilliane, here's the first container. I won't take so long next time."

She gave him a kind smile. "There's no rush. I made some dough with the last of the flour, so we'll be fine for now."

Just before he opened the swinging door, she called to him, "Could you be sure to bring one of the containers marked *Raisin*? Two plain and one raisin should do us for a while."

This time, Jeremiah glided past Bo's end of the counter. As Jeremiah passed, Bo glanced around, probably checking to see if anyone had accompanied him. By the time Jeremiah emerged from the refrigerator, Bo had draped himself over the counter to flirt with a pretty blonde *Englischer*. He shot Jeremiah a triumphant, *bet-you-wish-you-were-in-my-place* look. Bo would be mighty disappointed to know that rather than being jealous, Jeremiah was relieved Bo had turned his attention elsewhere, and the *Englischer* seemed to be enjoying Bo's attention.

After Jeremiah had delivered one raisin and another plain container, he resumed his position by the warmer and slipped back into the routine. Maleah stayed at the back table to help Rose prep more pretzels, so he was alone with Keturah—or as alone as he could be with long lines of customers staring at him.

Chapter Eleven

Keturah grew used to the rhythm of opening the white bags, turning, and waiting for Jeremiah to drop in the pretzels. She also liked his triumphant smile each time he succeeded. Seeing the gleam in his eyes warmed her heart.

Not only was he helping her; she was helping him. And that small joy kept her spirits up. Between the press of customers and the expectation of Jeremiah's smile each time she faced him, she rarely had time to think of missing Mamm.

When they finally reached a lull in customers, Keturah breathed a sigh of relief. "Let's all take a quick break."

No sooner had she said it than a man strode to the counter.

Lilliane headed in his direction. "You two take your break. I'll handle things here. Then I can eat after you're done."

Keturah headed to the table at the back where Daed usually sat to keep an eye on things and take care of the books. He also helped other businesses with their accounting. He'd been a whiz at numbers. No matter how deeply engrossed he'd been in figuring, though, he'd never missed anything going on in the stand.

Her feelings in a jumble, Keturah dug through the picnic cooler they used to store their meals. She'd packed fewer sandwiches than she used to, because two of their family would never be here with them again.

Her eyes stinging, she lifted out her sandwich. She'd give that to Jeremiah, along with the apple and chocolate chip cookies. He hadn't brought food, because he hadn't intended to stay. And they'd all been so busy, they'd skipped lunch. She also hadn't expected Maleah and Rose to be here. What would she feed them?

Jeremiah inhaled deeply. "That barbecued chicken smells delicious. Could you show me where the stand is?"

"I was going to offer you this sandwich, but barbecued chicken does sound good." She closed the lid on the lunch cooler.

"*Danke.* That smell's been calling to me since lunchtime and making me hungry."

He could easily follow his nose to find the stand, but she'd be glad to take him there. "Hartzler's is about halfway down the market by the central staircase." She went over and pushed open the swinging door. "Come on."

For some strange reason, she felt like a schoolgirl who'd just been let out for recess. They rarely bought food from other stands. Daed had been frugal, so they packed lunches. This would be a real treat.

"I never had a chance to tell you the rest of Mrs. Vandenberg's plans." Jeremiah moved into place beside her.

Once they got into the busy market aisles, though, they couldn't stay side by side. Keturah walked ahead of him but angled her body sideways so she could look back at him.

"Because handling coins and bills would be difficult for me and possibly others who'll come after me . . ." He appeared downcast as he trailed off, but then his upbeat expression returned. "Mrs. Vandenberg wants to install an automatic self-service terminal like they have in some supermarkets and stores. The kind where you insert cash or a charge card and the machine makes the change."

Keturah stopped so abruptly, he almost ran into her.

"What's the matter?"

"Daed would never let us—" She snapped her mouth shut. Sorrow expanded inside her chest, making her ribs hurt. Daed . . . and Mamm . . . weren't around to make decisions.

"Are you all right?"

Jeremiah's soft, caring voice helped soothe the blossoming ache in her heart.

"I'm sorry. For a minute, I forgot"—she swallowed back the rising pain—"my parents aren't here anymore."

"I understand." He waited until she'd regained her composure. "Your *daed* wouldn't have wanted the machine?"

"Definitely not."

"He'd have a problem with using electricity?"

"Well, originally, he did. But when he took over the stand, the ovens and refrigerator were already connected. Mamm convinced him to keep those."

"So you'd be all right with plugging in a self-service terminal?"

"I keep forgetting I have to make these decisions now. I don't like going against my parents' wishes. Daed wouldn't ever take credit cards."

"I guess that means no terminal, then."

"But Mrs. Vandenberg is the one who's doing it. I don't want to say *neh* to her. It's her expansion."

"She doesn't want to do anything you don't feel right about."

"I'm not sure how I feel." Once again, Keturah was torn between following her father's rules or doing what was best for the business. "I'll have to think about it."

"Excuse me." A woman holding two toddlers by the hand tried to squeeze around them.

"I'm so sorry. I didn't mean to block the aisle."

"You're not the one who's in the way," Jeremiah said. "I am."

Keturah didn't want him to blame himself. "Why don't we go over there to finish talking?" She pointed to some tables and chairs several aisles away. "Hartzler's is right beside that seating area."

"Let's get something to eat first. You look like you could use some food."

She wasn't sure she could choke anything down, but she headed toward the counter with him.

Gideon had already decorated his stand. He'd suspended a series of scrolls from the ceiling. It began with the prophecy in Isaiah: "*For unto us a Child is born, unto us a Son is given . . .*" Then each scroll told the Christmas story from Luke.

What a great idea! Maybe she could come up with something that focused on Christ's birth.

When they reached the front of the line, Gideon Hartzler smiled at both of them. "*Wie geht's?*"

"It's going fine. Jeremiah's been a big help."

"I doubt I'm much help." Jeremiah shrugged as if to dismiss his contribution.

"That's not true." Keturah wished he'd stop putting himself down.

"We should order." He waved for her to go first. "My treat. And please get whatever your sisters like too."

"*Neh*, we should be paying for you. You're working for us."

"I'm paying. I'll explain why later. We don't want to hold up the line."

Reluctantly, she ordered. She'd insist on repaying him. No point in arguing when people behind them were waiting.

Then Jeremiah added his order. "And please give us five orders of fries, an eight-piece bucket of chicken, and broccoli-raisin salad."

Keturah stared at him. "You must be hungry."

He laughed. "*Neh*, I want to be sure no one goes hungry. You only ordered one piece of chicken for each of you."

She hadn't expected such a huge bill. Mamm would be aghast. If she bought fries, which she only did once or twice, they got one small order for the family to share, never individual containers. And Mamm would never order more than one piece of chicken for each person.

Jeremiah paid the bill without blinking. He set the huge bag on his lap. "Did you want to eat here, or do you need to head back?"

"Let me take a peek to see how busy Lilliane is." Keturah walked behind the central staircase so she could see the aisle.

Rose seemed to be helping Lilliane. Olivia had a line, but it wasn't as long as it had been that morning.

She returned to Jeremiah. "If we don't take long, we can sit here for a while. They seem to be handling the customers." Keturah moved a chair aside so Jeremiah could pull up to the table.

"Not as busy as Saturday, then?"

"I think Friday and Saturday's constant stream of business was because it was our first week back at the market. People probably wanted to express their sympathy." Her eyes burned, and she squeezed them shut.

Jeremiah set a hand over hers. "It isn't easy. You're very brave to keep the stand running."

"Oh-ho, what have we here?" Bo Ridley waggled his eyebrows at Jeremiah. "Making a move already."

Jeremiah's jaw tightened. "I—"

"Go on," Bo urged. "I'd like to hear your excuse. Better yet"—he turned to Keturah—"tell me, is he a good kisser?"

She drew in a sharp breath. This was even worse than Bo's usual stares, the ones that made her uncomfortable. Jeremiah looked so unnerved, she wanted to reassure him. But he drew his hand back and set it stiffly in his lap. She missed the comfort of his touch.

Keturah had to say something to defend him, but what? "I don't know. You'll have to ask his wife."

"He's married?" Bo drew back in shock. "And he's fooling around with you?" His eyes squeezed into slits. "Wait a minute. He doesn't have a beard."

Keturah sat stony-faced, pretending to ignore him. Often when she did that, Bo went away.

"Well, from the way you were drooling over him, you'd obviously like to be that lucky woman." Bo clapped Jeremiah on the back. "Good luck avoiding that trap, man. Love 'em and leave 'em, I always say. Better that way." With a snicker, he took off.

Her cheeks on fire, Keturah ducked her head. "I'm sorry," she whispered to Jeremiah. "He's, um . . ." How could she describe Bo?

Jeremiah ground his teeth. "I know."

"I usually try to stay away from him."

"I don't blame you." With a grim expression, he pushed back from the table. "Maybe we should get back to help your sisters. Besides, we don't want their chicken and fries to get too cold."

"I'll pay you when we get back." She hadn't brought enough money with her, and she'd never have spent that much money on one meal, even if she could afford it.

"Absolutely not."

This time they stayed moving as they talked so they didn't block the aisle. "It's the least I can do for all your work."

"I feel like I should pay you for letting me work there." Jeremiah's eyes begged her to understand. "Ever since the accident, I've felt so helpless and useless. It means a lot to be able to do a job, any job." His rueful smile touched her. "*Danke* for putting up with me."

"Even if you don't believe it, having you has been a help." She wished she could get him to believe it. "You don't owe us anything. We owe you."

How could Jeremiah explain how much it meant to have his dignity back, to be able to contribute even a little to the business? Not to mention their kindness. It was a joy to work at the pretzel stand.

When they returned with the chicken, Maleah's eyes grew round. "We each get fries? And all this chicken?"

After he nodded, she ran over, threw her arms around his neck, and hugged him.

"*Danke,*" she whispered in his ear. "I'm so glad you're working here." She stepped back. "And not just because you brought us chicken."

In a stern voice, Keturah said, "Save some of that chicken. Jeremiah might want it for lunch tomorrow."

"Let them eat it all. That's why I bought it. If I want chicken tomorrow, I can go and get some."

"Keturah?" Lilliane called. "I could use some help."

So much for the brief respite they'd had. Long lines had formed. The lull had only been temporary. He headed for the warmer.

"I forgot to tell you," he said before Keturah took her place at the counter. "Mrs. Vandenberg plans to put another pretzel warmer over there." He waved to the opposite side of the stand. "That way those of us from the rehab center could fill orders on that side. She intends to put it beside the money machine, if you decide to allow that."

Her eyes sad, she studied him. "That machine would help you and the others, wouldn't it?"

"*Jah.*" He couldn't make change without it, but he didn't want to manipulate her into accepting something that went against her conscience.

Despite the guilt on her face, she straightened her shoulders. "Then I'll do it."

Jeremiah wanted to tell her not to if she didn't feel right about it. Before he could say anything, Lilliane interrupted.

"Are you coming, Keturah?"

At the desperate note in her sister's voice, Keturah whirled around. "I'm sorry." She beckoned to the next customer, and Jeremiah strained to hear the little girl's order.

He had the raisin pretzel ready when Keturah turned. Her smile almost made him miss the bag again.

As Keturah collected the money, Maleah piped up behind him, "See, I told you. You almost dropped that pretzel, but you didn't. I was right. You didn't make that mistake again."

He smiled at her. "Thanks for reminding me."

She grinned back. "You're welcome."

Again he missed the order while he talked to Maleah. Keturah turned, expecting a pretzel, and with a sheepish expression, he asked, "What kind?"

"If neither of you can keep your minds on your jobs, I'm going to have to separate you and Maleah." She said it with mock sternness.

The last thing he wanted to do was cause trouble or slow down her work. "I promise I'll keep quiet until closing."

Keturah laughed. "I'm not sure that's possible."

"Are you saying I'm too talkative?" He put on a wounded look.

"*Neh*, but Maleah can be." Keturah softened her words with a fond smile at her sister. "I need one plain and one raisin." She held out two bags.

Raisin pretzels went in separate bags because they were coated with glaze. Fighting to keep his hand steady, Jeremiah dropped that one in. Then he managed to do the plain one, only rattling the bag a little as he bumped the top edge.

"See," Maleah said, "you did it again."

After Keturah had folded the tops of the bags and put them in one hand, she shook her finger at her sister. "You need to stop distracting Jeremiah. If you want someone to talk to, try praying."

After Keturah turned around, Maleah shot Jeremiah a mischievous grin. "I'll pray, but I'll also whisper to you sometimes."

"I'd like that as long as I can hear the orders. Maybe we can talk while your sister counts out change."

Maleah's sweet little giggle followed him as he turned to pay attention to the next customer who'd stepped up to order.

As he reached for the correct pretzels, Maleah whispered, "You're nice, Jeremiah."

A wave of longing for a home and family swept over him. He hadn't realized how alone he'd been since Mamm had died. His brothers and most of his relatives lived in New York State. Friends from church visited him at the rehab center, but he had no family around.

Although the girls grieved for their lost parents, they had each other. Somehow little Maleah's chatter made him feel a part of their close-knit family. Lilliane reinforced that feeling a few minutes later when she returned from eating her lunch.

"*Danke* for the chicken and fries, Jeremiah." She gave him a shy smile as she passed. "It was good."

Rose joined them. "I liked it too. And *danke* for getting the dough when we needed it."

All he needed to feel complete was a comment from Keturah. Hers would hold the most meaning.

Chapter Twelve

Exhausted and drained, Jeremiah dragged himself to his room after he returned from the market. He'd gotten back so late he'd missed supper.

Too tired to eat anyway, he set the bag of pretzels Keturah had insisted on sending with him on the bedside table and then maneuvered himself onto the bed. He closed his eyes to replay the day and bask in the sunshine of Keturah's smile.

"Is something wrong?"

A concerned voice punctured Jeremiah's fantasies, which had progressed to Keturah's soft hand under his on the café table. Reluctantly, he opened his eyes to find Darryl framed in the doorway, a concerned expression pushing his thick brows together.

"You okay?"

"I'm fine. Just tired from working."

Darryl's eyes widened. "I didn't know you planned to work at the market."

Jeremiah's weak laugh revealed his exhaustion. "Neither did I."

"Do tell." Darryl entered the room. "Why don't I help you get ready for bed while we talk?"

"Isn't your shift over?"

"Yep, but I might as well be doing something useful rather than sitting around."

"But you won't be getting paid."

"I care more about helping people than making money. Besides, I'll save the evening shift some time tonight."

Actually, hadn't Jeremiah done the exact same thing today—insisting he didn't need to be paid? He'd happily worked with Keturah and her sisters for free.

Darryl helped Jeremiah get undressed and ready for bed. "So what happened?"

As Jeremiah explained Mrs. Vandenberg's plans for the stand and his own surprise employment, Darryl's smile grew wider and wider.

"She's quite a woman. And good on you for taking that job."

"I worry I'm more of a problem than a help."

"Naw, they need you. It sounds like you're doing the job their mother used to do."

"I am." Jeremiah gazed off into the distance. First Keturah had put him on one side of the stand. Then her face scrunched up as if she was holding back tears. Then she asked him to work on the opposite side.

"You look like you're far away."

Darryl's remark brought Jeremiah back to the room.

"I think Keturah had me in her *mamm*'s place at first. Then she moved me to the pretzel warmer." Keturah hadn't needed him there, but it saved her grief.

"Did you get along with everyone else?"

"Her seven-year-old sister liked having someone to talk to. She seems really lonely."

"It's hard to be an orphan when you're young." Darryl spoke with conviction, and his face reflected deep pain.

Jeremiah wanted to reach out. "You sound like you know what it feels like."

"Sure do. I was eight when I lost Mom. Never knew my father."

"That had to be hard. My *daed* died when I was six, and my whole world fell apart. I still had Mamm, though. I can't even imagine losing both parents at that age."

"Yeah, it was the hardest thing I've ever been through. Life was never the same after that." Darryl's face darkened.

"What happened?"

"Bounced around in foster care for a while until a family decided to adopt me. They were pretty nice, but then their little girl got sick. Leukemia or something. They couldn't take on another child." Darryl's Adam's apple bobbed up and down rapidly.

His heart aching for Darryl, Jeremiah waited. He'd never have guessed from Darryl's cheerful demeanor he'd had a rough childhood.

"Other than Mom dying, that was the second roughest day of my life. I thought I'd have a home, a family. And then I didn't." Darryl's eyes welled with tears. "I didn't know the worst was yet to come."

"I'm so sorry."

Darryl focused on the blank wall above Jeremiah's bed, and his face twisted. "If I'd known what was next, I'd've run away then instead of later." He broke off abruptly, and he switched into an accepting smile. "You don't want to hear all this. It's over and done."

But Darryl was wrong. "I do want to hear the rest. I want to know how you went from there to who you are now."

Darryl laughed. "There's an easy answer to that. God's love and forgiveness. And, of course, God's servants on earth—all the people who've helped me since."

"How old were you when you ran away?"

"Which time?"

"You ran away more than once?"

"About a dozen times. I kept hoping they'd put me with different foster parents, but they didn't. I tried telling them the truth about what was happening, but the other kids told children's services I was a liar. They were too scared to tell the truth."

Although Jeremiah had no idea what abuse Darryl had endured, he didn't deserve to be branded a liar.

"I didn't blame them. They knew what would happen if they backed me up. And they got special privileges if they insisted I was lying. What bugged me most back then was that no one questioned why the foster parents agreed to take me back each time."

Jeremiah wondered the same thing. "Why did they?"

"They made good money off me. And they loved punishing me."

How could anyone be so cruel?

Darryl exhaled a long sigh. "Thank God, Mrs. Vandenberg rescued me."

"She did?"

"Well, not her personally. At least, not at first. She supports shelters for runaways. One day when I was in one of her shelters, she stopped in, and we talked. She had a detective look into my foster family, and they ended up rescuing all the kids there. My foster parents are still in jail, but I visit them regularly."

"You do?" Jeremiah wouldn't want to go anywhere near people who'd abused him.

"Of course. They need to hear the message of God's love and forgiveness. My foster mom accepted Christ. I'm still praying for my foster dad."

Jeremiah was amazed that Darryl would call them his "foster mom and dad." He wished he had such a forgiving spirit.

"But back to Mrs. V. She's amazing, isn't she? She figured out exactly what I needed and made sure I got it. At first, I rebelled, but she made me finish my GED and encouraged me to go to church with her. That's the first I'd heard about God."

Mrs. Vandenberg found so many different ways to help people. Jeremiah could sing her praises too. But she'd really turned Darryl's life around. It was hard to believe he'd never heard about God. One more thing to go on Jeremiah's *To Be Grateful* list: learning about God since childhood. Oh, and having caring parents.

"This time of year is special to me," Darryl continued, "because I first asked Jesus into my heart during a Christmas Eve service. Before that, I thought Christmas was about Santa and reindeer. And about not getting gifts because I was on the naughty list."

He took a deep breath. "I never knew Christmas meant the birth of God's Son. That night I received the greatest gift of my life."

Darryl's heartfelt story, and the tears shining in his eyes, touched Jeremiah.

"Everyone wonders why I'm always so happy. That's why. When you get a gift like that, you can't help being grateful." Darryl's face broke into his usual wide smile. "Doesn't matter what time of year it is. It's always Christmas in my heart."

As she and her sisters sat down to supper the next evening, Keturah leaned back in her chair and stretched her arms overhead. Jeremiah had insisted they take the leftover chicken home because he had nowhere to store it. Her sisters all agreed to eat it cold with the broccoli salad and buttered bread. They'd been rushed off their feet all day preparing dough for tomorrow, so not having to fix a meal was a blessing.

Following the prayer, Keturah ate a few bites, then caught her sisters' attention. "I don't know if you could hear the conversation yesterday morning, but Mrs. Vandenberg talked to me about expanding our stand."

Lilliane frowned. "How will we afford that?"

"Mrs. Vandenberg plans to pay for it. She'd like to use the bigger space to help people from the rehab center get back to work."

"Like Jeremiah?" Maleah leaned so far forward, the front of her dress dipped into the dressing on the tops of her broccoli florets.

Suppressing a sigh, Keturah pointed a finger toward her sister's plate. Maleah straightened up and stared down at the greasy circles on her gray dress.

"Sorry," she muttered.

"You'll need to wash those out with lye soap after supper." But Maleah would need supervision to get it done, a task that would fall to Keturah. "To answer your question, *jah*, we'd be helping others like Jeremiah."

"But I want to keep him," Maleah wailed. "Can't he stay forever?"

Although her sister tended to be dramatic, it surprised Keturah that Maleah had gotten so attached to Jeremiah after only two days. Maybe in her sorrow, she'd latched onto the first male figure around.

Maleah's lower lip quivered. "He doesn't treat me like I'm a baby." She glared at each sister in turn.

Hmm . . . Maybe they needed to start giving her more responsibility. They did coddle her, even more so since the accident. Deciding when to help and when to step back proved difficult. Keturah was only starting to understand how hard it was to be a parent.

Rose set down her chicken leg. "I wish we could keep Jeremiah too. He's so nice. I can't believe he bought us all this chicken and everything."

"Even our own bags of fries." Maleah's eyes gleamed.

"I can't imagine what that cost." Lilliane turned to Keturah. "We should have paid him back. He's working for free."

"I tried, but he wouldn't let me. He said he owed us for letting him work at the stand."

Lilliane stared at Keturah with disbelief. "What? That doesn't make any sense."

"I didn't think so either, but he said having a job makes him feel less helpless. I guess he needs people to do things for him, so it's a chance for him to do something for himself and for others."

"I can understand that, but still . . ."

"I didn't want to accept, but paying for it might have made him feel like others were taking care of him."

"I suppose so." Lilliane's disgruntled expression revealed she disagreed.

"We could write him a thank-you note." Rose's cheerful peacemaking efforts brought smiles to everyone's faces, even Lilliane's. "Let's do that after supper."

One more chore to add to that evening's list, but this one wouldn't be a hardship. Like Maleah, Keturah wanted Jeremiah to stay. His ready smile lifted her mood each time she turned around to fill bags.

Usually, she sucked in a breath and held it while he inched each pretzel up from the rack. But after he succeeded, delight brightened his handsome features, and she released her pent-up air along with her tension.

Jeremiah also exuded a calmness that washed over her whenever she grew harried or overwhelmed. He might not accomplish a lot, but he'd become valuable for other, more important things.

"He'll work for us until he's ready to go out on his own." She'd made sure of that.

"I hope that never happens."

"Maleah!" Rose stared at her younger sister. "How can you say that? Don't you want him to get better?"

"'Course I do, but I don't want him to leave. He's nice, and I don't have anybody to talk to when he's not there."

Keturah hadn't thought about how being at a table alone affected her talkative sister. Why hadn't she noticed before?

Tears pooled in Maleah's eyes. "Mamm sometimes

whispered to me so I wouldn't be lonely. If Jeremiah goes, no one will be around to listen to me."

Daed must have moved Maleah to that worktable to prevent her chatter from distracting the other girls, but for Maleah to get so attached to a stranger—even a nice and kind one—signaled she needed company.

"When we expand, maybe we can change the layout so you don't feel so alone."

For now, Jeremiah would fill that role. Once they did increase the stand size, he'd move to the *Englischer* side. Keturah had decided to call it that to ease her conscience about the self-service terminal.

She needed to tell her sisters about that too. Taking a deep breath to give herself courage, she plunged in, dreading Lilliane's reaction. "Because the stand expansion is for rehab workers, Mrs. Vandenberg will install some equipment to help them."

Lilliane's eyes held suspicion. "What kind of equipment?"

"A pretzel warmer." Keturah hesitated. "And a self-service terminal."

Rose's forehead creased. "What's that?"

"You know those machines at the supermarket or stores where you check out yourself?"

"We're going to have a big thing like that in our pretzel stand?"

"I doubt it'll be that big, but it'll do the same job."

Rose broke in. "Will the machine take credit cards like they do at the stores?"

Keturah ran a finger around the edge of her water glass and avoided her sister's eyes. "I believe so."

Lilliane sucked in a breath. "But Daed . . ."

"I know he wouldn't have wanted that."

"Then why are you doing it?" Her sister's eyes blazed.

"We need to help Jeremiah and the others who come after him. And we won't be using the machine. The *Englischers* will."

Lilliane's brows drew together. "Won't we get the money from the charges?"

Keturah had tried to push away that idea to assuage her uneasiness. She'd hoped her sisters would accept that part of the business as *Englisch* and not really connect it with them.

But Lilliane's question pointed up Keturah's fibs to herself. Although she'd told herself accepting Mrs. Vandenberg's expansion wouldn't cause harm, had she been lying to herself?

An anguished cry came from Lilliane. "I always tried to obey Daed and do whatever he said."

Her sister spoke the truth. Of all the girls, Lilliane always listened to their parents and followed every command. And Rose did her best, so she rarely needed to be scolded, unlike Keturah and Maleah, who'd often ended up in trouble.

Lilliane stood. "If you go against Daed's wishes, I cannot work in the stand." She pivoted on her heel and rushed away.

What could Keturah do? She couldn't say *neh* to Mrs. Vandenberg, but she definitely couldn't lose her sister.

Chapter Thirteen

While Keturah and her sisters unloaded the buggy before dawn, a van pulled up nearby. Her spirits lifted. Jeremiah had returned.

Christmas Extravaganza lights flashed ribbons of green and red across his face as he emerged from the van with a huge smile and rolled over to help them. "If you load me up, I'll help you take everything in."

Lilliane and Keturah had each grasped one side of a heavy container.

"Put that in my lap," Jeremiah said.

They both hesitated.

"I can handle it. You should see the tortures my physical therapist puts me through."

Lilliane, her teeth clenched with the strain, appeared doubtful, but Jeremiah coaxed them again, and she gave in. Keturah tried to set it down gently. She wasn't positive, but when it landed, he might have bitten back a groan.

"I don't know how"—he drew in a breath and moved forward—"you two carried this."

"It's not easy, but we've been doing it since . . . since Daed . . ." Lilliane swallowed hard.

He turned a sympathetic glance in her direction. "I understand."

Those words sounded so genuine, so heartfelt. The same peace that fell over her when she read the letter in her pocket radiated from Jeremiah.

When they headed inside, lights and decorations sparkled from each stand they passed. The kosher meat stand had blue and white bunting draped behind a large menorah. Silvery stars of David hung from blue and white ribbons. A basket filled with plastic dreidels sat on a table under a sign saying, *Spin Me*.

A few stands down, Grandma's Cookies had a small table filled with holiday cookies labeled *Cookies for Santa and His Reindeer*. Underneath, the sign said, *Are you a reindeer?* Beside the table, they'd set a miniature sleigh filled with antler headbands and the invitation *Help yourself to antlers and a cookie*.

Maleah's eyes grew wider with each step. "Everyone's giving away presents. Can we do that too?"

"What would we give away?" The last thing Keturah needed was another project.

"How about small pretzels with a sign explaining they're praying hands?" Jeremiah suggested.

Keturah groaned. "When would we bake them?"

"They don't have to be soft pretzels, do they? What if I bought small, crispy ones from the bulk foods store?"

"I can pay for them." She wasn't about to let him incur another expense on their behalf.

"I'd like to do that. It'll get me in the Christmas spirit. Besides, I don't have anyone to buy gifts for."

He sounded so forlorn, Keturah couldn't turn him down.

Gina came bouncing up to them when they reached the stand. "I just wanted to remind you next Saturday will be opening day for the extravaganza. Please have your decorations and giveaways ready before then." Without waiting for an answer, she hurried off.

Lilliane thumped her container down on the table. "*Ach*, you should have told her we don't decorate for Christmas."

"At least we'll have Jeremiah's pretzels to give away." Rose smiled at him.

"If it's all right with you, I have an idea," Jeremiah said.

"Anything's all right with me." Keturah started out of the stand. "As long as it isn't Santa, lights, and reindeer."

Jeremiah laughed. "I promise even your sister will approve." He kept his voice low so Lilliane couldn't hear him.

Mrs. Vandenberg tottered toward Keturah. "Could Jeremiah help your sisters unload so we can discuss the plans for this weekend?"

This weekend? Keturah hadn't expected the expansion to happen so soon. The market closed early on Saturdays, and she preferred to go home and rest. Not to mention that this would be their first full work week without their parents, and judging by what had happened so far, it would be draining. Even more so, since Gina had extra events for Saturday that would bring in larger crowds. Plus, laundry and other chores awaited them at home on Saturdays.

"Is everything okay?" Mrs. Vandenberg studied Keturah closely. "You seem reluctant to do this. I don't want to pressure you into changing your stand if it doesn't feel right to you."

"It's not that. I'm tired." Something in Mrs. Vandenberg's eyes made Keturah confess the truth. "It's been a hard week with Mamm gone and me being in charge of all the decisions."

"I can understand that, and I don't want to add to your burdens. Would you like me to put off the stand expansion?"

"*Neh*, please do it whenever it works for you."

"I planned to have the workmen come Friday night after the market closes to rough out the side walls. They can finish whatever else needs to be completed after closing on Saturday or on Monday."

The new stand would be done before next Tuesday? And her fears of being asked to add something else to her schedule had been wrong. "Oh, I'm sorry. I should have realized that. I thought . . ."

"I was going to ask you to do more work?" Mrs. Vandenberg tilted one eyebrow in a comical expression.

Keturah laughed. "*Jah*, something like that."

"It might not feel like it right now, but I'm trying to make your load lighter and easier."

"I know that, and I'm sorry to seem so grumpy."

"You're only being honest. Nothing wrong with that."

"My parents would disagree. They'd say I'm being *mürrisch*." She'd spoken as if they were still alive before it struck her that they were no longer around. For a brief moment, she'd forgotten. Reality smacked into her, almost knocking her off her feet.

When she teetered, Mrs. Vandenberg reached out to steady her, and a few of the tears Keturah had been suppressing slipped down her cheeks.

This ninety-two-year-old woman, who needs a cane and a helping hand tried to support me with no thought for herself. She could have fallen and broken bones, but she only thought of me.

"It's hard to be the strong one in the family." Mrs. Vandenberg's sympathetic voice made the tears come faster. "You've been through a lot. Nothing wrong with crying."

"I'm sorry." Keturah tried to stop the flow.

"Never be sorry for expressing your emotions."

But Keturah shouldn't be crying in public. She had her back to her sisters and hoped they couldn't tell. But Jeremiah had moved past her and turned to look. His eyes filled with pity. And understanding.

Knuckling away the moisture on her cheeks, Keturah stood straighter.

"I find I'm a little shaky on my feet." Mrs. Vandenberg reached out and grasped Keturah's arm. "Could I lean on you for a bit?"

Keturah studied the elderly woman with suspicion. *Is she doing this to ease my embarrassment at being dependent a few minutes ago?*

Mrs. Vandenberg's face remained guileless.

"*Danke,*" Keturah whispered, her throat thick.

"I should be thanking you, dear. This old body isn't what it used to be."

With Mrs. Vandenberg clinging tightly to Keturah's arm, they made their way into the pretzel stand. Keturah seated Mrs. Vandenberg at the table in the back where her father had sat to do the accounting. They had one chair, so she stood while Mrs. Vandenberg pulled a zippered leather folder from her handbag.

"Sit, dear." Mrs. Vandenberg motioned with her chin to the opposite side of the table as she opened her folder and removed some papers.

"We, um, only have one chair." Her father did not believe in encouraging idleness.

"Oh, my goodness. I can add chairs to my list."

"*Neh*, we don't have time to sit." And Keturah didn't want to upset Lilliane any more than she already had.

"That's true." The cobwebby lines around Mrs. Vandenberg's mouth deepened as she pursed her lips. "You all need more leisure time. We'll need to find a solution for that, won't we? Right now, though, here's the timetable for renovations."

Keturah ran her finger down the list. "How did you get this done so fast?"

"I have my ways. It also helps to have a good contact list. And money doesn't hurt."

Keturah had heard many stories of Mrs. Vandenberg's wealth and her charity. But this seemed unbelievable.

"Will this be okay? I don't want to disrupt your business, so I've scheduled all the work for times when the market is closed."

"They can really have all of this done in such a short time?"

"I've found them to be quite reliable."

Wait a minute. Keturah pointed to next week's dates. "What's this?"

"That's when the new refrigerator and the shelved cooler will be installed."

"I haven't even ordered them yet." When would she get

the time to do that? They spent their days off making batches of pretzel dough and catching up on housecleaning.

"I took care of that. I hope you'll like what I picked out."

Ach, what would that cost? She'd had no time yet to go over their finances to see what they'd need for household expenses and stand rental.

"I was planning to do that, but—" She nibbled on her lower lip. Would a woman as rich as Mrs. Vandenberg understand that making major purchases meant carefully considering options within your budget? "I don't know yet what I can spend."

"That's no problem. It's coming out of my renovation budget."

"But I can't let you do that."

"All these updates to the stand are capital improvements. In other words, they'll make my business more valuable and serve as tax deductions. That way, they'll be considered market property if you ever give up the stand."

That made sense, but Keturah had no intention of giving up the stand.

Mrs. Vandenberg reached out and patted Keturah's hand holding down the paper. "Not that I'd ever want you to leave." She smiled. "I'd like to see you do what some owners have done and pass your stand down to the next generation."

"If I keep the stand that long, the refrigerators will need to be replaced."

"Don't worry about that. I'm sure the market owners will take care of that."

"It doesn't seem right. I should pay for them."

"Do you plan to take them with you if you ever leave the business?"

Keturah couldn't imagine doing that. They'd have no use or space for commercial refrigerators. She shook her head.

"See. That means they'd be mine."

"But . . ." Keturah sputtered to a stop. She'd run out of arguments. She didn't envy any of the people Mrs. Vandenberg did business with. She'd get them to agree to any terms she set.

Mrs. Vandenberg pushed herself to her feet. "Now that this is all settled, I have some other business to attend to at other stands. I'd like to adapt more stands for rehab workers."

Keturah sucked in a breath. Did that mean they might lose Jeremiah? He might prefer to work elsewhere.

"Don't worry about that, dear." Mrs. Vandenberg patted Keturah's arm as she passed. "I think God has a very special reason for bringing Jeremiah to your stand. Trust me on that." She laughed. "I guess I should have said, *Trust Him on that.*"

Keturah puzzled over that as Mrs. Vandenberg limped away. What did she mean? And when she'd said *him*, had she meant Jeremiah or God? Or both?

Jeremiah entered the stand with another heavy container to find Keturah staring off into space, her brow furrowed. "Did Mrs. Vandenberg upset you?"

"What?" Keturah jumped. "*Neh*, I just wonder what she meant."

He hadn't intended to startle her. "About what?"

"I, um, well, I'm overwhelmed by all her plans."

"She does seem to move quickly." Jeremiah could attest to that. One minute he was meeting her, and less than a day later, he had a job in the pretzel stand. But Keturah's concerns seemed deeper. "Are there things you don't want to do?"

Keturah seemed to be struggling to bring her mind back from faraway thoughts. "I don't like her paying for all the new equipment. She called them capital, um—"

"Expenditures? That makes sense. She'll be investing in her own business." Once again, Jeremiah admired Mrs. Vandenberg's methods.

"I don't think that's the word she used, but what you're saying sounds like what she explained. How do you know so much about that?"

"I used to own my own business. Back before—" He waved toward his wheelchair.

Keturah looked as if she wanted to ask more questions, but Gideon passed by, keys jingling in his hand. "*Ach*, we're not even unloaded yet."

"I brought everything in except for the extra dough. And Lilliane and Olivia are almost ready to fill the pretzel warmer, so you should be all right."

Keturah blinked and gazed around her as if surprised so much had been done. "About the extra dough, I hate to ask this, but would you mind taking that to Ridley's refrigerator?"

Jeremiah grimaced, then tried to adjust his face into a neutral expression.

Keturah must have noticed his first reaction. "I can go if you'd rather not."

"Absolutely not. Better me than you." Bo might make

crude comments to another man, but Jeremiah had no idea what Bo might do to a woman. Suppose he trapped Keturah in the refrigerator or something?

"Are you all right?" Keturah watched him worriedly.

"Just thinking about meeting Bo."

She laid a hand on his arm. "You don't have to do it. If Lilliane can't make enough dough, we can tell customers we ran out."

The warmth of her soft skin on his flesh drove all thoughts of Bo from his mind and replaced them with other, more tantalizing ones. He wished Bo hadn't mentioned kissing Keturah, because Jeremiah's gaze drifted to her soft, full lips.

He jerked his attention back to Bo. "I, um, I'll go now."

Even though she lifted her hand, her fingers left a gentle tingling behind. He struggled not to touch the spot or to stare at her with the longing she'd raised in him.

"I-I'd better go so I can get back here before you get too busy."

The faster he did this chore, the faster he could return. He hurried to the buggy, but once he'd loaded the first container, his movements slowed. He disliked facing Bo.

Perhaps he'd be lucky enough to avoid Bo today. Jeremiah sneaked past several times with boxes while Bo had his back turned, directing the installation of a winter wonderland scene with waving snowmen in candy-striped scarves. But when Jeremiah emerged from the refrigerator one final time and tried to slip off, Bo yelled to him.

"Hey, Jerry, hang on."

Jeremiah cringed at the nickname. He wanted to pretend he hadn't heard Bo's call, but that would be dishonest. He stopped and turned his head.

With a *cat-playing-with-a-mouse* grin, Bo scurried toward him. "Were you trying to sneak by without speaking, Jerry?"

"It's Jeremiah," he corrected, hoping he didn't sound too judgmental.

"Jerry sounds friendlier—not so stuck-up."

"I prefer my full name."

"Sheesh. You sound like an uptight old man."

"It's just that I'm named after a prophet in the Bible, so I don't feel right shortening it."

"A prophet? What'd he do?"

"Called people to repent for their sins."

Holding up his hands as if to ward off an attack, Bo backed up. "I'd better not get too close to you then. I'd rather not confess my sins."

"Might do you good."

"I doubt it. I gotta go." With a sickly smile, Bo hightailed it toward his counter and disappeared.

Jeremiah hummed a little tune as he headed back to the pretzel stand. Maybe he wouldn't have to worry about Bo bothering him anymore.

But he tried not to think of another fact about the prophet he'd been named after. God had called that Jeremiah never to marry. As much as Jeremiah wanted to be like the holy man of God, he hoped he wouldn't suffer the same fate. But it seemed as if he might not have a choice.

Chapter Fourteen

After spending a full day at the market, Jeremiah longed to go to sleep. Exhaustion had seeped into every bone in his body. He'd enjoyed being busy and interacting with people at the market. But no matter how hard he tried not to dwell on the one person who'd added the most to his days, Keturah kept popping into his thoughts.

He glanced at *Die Botschaft*, which he'd kept open to her message asking for permission to send him another letter. He sifted through the time schedule again. Depending on when she received his letter, how long it took her to reply, how long it took the post office to deliver it . . .

She might have sent back a letter, which he'd get soon, or he might not hear from her for a while. She'd had a lot going on this week. Or maybe she'd decide not to write back. That might actually be best. Although he liked the idea of writing to her, he'd rather have their correspondence end. Then he wouldn't wrestle with his conscience over whether or not to tell her the truth.

Once he'd decided that, he called the Christmas Year 'Round Shop. They'd already closed for the evening, so he left a detailed message. He knew exactly what he wanted, but he didn't know all the prices. He only hoped someone could pick everything up for him.

A tap on the doorjamb startled him. Had they come to prepare him for bed already? When he wheeled around, Zeke stood in the doorway.

"Hope I'm not too late, but with milking, cleanup, and supper, my days are pretty long now."

For a moment, a sharp stab went through Jeremiah. He'd relished those long, hard days. The early risings. The physical labor. The— He snapped his mind away from those memories. They belonged to the past. A past he'd left, never again to return. Before he could drown in self-pity, he reminded himself of the market job he'd been so eager for. He looked forward to working there.

"I had a few questions I'd like you to answer if you have time." Zeke stood hesitantly in the doorway, as if he didn't want to intrude.

"Of course. Come on in." Jeremiah waved to the chair near his bed. "Why don't you bring that over here so we can talk?"

Zeke grabbed the chair and headed over. Before he sat down, he pulled a pink envelope from his pocket. "I assume this is for you." His tilted eyebrows indicated curiosity. "Maybe you should open it to check."

Jeremiah's heart thumped hard. One glance at the return address told him the letter belonged to him. All he wanted to do was open the envelope and read the letter inside, but he couldn't savor it with Zeke watching. "You're right. It's mine."

"Is this the Keturah Esch who works at the pretzel stand at the market?"

"*Jah,*" he answered reluctantly. Zeke's family worked

in the auction building across the parking lot from the market. Jeremiah should have thought about that before asking Zeke to be his messenger.

"I heard a rumor that you're working at their market stand. Is that true?"

Would this visit turn into Twenty Questions? Again, Jeremiah preferred not to answer. "Mrs. Vandenberg wants to place rehab workers at the market. She asked me to try it first to see how it goes."

"And how is it going?"

"Pretty well, I guess. I'm not sure I'm much help, but I manage to do a few jobs." Like getting the dough from Bo. Thank the Lord, the refrigerators would be installed soon, so he wouldn't have to keep doing that odious chore.

"But if you're working there, why do you need to send letters to Keturah?"

"It's a long story. She doesn't know I'm the one who sent the letter. I didn't know her or that I'd be working for her business when I sent the first letter. I didn't sign my name."

"I see. But now that you're working there, you can talk in person."

Jeremiah didn't respond. He still hadn't figured out what to do about that. He should have confessed as soon as he met her. His hesitation had now made it awkward.

"You can, can't you?" Zeke studied him. "You're not like me—tongue-tied around girls. Right?"

"Not usually."

Now Zeke's eyebrows slanted questioningly. "You are around her? That's a first. Does that mean what I think it means?"

"Don't be ridiculous." Jeremiah regretted being snappish. "She wouldn't be interested in me."

"Why not?"

Keturah was sweet, beautiful, and well out of his league. Even if he didn't have so many physical problems to overcome, she wouldn't consider him. For all he knew, she was already courting.

"I'm serious, Jeremiah. Why not?"

With a sigh, Jeremiah asked, "Aside from this?" He indicated his wheelchair.

"You're not going to let that stop you if you're interested in her, are you?"

Zeke had no idea how much Jeremiah had to rely on Darryl and other staff members for daily tasks. Jeremiah tried to explain, "I couldn't ask a woman to take care of me. Besides, how would I support a wife? I'm working part-time hours in a market stand." *For free.* He did have plenty of money in the bank, but he'd want to be able to care for and support himself before he asked anyone to date.

"Your loss."

"What about you?" Jeremiah needed to take this conversation in a new direction. "Are you interested in anyone?"

Scarlet suffused Zeke's face. That, and the fact that he didn't answer, indicated Jeremiah should probe further.

"Who is she?"

Zeke waved a hand. "Nobody you'd know. And she wouldn't be interested in me anyway."

"Well, if I wouldn't know her, you could at least give me her name."

"Sadie," he mumbled.

"And how did you meet her?"

"My sister Leanne brought her to Sunday dinner yesterday. She's visiting from the Midwest."

"So she won't be staying long, then?"

"*Neh.*"

Zeke looked so downcast, Jeremiah wanted to help him.

"Why not ask about writing to her?" As soon as he said it, Jeremiah wished he'd kept quiet. He'd been trying to take the heat off himself and distract Zeke from the letter.

To his surprise, Zeke laughed. "Maybe I'd have better luck with a girl I didn't have to talk to in person. But she's my sister's friend. She'll think it's odd if I ask her about sending her letters." He appeared as eager as Jeremiah to change the subject. "For now, though, can I ask you some questions about the dairy?"

"Ask away." For Jeremiah, talking about cows would be easier—and less painful—than talking about women and courting.

For the next hour, Zeke asked question after question, and Jeremiah did his best to explain how he'd handled the various problems and concerns. But the whole while, his focus remained on the pink envelope he'd set on the desk behind him.

When Zeke finally rose, excitement flooded through Jeremiah. He couldn't wait to read the letter.

But Zeke stopped in the doorway. "I forgot. Isaac wants to know if you want him to talk to the trainers about Snickers. He might not have any say in who Happy Helpers gives the dogs to, but he'd be glad to ask them."

Jeremiah had gone to the market last week intending to talk to Isaac. He'd gotten sidetracked by working in the pretzel stand. "I would like Snickers if I can have her. I planned to talk to Isaac, but it's hard to get away from the stand. They've been so busy."

"*Jah*, my brothers said they've been passing the word around the market and to the community to buy pretzels to help the girls. Isaac said the lines are wrapping around several aisles."

"They sure are."

"I also heard they're doing some kind of Christmas event and they'll be bringing in busloads of people. The lady in charge wants Isaac and Andrew to use some auction animals to set up a live nativity scene."

Jeremiah hadn't heard about the buses or the live nativity. That'd increase Keturah's business. Who knew when he'd get time to talk to Isaac? "If your brother can stop by sometime, I'd like to talk to him."

"I have a better idea. Mamm misses your visits. Why don't you come for a meal on Saturday? I know she'd love to have you, and so would my brothers."

"I have to work." Saying those words gave Jeremiah a sense of pride. Two weeks ago, he'd despaired of ever being capable of doing something useful.

"Market closes at four. You can ride home with Isaac and Andrew. I'll drop you off here on my way back to the farm."

"You still eat at your *mamm*'s house every night?" Jeremiah teased.

"Not every night." Zeke's face flushed. "Besides, what would you rather eat? My cooking or my *mamm*'s?"

"Well, if those are your choices . . ." Jeremiah laughed. Everyone in their youth group considered Zeke's *mamm* the best cook in the church.

"Exactly. See you on Saturday night. And I can pick you up for church on Sunday as usual." Zeke waved and headed out into the hall.

Jeremiah couldn't wait until Saturday. Not only would he have a delicious meal, he'd have good company. The weekends, especially those with off-Sundays, seemed so empty. Now he had work at the pretzel stand, a supper invitation, and church to anticipate. Along with a letter from Keturah.

After waiting impatiently for the door to close behind Zeke, Jeremiah opened the letter and eagerly read every word.

He was rereading it when Darryl showed up for the evening routine.

"Looks like a good letter." He flashed his usual broad smile. "Pink, huh? You got a girlfriend?"

"Just a friend."

"She sure does make you smile."

Not wanting to reply to that, Jeremiah asked, "Are you working night shift this week?"

"Naw, I'll be in to get you ready tomorrow morning. Just helping a friend out for a few hours."

"You seem to help a lot of people."

"You do too, don't you? That's what God wants us to do."

Jeremiah put the letter upside down on the bedside table so he could finish rereading it once Darryl helped him into bed.

Darryl glanced at the pink stationery. "Seems like that's a special letter."

"It is. The writer lost her parents recently, so I've been trying to comfort her and offer advice."

"Sometimes God lets us go through rough times so we can help others. You just lost your mom, right?"

"*Jah*. That's what gave me the idea to write to people who've been through deaths in their families. She's the first one who's written back."

"See. You're helping people too. Just think what this world would be like if everyone helped even one person. I really like the idea of random acts of kindness."

"I do too." Jeremiah had always tried to do that. Maybe he could look on the letter writing that way. Then he wouldn't feel so bad about staying anonymous. Except . . . how was he going to do that without using the Lantzes' address?

"Is everything okay? You're frowning?"

"Just a minor problem."

"Can I help?"

"Well, I don't want the letters coming here to the rehab center. If she sees that address, she'll pity me."

"What about a post office box?"

Why hadn't he thought of that? "That'd be great, except how would I get to the post office? Does the van go there?"

"No need for the van. I walk past the post office on my way here. I can bring your mail. Only problem is you'd have to go in to show them your ID." Darryl grinned. "I'm guessing you don't have a driver's license."

"But you do, right?"

"Sure. You want me to open a box for you? But it'll have to be in my name."

"That's all right." Jeremiah slid open the drawer in the bedside table where he kept his Bible and where he'd just put his checkbook. "How much do you think it costs?"

"Let me see." Darryl pulled out his phone and looked it up.

After he listed the prices, Jeremiah selected the smallest box. The only thing he'd need it for was Keturah's letters. Then he made out the check to Darryl and added twenty dollars extra.

"Wait. This isn't right. I said—"

"I know what you said. The extra is payment for your time."

"I can't take that. I'm doing this as a favor, not for money."

"If you don't want the extra, donate it somewhere."

Darryl brightened. "I can think of plenty of ideas for that. Thanks!"

"I'm the one who should be thanking you." Darryl had solved one major problem. Now Jeremiah needed to deal with another concern—how to answer Keturah's questions.

Lord, please give me the wisdom to help her.

Chapter Fifteen

Although Keturah had told her sisters to expect changes to the stand, when they arrived on Saturday morning, all of them gaped. The stand had almost doubled in width. The waist-height swinging door had been reinstalled in the new sidewall. The only unfinished parts included a wooden build-out that must be for Jeremiah's lower counter, along with a spot for installing the self-service checkout.

Lilliane bit her lip as she stared at it. Then she turned and marched to the back of the stand to begin making pretzels.

Keturah didn't know whether it would be better to talk to her sister or to give her time to adjust. Before she could decide, Jeremiah arrived.

He let out a low whistle. "I wasn't expecting the stand to look this different. What do you think about it?"

He directed his question to Keturah, but Lilliane blew out a frustrated breath.

"Is everything all right?" he asked her, with genuine caring in his voice.

She shook her head but didn't elaborate.

Jeremiah turned to Keturah, his eyebrows raised in question.

Tell you later, she mouthed. After he nodded, she pointed to the right side of the front counter, which had been built at the perfect height for him. Rather than having shelving and room for a cash box under the counter like Keturah's area had, his side had an opening so his wheelchair could fit underneath.

Jeremiah beamed and rolled over to check it out. "Perfect," he said as he slid his chair into place. "All I need is the pretzel warmer and the checkout terminal."

Keturah winced and glanced at Lilliane, whose lips pinched together.

Jeremiah looked from one to the other, his forehead wrinkled.

Keturah wanted to explain her sister's reaction, but in private. "We haven't unpacked the dough for Ridley's refrigerator yet. Could you help me with that?"

"Of course, but I can get it myself so you don't have to go to Ridley's." His eyes held concern.

"I have a few other things to bring in, and I need to check on Rose and Maleah. They should have been back by now."

Jeremiah released a tense breath. Keturah liked that he wanted to protect her from Bo. She found herself being more and more drawn to Jeremiah. His kindness and consideration made her feel safe and secure.

He exited the stand and held the door open for her. Keturah added politeness to his list of positive qualities.

When they were out of earshot of the stand, Jeremiah brought up Lilliane. "Did I say something to upset her?"

If Keturah were keeping a running tally of his good

points, she'd also jot down understanding and caring. He seemed genuinely concerned about her sister.

"Lilliane doesn't want to do anything our parents might have disliked. I agree, but . . ."

"But you don't want to say *neh* to Mrs. Vandenberg?"

"Exactly. I'm so torn about this. And if Mrs. Vandenberg had asked Daed about doing this, would she have convinced him to expand the stand?"

"What do you think?"

"I don't know, but I feel like God would want me to help people, and most of the people who'll come from the rehab center won't be Amish, so it won't bother them."

Distress flared in Jeremiah's eyes, and Keturah wondered if she'd hurt his feelings by mentioning the people who'd replace him. She didn't want him to think she looked forward to getting rid of him.

"We're so happy to have you right now, and I hope you'll stay for a long time." *Ach!* In her haste to reassure him, she'd made it sound like she didn't want him to recover. "I'm sorry, I didn't mean I don't want you to get better, it's just that—"

"It's all right." A smile played across his lips. "I'm glad you find me useful. I've been worried I'm more of a problem than a help."

"Why would you think that? You've done a lot. Since you've started working here, we rarely run out of pretzels, and you don't know how glad I am that you're willing to pick up the dough from the refrigerator."

"I can imagine," he said dryly.

Keturah wished he didn't have to endure the sharp side of Bo's tongue, but Jeremiah had definitely picked up on her unspoken distaste at being around Bo. Her stomach curdled even thinking his name.

"Are those your sisters over there?" Jeremiah pointed to the candy stand, which had been transformed into a gingerbread house.

The huge Styrofoam cutout surrounding the stand looked so real, Keturah wanted to break off a piece to see. Nick had small baskets filled with peppermints glued on each side of the doorway. But what shocked her most was Nick himself in a Santa hat.

Rose and Maleah were talking to him. Neither of them had unloaded supplies from the buggy. Instead, they stood enraptured, staring at something in Nick's hand.

"I'd better round them up." Keturah headed in that direction, and Jeremiah followed.

"Girls, we need to get everything unpacked before the market opens."

Maleah bounced up and down on her toes. "Look at this, Keturah. Do it again, Nick."

He slid something into his mouth that made his cheeks glow green.

"It's a light-up lollipop. You push a button on the lollipop to make it flash." Maleah turned pleading eyes to Keturah. "Can we get one?"

"Not now. You just had breakfast, and we have work to do." Besides, she couldn't justify spending that much money on a lollipop.

As Keturah herded her sisters toward the buggy, she tried to ignore their disappointed faces. Her father's voice in her head convinced her she'd done the right thing. He would have balked at buying expensive lollipops just for show.

Maleah dragged her feet. "Please?"

"What would Daed have said?" Keturah asked her.

"*Neh*, but he's not here now."

"But his advice is still good." She repeated their father's standard answer when they asked for things they didn't need: "*Don't waste money on worldly things. Use it for things that help others and glorify God.*"

Rose sighed. "We shouldn't get them."

But Maleah stopped in front of Keturah and planted her feet. "But doesn't God want us to have any fun?"

"We can have plenty of fun without spending money." Keturah felt bad. Maleah had been through a lot, and the lollipop would be harmless, but she couldn't bring herself to go against their childhood training.

Yet wasn't she being hypocritical in insisting on following Daed's directives in this small matter while ignoring them for a much larger issue? How could she justify allowing the self-service checkout?

Jeremiah felt bad for Maleah. Even Rose's face drooped. If he were their age, he'd want a lollipop like that too. Back then, though, Mamm had had little money, so he'd had to forego special treats. Perhaps Keturah couldn't afford them either.

All thoughts of lollipops fled from his mind as they passed Bo's stand. Bo propped his elbows on the top of his high glass counter, set his chin in his cupped hands, and ogled Keturah as she passed. Jeremiah ground his teeth together. If he could walk, he'd step between Bo and Keturah to block Bo's view.

Once again, he railed against being confined to a

wheelchair. Then and there, he vowed he'd work harder than ever to regain the use of his legs so he could protect Keturah—and maybe someday be able to ask her out.

If she didn't find someone else first. Or maybe she already had a boyfriend. How could he find out? It wasn't a question that would come up in casual conversation.

Perhaps he could slip it into the letter when he wrote back to her. She'd asked him about himself. If she was courting and she discovered he was a male close to her age, most likely she'd never write back.

While Keturah and her sisters unloaded the last of the supplies, Jeremiah headed for Bo's refrigerator with the first container of dough.

"Hey, Jerry-miah," Bo called.

It seemed Bo was determined to call him *Jerry*.

Jeremiah couldn't wave because he needed both hands—one to steady the huge container on his lap and the other to keep the wheelchair moving. But he didn't want to be rude. "Hi, Bo," he called over his shoulder as he passed.

"You ignoring me?" Bo's tone signaled his annoyance.

"Sorry. The market opens soon, and I need to get these stored and hurry to the stand."

"I'm sure they won't miss you. Seems like all you are is an errand boy."

Bo's barb pointed up Jeremiah's own insecurities. He worried that his work was useless. The girls could remove the pretzels from the warmer and deliver these containers to Bo's refrigerator, although Jeremiah did save them from contact with a snake.

A customer drew Bo's attention, and Jeremiah breathed out a long exhale. He hadn't realized how tense he'd been since Bo had called *Jerry-miah*. Praying Bo's distraction would last, Jeremiah moved as quickly as he could to store the other containers.

When he headed out of the refrigerator the final time, Bo stood waiting, blocking the exit.

"Thanks for the use of the refrigerator." Jeremiah redirected his chair to get around Bo, who moved again to obstruct Jeremiah's path.

"You avoiding me?" Bo's challenging tone sounded as if he was spoiling for a fight.

But why? Jeremiah hadn't done anything to Bo. At least not that he knew about. In fact, last time, Bo had practically run away.

Suppressing the urge to laugh, Jeremiah pasted an innocent expression on his face. "Oh, I'm sorry. I thought you'd rather not hear my thoughts on repenting for sins."

Bo paled and clenched his teeth. "I'm sure we can find other topics to discuss." He leaned one elbow on the nearby counter as if he had all day for a conversation, but kept his body angled so his feet and legs obstructed Jeremiah's path. "We could always chat about the lovely Keturah."

The very last topic Jeremiah wanted to talk about with Bo. "I really need to go. Gideon's heading over to open the doors."

Bo straightened up to look. And with one rapid move, Jeremiah rushed around Bo, who didn't react in time to block the wheelchair.

"I don't know what your plans are," Bo called after Jeremiah, "but don't get your hopes up. She's too good for you."

No kidding. Jeremiah didn't need Bo to rub it in. But

did his belligerent attitude stem from rivalry? If so, he was wasting his time. First of all, Jeremiah would never attract Keturah's attention, not in any romantic way. And secondly, whether Bo knew it or not, Keturah was with the church, so she'd never get involved with an *Englischer*.

As Jeremiah passed the candy stand, he stopped. He couldn't erase Maleah's pleading eyes from his mind. Although he understood Keturah choosing not to spend money on frivolous purchases, he wanted Maleah to have fun.

After a brief internal debate, he veered toward that aisle. Nick didn't have any customers yet, so it shouldn't take long. "Five of those light-up lollipops." Jeremiah pointed to the new display.

Nick's eyebrows shot up. "You know how much they cost?"

"*Jah.*" Money was no object. He had plenty of it and few ways to spend it. Making a little girl happy, and perhaps bringing some humor to her older sisters, seemed like a good investment.

Jeremiah paid Nick and tucked the bag beside him so it stayed hidden. He'd wait until after school to present the lollipops.

Humming, he headed down the aisle to the pretzel stand.

The tension lines on Keturah's face relaxed when she spotted him heading toward the stand. "I thought maybe you'd decided not to come back."

"I wouldn't do that to you." Had she really been worried about that? Her change of expression seemed to indicate she had. But why? His contribution to the stand wasn't very valuable.

"I miss you when you're not here," Maleah said from behind him. "But I can't talk to you as much now."

Jeremiah turned to face her. He'd been so intent on studying Keturah's face, he hadn't noticed the changes they'd made while he was gone. The wider stand had allowed them to rearrange the furniture, and they'd moved Maleah's table closer to her sisters' work space.

"Look on the bright side," Jeremiah said. "You have two people to talk to instead of one."

A sweet smile lit Maleah's face. "That's true." Then she frowned. "But I really like talking to you."

"I like talking to you too, but we can still do that when you fill the warmer."

Keturah raised a hand warningly. "As long as you both pay attention to your jobs." But her eyes twinkled.

Jeremiah pressed a hand to his heart as if making a promise. "We'd never let talking interfere with working."

Maleah giggled.

"We'll see about that." Keturah scurried over to the counter, where customers had begun lining up. "I hope the changes will make it easier for you to hear customer orders," she said as she passed Jeremiah.

He hoped so too. Missing the orders had embarrassed him, and today he planned to pay closer attention.

The morning went smoothly. Jeremiah also focused on keeping the warmer stocked, and they never ran out all morning. They stayed so busy they had to take staggered lunch breaks.

When Jeremiah's turn came, he planned to go to the barbecue stand, but Lilliane stopped him by handing him a sandwich, a plastic bag of chips, a red beet egg, and a mug she'd filled with lemonade.

"*Danke*, but you didn't need to do this."

"We wanted to." She ducked her head. "We all really liked the chicken and wanted to do something for you."

"It looks delicious." He bit into the ham and cheese sandwich with mustard and enjoyed every bite. But his pleasure wasn't only tied to the food. He appreciated them taking the time to fix him lunch. Even if it hadn't been their intention, their including him made him feel as if he were part of their family.

He swallowed hard at that thought. He'd spent several lonely months. Friends and relatives still sent cards or letters, and some stopped in at the rehab center when they could. But he hadn't realized how much he missed the little things—homemade sandwiches, warm meals, and company.

"Are you okay, Jeremiah?" Rose asked softly.

"More than all right."

"Oh. You looked sad."

He cleared his throat to dislodge the lump. "Just enjoying the sandwich."

Maleah studied him too. "Why does that make you sad?"

"My *mamm* made me sandwiches like these."

"She doesn't anymore?" Maleah gave him a sympathetic look. "Are you too big?"

Jeremiah tried not to smile at her question. That was easy to do if he remembered how much he missed Mamm. "My *mamm* died."

Rose sucked in a breath. "I'm sorry."

Maleah's eyes overflowed with tears. "Our *mamm* did too, and so did our *daed*."

"I know. I'm sure it's hard."

Lilliane's strained face showed she was listening.

Maleah swiped at her eyes with her sleeve. "Do you have a *daed*?"

"He died when I was six."

"Almost like me," Maleah said softly.

"*Ach*, Jeremiah. I'm sorry." Lilliane gazed at him with pity.

At the front of the stand, Keturah called back, "I thought we decided to take turns at lunch breaks."

They all turned to find a long line of customers and an almost empty pretzel warmer. Jeremiah crumpled his sandwich wrapper awkwardly and tossed it into the trash can.

Maleah cheered. "*Gut* shot."

"I'd better help your sister. And it looks like we're almost out of all the pretzels."

"We'll get to work." Rose and Lilliane went back to shaping pretzels.

Jeremiah hurried to the pretzel warmer. "I'm sorry I wasn't paying attention."

She shook her head. "All along, I've been blaming Maleah for distracting you." Her light tone indicated she was only teasing.

But he regretted not keeping a better eye on things. He listened carefully to the order and had the pretzels ready when Keturah turned with the bag.

"What were you talking about?" She waited for him to drop in two raisin pretzels.

"I told Maleah my *daed* died when I was six." He'd had plenty of practice saying that over the years, so he could do it without outwardly showing his pain.

"Oh, Jeremiah. I'm so sorry. That must have been hard."

"It was." But it didn't ache quite as much as the recent loss of his *mamm*.

Her sympathetic expression eased some of his sorrow. He could stay like this all day, just staring into her eyes. But customers were waiting. Reluctantly, he motioned to the bag in her hand, breaking the spell.

She followed his hand motion. "*Ach*, the line." She blinked, as if waking from a dream, and focused on the pretzels.

And he ached inside with losing their momentary, deep, heartfelt connection.

What was happening to her? Keturah couldn't believe she'd forgotten all about the customers, the pretzels, and her job as she'd stared into Jeremiah's eyes. Something about him distracted her, mesmerized her.

"I'm sorry for the delay." She handed the woman her bag and the change.

The customer laughed. "If I were your age and had that handsome man to stare at, I'm sure I'd be just as enamored."

Keturah's cheeks burned. She hoped Jeremiah hadn't heard, but he'd be listening carefully for orders. For the first time ever, she wished her little sister had been chattering to him.

Not only had Keturah made her interest clear to Jeremiah, she'd also broadcast it to everyone in the market. All the stand owners waiting in line would spread the news.

"Don't worry about it." The woman smiled and sighed

with a dreamy expression on her face. "It's nice to see young love."

Love? Keturah's stomach clenched, and not just from missing lunch. Had the others watching her interpreted it the same way?

She barely heard the next order. Hopefully, Jeremiah had. She turned and, without looking at him, held out a bag.

He dropped in a raisin pretzel. "Don't you want another bag for the cinnamon sugar?"

"Of course." She turned and fumbled with the bags. She tried to tell herself her clumsiness came from holding another bag in her hand, but her shaky hands belied that explanation. Perhaps her reaction resulted from hunger. She hadn't had lunch yet. That had to be the reason.

Finally, she got the bag open and, barely able to breathe, held it out to Jeremiah. Hunger wouldn't cause her lungs to constrict like this. Was she having a panic attack?

"Lilliane, can you help?" Her words came out strangled.

Her sister dropped the dough and rushed over. "What's the matter? You look flushed, and you sound hoarse."

Keturah shook her head. "I—I just need lunch."

"Sit down for a while until you feel better."

Both Jeremiah and Lilliane studied her with concern. The unusual ruddiness of Jeremiah's cheeks made Keturah wonder if he'd been as embarrassed by the woman's comments as she had.

Keturah fled to the back of the stand to recover her equilibrium. She plowed into Maleah's table. "*Oof.* I forgot we moved that."

Why hadn't she watched where she was going? Were

Lilliane and Jeremiah still watching her, or had they turned back to serving customers?

"Did you hurt yourself?" Rose gazed at her sympathetically.

"I'll be fine." Keturah's answer came out gruff. To make up for it, she smiled at her sister. "*Danke* for asking."

She passed the other worktables without incident and sank onto their only chair. After retrieving a sandwich from the cooler, she prayed. Then she drew in a calming breath and cleared her mind of the whirling thoughts and questions.

Rose headed for the water bath near where Keturah sat. "Poor Jeremiah. I guess you couldn't hear what he told us back here."

"*Neh*, I didn't." Keturah had come back here to escape thoughts about Jeremiah. It seemed she'd failed.

"His *daed* died when he was six. His *mamm*'s dead too."

"Did it happen at the same time?"

"I don't know. He didn't say."

So Jeremiah had also experienced being an orphan. That might be why he was so kind to them. She'd almost mistaken his caring for interest in her, but he'd been treating her sisters the same way. And he'd really bonded with Maleah. Perhaps he understood her more because of his own loss as a young boy.

Keturah had nothing to worry about. She'd misinterpreted his nervousness. Her tense muscles relaxed temporarily. But was that what she wanted?

Chapter Sixteen

After Keturah returned from her lunch break, she avoided looking at him. Her change of attitude hurt Jeremiah. She'd been upset and had rushed back to the lunch table after that woman had mistakenly assumed Keturah was interested in him.

Her blush, her stiffness, and her pinched face all revealed how much the idea had bothered her. She now appeared determined not to give any wrong impressions. She evaded his eyes, extended rigid arms, nodded cursory thanks, and pivoted quickly to face her customers. No talking, no teasing, no friendship.

It saddened him. He wished he could reassure her that he understood they couldn't have a relationship. But would bringing it up make things worse? And could he say the words to calm her worries if it meant denying his own feelings?

They rushed through the rest of the afternoon, each minute harder than the next. For the first time, Jeremiah was almost relieved the work day had ended. As he helped clean up, the bag beside him crinkled. He'd forgotten about the lollipops.

They could all use cheering up. He waited until everyone had finished the chores to pull out the bag, and then he beckoned to Maleah.

"You get first choice of color." He only opened the bag enough for her to peek in. "Don't let your sisters see."

She squealed and hugged him. "*Danke, danke, danke!*" Bouncing up and down on her toes, she picked up one color and then another, dropping each of them back into the bag at least twice before settling on pink. Then she cupped her lollipop in two hands so her sisters couldn't see it as she lifted it out of the bag.

The other girls stared at the bag and then at Maleah and Jeremiah.

"What do you think?" he asked Maleah. "Should we let your sisters pick their own, or do you want to choose for them?"

She pursed her lips. "They can pick, but tell them to do it fast, fast, fast."

"Rose?" Jeremiah lifted the bag, and she headed over. When she peeked into the bag, she laughed.

"Don't let your sisters see," he warned again.

Giggling, she picked green and palmed it out of the bag.

"You're next, Lilliane."

She headed over with a puzzled frown that only deepened as she glanced inside. "What is this?"

"You'll see in a minute. Just take your favorite color without letting Keturah see."

"I don't know." She nibbled on her lower lip. "It depends on what it is."

"Come on, Lilliane." Maleah sounded as if she'd explode if she had to wait any longer. "Pick blue. I know you like that."

"All right." She took her selection and tucked it behind the edge of her apron.

"Now for Keturah."

As Jeremiah extended the bag, Rose and Maleah burst out laughing. Keturah stepped toward him as cautiously as if she expected a snake to jump out and bite her.

She peered into the bag. "Jeremiah." Her tone wavered between scolding and disbelief. "You shouldn't have done this."

"I'm sorry you don't have a choice of colors, but at least we'll match." That made him extremely happy. But she might assume he'd done that on purpose. "Nick only had four colors." And Jeremiah had picked orange, his favorite. He hoped she'd like that flavor too.

Her cheeks flushed, reminding him of pink envelopes. Perhaps he should have gotten a different color.

"I can exchange it for another flavor if you want."

She shook her head. "But these are for little children."

"Today they aren't."

"Would someone please tell me what's going on?" Lilliane's voice matched her petulant expression.

"We're all going to enjoy a little treat." Jeremiah waved in her direction. "Do you want to taste yours first?"

She looked around at everyone else suspiciously. "Is this a joke?"

"Try it," Maleah begged. "Go on, Lilliane."

Her face twisted. Once she put the lollipop in her mouth, though, her tense features relaxed. "It tastes like a normal lollipop."

"Push the little button."

"Is something bad going to happen?"

"*Neh, neh*, just do it," Maleah encouraged her.

Blue light pulsed from her mouth.

Maleah doubled over with laughter. Even Rose and Keturah giggled. Lilliane frowned.

"Watch. Here's what you look like." Maleah opened hers, stuck it in her mouth, and pushed the button to create a steady glow. "Mine's pink," she mumbled with her mouth full.

"Come on." Jeremiah motioned to Keturah as Rose eagerly unwrapped hers. "You too."

With a broad grin, Keturah challenged him. "You first."

He accepted her challenge. Soon, orange light radiated from his mouth. The merriment in her eyes filled him with joy. Then she unwrapped hers, and she glowed with a matching color.

All four girls doubled over with laughter, and Jeremiah's heart couldn't be fuller. He'd brought them some much-needed fun.

Keturah and her sisters had their backs to the counter, so only Jeremiah noticed Bo passing by. Bo's eyes shot daggers at Jeremiah.

What had he done to make Bo react like that?

Jeremiah was enjoying himself too much to care. But seeing Bo reminded Jeremiah of the kiss comment, and his gaze strayed to Keturah's lips as she slid the shimmering lollipop in and out of her mouth. He couldn't help wondering what it would be like to kiss her, and then his eyes met hers.

* * *

Keturah licked her lollipop, enjoying the orange flavor and her sisters' giggles. Even Lilliane had unbent enough to chuckle at Maleah's antics. They'd all needed some lighthearted fun. And although she was a little embarrassed at how heartily she'd joined in, she had to admit, it was nice to relax and act silly.

She glanced in Jeremiah's direction to thank him, but their gazes caught and held. And held . . .

Before she knew it, she was drowning in the gentlest, warmest honey brown eyes she'd ever seen. So full of kindness, caring, and . . . ? And something she couldn't identify. Or maybe something she was afraid to name.

She sobered and forced herself to look away. Of course she'd been mistaken. After all she'd been through recently, she'd mixed up sympathy and attraction. Even if she wasn't wrong, she had no business responding. She had three sisters to parent and a business and a household to run. Entertaining such ideas was foolishness.

Steeling herself not to let her interest show, Keturah tried to push away those thoughts and rejoin the playfulness. When she finally had enough courage to return Jeremiah's look, she found it innocuous and friendly, similar to the glances he shared with her younger sisters. She must have misread the emotions flowing from him.

The jangle of Gideon's keys alerted her that they needed to pack up and leave. "We should hurry before we get locked in here for the night."

"That sounds like it might be interesting. We can sneak a new supply of lollipops from Nick's stand to light the building." Jeremiah winked at Maleah. "I'll pay him in the morning."

Her eyes gleamed. "*Jah*, let's do that."

Keturah smiled at her sister's exuberance. Jeremiah had lifted all their spirits, and Keturah hesitated to squash Maleah's excitement. Suddenly, Keturah understood how hard it must be for parents to say *neh*, to insist their children had to do their chores and to remind them of other duties. She wished she could be a sister rather than a guardian.

Jeremiah glanced at the clock on the wall across the room. "I should go. My ride is probably already waiting for me. But let me help you pack up."

She smiled her gratitude. He'd rallied her sisters, who began rushing around to finish cleaning and loading Jeremiah with items to carry. He smiled good-naturedly.

Rose sidled up to Keturah and whispered, "Could we invite Jeremiah for supper? I think he's lonely."

"What would we feed him?"

"He liked our sandwiches. Maybe some spaghetti soup?"

"I guess so." Keturah had to admit she'd like him to visit as much as her sisters would.

"Jeremiah?" Rose called as he started from the stand with Lilliane and Maleah, who had their arms as full as his.

He stopped and glanced over his shoulder.

"Would you like to come for supper?"

"*Jah*, he would," Maleah declared, turning to him. "Wouldn't you?"

"I certainly would, but I already have a supper invitation for tonight." He appeared regretful, but perhaps he was only being nice.

Her sisters' faces reflected their disappointment. Keturah

tried to hide hers. Someone as charming as Jeremiah probably had many friends. Maybe even a girlfriend. Why did that bother her so much?

Evidently, Rose didn't intend to take *neh* for an answer. "What about tomorrow? No, wait, that's Sunday. Could you come on Monday?"

Keturah held her breath as she waited for his answer.

"I suppose I could do that."

"Yay!!" Maleah jumped up and down.

"Careful." Keturah reached out to catch any items that might fall, although she had to admit she'd enjoy his visit as much as her sister.

"That would be nice." Even Lilliane seemed pleased.

"Give him our address, Keturah." Maleah's smile spread across her face.

"I don't—" Jeremiah broke off abruptly. "Um, never mind. I'm looking forward to it."

Maleah looked at Rose. "I can't wait for him to come!"

"Me either." Rose had gathered another batch of empty containers, so Keturah jotted the address on a piece of paper she tore from the back of one of her father's ledgers.

"At least this book is useful for something." She held out the page, and Jeremiah took it.

"Isn't that your accounts book?" He studied it as she returned it to the drawer.

"*Jah*, but we've been so busy, I haven't had time to figure them out." Even if she had the time, she wasn't sure she'd be able to make sense of it. She'd never been good at math.

"If you want, I'd be happy to help you. You really should keep up with it so you're not overwhelmed when it's time to pay taxes."

Keturah sent him a doubtful look. "*Danke* for offering, but I'm not sure when I'll get around to it." If she had her way, the answer would be never—for the accounting, that was. Not for spending time with him. But she should probably skip that too.

"Speaking of time, what time do you want me to come on Monday?"

"Would six work?" Keturah hoped they'd have finished making dough before that, giving them time to clean the kitchen and prepare a meal. One part of her dreaded his coming, but the rest of her bubbled with anticipation.

He'd have to hire a van and find a driver, but Jeremiah wouldn't let that stop him. "I'll be there," he promised. A promise that thrilled him.

Despite the frigid winds determined to rip his hat from his head, Jeremiah held it down with one hand and hummed as he sped across the parking lot to the auction building. Even though Keturah hadn't been the one who'd invited him, she'd given him their address, signaling she wanted him to come. Or maybe she couldn't find a polite way to decline after her sisters had invited him. Either way, he had Monday to look forward to, and he could hardly wait.

"Whoa!" Andrew, one of Zeke's younger twin brothers, stopped to stare at him. "You look like someone gave you the best news in the world."

They had, but Jeremiah had no intention of sharing it with Andrew, who loved to tease. Besides, until he'd started courting Ruthie, Andrew had always been surrounded by girls at youth group meetings, so he'd have no idea how exciting a simple supper invitation could be to someone like Jeremiah.

He needed to distract Andrew from more questioning. "Is Zeke here?"

"He's loading the empty chicken crates into Myron's truck. Shouldn't be long." The wind almost ripped the door from Andrew's hand. "It's freezing. Why don't you wait inside?" He held the door so Jeremiah could enter.

"*Danke.*"

"I have to go, but I'll see you at supper." With a quick wave, Andrew took off, leaving Jeremiah alone inside the cavernous, warehouse-like building. Well, not exactly alone. Many sellers were packing up containers, and buyers banged in and out of the doors, sending icy blasts into the already chilly space as they claimed their livestock or produce.

During the ten minutes he waited, Jeremiah analyzed his earlier encounter with Keturah. Their eyes had met and held. The connection had been unmistakable. But had her response matched his? She'd broken their gaze before he could evaluate the emotions brimming in her eyes.

Joyfulness and gratitude had changed into something deeper. His pulse had thrummed at what he'd hoped he'd read in her glance. He hadn't wanted to reveal deeper feelings or overwhelm her. And when she'd focused elsewhere, he'd shuttered his own messages. Although he'd told Zeke that Keturah would have no interest in him, part of him wondered and hoped.

A hand waved in front of his face, interrupting his daydreams. "Are you all right?" Zeke peered at him curiously. "You looked like you were a million miles away. Ready to go?"

Jeremiah must have answered, but he paid little attention to the conversation. Zeke didn't notice. He nattered away about Sadie, who'd walked over to their house with Sovilla yesterday to see the puppies. Isaac and Sovilla had spent so much time staring into each other's eyes, Zeke had had to entertain Sadie.

"That's great." Jeremiah infused his response with enthusiasm.

Although he was excited for his friend, the possibility of a relationship with Keturah floated tantalizingly in Jeremiah's mind and distracted him. At the meal, he barely heard the supper table banter. Each time they directed a question his way, he had to ask them to repeat it.

As much as he enjoyed their company, part of his mind kept straying to the letter on his desk. He had another way to communicate with Keturah. He couldn't wait to get back to his room to reread her letter.

Andrew leaned toward him. "Zeke said you'd like to have Snickers for a service dog."

Snickers? Jeremiah struggled to return to the conversation. Had Andrew asked if he wanted a candy bar? "*Jah*, I do."

His twin Isaac beamed. "G-great. I—I talked to Happy Helpers." With only a little stuttering, he explained that the service organization had agreed to place Snickers with Jeremiah once she'd completed her training.

Andrew broke in. "They have a waiting list for assigning dogs, but because Isaac supplies so many of their service puppies, they're willing to bend their rules for one of his friends."

Ach, Isaac and Andrew had been talking about a dog. Jeremiah hoped his earlier answer had made sense. He needed to pay more attention. "*Danke.* I'd like to have Snickers."

Isaac invited Jeremiah out to the kennel after supper, and Jeremiah enjoyed playing with and cuddling the puppies. He also appreciated Isaac's company. Because Isaac sometimes stuttered, he rarely spoke, giving Jeremiah time to indulge in thoughts of Keturah.

Zeke popped his head into the kennel. "You ready to go?"

Jeremiah nodded. For the first time ever, he couldn't wait to return to the rehab center.

As Zeke stopped at a light on the way home, he studied Jeremiah. "All night you've seemed lost in your thoughts. From the smile on your face, they're mainly good ones. Want to share?"

Not really. His budding relationship with Keturah—if there even was one—remained too personal and precious. He didn't want to bandy his feelings about to others. Suppose he'd been mistaken and her only feelings were kindness or, worse yet, pity.

Better to wait to be sure.

Back at the rehab center, he reread Keturah's letter one more time. He'd wait until tomorrow to answer it. That would keep him occupied after church and make the day go by faster.

Darryl tapped at the door. "Wow, you're looking chipper. I thought you might want your mailbox info." He held out paperwork and a key.

"Why don't you keep the key for checking the box?"

"I asked for two keys. You can have that one for safekeeping."

"Smart idea." Jeremiah put it in the drawer with his Bible and checkbook. "It'll be in here if you need it."

Darryl nodded. "Did you want help getting ready for bed?"

"Aren't you on day shift?"

"Yes, but like I told you last night, I'm happy to help anytime."

"I'll wait for Greg, but you might be the answer to my prayers."

"How so?"

"Would you like to earn some money after work?"

"Sure. I'm trying to save up for college."

Hmm. Maybe they could help each other. "What would you think about being my driver?"

"Huh?" Darryl looked at him blankly. "What do you mean?"

"You don't have a car, do you?" When Darryl shook his head, Jeremiah explained his plan. "I'm thinking of buying a van so I can get around, but I'll need a driver. I'll pay you for your time."

"I'm happy to do it for free."

"I know, but I'd rather hire someone. Would you be willing to do it? I think Harrisburg is the closest place to get specialized vans."

"Of course. This is for Monday, then?"

"That'll be the first time. But I'd like to do more things. Only on your days off or in the evenings. I don't want to take up all your time."

"Right now, except for church activities and this job, I haven't been doing much. Mainly studying for the SATs so I can get into college. I want to be a social worker and help troubled kids."

"Glad to do what I can to support that. What time are

you done with work Monday? And do you have other things you need to do?"

"I start early, so I'll be off by two thirty, or two, if I skip my lunch break."

"If you can leave at two, I'll buy you lunch." If they left then, they could make it to Harrisburg and back before six. He didn't want to be late for dinner at Keturah's.

Chapter Seventeen

Jeremiah woke early Monday morning eager to start the day, and Darryl showed up as the gray skies lightened just before dawn.

"Rise and shine. It's already a little after six."

"I've been waiting for hours." Although Jeremiah was exaggerating, waiting for Darryl to arrive had seemed that long.

Now that he was here, Jeremiah wasted no time in getting ready. He'd have two hours to write to Keturah, followed by breakfast and therapy. Then they had the trip to Harrisburg and, finally, the highlight of his day, supper with Keturah. And her sisters, of course.

"You're doing good at this." Darryl smiled. "The faster you can do this stuff for yourself, the sooner you can get out of here."

Get out of here? Some of the joy and excitement leaked out of the day. Jeremiah had mixed feelings about being discharged. How would he manage to do all this on his own? And worse yet, he had nowhere to go.

"You okay?" With a concerned expression, Darryl studied Jeremiah's face.

Why did Darryl have to be so perceptive? Jeremiah didn't feel like talking about the worries he regularly pushed out of his mind, but Darryl's quirked eyebrows indicated he expected an answer.

"Just thinking about the future. I don't have a place to go when I leave."

"You're homeless?"

Not in the way Darryl meant, but, *jah*, he had no home. "I sold my farm, and the house along with it, so I suppose you could say I'm homeless."

"But you have money to get another place?"

More than enough. Jeremiah nodded.

"That's good." The glint in Darryl's eyes matched his cheeky grin. "I was going to suggest you live in the van. Having a roof over your head beats living in the streets." He sobered, and his expression melted into sadness as he stared off into the distance.

He looked as if he was familiar with that experience. Now wasn't the time to ask him about it. He had work to do, and Jeremiah had a letter to write and therapy to attend. Perhaps on the way home from Harrisburg, when the two of them were alone in the van, Jeremiah could probe for that story.

Darryl snapped out of his sorrow with a jerk and put on his usual happy smile. "Aren't we lucky to have such a wonderful day?"

"*Jah!*" Jeremiah agreed one hundred percent. A letter to read, a van to buy, and a supper with Keturah. What more could he ask for?

Well, maybe a healed body, a home, and a family.

Darryl headed for the door, then turned. "Listen, man, if you need a place to stay when you get out, you're welcome at my place. It's not ideal, but it's a first-floor apartment with an open floor plan, so you could get around okay."

Darryl's offer touched Jeremiah. "Thank you." His voice came out husky. He'd never met a more bighearted teenager. More than ever, Jeremiah was glad he'd planned to give Darryl the van.

"See you at two." Darryl waved and hurried out the door.

Jeremiah couldn't wait. Right now, though, he had a letter to compose. All last evening, he'd thought about how he wanted to answer most of her questions. A few of them he still needed to consider. He prayed for wisdom on the questions of faith.

As he slid his hand into the pen holder, he recalled the day the pen had fallen under the desk. His frustration and inability to pick up a simple object came rushing back. His struggle to open bags that first day at the market. His inability to care for his own bodily needs. How could he ever live alone?

Once he had a van, he'd have more flexibility in his schedule, depending on Darryl's availability. Perhaps Jeremiah could find one more driver to transport him during the hours when Darryl was working. At least he'd have the freedom to travel places. And he'd postpone thinking about his future housing for the moment to concentrate on responding to Keturah.

Setting out the yellow stationery, Jeremiah began the easiest part of the letter:

Dear Keturah,

I'm glad the Scripture verses are helping you. The Lord has given us many promises of comfort.

*I pray they will continue to bless you and your
sisters.*

He planned to add more verses at the bottom of this
letter, but first he had to deal with some thorny questions.
She wanted to know about him. Last night, he'd agonized
over this. He should be honest and tell her his name, but
would she be embarrassed that she'd written about him in
the letter?

In the letter, she'd described a stranger who'd helped
out in the stand. She'd surprised him by not complaining
about his inability to do the job well. In fact, she'd mentioned him as a blessing. Each time he reread that part of
the letter, his heart warmed. She credited him with doing
something significant for her and Maleah. Perhaps he
wasn't as useless as he sometimes felt.

Pondering her compliments, as slight as they were, prevented him from writing. He scolded himself for the delay
and for the pride that kept him returning again and again
to that particular paragraph. Time to move on.

*I'm an Amish man of twenty-five who enjoys
reading* Die Botschaft. *Your letter caught my eye.
God seemed to be calling me to write to you, and
I'm glad I listened. I continue to pray for you and
your sisters.*

*As for me, I've had some sad times in life, so
I've learned to depend on God. I understand the
middle-of-the-night questions. I've asked God
some of the same ones. I've found taking them to
the Lord in prayer is the best solution.*

I also believe that many times tragedies occur

*to teach us to help others who are hurting. So I've
been trying to ask God who He wants me to help.
It may be too soon for you to reach out to others,
although I'm sure you're already helping your
younger sisters.*

He did know that for sure. He'd watched her over the
short time he'd known her. Jeremiah skimmed that last
sentence. Did it sound as if he'd met her or seen her with
her sisters? After deciding it could have been written by a
stranger, he continued:

*The one promise I've been clinging to is that
"all things work together for good to them that
love God." I don't know what the future holds for
you, but I pray you will soon see God working
good in your life.*

In fact, he prayed for that every night and lifted her and
her sisters up to the Lord, asking for their comfort. He also
asked God to show him how to assist them more. Working
in the stand might help some, despite his slowness and
awkwardness, but maybe he could do more small things
to cheer them. The chicken and the lollipops seemed to be
a hit, even with Lilliane and Keturah.

Once he had the van, he might find other ways to
lighten Keturah's load. He didn't know how yet, but he'd
be open to it.

Besides her request to tell her about himself, one of the
hardest questions to answer turned out to be the one about
her father. He didn't want to encourage her to go against
what she'd been taught. And he certainly didn't want her
to disobey the Bible. He didn't know what he'd do if he

had to choose to go against Mamm's wishes. He couldn't imagine a situation like that coming up.

The only thing I can tell you about obeying your parents is that I would do what they said unless you feel very strongly God is calling you to do something different.

Was that a sufficient answer? She'd written this before Mrs. Vandenberg had proposed the self-service terminal. Her main concern in the letter seemed to be making the dough ahead. He could reassure her about that, at least.

I don't want to steer you wrong, but it seems to me if you're baking the pretzels every day, they'd be "freshly baked."
If I can ever help again, feel free to write.

With many prayers,

Should he sign his real name? Keturah had poured out her doubts to a stranger. The fact she'd done that made him wonder if she had anyone else to talk to about her concerns.

How would she feel if someone she worked with knew those intimate thoughts? If he'd shared his late-night fears and daytime struggles with someone anonymously and then discovered he knew the person, he'd be embarrassed. It would make their working relationship uncomfortable. And she'd never share anything else with him in person or by letter. He didn't want her to bottle her pain up inside.

Jeremiah tried to excuse remaining anonymous. He wouldn't be at the stand long. It would be better not to let her know. They'd go their separate ways once he'd finished working there.

As much as he'd fantasized about the look they'd exchanged, Jeremiah had to face reality. Keturah's joy at forgetting her tragedy for a short while likely had prompted that connection. She'd forget him as soon as his job ended. But maybe they could keep corresponding afterward—if she wrote back after this letter.

He also had to admit he didn't want to damage the friendship and working relationship. If she found out, would she ever trust him again?

He settled for signing the letter:

A Friend Who Cares

Although he doubted she'd do more than send a polite *danke* for his letter, he didn't want her to send it to the farm if she did respond. But he also didn't want to make her think he expected an answer.

Underneath the signature, he printed *c/o Darryl Nissly* and added the post office box. Because he'd used the whole sheet of stationery, Jeremiah took out a fresh page and filled it with encouraging verses. He hoped they'd remind her of God's comfort.

After sealing the envelope, he took it out to the front desk to mail it. Then he ate breakfast and worked hard at his therapy sessions, because he now had even more of an incentive to recover. He wanted to be a bigger help in the pretzel stand.

Occupational therapy with Bert after lunch turned out to be a surprise. Bert presented Jeremiah with a metal box enclosed on three sides. It held a thick stack of white bakery bags like the ones they used in the pretzel stand.

"Mrs. Vandenberg had this designed for you." Bert pushed on the bags to lower them. When he removed his hand, the bags rose. "It reminds me of those napkin containers in restaurants that move the napkins closer whenever you take some out."

Jeremiah examined it. "Or maybe a postal scale? One that sinks under the weight of packages."

"Yeah, like that. This'll keep the bags moving up as you remove them."

Although he didn't want to be critical, Jeremiah failed to see how a stack of bags lying on their sides could help him when he couldn't pick them up.

Bert noticed his puzzled expression. "You'll have to do some work. That's what we'll practice today." He handed Jeremiah what looked like a metal nail file, only thinner and much wider. "The point's dull, so you won't hurt yourself."

"You want me to stab the bags?"

"Stop being a wise guy." Bert demonstrated sliding the metal tool inside the bag and flicking it upward to open the bag and then flip it upright. "I thought we could rig a penholder so we can attach this. That way you won't drop it."

"Smart idea."

"I know. Only problem is we'll have to attach it to your left hand, because you'll be using your right one to lift pretzels."

Jeremiah started to protest, but stopped himself. Before the accident, he'd used both hands to care for the cows and handle the milking machine. Besides, at the moment, both of his hands performed tasks equally clumsily.

After letting Bert strap the tool to his left hand, Jeremiah attempted to slide it into the top bag and execute the simple but elegant maneuver Bert had. Ten minutes passed as Jeremiah miscalculated and missed bags, poked holes in bags, and flipped them onto the floor.

"You can do it," Bert encouraged when Jeremiah almost quit. "Mrs. Vandenberg brought a lot of practice bags." He opened his supply closet to reveal hundreds.

It seemed a waste to use all those bags for practice, but Jeremiah kept going. "I'll never get this."

Following ten more minutes of practice, Jeremiah finally opened two bags in a row.

"See, you did it." Bert acted like a cheerleader. "Pretty soon, you'll be doing this flawlessly."

Beads of sweat popped out on Jeremiah's forehead as he slipped the opener into a bag. He had to get this. He just had to. One bag opened. Then another. Soon he had a row of ten before he made an error.

When the session ended, Bert pointed to the container holding the bags. "Mrs. Vandenberg will take that to the market and have it installed. She also brought you this."

He held up an unmarked yardstick. *Neh*, not a yardstick. Too short.

"This should make it easier to pick up the pretzels."

Longer than tongs, that flat stick would work better. It also had a small ledge to prevent the pretzels from sliding down to his arm. So far, so good. Except for one thing. "I'm not sure I can use both arms at the same time."

"You're in luck. We both have time before our next

appointments, so I requested an extra session with you. Guess what we're going to practice?"

By the time his appointment with Bert ended, Jeremiah's energy had trickled away. And he still had several more hours of therapy to face. Doing three hours a day plus working in the market had been grueling. Today, he only had therapy, and it tired him more than last week in the pretzel stand.

As Jeremiah headed out the door, Bert called after him, "By the way, I've set up a meeting with Tina and the rest of the team for Wednesday afternoon. Now that you have a job and you're doing so well with your therapy, it's time for you to transition to outpatient treatment."

Outpatient treatment? Fears and questions collided in Jeremiah's brain, and his weariness increased tenfold. How would he care for himself?

"Don't look so anxious. We'll all work together to prepare you for the move. And we'll see that you get any in-home help you need."

After that bombshell, Jeremiah went to his room for a short break before his next therapy session. He'd have a van to get back and forth to his outpatient appointments, but he'd need to find a place to live. Darryl's offer came to mind. Depending on how soon the rehab team planned the discharge, Jeremiah might need to take him up on it. Staying in Darryl's apartment would only provide a temporary solution, though. Jeremiah should find his own home.

Dear Lord, I'm trusting You to guide me.

He poured out his anxieties and left them all in God's hands before he headed to his next session. Then he concentrated on appreciating the blessings in his life. He also had a new van and supper at Keturah's to look forward to today.

As he'd suggested Keturah do, Jeremiah looked for the good. At first, being discharged brought up only insurmountable obstacles. On the positive side, the doctors considered him ready to live on his own. That meant his healing had progressed.

By the time Darryl arrived promptly at two, Jeremiah had come up with several other benefits, along with a few plans. He also had a list of requests for Darryl.

"I hope you're ready for a long trip," Jeremiah said. "I've lined up a driver to drop us at a Harrisburg dealership that sells vans with lifts. I checked with PennDOT, and we'll need your driver's license for the tags and title. I'll pay for the van, all the registration fees, and the insurance."

Darryl looked hesitant, and Jeremiah realized he should have asked Darryl's permission first. "If you're willing to help me buy the van, that is." If Darryl didn't agree, all of Jeremiah's transportation plans would come crashing down. He didn't know anyone else he could ask.

"I don't mind helping you buy a van, I guess. It feels odd, but I can see you can't do it yourself."

"The van will be in your name, so it'll be yours to take to work and wherever else you want. And you can use it to drive people if you want to make extra money. All I ask is that you take me a few places each week."

"I can't accept that."

"Let's argue about it on the way to Harrisburg. We don't have much time. If we buy the van, we can get all the paperwork taken care of to get it titled and licensed. I need to be back here before six."

By the time they arrived at the dealership, Jeremiah had convinced a reluctant Darryl to agree to the plans. He pushed Jeremiah's wheelchair around the lot as they examined the choices. They went for a test drive in two different vehicles, and Jeremiah insisted Darryl make the final decision.

"You're the one who'll be driving it the most, so you need to be comfortable. You probably have a better idea than I do which one has the better engine."

Although he protested against making the choice, Darryl finally selected the blue van. Jeremiah preferred that one too. After haggling with the salesman, Jeremiah got him down to a price that seemed fair. Then Darryl filled out the paperwork and took care of the insurance, and Jeremiah paid. After the dealership completed a quick prep, they got on the road and headed home.

As Darryl drove, Jeremiah suggested ways to make money. "You could be a driver for the Amish, plus you could take patients at the rehab center out when the vans are busy."

"This seems too good to be true."

"Look at it as a gift from God. And you'll be a gift to me."

"If you say so." Darryl sounded unconvinced, but as they traveled, he seemed to be warming to the idea.

Jeremiah had a big favor to ask. "You've already been a big help. But today I learned I'm being discharged soon."

"Hey, that's great news."

"Except I can't take care of myself and have nowhere to go."

"I already said you can stay with me."

"But how will I do all the things I need to do?"

"They usually pay people to help. One of my friends stays overnight with a quadriplegic, and the man has someone else come in during the day. If you stay with me, I could be your overnight person. And I could get you ready in the morning and at bedtime. That's no problem."

"I'd like that. We'll have to be sure they pay you."

Darryl waved a hand. "I don't need them to. Consider it payback for the van."

Jeremiah didn't argue, but he intended to see that Darryl got paid. "I don't want to take up your time. Or interfere with your plans."

"Like I told you, I don't do much except church activities and work." He grinned. "If you don't mind going to the market early, I could drop you off in the morning before I go to rehab. Picking you up after work is no problem."

Jeremiah sat there stunned.

Had God answered all his prayers at once?

Chapter Eighteen

Keturah had woken with four things on her mind that morning—getting the dough made, cleaning the house before Jeremiah arrived, fixing a meal a little more substantial than spaghetti soup, and preparing Lillianc for the changes to the stand tomorrow.

According to Mrs. Vandenberg's schedule, the second pretzel warmer and the self-service checkout were being installed today. Jeremiah could start waiting on customers tomorrow. That would be a huge help.

Although Keturah managed to keep her mind on her work and complete three of the four items on her list, she dreaded facing Lilliane's reaction. But now, as the meatloaf and baked potatoes cooked, they only had twenty minutes before Jeremiah's arrival. Keturah didn't want him to arrive to find Lilliane in tears or to have her sister flee upstairs and refuse to eat supper.

By the time Jeremiah left, Keturah would be too exhausted or worked up to have an emotional conversation with her sister. If she postponed it tonight, she'd only have tomorrow before they drove to work. That wouldn't give Lilliane much time to get used to the idea.

With guilt laying heavy in her stomach, Keturah finished the last-minute preparations. She had to find a way to smooth these changes over, even though she had her own doubts about whether she should have agreed to the plan. It was too late to have reservations. By now, the workers would have already installed everything.

"He's here," Maleah called. She'd been waiting by the window since five thirty in case Jeremiah arrived early.

How could a stomach that had been so sick a few moments before suddenly explode into flutters?

By the time Darryl pulled into Keturah's driveway, Jeremiah's heart had kicked into double time. Although he kept telling himself the invitation had only been kindness on her part, actually going to her house made the visit seem more significant.

Then Keturah appeared in the doorway, and blood pounded in his ears.

His eyes alight with curiosity, Darryl looked at her and then at Jeremiah. "Is that your girlfriend?"

I wish. "*Neh.*"

"But she invited you for dinner."

"Her little sister did. She agreed, but probably just to be polite."

"She's smiling like she's happy to see you."

Darryl's observation gave Jeremiah some hope. But he had to be honest. "She's friendly to everyone."

"You sound disappointed." Darryl examined Jeremiah's face. "You like her, don't you?"

"She's very nice." Although he spoke the truth, Keturah far surpassed that description. He had many other words to describe her. "Besides, she wouldn't be interested in me."

"Why not?" Darryl looked genuinely puzzled.

"Because." Jeremiah motioned toward his body. "I can't ask anyone to date. Courtship leads to marriage. How could I ask anyone to do all the jobs you do?"

"I don't mind."

"Really?" Jeremiah found that hard to believe.

"Really." Darryl's matter-of-fact answer made it clear he meant what he said. "She might not mind either. Give her a chance. You might be surprised."

Jeremiah didn't even want to think about it. He'd never want to be a burden on a wife. And Keturah already had too many responsibilities. Adding more was the last thing he wanted to do.

The sudden realization that he'd been sitting here all this time increased Jeremiah's nervousness and embarrassment. "I should go."

"Would it be okay if I visit a friend? I can come back whenever you need me."

"Sure. Take your friends out. Have fun." Jeremiah had no doubt he could trust Darryl to be responsible.

Maleah dashed from the house and tapped on Jeremiah's window. Darryl opened the automatic van door.

"Don't you want to come in?" she demanded.

Jeremiah grinned at her eagerness. At least one person in the family welcomed his visit. "I'll be right there."

Darryl hopped out of the van and came around to slide out the ramp while Maleah watched wide-eyed. Then he undid the tie-downs and kept one hand on the wheelchair while Jeremiah rolled out.

With Keturah's eyes on him, Jeremiah's thumping pulse increased, and he had to steady his hands to move himself along. Could you want two things at once? He never wanted this walkway to end so he could gaze at Keturah framed in the doorway, yet he also wanted to hurry toward her as quickly as possible.

With Maleah urging him on, it seemed she'd chosen the second option for him. "Want me to push you?" she asked, evidently believing he was moving too slowly.

"Maleah, leave Jeremiah alone." Keturah greeted him with a heart-stopping smile. "We're glad you could come."

The word *we're* depressed him a little, but her smile made up for it.

Seeing Jeremiah made Keturah's heart bump a little faster. He had the nicest smile, one that made her comfortable and happy. If Lilliane hadn't called from the kitchen, Keturah might have kept staring at Jeremiah without inviting him in. He didn't seem to notice she'd been keeping him waiting outside the door.

"The meatloaf's done," Lilliane called again.

"Are you ready to eat?" Keturah asked. "I mean, come in." She stepped to one side so he could get by.

Maleah followed him in but bounced around to the front of his chair. "Want me to show you where to go?"

"That would be nice."

Beaming, she led him down the hallway. "Our kitchen's back here."

Keturah wished she could walk beside Jeremiah, but his chair took up most of the hallway. She should have thought about making things accessible for him. When they reached the kitchen, Rose was filling glasses, and Lilliane was slicing the meatloaf.

"It smells delicious." Jeremiah sounded delighted. "It's been a long time since I had meatloaf." That faraway sadness entered his eyes for a moment. Soon, though, he glanced around, and his smile returned.

Why hadn't she thought about where to seat him? Keturah scrambled to remove the chair at the head of the table.

"Hi, Rose. And Lilliane."

They both greeted him enthusiastically.

"*Danke* for inviting me. Everything looks delicious." His cheerfulness lifted Keturah's mood a little.

The girls sat in their usual spots, but Maleah scooted closer to Jeremiah before they all bowed their heads for silent prayer.

When they finished, Jeremiah tucked his hands under the table to secure the holder for his fork. He wrapped the cuff around his hand so he wouldn't drop his utensils.

When he lifted his hand to eat, Maleah stopped and stared. "What's that?"

"A holder for my fork so I don't drop it."

"I need one of those. I'm always dropping my silverware. Daed always said—" She stopped short, and her eyes filled with pain.

"Why don't you let Jeremiah eat, Maleah?" Keturah suggested.

Her sister kept quiet for a few minutes but soon returned to chattering. Jeremiah tried to include everyone in the conversation while they ate supper and dessert, and soon even Lilliane had lost her usual sour expression.

By that time, Keturah and Rose had cleared the table, and Lilliane had put water on to boil for tea and coffee.

Jeremiah offered to help, but Keturah suggested he keep Maleah company. Her sister often dropped and spilled things. That would keep her from having an accident in front of company.

He entertained Maleah, telling her about his trials opening the paper bags that morning. She giggled as he described all his mishaps, but Keturah's heart went out to him. She couldn't believe how hard he had to work to do even that simple task.

"That reminds me." He looked over at her as she filled the sink with water. "Did Mrs. Vandenberg say when the self-serve checkout would be coming?"

Her spirits sank. She'd planned to break the news to her sister gently. "Tomorrow."

Lilliane whirled to face Keturah, her face ashen. "You told Mrs. Vandenberg *jah*?"

Keturah's pained expression must have given Lilliane a clear answer.

"I can't believe you did that." Lilliane threw down the dish towel and rushed from the room.

Keturah called after her, but Lilliane ignored her and banged open the front door, leaving it swinging in the wind.

"I'm sorry." Jeremiah looked stricken. "I didn't mean to upset her."

"It's not your fault. You didn't know." Keturah's stomach twisted into tight knots.

"Let me go after her." Jeremiah pushed back from the table.

Keturah longed to stop him, but he appeared determined.

Maybe Lilliane would respond better to him. As he headed for the door, a pang of disappointment zinged through Keturah. She'd hoped to spend time with Jeremiah, but right now, her sister needed him more.

By the time Jeremiah got outside, Lilliane had marched off down the street.

"Lilliane, wait." Jeremiah hurried after her.

She turned her head, her eyes glimmering with tears, but she didn't stop.

Exerting himself, Jeremiah rushed to catch up. By the time he reached her, his breath came in gasps. Lilliane didn't look happy to see him.

"I know . . . you're upset . . ."

Her damp eyes reflected pity for his exhaustion, but with her fists clenched as tightly as her jaw, she walked faster, trying to escape. Jeremiah managed to keep pace. He had something he had to say to her, and he intended to do it, even if she didn't want to listen.

"I'll ask . . . Mrs. Vandenberg to . . . take out . . . the machine." He gulped in a little air. "I don't . . . have to work . . . at the stand."

She stopped so abruptly, Jeremiah rolled past her and had to back up.

"*Neh*, we need you." She stared at him incredulously. "You'd really give up the job to make me feel better?"

"Of course." He took a few deep breaths to fill his lungs. "The stand belongs to your family. I didn't mean to come in and disrupt the business."

Lilliane stared at the ground. "It's not your fault."

"If I hadn't come to work there, none of this would

have happened. I'll give up the job." He only wanted to help. So did Mrs. Vandenberg. But neither of them had considered the consequences.

"I can't ask you to do that." Lilliane scuffed a foot on the asphalt and didn't meet his eyes. "That wouldn't be fair."

Jeremiah had to get through to her. "I don't want you to go against your conscience. If you still need me, I can go back to working the way we have been."

"*Neh*, the machine will make it easier for you and for Keturah. She could use more help with customers. Besides, the machine is already there, isn't it?"

"I expect so." Or it would be there tomorrow.

Lilliane shrugged and resumed walking, but she'd slowed her pace. "Then what's done is done."

"Not necessarily. Mrs. Vandenberg plans to help other people from the rehab center. I can ask her to move the checkout to another business. I'm sure she'd do it if we asked." And he'd pay the costs of removing and reinstalling it elsewhere.

Once again, Lilliane stopped suddenly. "But what about you?"

"I'm more concerned about your feelings, and I don't want to come between you and your sister."

She spun toward him. "You can tell Keturah I'm not upset with her. I understand why she did it."

"If it helps, Keturah was really torn over this. I think she did it to help me."

"I want to help you too, but—" She lowered her lashes and squeezed out one word, "Daed."

Her voice held so much agony that Jeremiah's chest

contracted. He wanted to do something, anything to ease her pain.

Then she lifted eyes that begged him to understand. "My *daed* was strict. Very strict. I always tried to do what he said. Not like the others." She bit her lip. "Rose is more like me. But Maleah and Keturah sometimes get—I mean, used to get—in trouble." A small sob escaped.

Jeremiah could easily picture lively Maleah getting in trouble, but Keturah? That seemed out of character.

"We had a lot more rules than everyone else at school and church. Rose and I didn't mind, but the other two did. They didn't deliberately disobey, but they forgot. Or made mistakes. Or they broke the rules to help someone else."

Breaking the rules to help others fit Keturah perfectly. Hadn't she made dough ahead of time against her father's pretzel-making directive? In the letter, she'd explained she'd done it to keep from overworking Lilliane and to give better customer service. Presumably, that would have gotten her in trouble with her father. And now she'd agreed to the self-service checkout to give him a job and assist Mrs. Vandenberg's project.

Though her *daed* was no longer around, Keturah still carried the guilt of disobeying. She'd made that clear in the letter.

Lilliane shifted from one foot to the other. "Not to be rude, but I'd like to be alone to think and pray."

"Sure. And I'll be praying for you." *And the rest of the family.*

"*Danke.* I'm sorry I've been so *mürrisch.*" She whirled and rushed off before he could answer.

Jeremiah headed back to the house, his spirit burdened for Lilliane and his mind whirling.

How did you decide right from wrong when the Bible instructed children to obey their parents, but it also said to love and help others? He'd wrestled with this when he'd read Keturah's letter. And he still had no solution. Praying and being open to God's leading seemed the best path forward.

When he reached the house, Maleah raced out to greet him. "I thought you were never coming back." She peered behind him. "Where's Lilliane?"

"She wants to walk and pray."

Keturah came outside. She stood beside Maleah and put a hand on her shoulder. "Lilliane likes to walk and pray when she's upset. She'll be back, but I hope she didn't act, well . . ."

"I like her honesty. And she's determined to do the right thing."

"I know." She lowered her head as if weighed down by guilt.

"You are too, aren't you?"

She lifted her chin, her eyes filled with surprise. "I thought I was. Now I'm not so sure. Lilliane and I often see the same things in different ways."

Jeremiah didn't want to give away that he'd read about her dilemma with the dough, but he did want to ease her mind. "It seems like the Bible doesn't directly cover these decisions you're making, so you have to figure out what Scripture verses apply."

"That's exactly my problem. I want to help people, but Lilliane thinks obeying Daed is more important."

"She mentioned that."

Keturah's eyes widened. "She did? Lilliane usually doesn't open up to people. She must really trust you."

"Oh, and Lilliane said to tell you she isn't upset with you. She understands why you agreed to having the machine."

"Are you a miracle worker?" A bemused expression on her face, Keturah kept shaking her head.

Neh, he'd only listened and tried to understand. But when Keturah smiled at him, Jeremiah thanked God for his own special miracle.

Keturah couldn't believe Lilliane had told Jeremiah so much about herself and her feelings. Although Keturah had to admit that Jeremiah inspired trust. He had a good heart, and although she had no proof, she sensed that whatever anyone told him, he'd understand and hold in confidence. And his kindness and caring made it easy to talk to him.

"It's hard to know what to do in these situations." Jeremiah's eyes met hers with sympathy. "I've found praying about it and following what God lays on my heart seems to help."

Keturah had prayed, and God had given her peace about the decision. But what if Lilliane did the same and came to a different conclusion? Keturah hesitated to ask Jeremiah that question. He hadn't come here to settle family problems, and he'd already counseled her sister. Maybe she could write another letter to *A Friend Who Cares*. She'd found that writing down problems and dilemmas helped. Even if she never sent the letter, it might clear her mind.

"Want to play a game?" Maleah waved a pack of cards in Jeremiah's face.

"Maleah." Keturah struggled to keep impatience from her tone. "Jeremiah may have other things to do tonight."

"I don't, but you might have plans?" He looked toward her for an answer.

"Only chores, and I'm happy to put those off for a while." *More than happy.*

They'd played for almost an hour before Lilliane returned. With a weak smile, she walked past them and headed for the stairs.

"I'm going up to bed. Good night, everyone." Over her shoulder, she added, "And thanks for talking to me, Jeremiah. I don't want you to stop working in the stand."

Stop working in the stand? Keturah sat there, shocked. "What did she mean by that? Are you planning to quit?" After all her worries over installing the new equipment, would Jeremiah not even be there to use it?

He cleared his throat and didn't meet her eye, which raised her anxiety. How would she cope with one less person in the stand?

"I told Lilliane I could ask Mrs. Vandenberg to move the checkout machine to a different stand."

"You're leaving us?" Keturah was struggling to understand.

"*Neh!*" Maleah shouted. "Don't go."

His voice husky, he explained, "I'm worried the machine is coming between you and your sister. I don't want to do that."

"You'd rather work somewhere else?"

Jeremiah hesitated as if unsure how to answer, and Keturah braced herself for news she'd rather not hear.

"I don't want to leave, but I also don't want to cause trouble for your family."

Expelling a long sigh, Keturah said, "We need you, and we'd like you to stay."

Rose, her face filled with anxiety, spoke up for the first time. "Jeremiah, please don't go."

"We might need to hire someone to help even if you stay to wait on customers. But if you go . . ." Keturah couldn't even contemplate that.

"I won't leave if you need me, but I wish I could do more."

"Waiting on customers will be a big help. It'll free me to make pretzels sometimes, but if we stay as busy as we have been—"

"Do you know anyone who can help?" Jeremiah's calm voice, his logical thinking soothed Keturah's panic.

Her anxiety had subsided ever since he'd assured her that he'd stay. But for some reason, her heartbeat hadn't slowed. Instead, it had picked up its pace. Maybe she shouldn't have selected a seat so close to Jeremiah.

Keturah forced her thoughts back to the business. "*Neh*, and I'm not even sure if we can afford to pay a worker." She hadn't managed to make sense of her father's bookkeeping yet. Not that she'd tried. Her dislike of math had made her put off that chore.

"I can pay someone if that's a problem."

"I can't ask you to do that. We may be able to afford it, but—" They'd had a lot more customers than usual. She wouldn't know how much they'd been making, though, unless she did the accounting.

"But what?" Jeremiah prompted.

Keturah ducked her head and mumbled, "I haven't been keeping up with Daed's books."

"Is that something I could help with? I did the book-keeping for my business before I sold it. I remember how confusing the ledgers were at first."

Keturah hesitated. Daed would have been upset at letting a stranger see their books. And he'd never been quick to trust people, but Keturah had just labeled Jeremiah trustworthy. Could she extend that to something as personal as their finances?

If she didn't accept his offer, she'd have to find someone to teach her. And she'd have to give them access to the books. Or she'd have to find time to read a book about it and teach herself.

"I shouldn't have asked." Jeremiah sounded apologetic. "I'm sure you don't want a stranger looking over your finances."

She hadn't meant to hurt his feelings. "It's not that." The truth of the matter was her embarrassment over her inadequacy. "I'm not good at math, and—" If she let him help, he'd see her struggles.

"I'd be happy to teach you or do it all myself, if you'd trust me."

"You mean like a bookkeeper?"

Daed had done that for other businesses, so he wouldn't have objected to that. Actually, that wasn't true. He would have insisted she learn and do it herself rather than pass off a chore she despised.

But Daed wasn't here. And Keturah had no time or desire to learn. The thought of handing over the books lifted a huge burden from her shoulders.

"How much would you charge?" Whatever he asked, she'd find a way to pay it, even if it meant not hiring another worker.

"You don't have to pay me. I enjoy math and bookkeeping."

"Enjoy it?" Keturah had a hard time imagining anyone liking that tangle of numbers. "Still, I can't let you do it for free."

"Why don't I look over the books first to see how much time it'll take and then tell you?"

Keturah's smile stretched her cheeks until they ached, but at the same time, she wanted to burst into tears. Jeremiah turned her feelings upside down.

Chapter Nineteen

The next morning, Jeremiah arrived at the market early to handle the bookkeeping and tackle the new skills of waiting on customers, opening bags, and filling orders. For the first time since the accident, he approached the morning feeling both competent and useful.

That confidence lasted throughout the first hour as he worked through the books, inputting the receipts Keturah had given him, along with a list of their daily sales. Every once in a while, he couldn't resist flipping the pages to brush a finger over the stub of paper in the back, where Keturah had torn out the page to write her address on it.

He still couldn't believe he'd been at her house last night. And he'd ended up with more responsibilities at the pretzel stand. He only wished he could be a part of her life in other ways. But having her friendship was all he could aspire to right now, and he treasured that.

"Are there problems with the books?" Keturah stood behind him, looking over his shoulder.

He flipped back to the columns he'd been working on, embarrassed that she'd caught him and also discomfited by the messiness of his numbers. "I, um, hope you can read these." He gestured toward the penholder strapped to his right hand. "I still don't have good coordination yet."

"As long as you can read them, that's all that counts. I can't thank you enough for doing this for me. You don't know how much I was dreading it."

At her words, a lump rose in his throat. He'd definitely done something useful. "Glad I can do something for you."

"You've been a big help. We couldn't have done a lot of things without you."

Perhaps her excessive gratitude came from avoiding the bookwork she disliked rather than from his actual contributions, but Jeremiah's spirits soared.

He closed the ledgers. "I guess I should practice with the machine and everything else." He didn't relish the idea of Keturah seeing him struggling with the bags, but he needed to be sure he could do it. He didn't want to be fumbling to open bags once he had a line of customers.

But he needed Keturah's help. "Would you be able to refold the bags after I'm done?"

"I'll do it." Maleah rushed over.

In one way, Jeremiah preferred to work with Maleah. He didn't mind her seeing his mistakes. But he'd been hoping for time with Keturah.

Good thing only Maleah was watching, because he messed up time after time.

"You're not making the same mistake twice, are you?" she asked.

It seemed like it to him, but he couldn't be sure. Finally,

he managed to do several in a row. Maleah cheered. Then she refolded the bags and pressed them down carefully.

"Did I do that right?" She looked to him for confirmation.

"Perfect," he assured her.

"If you're done," Lilliane called, "we need you back here. The pretzel warmers need to be filled before you leave for school." Lilliane had come into the stand that morning and nodded to him, but then pointedly kept her back turned to his side of the counter. And to the machine.

Maleah scampered off, leaving Jeremiah with a neat stack of bags, along with worries fluttering in his stomach. Would he be able to do this when he had a long line of customers?

He'd soon find out. Mrs. Vandenberg's driver picked up Maleah and Rose to take them to school, and Olivia arrived about ten minutes before Gideon opened the doors and crowds streamed in. Most people lined up in their usual place in front of Keturah's counter, but several curious customers examined the checkout.

"What's this?" Nick's voice boomed around the market. "You going high-tech on us, Keturah? Even I don't have anything this fancy."

Her face reddened, and Jeremiah could only imagine Lilliane's expression as Nick broadcast the news. He didn't turn to check.

"Mrs. Vandenberg put it in." Keturah's words came out defensive, and Jeremiah wondered if she'd face problems with people criticizing her.

Nick glanced at Jeremiah. "I suppose this is for you?"

Jeremiah couldn't tell from Nick's tone if he meant it as a friendly question or a jab, but it'd be better to respond with politeness. "*Jah*, it is. Mrs. Vandenberg wants to put them in a few stands."

"Well, tell her to visit mine. It would be nice not to have to make change."

"She's doing it to help people at the rehab center." Keturah sent him an apologetic smile.

"Oh." That deflated Nick. He switched his attention to Jeremiah. "Well, I guess I can be your first customer, then. I'll take a raisin pretzel."

Nick leaned over the counter to watch, and Jeremiah's nervous fingers made several unsuccessful attempts to open the bag. *Please, Lord, help me to do this.* Finally, he flipped a bag open and upright.

"That's a pretty nifty trick. Maybe you could work at my stand."

"Definitely not." Keturah pretended to frown. "We don't want to lose Jeremiah."

Her words suffused Jeremiah with warmth. Perhaps too much of that heat flooded onto his face, because a sly grin crossed Nick's face.

"Seems like he's pretty happy to be working here. Look at that smile."

If Jeremiah's face hadn't already been burning, it would now be aflame. Some customers stared at him, and others tittered. Could he be any more uncomfortable?

The answer to that happened to be *jah*, because Bo stood several customers behind Nick, smirking.

Great. Jeremiah would face more heckling.

Fretting about Bo increased his bumbling motions, and he flipped the next customer's bag onto the floor. At least it had been empty. Then it took him six tries to insert the tool into the next bag.

One good thing was that customers paid more attention to inserting their money and collecting their change than they did to his movements, and he finished the next few people in line with less clumsiness. Another positive was that Mrs. Vandenberg had planned room beside the stand for his line, so he and Keturah didn't have two lines blocking the aisle.

"Nice move." Bo patted the machine. "This got you closer to the object of your desire, huh?"

Jeremiah didn't answer. "May I take your order?"

"Well, you can take it, but I'm not sure you can fill it." A lazy smile slid across Bo's face. "Unless you can convince Beautiful over there to give me the time of day."

Keturah gritted her teeth and ignored him. Jeremiah wondered why Bo had gotten into this line instead of hers, but Bo propped his elbow on the higher display shelf between the two counters and inspected Keturah while Jeremiah struggled through the order.

"Did you put your money in the machine?"

Bo dragged his gaze back to Jeremiah and inserted his money. "Sorry. The view's so good here, I forgot."

Irritation had propelled Jeremiah to stab the tool into Bo's bag, leaving it with a ripped and ragged top. Jeremiah folded it over, hoping Bo wouldn't notice. But, of course, he did.

"Looks like someone's a little jealous, eh?" With a snide laugh, he headed off.

Keturah's jaw and shoulders relaxed, but Jeremiah's tensed. Had Keturah heard Bo's comments? Would she realize the truth?

* * *

Keturah did her best to ignore Bo Ridley, but she always wanted to take a long, hot shower after she was around him to wash away the icky residue. And poor Jeremiah had to endure Bo's crude humor.

Her day only went downhill from there. Mrs. Vandenberg stopped by at lunchtime to announce the new refrigerators would be delivered after work that day. The news itself thrilled Keturah, but it meant telling Lilliane, who was already struggling to accept the new checkout machine.

"Is something wrong?" The concern in Jeremiah's eyes warmed Keturah.

"The refrigerators are coming today instead of next week."

"That's great news, isn't it?"

"Not for Lilliane," she said glumly. "I haven't told her. She's already upset about making dough ahead, and she won't like my idea of premaking pretzels."

"Look on the bright side." Jeremiah's eyes danced. "We can say goodbye to Bo."

Keturah laughed. "You always manage to cheer me up."

"I'm glad I can contribute something."

"Jeremiah, like I said this morning, you've been a huge help."

He had no idea of the many ways he supported her. His smile, which lifted her spirits when she was tired. His willingness to tackle any job without complaining. His diverting half of her line today. His kindness and friendliness to her sisters. His agreement to take on the bookkeeping. She couldn't even explain the heavy load he'd taken off her shoulders.

Oh, and the barbecued chicken and light-up lollipops.

He made her want to come to work every day, a major accomplishment. Ever since the accident, Keturah had put one foot in front of the other and trudged through each day. Her body had returned to the natural rhythm of market days, but she'd lost her energy and interest. Jeremiah had changed that.

"Want me to talk to her?"

"Huh?" Keturah had been so lost in thought, she'd forgotten what they'd been talking about.

"Would it help if I talked to Lilliane?"

Her sister's name brought it all crashing back. She'd be asking Lilliane to make another adjustment. It didn't seem fair to her sister. And she couldn't ask Jeremiah to handle it, although he'd done a wonderful job last night.

"I should tell her." Keturah dreaded the thought.

Jeremiah read the distress on Keturah's face. He wanted to help, but he waited until Rose and Maleah had arrived that afternoon and they had a lull in customers.

"Need more dough?" he asked Lilliane. After she nodded, he added, "Could you go with me? I want to get something else, but I'll need help carrying it."

"Me?"

"You always work so hard. You could use a break."

Lilliane gave him a shy smile. "I can't stay long."

"We can hurry." Jeremiah moved as fast as possible through the aisles. He'd get the dough first, but he didn't want Lilliane to go near Ridley's. "Can you wait over by Hartzler's? I want to get some pastries."

"*Danke.*" With a nervous frown in Bo's direction, she took off, but not before Bo noticed her.

"Hey, Jerry-miah, you two-timing Keturah? The more the merrier, I always say."

Jeremiah's teeth clenched at Bo's slimy smile. He couldn't wait for the refrigerators to arrive. Then he'd avoid seeing Bo several times each market day.

With the container on his lap, Jeremiah joined Lilliane at the baked goods stand. "If you don't mind ordering, I'd like a cinnamon bun. Then I'd like you to pick out pastries for you and your sisters. Be sure to get one for Olivia too."

"I can't. I don't have money with me."

"It's my treat."

She shook her head. "You already bought us chicken and those silly lollipops." Although her tone was critical, her lips curved up a little when she said *lollipops*.

He needed to encourage her to have more fun. "And you've given me a job when nobody else would. I can never pay all of you back for that."

"You don't owe us anything. We're happy to do it."

"That's how I feel too."

Lilliane looked puzzled for a moment, then his meaning dawned on her. "You always make me want to take back what I've said."

He laughed. "But you said it, so now you have to let me buy the pastries."

With a trace of a smile, she stepped into line.

So far, so *gut*, but Jeremiah hadn't broached the topic he intended to discuss. He waited until Lilliane returned carrying a white bakery box. "I'm so glad the refrigerators will be delivered today so we don't have to use Bo's anymore."

She shivered at Bo's name. "Me too." Then her brows

drew together. "Refrigerators? We're getting more than one?"

Jeremiah took a deep breath. "*Jah*, that's what I wanted to talk to you about. Keturah's worried about upsetting you."

"Why? I don't think we need two, but Mrs. Vandenberg's putting them in. They really belong to her."

"Well, one of them isn't a regular refrigerator."

"Huh?" She stopped walking.

"Your sister wants to make your job easier."

Before he could say more, Lilliane snapped, "Daed always warned us not to take the easy way out."

Jeremiah didn't want to contradict her *daed*, but in his business, he'd found certain shortcuts improved efficiency. "She also wants to serve customers quickly and not run out of pretzels."

The tightening of Lilliane's jaw did not bode well for what he planned to tell her.

He hoped she'd see things Keturah's way, although he suspected she wouldn't. "The second refrigerator will hold preformed pretzels."

Lilliane blinked several times as though trying to comprehend what he'd said. When she spoke, her words held a dangerous edge. "You mean we'd shape the pretzels ahead of time and put them in this refrigerator?"

"*Jah*."

"Like they do at the mall? Daed insisted we needed to keep to higher standards."

Jeremiah wanted to be understanding. "I heard they'll be busing people to the Christmas Extravaganza. You'll probably have ten times the customers."

Lilliane stuck out her chin defiantly. "Daed insisted we make everything fresh, the way our sign says."

"The sign says *Baked Fresh Daily*, it doesn't say *Made Fresh Daily*."

"You sound like Keturah. Did she put you up to this?"

"*Neh*, she doesn't know I'm doing this."

"But she'll be happy if you talk me into accepting it the way you did with that—that machine." Bitterness dripped from her words. "All we hear at the supper table is *Jeremiah did this, Jeremiah said this, Jeremiah's so wonderful, so much fun, so nice*."

As much as he liked hearing that they talked about him positively—and he hoped Keturah said some of it but guessed most of it came from Maleah—Lilliane's mocking tone had a sarcastic edge that bit into him. "I'm sorry you have to endure that."

"What?" Then, as if realizing what she'd said, she crushed the bakery box to her and stammered, "I'm sorry . . . I didn't mean that . . . Forget I said it. I'm glad you're working at the stand."

"Lilliane," he said gently, "some people might not like hearing the truth, but I don't mind. And when you disagree with Keturah's changes, it's because you want to do the right thing."

Her grip on the box loosened, and Jeremiah hoped the pastries hadn't been too squashed. "*Jah*, I want to follow Daed's rules."

"And Keturah wants to make things more efficient for everyone. Judging from what I've seen in the books, your business has more than tripled in the last few weeks."

Lilliane squared her shoulders. "I can handle it."

"That's a lot of work, especially when your sisters are

in school. Keturah doesn't want you and Olivia to have to work so hard." As soon as he said that, Jeremiah regretted it. She'd already pointed out her father's philosophy.

Lilliane jumped on his statement right away. "Daed believed in doing things the hard way. He said it builds character."

"What about the customers?"

Some of the fight leaked from her. "Once again, I guess I don't have any choice."

"I'm sorry. I wish things could be different." He'd learned that sometimes you didn't get to choose; you just had to accept what happened.

"But I don't have to like it." She started to stalk off but then whirled around. "Since you're my sister's messenger, tell her that if she changes one more thing, I quit."

"I'll let her know. And I understand how hard this is for you."

"*Neh*, you don't. Nobody does." She pivoted on her heel, and with her back ramrod straight, she stomped off.

He wanted to chase after her, but the scrolls with Scripture verses hanging over the pastry stand caught his eye. They matched the ones around the corner at the barbecued chicken place.

"Could you tell me where you got your signs?" he asked.

"My sister-in-law Nettie made them." The cashier gestured toward a woman making salads at the end of the barbecue stand.

"Do you think she'd make one for the pretzel stand?"

Nettie came when beckoned and agreed to make a sign explaining the praying hands. She jotted down the words Jeremiah wanted. "I'll bring it on Thursday."

That taken care of, Jeremiah wove through the crowds. To his surprise, Lilliane stood a short distance from the pretzel stand, waiting for him.

"Jeremiah, I'm sorry. What I did and said was rude. Will you forgive me?"

He smiled at her. "Of course." That apology must have cost her a lot.

She walked beside him to the stand. "My temper often gets the better of me. I didn't mean to hurt you."

"You didn't. I know we're asking a lot—"

A loud yell interrupted them. "What's that?" Maleah pointed at the bakery box.

"Can you give them out?" Jeremiah asked Lilliane. "I don't know whose is whose."

He set the dough container on the nearest table while Lilliane distributed the treats. Her choices seemed to be hits with her sisters, except Maleah.

She pouted. "I want the cinnamon roll."

"*Neh*, that's Jeremiah's. You love blueberry Danish."

"Do you want to switch with me, Maleah?" Jeremiah asked. "I like blueberries."

Her thrilled expression was the perfect reward for giving up his favorite snack. But Lilliane eyed him. Evidently, she believed Maleah should eat what she'd been given.

When Lilliane turned her back, Jeremiah beckoned to Maleah. "Can you bring me my pastry?"

She scurried over, her eyes hopeful.

Jeremiah wrestled with his conscience. He'd already asked Lilliane to go against her *daed*'s wishes twice. He should at least support her in one thing. But he wanted to make Maleah happy.

He peered into the box when she held it out. "Hmm. That blueberry Danish looks good, but cinnamon rolls are my favorite."

Her face fell.

"I could take it, but then you'd be disappointed."

"*Jah*, and if I eat it, you'll be sad." She closed her eyes for a moment. "You take it." The words sounded wrenched out of her.

"I have a better idea. What if we both eat it?"

"We can't." Then she giggled. "Oh, you mean share it? You can have half of mine too."

"Perfect." They split both treats, and Maleah danced back to her worktable with half a pastry in each hand.

Keturah smiled. "You're really good at solving problems." The strain lines around her eyes and mouth eased temporarily. She'd wrapped her raspberry Danish in bakery paper and set it on the shelf near the cash box so she could wait on customers.

Jeremiah couldn't tell if her stress came from the long lines or from worry over Lilliane. He could help with both of those worries. "You haven't eaten your Danish. Now that I'm back, do you want to take a break?"

"Not yet. Maybe once the line goes down a little."

"You need a rest. Rose and Maleah are here, so Olivia could take your place."

"Good idea." Keturah nodded to the pastry. "I guess that was your idea too."

"Actually"—he leaned close to whisper—"I used it as an excuse to talk to Lilliane. She's not happy about the refrigerator, but I think she'll accept it."

"Oh, Jeremiah." Keturah's eyes shone, and her face smoothed out. "*Danke.* You've been such a blessing to all of us." The smile she directed his way set his spirits soaring.

Chapter Twenty

Jeremiah's excitement took a nosedive the next afternoon as he headed into his rehab appointment. Everyone on the team had gathered around the conference table with computers, folders, pens, and notepads at the ready. They all looked cheerful. A lot more upbeat than Jeremiah.

As much as he'd railed against staying at the rehab center, knowing the time had come for him to leave triggered growing fears and nagging doubts. He depended on so many different people every day. How would he ever take care of himself?

The meeting progressed from a discussion based on the doctor's most recent evaluation, clearing Jeremiah for discharge, to all the practicalities of his day-to-day living and therapy appointments. He'd still be expected to attend his usual sessions even after he moved home.

The word *home* twisted his gut. *Home* to him meant the farm and Mamm. Both were gone.

The social worker tapped a finger on the address she had listed. "I assume you'll be going here? I tried several times to get ahold of someone over the past few days, but nobody answered."

That phone had been installed in the barn. Zeke worked part-time at the auction house during the day. He wouldn't be around to answer.

Jeremiah shook his head. "I sold the farm."

Her eyebrows rose. "So where will you be living? With relatives? If so, we'll need to have them attend trainings this coming week to prepare them."

"I don't have any relatives in this area."

Deep lines appeared between the social worker's brow. "Where did you plan to go after you're discharged?"

If he explained he was homeless, would they keep him here longer? "I don't really have anywhere to go."

The shuffling of papers quieted, and a roomful of concerned faces turned in his direction.

A hiss escaped from the social worker's lips. "I wish someone had alerted me to this."

"Nobody else knew either."

Before she could get even more upset and flustered, Jeremiah added, "Darryl Nissly offered to let me stay with him temporarily."

"The Darryl who works here?" At his nod, the tension in her face relaxed. "That'd be perfect. He already knows how to care for you."

"Why don't we get him in here so we can make plans?" one of the therapists suggested. "He'll be getting off work soon."

A short while later, Darryl arrived, and plans progressed around Jeremiah. By the time everyone finished speaking and getting approvals, Darryl had been approved for a paid position as Jeremiah's caretaker, and Darryl's work hours at the rehab center had been rescheduled so he could take Jeremiah to and from work and pick him up for therapy sessions.

Both Jeremiah and Darryl left the room in a daze. Jeremiah had been cleared to move into Darryl's apartment next Wednesday.

"*Danke* for doing this." Although Jeremiah appreciated having a place to stay, eventually he wanted to find or build a home of his own. That meant working even harder to recover so he could care for himself.

"I still can't believe they're paying me for this. I'd gladly do it for free. Maybe I'll be able to go to college sooner than I thought."

"If you'd like to earn a little more money, I have a few errands to run in town."

"Wow. Just wow. God is so good."

Several hours later, after treating Darryl to supper at a restaurant, Jeremiah arrived back at the rehab center with the back of the van loaded with surprises for tomorrow.

Keturah's heart sang as she touched her pocket. Not even the gray skies, icy wind, and dirty piles of slush in the market parking lot dented her joy. Another letter had arrived in a yellow envelope. She'd only pulled yesterday's mail from the box this morning as they headed to the market, so she hadn't had time to read it yet.

As soon as they unpacked everything, she'd pull the horse into the shelter and take a few minutes for a quick read. Then, tonight, after her sisters went to bed, she'd savor the whole letter again and again, the way she had his other two. But they'd only unpacked half their supplies when Jeremiah and Mrs. Vandenberg arrived within minutes of each other.

Keturah sighed. As happy as she was to see both of them, she'd have no time to open the yellow envelope. She hoped for a break today so she could sneak off for a few minutes. Having this secret in her pocket made her impatient for privacy.

But first, she had to help her sisters prep extra pretzels to fill the shiny new refrigerator that had been installed last night after closing. With twelve racks wide enough to hold two baking sheets each, the glass case could chill two dozen trays. Lilliane glowered and pointedly ignored the gleaming appliances, but Maleah and Rose both exclaimed over them.

After a quick glance at Lilliane, Jeremiah whispered his comment so softly only Keturah heard. "Those will be a big help." Then, in a louder voice, he added, "I need to bring in a few things from the van. After that, should I collect all the dough from Ridley's?"

"Would you?" Keturah tried to convey her appreciation for both of his comments. What a relief to have no more reasons to head to Bo's. "I'm sorry you have to deal with him."

"Me too." Jeremiah's teasing tone made it sound like a joke, but Keturah had seen how Bo tormented Jeremiah.

"I'm so glad you won't have to go there after today."

Startled, they both looked at Lilliane.

"What?" she said defensively. "Bo's mean to Jeremiah."

Jeremiah sent Lilliane a sunny smile along with a *danke*. For some reason, that irritated Keturah. She couldn't possibly be jealous of her younger sister, could she?

The letter crinkled in her pocket. Although Keturah

hadn't read it, knowing *A Friend Who Cares* had written back soothed her.

Jeremiah returned with an *Englischer*. They both carried boxes and parcels. While Jeremiah set out a gorgeous nativity set on the higher shelf between her counter and his, the young man set up a table outside the stand, placed a large glass bowl on it, and filled it with mini pretzels.

Keturah stood there speechless. Her sisters stopped working to crowd around and admire the hand-carved figures.

"They're beautiful," Rose said reverently. She stroked the wooden baby Jesus in His cradle.

The *Englischer* returned carrying a foldable ladder. He hung a glittering star from the ceiling, right over the spot where baby Jesus lay. Then he dangled angels at different heights on both sides.

Misty-eyed, Keturah scolded Jeremiah. "You shouldn't have done all this."

"I want the stand to be ready for the Christmas Extravaganza."

The *Englischer* cleaned up the boxes and wrappings. "I'll take this to recycle."

Jeremiah accompanied him with the rest of the boxes and returned a short while later with a sign. The calligraphy explained about pretzels being praying hands.

"*Danke.*" All of Keturah's gratitude could never fit into that one word. She wished she had a way to let Jeremiah know how much she appreciated what he'd done.

"I enjoyed doing this, and I've wanted to buy one of Luke Bontrager's nativity sets ever since I saw them in the window of the Christmas Year 'Round Shop."

"I can't believe this." Keturah shook her head. "I'd been thinking of draping a pine garland in front of the stand."

Lilliane stepped out of the stand and studied the scene. "It's beautiful, Jeremiah."

She waved toward the U-shaped quilting and fabric booth catty-corner to their stand. It had a three-sided cardboard fireplace holding a glowing fake fire. Quilted stockings hung from the mantel, and Christmas-themed quilts lined the walls. Then she gestured at Gina's stand.

"Our stand looks better because it shows the true meaning of Christmas."

Keturah agreed. Although Lilliane hadn't said it, even Daed would have been happy with these decorations.

Before Rose and Maleah left for school, they filled all the refrigerator shelves, which Keturah appreciated once the market opened. An impending snowstorm brought in throngs of customers, who stocked up on meats, produce, and baked goods. Most of them stopped for a pretzel to warm themselves before heading back out into the cold. Keturah barely had time to breathe for the rest of the day. Neither did anyone else.

Despite Lilliane's aversion to the refrigerator, they needed all the pretzels they'd stored and more. She refused to go near the shelves, so Olivia removed the trays and put those pretzels in the oven whenever they ran low. The day flew by, and after closing, the letter remained unread in Keturah's pocket. Now she'd have to wait until after supper for some privacy.

By the time they'd finished the dishes, stars sparkled overhead and newly fallen snow glistened in the moon's bluish beams. Keturah slipped upstairs with pink stationery and the DeWalt. Once she'd prepared for sleep and closed her bedroom door, she hung the hook of the battery-powered light over the bed's headboard and curled up under the covers.

Although she'd been eager to read the letter all day, she waited a moment to open it. Her heart overflowed with thanksgiving. God had surely blessed her today. First, Mrs. Vandenberg and the refrigerators. Then, Jeremiah's kindness with the decorations. Now, the letter. After whispering a prayer, Keturah lifted the envelope flap.

She reread the letter twice, gaining comfort and reassurance. Once again, the verses—this time a whole page full—touched her.

A Friend reinforced her belief that making the pretzels ahead didn't violate their advertisement. That eased some of her worries, and he encouraged her to pray about her decisions. He understood how torn she'd been over following Daed's directives or helping others, but he nudged her back to seeking the Lord's guidance for these thorny issues.

Finding out he was close to her age made her a little self-conscious, but he'd encouraged her to share her thoughts and problems. She wished she knew his name, but if he wanted to tell her, he would have. She decided to respect his desire to remain anonymous and addressed her response to *Dear Friend*. He did seem like a dear friend—in her mind at least—but she couldn't leave it like that. Not when she was writing to a man. She changed it to read, *Dear Friend Who Cares.*

> *Like you said, I'm finding that God has been bringing good into my life.* Danke *for reminding*

*me again to look for it and to trust God for the
future.*

This time, Keturah decided to start with the positive
news and told him all about how helpful Mrs. Vandenberg
and Jeremiah had been. She finished up by describing Jeremiah's talks with Lilliane.

> *I can't tell you how much that lifted my burdens.
> Jeremiah hasn't been here long, but already he
> seems like an important part of our business. One
> of the best things about him is the way he
> brightens our days.*

Keturah told her *friend* about the chicken, the pastries,
and the lollipops.

> *You should have seen how our mouths lit up.
> Can you picture all of us with pulsing, colored
> lights? We all acted like children. I still laugh
> when I remember it. I admit it felt good to be so
> silly, and my younger sisters needed the fun. Even
> Lilliane unbent enough to laugh. That was quite a
> miracle.*

After detailing her conflicts with Lilliane and her own
conscience nagging her over Daed's rules, she added, *To
be honest, I'm still not sure I've done the right thing. I appreciate your advice about praying. I've been trying to
follow God's will, but I'm still torn.*

Once she'd opened that floodgate, she poured out her
heart and asked some new questions she'd been grappling
with over the past few days. She lightly touched on one

subject that had been haunting her—guilt—but she didn't delve into it, because she needed her sleep. She'd stayed up much too late already, and they'd be getting up early tomorrow for market. Time to end the letter.

> *Again,* danke *for your letters. I can't tell you how much they mean to me. I reread them often to remember your words, and they remind me to lean on God. And they also reassure me someone cares.*

The week flew by faster than Jeremiah wished. He had to leave the market early on Tuesday afternoon for his last meeting at the rehab center before he moved to Darryl's. He'd warned Keturah of his changed schedule but didn't mention moving out of the center tomorrow, mostly because he avoided thinking about it. He'd also worked hard to appear competent here at work, so he didn't want her to realize he needed a full-time caretaker.

Right before he left, Lilliane insisted Keturah hang a sign on the self-serve checkout stating *Not in Service.* Keturah had agreed to work on that side of the stand but not to let her customers use the machine.

While Jeremiah maneuvered through the market aisles, Olivia hurried past him and out the door. Tall banks of plowed snow dotted the parking lot, and car tires splashed slush as he exited. He pulled a black stocking cap down over his ears and huddled into his coat.

"Watch out for ice patches," Darryl called as he hopped from the idling van to pull down the ramp. "I almost slipped earlier." He shivered as he affixed the tie-downs. "Boy, is it cold out here."

Jeremiah's teeth chattered. "Freezing." Once the van door slid shut, the blasting heat warmed him.

Darryl waited in a long line of cars exiting the parking lot, but more vehicles flooded into the entrances. "I hope the stand isn't too busy. Both Olivia and I left around the same time."

As they headed down the road, Jeremiah pointed to a girl struggling through the snow on the shoulder, her head bent against the wind. "That's dangerous. Maybe we could give her a ride."

"Fine with me." Darryl steered to the side of the road far enough ahead of the girl so he wouldn't spray her with snow.

Jeremiah marveled at Darryl's thoughtfulness. The girl shook her head when Darryl offered her a ride. Jeremiah didn't blame her for not taking a ride with two men, but they only wanted to help. Then the wind whipped the scarf from the girl's face.

"Olivia?" Jeremiah called. "Please get in."

"Jeremiah?" Her voice trembled. "Thanks. It's cold out here, but I don't want to take you out of your way."

"You won't."

Olivia, her nose and cheeks red from the cold, settled in the front seat, and Jeremiah introduced her to Darryl. After they dropped her off, which took them a few miles beyond their destination, Darryl remarked on what a nice girl she was.

"And she's Mennonite."

"I could tell."

Jeremiah smiled to himself. "Maybe you could pick her up and drive her home from market every day during the winter weather."

"I'd be happy to, if you're all right with me using the van. I don't like to think of cars spinning out of control and hitting her, not to mention her walking in such bad weather."

"I'm fine with you driving her. Actually, maybe you could also drop Keturah's younger sisters at school when you head back to the rehab center in the mornings and bring them to the market in the afternoons when you come to get me. You go right past the turnoff for their school. I'd be happy to pay you for your time."

"No need for payment. I'd be glad to do it."

"I'll let Mrs. Vandenberg's driver know. That'll save him the trip."

Once Jeremiah had made the plans, though, he wondered how long he'd be going back and forth to the market. Now that he was moving out of the rehab center, would Mrs. Vandenberg replace him with someone else?

The minute Jeremiah left, Keturah was swamped with customers. Thank heavens, Rose and Maleah had arrived.

Maleah glanced around. "Where's Jeremiah?"

"He had a meeting."

"Aww. I wanted to show him something."

"It'll have to wait until Thursday." Lilliane brushed past Maleah. "I'm going to wait on customers with Keturah. You and Rose need to make more pretzels. Olivia had to leave early too."

As Lilliane approached the front counter, her face twisted. Despite her own discomfort, Keturah moved into Jeremiah's spot. Lilliane kept her body angled away from the self-serve checkout.

Keturah sighed. Except for the fact that the machine helped Jeremiah, which was definitely important, she wished she'd never agreed to have it installed. Too late now for regret. She needed to make the best of the situation.

"I'll take two dozen, evenly divided among the flavors."

They'd need to bake more. Keturah had to take some pretzels from Lilliane's warmer. She checked to see if her sisters had used up all the premade pretzels. Catching Rose's attention, Keturah mouthed, *Two dozen mixed*.

Rose's eyes widened, and she glanced at Lilliane's warmer. With a quick nod, she notified Maleah and then went back to dipping pretzels in the baking soda bath.

The *Englischer* glanced at the sign on the checkout. "Wait. Is the machine broken?"

"*Neh*, but we'd prefer cash."

"I came out of my way to get pretzels because I'd heard I could charge them. All I have is this." He waved a credit card in front of her. "And I have twenty employees waiting for the treat I promised."

What should she do now? Pass up this large order and send away an unhappy customer and disappoint twenty other people, or take care of him in a kind and caring manner?

Jeremiah's advice guided her choice. Would God consider taking charge cards sinful? If so, why did some Amish and Mennonite vendors take charges? Even ones she respected, like Gideon Hartzler, took charge cards. And this man had no other way to pay.

She glanced at Lilliane, who had her back turned as she lifted two pretzels from the warmer.

"You may use the machine," she said softly, but she'd forgotten about the beeps.

At the sound, Lilliane whirled around and stared at Keturah in horror. "You promised."

"We'll talk later."

Her face scrunched up as if she were about to cry, Lilliane returned to her customer, and Keturah filled a large shopping bag with pretzels.

"Oh, good," the next man in line said. "I'll use a credit card too."

Before she knew it, people started slipping out of Lilliane's line to use the machine. If she let one person do it, she couldn't deny the others.

As the machine beeped and hummed, Lilliane's jaw grew tighter and tighter until she looked as if she'd explode.

"We can't wait on many more customers unless we get more pretzels. Maybe you could help Rose." Keturah moved to take over Lilliane's spot, and some of the tension drained from her sister's face.

Pretzel baking would take a while, and Lilliane wouldn't lose her temper in front of the customers. At least Keturah hoped her sister wouldn't. Maybe by the time Lilliane finished, she'd forget about her anger.

More than ever, Keturah missed Jeremiah. For more reasons than one.

Chapter Twenty-One

After his final meeting at the rehab center, Jeremiah headed for his room with stacks of material, names and phone numbers, schedules for outpatient visits, exercises to do between appointments, paperwork for the home health workers who'd be stopping by, and plans for his on-going recovery. The various therapists, along with the social worker, had assisted Jeremiah in ordering equipment and tools that would be delivered to the apartment, and they'd ensured he and Darryl would have ample help.

Darryl waved as he headed off with his own sheaf of papers. Tomorrow at ten, he'd return to pick up Jeremiah and take him to the apartment. Instead of taking his scheduled day off, Darryl planned to give it up to spend time moving Jeremiah.

Jeremiah still couldn't believe he'd be out of the center in less than a day. Instead of reading the newspaper after dinner, he went over all the paperwork several times to be sure he hadn't missed anything important. He also called Zeke to give him the new address.

"Great! I'll stop by to visit on the weekend. And I'll let Isaac know you'll be ready for Snickers soon."

Jeremiah had forgotten to ask Darryl about a guide dog. He'd needn't have worried. When Darryl arrived the next morning, he said he loved the idea of a dog.

"Oh." Darryl reached into his coat pocket and pulled out a pink envelope. "Thought you might want this."

Jeremiah forced himself to reach out slowly rather than snatching the letter. He wished he could open and read it right away, but he'd have to wait until he got settled into his new room.

Several hours later, Jeremiah had moved his meager possessions into Darryl's second bedroom and taken a tour of the apartment. Darryl had rearranged everything except his own bedroom to make the apartment as accessible as possible. After they had everything in place, Jeremiah returned to the rehab building for his usual Wednesday therapy sessions, only this time as an outpatient. He'd tucked the letter into a drawer, and it called to him while he ate supper, chatted with Darryl for an hour, and got ready for bed with Darryl's assistance.

"I know you'd rather not use electricity," Darryl said as they reentered the bedroom, "so the lamps on both bedside tables are battery operated. All you need to do to turn them on is to wave your hand near them." He demonstrated.

Jeremiah couldn't get over how thoughtful Darryl was. Somehow, some way, Jeremiah hoped to find a way to repay this generosity.

Right now, reading Keturah's letter took first priority. After a bit of a tussle with the drawer handle of the bedside table, he extracted his Bible, stationery, pen holder, and the pink envelope from the drawer. He started with Keturah's letter.

Part of him flushed with pleasure when he read her descriptions of how he'd helped her. Another part of him squirmed. Keturah would be so embarrassed if she knew she'd been writing to him. As he planned his reply, he debated about whether to reveal the truth in a letter or in person. Doing it in writing seemed cowardly, but how would he get a chance to talk to her alone?

He pushed aside that thought to concentrate on the rest of her note. One sentence stood out to him.

> *One other concern keeping me awake at night is guilt. Disbelief and confusion clouded it at first, but the more I accept the truth of what happened, the guiltier I feel.*

Jeremiah had been struggling with guilt too. Survivor's guilt.

It didn't seem fair that he'd survived when his mother and several other people had paid with their lives. All because Jeremiah had begged Mamm to come along on a trip he'd organized with an *Englisch* van driver to see the Pennsylvania Grand Canyon.

The driver wanted to fill the seventeen-person van. He'd invited several Amish couples from Ephrata, but he'd counted on Jeremiah for the rest of the passengers. One of his friends had canceled at the last minute, so Jeremiah had an empty seat to fill.

He'd begged Mamm, reminding her that he'd always wanted to go to Arizona. Daed had promised to take six-year-old Jeremiah someday. Then Daed had died.

Chances were, Jeremiah might never get to see the magnificent Grand Canyon in Arizona. He'd pored over photos of that wonder of the world. He'd barely ever been out of Lancaster County. As a dairy farmer, he didn't get days off. Cows needed to be milked twice a day, seven days a week. Zeke had agreed to take over the milking for one day, skipping his own family's auction business because he wanted to support Jeremiah's desire to go on this trip.

When Jeremiah couldn't find anyone else to take the seat, Mamm gave in. If only he'd known what would happen, he'd have accepted her refusal. If only he'd known, he'd never have organized the trip.

He'd paid for his selfishness many times over. Not only in the loss of his mobility and in the loss of his livelihood, but worst of all, in the loss of his mother. All gone in one day. The day he'd dreamed of for weeks before the trip. The day he'd pleaded and begged Mamm to take that empty seat. The day that was supposed to be one of the highlights of his life.

The day that had turned into a nightmare. A nightmare that had destroyed his life.

A dark cloud engulfed Jeremiah as he traveled back in time to the accident. An oncoming car weaving. The van swerving. Brakes squealing. Metal screeching. Loud booms. People screaming, groaning, crying out.

Then sharp, searing pain shot through him. Blackness descended.

When he woke after the operation, he had no idea of the damages to his body or any of the losses. He drifted in and out of consciousness, didn't recognize people for days. Then he had to deal with the reality of Mamm's death.

The politician had kept all but a brief mention out of

the paper. The only write-up Jeremiah had seen was a brief paragraph saying a two-vehicle crash on I-80 W was under investigation. The names of the injured and dead had not been listed, pending notification of family members.

By the time he'd recovered enough to be aware of what had happened, Jeremiah had missed all the articles about the collision. He didn't know the names of the people from other districts who'd been on the trip, so he wrote to everyone he read about in *Die Botschaft* who'd lost loved ones. He longed to reach out to anyone who was hurting. Perhaps he'd also sent those letters to salve his guilt.

Right now, though, he should be concentrating on Keturah's problems rather than his own. He wanted to support her, so he prayed for wisdom.

> *You may be racked with guilt over things you said, or those you left unsaid.*

Jeremiah had no idea why he'd written those words. It seemed as if God had dictated that sentence, but the rest of the paragraph came straight from his heart.

> *At first, you walk around numb, but once reality sinks in, the guilt begins. Regrets whirl in continuous circles like a dog chasing its tail. "If only . . ." So much you could have done differently. Remorse keeps you up at night and haunts you during the day.*

In his lifetime, Jeremiah had left so much unsaid and undone. He jotted down several verses he clung to during those times.

We believe God forgives us as we forgive others. But His forgiveness is not as limited as ours. Each time one of those memories bothers you, take it to the Lord in prayer.

After he finished answering what seemed to be her deepest need, he moved on to the other events she'd mentioned. He tried to reassure her she'd been doing a good job caring for her sisters—one of her persistent worries—and in her business choices. This time, as he chose verses, he concentrated on God's power to help her.

Remember, you don't need to make any of these decisions alone. When you're feeling unsure of what to do, read James 1:5 and Philippians 4:6–7. Those are my favorite verses when I'm facing uncertainty. God has promised to give us wisdom and understanding. And I find He gives me peace when I've made the right choice. I'm sure He'll do the same for you.

Jeremiah tried to address everything she'd written, with the exception of her praise about him. As to that, he only mentioned he was glad she'd had some fun. But his heart rejoiced that he'd been the one to bring her that joy.

Over the next few days, Jeremiah seemed distracted and nervous. Keturah debated about asking him if anything was wrong. But they stayed so busy, they rarely had a moment for conversation.

On Saturday afternoon after they returned home from the market, Maleah pranced in from the mailbox with a stack of mail. Spying a yellow envelope, Keturah distracted her sister by suggesting she open some of the cards addressed to the whole family. Once Maleah tore the first one open, Keturah slid the letter into her pocket. Tonight, she'd have another flashlight reading marathon. She couldn't wait.

The rest of the day progressed too slowly to suit Keturah, but finally, she adjusted the light so she could read. He'd sent two pages again.

Delighted, she lingered over every word, then went back to the beginning, where he'd written about *guilt*.

She shivered. It was as if he'd tiptoed around inside her mind. How did he know she regretted the things she'd said and done?

The verses he'd mentioned brought up all her self-blame. Although she'd tried to shove it out of her mind, guilt over her last interaction with her father overwhelmed her. Now she had no way to ask his forgiveness, and if she were honest, she didn't want to, which added to the shame. She still harbored resentment, and each time the scene crossed her mind, a flash of anger shot through her.

The night before her parents left on their trip, Maleah had upset her milk at supper.

"How many times have I told you to be careful?" Daed thundered.

Maleah hung her head. "I-I'm s-sorry."

Keturah hopped up to get a rag.

Daed jabbed a thick finger in Keturah's direction. "Sit down!" he yelled.

Maleah jumped. Teardrops trembled on her lashes as she stared at the spreading puddle.

Daed turned in her direction. "Why are you sitting

there? Clean it up before it splashes all over the floor. And stop sniveling."

When her sister sat frozen, Keturah hurried to the sink, grabbed the rag, and held it out. "Here, Maleah."

His face red and furious, Daed shoved his chair back from the table. "What do you think you're doing?" He pinned Keturah with rage-filled eyes. "How dare you disobey me?"

Torn between obedience to her parents, which Scripture demanded, and her quaking sister, Keturah chose to defend Maleah. "It was an accident. She's only seven."

Daed's eyes narrowed. "You're talking back to me?" He glowered at her. "Go to your room now. I'll deal with you later." His voice had gone cold and hard.

Keturah hesitated a second. She debated challenging him again, but she worried what might happen to Maleah. She whirled and fled up the stairs, her hands and jaw clenched. *It's so unfair. Why is he like this?*

She'd asked that question many times but never received an answer.

Although it would add to her punishment, she slammed the door behind her. She flung herself on the bed and covered her ears, but she couldn't block out the noise downstairs. Daed berated Maleah while she whimpered.

Keturah had developed an inner strength that allowed her to withstand Daed's temper, but Maleah, with her tender and easily bruised heart, went through life cowed and shivering.

God, I can't forgive him. I just can't.

Someone pounded on the front door. Keturah tiptoed to the window. Their *Englisch* neighbor stood there, a look of consternation on his face.

When Mamm answered, he asked for Daed. She called out, "Melvin, Rod is here."

"I'll be right there." In a less strident tone than he'd used with Maleah earlier, he snapped, "Get that mess cleaned up."

In a concerned voice, Rod asked, "Is everything okay?"

"Of course," Daed blustered.

"Well, then, could you help me with some tree limbs? That lightning strike last weekend left some big branches dangling, and I'm afraid they might come crashing down on our dogs or kids."

"Sure, sure." Daed exited the house, and the door banged behind him.

Had Rod made up an excuse to get Daed out of the house? He often seemed to show up at the perfect time to defuse some of Daed's fury. Her father would never say *neh* to helping a neighbor, and Rod's requests always involved physical labor.

By the time Daed returned, he'd usually forgotten about his anger.

Not long after he left, the bedroom door clicked open. Keturah's head snapped up. Mamm entered with Keturah's uneaten supper.

Mamm never interfered with Daed's discipline. But she offered comfort when she could.

"*Ach, liebchen,* I'm sorry you missed supper. You were only trying to help."

Although the food had gone cold, Keturah ate every bite. Not only because she'd been trained to eat everything on her plate, but also because she wanted to show Mamm her kindness was appreciated.

"*Danke.*" She handed back the plate. "Can I help with the dishes?"

"*Neh.* I don't know how long your *daed* will be gone. It'll upset him to come home and find you out of your room. The other girls and I will help Maleah until he returns."

Those last three words struck dread into Keturah's heart. *Until he returns.* Then she'd learn her punishment.

Mamm must have read Keturah's expression and sensed her distress. "You could go to sleep early. If Rod keeps your *daed* out there for a while, he might head straight to bed. We need to leave much earlier than usual tomorrow morning for our trip."

Keturah had almost forgotten about their plans. Her parents had chosen a day when the market was closed, and Keturah had been put in charge of the household for the day. She'd already planned to ask her sisters to help her do extra chores to surprise Mamm.

"Perhaps by the time we get back, your *daed* will have forgotten all about tonight." Mamm's face filled with pity. But her eyes told the truth. Daed would never forget. He might even double the punishment, figuring Keturah had taken advantage of her time off.

If only I never had to face Daed again . . .

If only . . .

Keturah had gotten her wish. Maybe God had punished her for thinking such a thing. She'd more than paid for that terrible desire by losing Mamm too.

Maleah had been afraid her wish had caused the accident, and Keturah had reassured her sister it hadn't been her fault. If only Keturah could convince herself she hadn't been to blame either.

Even more than the shame over her unforgiving spirit

toward her *daed*, her mother's passing had left her with a deep regret. If only she'd known that evening would be the last time she'd see her mother, Keturah would have hugged Mamm, told her how much she loved her. Instead, Keturah had barely thanked Mamm for caring enough to bring the meal.

That was probably the kind of guilt *A Friend* had meant. The regret of not expressing all the love in her heart. She doubted he had any idea of the depth of her bitterness, her unforgiveness. Not only did Keturah still harbor anger at her father's treatment of her over the years—the incident over Maleah's spilled milk was mild compared to most of his cruelties—but she also refused to release her anger.

She dragged around a heavy iron ball of guilt that weighed her down.

Keturah slid a piece of stationery from the drawer and penned a thank-you.

> *I'm not sure how you always touch and soothe the sore spots in my soul, but you've done it once again. God has been using your letters to speak to me.*

She started with the easiest confession, unsure if she could share her conflicts with Daed in this letter or in any other.

> *I wish I could go back to the night before the accident. My heart aches that I took Mamm for granted. I appreciated what she did that evening, but I didn't let her know. And every day brings fresh memories and heartache.*

*So many times I didn't help her when I should
have. So many times I didn't do what she asked.
So many times I didn't thank her.*

Keturah set down her pen to wipe her blurry eyes.

*So many times I didn't tell her what she meant
to me.*

All the times Mamm had dried Keturah's tears, ban-
daged her skinned knees, read her stories, taught her how
to sew, how to keep house . . . Now each of those ordinary
moments had become precious. Each memory repre-
sented a jewel strung on a necklace of blessings she'd been
given daily. Blessings she'd neglected to appreciate.

But what of Daed? *A Friend Who Cares* had included
verses about forgiveness. Had God sent this message to
encourage her to let go of her resentment?

Chapter Twenty-Two

Keturah fell asleep with the unfinished letter beside her. And she woke before dawn with the unfinished business of Daed on her mind. Because today was an off-Sunday, she could take time to ponder both.

After a few minutes of reflection, she turned on the light she'd hung on her headboard last night and picked up her pen.

When I was younger, Mamm always warned me to think only good and true thoughts, because each of our thoughts forms a prayer. And after I was old enough to wear a kapp *every day, she reminded me that covering my head meant my heart should always remain in prayer. I tried to do what she suggested, but I had—and still have—a huge dark spot of anger and unforgiveness deep inside, and some days I wonder if losing my parents is God's punishment for those feelings.*

She'd comforted Maleah, who'd had the same worry, but guilt kept raising doubts. Maybe confessing her feelings about Daed might help her heal.

A Friend always understood, and he might have some wisdom to share. He'd already sent verses about forgiveness. Verses she seemed unable—or unwilling—to apply.

> *I've never told anyone this, because Daed*
> *always insisted we keep family life private . . .*

Daed's glowering presence loomed over Keturah as she touched the pen to the paper. Old fears stilled her hand. She couldn't do this. She shouldn't do this.

For a moment, her fingers trembled. She'd be punished. Once again, she was defying her father. He'd never forgive her for this betrayal.

But he was no longer here.

Her writing shaky, Keturah recounted several childhood memories and then her final confrontation with Daed. As the story flowed from her pen, some of the poison seeped out and spilled onto the page.

When she finished, she slumped back against the headboard. Telling the truth about the past left her drained and exhausted.

"Keturah?" Rose called from the kitchen. "Are you coming for breakfast?"

Two hours had disappeared while she wrote. Keturah scrambled from bed and dressed hurriedly. Then she secreted the letter, which now contained several pages, in her dresser drawer before heading downstairs.

Irritation flashed in Lilliane's eyes as Keturah entered

the kitchen. Her sister's annoyance clearly held more than impatience. They'd never discussed Keturah's use of the self-serve checkout yesterday. Already raw from her emotional experience this morning, the last thing Keturah wanted was to get into an argument. But they had to talk about it.

"I'm sorry, Lilliane. I broke my promise."

"Daed always said our word was our bond." Her face blotchy, Lilliane glared at Keturah. "It's like you want to destroy everything Daed taught us."

Lilliane's words slammed into Keturah. Was her sister right? Had Keturah's decisions been a rebellion against their father?

Daed had been a principled man, a helpful friend, a wise counselor. He'd done a lot of good for others and for the family. But he'd had a dark side. Lilliane saw the best of him; Keturah focused on the worst.

Unforgiveness colored everything with ugliness.

Rose's gentle voice smoothed over the disagreement. "Why don't we pray before the food gets cold?"

Grateful to her younger sister for easing the tension, Keturah slid into her place at the table.

Lord, please help me to examine my own life rather than concentrating on the faults of others.

Keturah waited until they'd all eaten a few bites before broaching the touchy subject with Lilliane. While Keturah explained why she'd let the *Englischer* use the machine, Lilliane dropped her fork and crossed her arms.

The minute Keturah finished, her sister exploded, "It would be better to lose that large sale than to disobey."

Once again, Rose's calming voice interrupted. "I'm

sure Keturah regrets what she did. It's over. What's done is done. The only thing you can do now is forgive."

Lilliane lowered her head and muttered, "What if you forgive, and the person keeps doing the same thing over and over?"

"You know the answer to that," Rose said gently. "*Seventy times seven.*"

Rose's words echoed in Keturah's mind long after breakfast ended.

It's over. What's done is done. The only thing you can do now is forgive. Seventy times seven.

On Tuesday, Jeremiah entered the market tense and nervous. He needed to tell Mrs. Vandenberg and Keturah he'd left rehab. He hated to lose this job and the chance to be near Keturah, but he had to be honest.

He didn't have long to wait. Mrs. Vandenberg arrived as he headed over to assist Keturah and her sisters with unloading the buggy. She waved and tottered by them. Although the parking lot had been salted, Jeremiah worried she might slip on slush.

"Wait," he called after her. "Let me help you to the door."

"Why, thank you."

From the smile she gave him, she looked as if he'd given her a million dollars. Although that might not be the best comparison. She already had millions.

When he reached her, she clamped a hand on his chair arm and walked beside him into the building, giving Jeremiah time to discuss Darryl taking Maleah and Rose to school and picking them up after school. And he'd be transporting Olivia back and forth.

Mrs. Vandenberg nodded. "Perfect. That fits into my plans—or, rather, the plans God's laid on my heart. I have a good feeling about that."

Jeremiah took a deep breath to prepare himself for the talk he dreaded.

But Mrs. Vandenberg spoke first. "How are you enjoying living at Darryl's?"

"You know about that?"

"Of course. Darryl goes to my church, and I'm working with Tina to set up more market stands. That's why I'm here this morning."

"I wanted to talk to you about leaving the pretzel stand."

Mrs. Vandenberg stopped so abruptly, Jeremiah almost pulled her off her feet. He glided to a stop.

"You're not happy there?"

"I'm very happy, but you said you wanted me to train someone else from the rehab center."

"Oh." She fanned herself with one hand, which seemed odd after coming in from the wintery weather. "I thought you planned to leave Keturah. And that just wouldn't do."

The way Mrs. Vandenberg phrased it, she made it sound as if he planned to break up with Keturah. Something he'd never do—because that was a total impossibility.

"Why don't you check with Keturah?" The frown lines between Mrs. Vandenberg's eyes smoothed out. "With Christmas coming, I doubt she'll want to lose you, and it's not easy to train someone else this time of year. But if you want to move to a different stand . . ."

Neh, that's the last thing he wanted.

"Never mind. I can tell by the look on your face you don't want to leave her."

"I like working there." His words came out too defensive, but he needed to counter what Mrs. V had implied. Twice now, she'd emphasized the word *leave* as if he and Keturah had a relationship. "I'm just glad to have a job."

The twinkle in her eye made it clear his effort to hide his interest in Keturah hadn't fooled her. "And she's extremely grateful to have you. I believe the Lord has brought you together."

When Mrs. Vandenberg said that, Jeremiah experienced a longing deep in his soul.

She patted his arm. "Trust Him for your future."

Had she been reading his mind again? The tips of Jeremiah's ears burned.

"I'm headed over there"—she waved to her right—"and you should get back to Keturah. She needs you." She hobbled toward the next aisle over. "Just remember, Jeremiah, God doesn't plant desires in our hearts that He doesn't intend to fulfill."

Jeremiah sat, staring after her, lost in thought. But what if the desires of your heart conflicted with what you believed possible?

He roused himself. He had to take the container he held to the stand. Behind him, someone called out, and he cringed.

"Jerry-miah, wait a minute." Bo hurried to catch up. "You taking that to my fridge?"

"*Neh*, Keturah has a new refrigerator big enough to hold her dough." Jeremiah should be polite. "Thank you for letting us—um, her—borrow yours."

Bo smirked at Jeremiah's slipup. "So that's it? No goodbye? No payment?"

"How much do I owe you?"

"I already told you what I wanted."

And that price was too much to pay. Money, Jeremiah was willing to give. But he'd never let Keturah get near Bo. Never.

"Aww, come on." Bo pushed his lips into a pretend pout, but a calculating look flared in his eyes. "Well, then, I'd say a thousand dollars would take care of it."

"I'll write you a check and bring it on Thursday."

"Just like that? No questions asked? You don't even want to bargain me down?"

"If you say that's a fair price, I believe you."

"You're something else, man. Forget it. You don't owe me anything. I was only kidding. Do you ever lighten up?"

"Sometimes." Jeremiah bit back a smile at the memory of the lollipops. He guessed his idea of fun wouldn't match Bo's. "I'd better get this to the stand." He patted the container on his lap.

"I can't believe your luck, spending all day with those girls. And they even added another girl. A Mennonite this time. It's like you have your own private harem." He whistled. "What I wouldn't give to be in your place."

"Really?" Jeremiah couldn't keep the ice from his voice. Would Bo actually want to deal with everything Jeremiah faced each day?

"You know what I mean. Not that." He gestured to the wheelchair. "I meant the girls. One of these days, I'm gonna get you to spill all your dirt."

Bo would be waiting a long time.

By the time Jeremiah reached the stand, the girls had

unloaded everything. He should have been here to help. As he stowed the container in the refrigerator, he worried about talking to Keturah. What if she said *neh*?

She studied him, and her brow creased into a concerned frown. "Is everything all right?"

Jeremiah took a deep breath. "I'm moving out of the rehab center into a friend's apartment."

"That's wonderful." She seemed genuinely happy for him.

"I talked to Mrs. Vandenberg about training a replacement, and—"

Keturah sucked in a breath. "You're going to leave us?"

"I don't want to, but Mrs. Vandenberg put in the machine to help people from the center."

"Can we ask her if it's all right to keep you?"

"She said it's up to you."

"Then I'd like you to keep working here. If you still want to?"

Keturah wanted him to stay. Jeremiah held his smile inside to keep it from bursting across his face. "*Jah*, I enjoy working here. *Danke*."

"*Gut*. It would be hard to adjust to someone new."

He came down to earth with a hard thud. He'd become part of their routine. Nothing more.

That evening, Keturah flicked on the flashlight and added a PS to her letter.

I had a bit of a scare today. Jeremiah told me
he moved out of the rehab center, so he was
planning to train someone to take his place. When

*I told him we need him, he agreed to stay. I was so
relieved. And not only because he helps with the
business. I can't even describe how much I'd miss
him if he goes.*

She reread what she'd written. Had she revealed too
much of her confusing, but possibly growing, attraction
to Jeremiah? She trusted her *Friend* enough to open up
about her deepest secrets, but her feelings were still too
nebulous to put into words. As he often did, he might read
more into what she'd already said.

She'd save her feelings for Jeremiah for another letter.
Maybe by then she'd have sorted them out. Right now, she
needed to deal with her bottled-up feelings toward Daed.

As she sealed the envelope, her sister's words replayed in
an endless loop. *The only thing you can do now is forgive.*

Keturah picked up the verses *A Friend* had sent. He,
too, had written about forgiveness. God spoke to her. She
needed to let go.

Daed was no longer here, so she couldn't ask for his
forgiveness. Even if he had been, she'd struggle with
doing this. She'd held on to every grievance, no matter
how small. Would her list reach the *seventy times seven*
the Bible suggested? What if all the wrongdoings ex-
ceeded that?

Keturah already knew the answer to that. God meant
for forgiveness to be unlimited. He'd stressed that in many
places in the Bible.

But if she forgave, would she be condoning her father's
actions? She no longer had to face him every day and feel
the sting of his words. Or watch him yell at her younger

sisters. But what if Daed were alive? Would forgiveness allow his cruelty to continue unchecked?

She pulled out another sheet of paper to write her question to *A Friend*, but she'd already sealed the envelope. Maybe she'd save this dilemma for another time. Or, perhaps, she could write out her questions and concerns and come to her own conclusions. Writing to someone else had proved how beneficial that could be.

So Keturah bent her head over the paper and wrote. And wrote. And wrote. She'd been unaware of all this bitterness. All these resentments had clouded her judgment.

Too tired to continue, she set aside the papers and turned off the light. She hadn't finished, and she still couldn't let all the old pain go. She wasn't ready. Not yet. And maybe she never would be.

Chapter Twenty-Three

For the next few weeks, letters flew back and forth between Keturah and Jeremiah. And each letter made him happier and guiltier. Keturah wrote so much about him in glowing, positive words, and reading between the lines, he detected a growing attraction that she didn't show at work.

From time to time, he surprised her looking at him with what he hoped was interest. Yet sometimes, she got a faraway look on her face as she stared off into the distance. The softness in her eyes and the dreaminess of her expression spoke of longing and love.

Who was she thinking of when she looked like that? Did she have a boyfriend? If so, he never visited her at work. And she never mentioned him in her letters. But that didn't mean anything. Her letters dealt with coming to terms with her grief and her past.

She carried a deep burden over her anger toward her *daed* she needed to heal. Jeremiah tried to provide a safe space for her to express her pent-up emotions. He prayed for her daily and hoped the words and verses touched her soul the way her sharing touched his.

The hardest letter to answer contained her question about forgiving verbal abuse if you were still enduring it. Jeremiah spent a long time in thought and prayer before he replied.

> *I've been struggling to answer your question about forgiving someone who continues to hurt you. It does seem like offering forgiveness again and again might enable that person to keep mistreating you.*
>
> *I've often found forgiveness works two ways— it heals the forgiver and the one forgiven. If you harbor anger or resentment, it can eat away at you. You're actually punishing yourself by not letting it go.*

In Keturah's case, she no longer had to face her father's wrath. She was the only person who'd benefit from forgiving. He wrote a bit more, trying to get that across as gently as possible. He didn't want her to feel he blamed her. He still hadn't addressed her concerns completely.

> *At the same time, that doesn't mean you shouldn't do something to try to stop abuse if you can. Forgiving the person doesn't mean allowing them to continue hurting you.*

Many times, though, the victim didn't have any way to stop the aggressor.

> *If you're in a situation where the person has power over you, it can leave you feeling helpless.*

Getting outside support is usually necessary.
Telling the truth to someone else might be a way to
get the needed help.

In your case, you provided that for your sisters
when you could, and it sounds as if God sent the
neighbor to your rescue sometimes. My heart
aches to think of you in that situation, and I wish I
could have been there to protect you.

Oh, how he wished he could have done something to shield her from that hurt. The only thing he could do now was to help her heal.

Although I'm deeply sorry you've lost your
parents, I'm also relieved you are no longer in that
situation. And I'm praying daily that you can
release all the painful memories and allow God's
healing forgiveness to cleanse away the past.

Please remember, I'm here whenever you need
someone to listen.

He lifted her up in prayer as he signed the letter and sealed it. More than ever, he wished he'd been honest with Keturah from the start. Then he would be able to extend emotional support to her at the market rather than just assisting with the sales and bookkeeping.

They had a good in-person rapport and an even deeper connection through their letters. Only one thing marred their relationship—he'd withheld his true identity. With each letter they exchanged, his guilt grew. He had to tell her, but how and when?

Every time he made up his mind to confess, another letter arrived, and he put it off. He should have told Keturah he was the letter writer when he first met her. Now he'd put himself in an impossible position.

This is why you don't lie.

A Scripture verse kept scrolling through his mind, increasing his guilt. *Lie not one to another. . . Lie not to one another . . .*

Why had he done that in the first place? And why had he kept up the false identity after he'd started working there? He had only one answer: *hochmut*. And what did God have to say about pride? The same thing He said about lying. The Bible condemned both. Shame filled Jeremiah's heart.

He had to face what he'd done. He had to tell Keturah the truth. Once he did, she'd despise him. She'd never trust him again.

He wanted to get everything off his mind now. But it might be better to tell her about being the letter writer when they were alone. He should do it outside work, because he wouldn't want to upset her in front of the customers. Or was he only making excuses to put off admitting the truth?

Keturah had torn up the pages of her grievances, but she shared a few in the letters she wrote. She found writing and receiving *A Friend*'s letters to be comforting. Slowly, she let down her guard and poured her true self out onto the paper.

She'd never experienced such a close spiritual connection with anyone. She shared her innermost feelings and deepest secrets. *A Friend* encouraged her to examine her life and open her heart.

When his latest letter came, tears rolled down her cheeks as she read. She'd always carried tremendous guilt over the times she'd interfered with her father's discipline. She'd never considered her role as that of protector.

But the line in the letter that brought a fresh flood of tears was the declaration *I wish I could have been there to protect you.*

Each time she reread it, her spirit welled with gratitude for his caring.

> *Oh, Friend, if only you could have been there with me. I felt God's presence as I read your words. Ever since we've been writing to each other, I've been keeping your letters in my pocket as I go about my day. They bring me such strength and comfort. I hope someday we can meet in person.*

The latest letter had arrived on Saturday, and Keturah skimmed it again before dressing for church the next morning. Before she left the room, she hugged the letter to her chest and imagined the man who'd sent it.

How wonderful it would be to meet a man with such a godly spirit and loving heart. He'd sent a message to a stranger and continued to pray for and support her on her spiritual journey. Each of his letters had encouraged her to move farther along the path to forgiveness.

Sitting in church later that morning, the Lord brought those messages to mind. The first sermon focused on Colossians 3:13. The end of the verse, *even as Christ forgave you, so also do ye*, stayed with Keturah as the minister emphasized that, if you have a grievance against another, you must forgive the way the Lord does.

Could she have any clearer direction?

As Keturah pulled out of the driveway following the church meal, Lilliane twisted her hands in her lap. "Ever since you made the changes at the market, I've been holding a grudge. Listening to the sermon today, I know I need to forgive you. Will you forgive me?"

"Of course." Knowing how difficult asking for forgiveness must have been for Lilliane dug another arrow into Keturah's conscience.

When she arrived home, she asked Maleah to see to the horse. Keturah had decided her younger sister needed more responsibility, and Keturah wanted to retreat to her room. She reread the letter and the verses *A Friend* had sent. Then she let the morning's sermons replay in her mind.

Alone in the silence, she wrestled with her anger and pain. Falling to her knees, she begged God to give her a willing heart. "I can't do this, Lord, but I want to do what You commanded."

One by one, she released her many burdens. The heavy weights rolled from her spirit until she managed to say, "Daed, I may not agree with what you did to all of us, but I forgive you."

With these words torn from the depths of her soul, she surrendered to God's will totally and completely. And this time when the tears came, they were cleansing tears.

Jeremiah flopped onto the bed, still sweaty after a torturous workout in rehab. He'd been learning to pull himself to his feet on the parallel bars and moving forward a few steps. He was determined to walk as soon as he could, and Darryl helped with extra leg exercises at home.

Writing to Keturah almost every night and working at the market had improved his finger dexterity. Soon he'd be able to open the bags without his tool. Maybe he could even learn to use tongs on the pretzels.

Meanwhile, he'd just picked up Snickers on the way home from the rehab center. He'd gone to training with the Happy Helpers to learn how to command the dog. And now the Labrador retriever, in her yellow harness, hopped onto the bed and curled up beside him, ready to help whenever needed.

Having a warm, furry body snuggled close helped to ease his loneliness. Most nights, he also had Darryl to talk to, but tonight, Darryl had driven Olivia to an evening event at the community college. She'd invited him to see how he'd like the campus. And for once, Jeremiah preferred being alone, so he could read Keturah's latest letter.

He stopped and reread the parts where she talked about how important he was to the business and how she hoped he'd never leave. She'd written something similar in each letter. And once again, he wondered if she meant more than just because of his work? He'd been noticing subtle signals that made him hope she was interested in him.

But she really touched him when she said she carried his letters in her pocket. He'd noticed her fingering something in her pocket, especially when she was stressed. Had it been his letters all along?

Her last line set his pulse tingling. She wanted to meet in person. But they already had. How did he tell her that?

Maybe he could ask her out and let her know the truth

when they were alone. One of his friends gave sleigh rides. With the newly fallen snow, it'd be a perfect time. He called Paul Burkhart and made an appointment for Saturday evening.

He penned a brief note to Keturah, praising God for her change of heart. He'd noticed a difference in her last week at work. Her face glowed with a new light, and she appeared less stressed and more peaceful. He'd hoped she'd managed to let go of her old pain, but he couldn't ask. Evidently, he'd guessed correctly.

Finally telling her the truth would allow him to be as open in person as he had been in his letters. Although he answered her other questions briefly, he struggled to keep his mind on the words as he pictured having time alone with her. Could he actually get up the nerve to invite her? And would she agree?

More snow fell on Saturday morning, making it nicer for a sleigh ride, but it kept many of the usual customers away from the market. Even the busloads of tourists didn't show up.

Gina had planned a Mrs. Claus story time at nine, but only a handful of children arrived. Although she read enthusiastically, Jeremiah sensed her disappointment. Her preteen daughter pranced around the market in reindeer antlers and a light-up red nose, selling raffle tickets to adults and handing candy canes to children.

He made a point to stop Gina after the children left. "The Christmas Extravaganza has brought a lot of customers to the market. You've really done a lot of work."

With a wan smile, she thanked him, but her shoulders straightened as she walked away.

"That was kind of you," Keturah said behind him.

He hadn't realized she'd been watching. "She looked so discouraged."

"She shouldn't be. Until today, we had nonstop customers."

Business had been so slow, Maleah and Rose had taken a break to walk around the market and admire all the decorations. Lilliane was at the worktable with her back to them.

Maybe now was his opportunity. Taking a deep breath, he let it out slowly, trying to calm his nerves. "Keturah, I really like spending time with you. I wondered if you would like to go on a sleigh ride tonight after work."

Her face lit up. "The girls would love that."

His heart sank. "I, um, meant you and me."

"Just the two of us?" She sounded stunned.

He braced for her answer. If she said *neh*, he didn't think he could bear it.

Keturah's mind whirled. Was he asking her on a date? It sounded like it. She enjoyed Jeremiah's company, and they'd been spending a lot of time together. If she were honest with herself, she'd been attracted to him for a while now, but . . .

The letter writer. She'd bonded with him, and she'd been sharing her innermost thoughts and feelings. If she agreed to go out with Jeremiah, she'd have to end that relationship. Keturah wasn't sure she could do it.

"I . . . don't . . . know. My sisters and I like being around you, but—"

He didn't let her finish. "I see."

From the look on his face, she'd hurt him deeply. She hadn't meant to do that. She really cared for him.

"Jeremiah, I enjoy spending time with you. We always have fun together, but I'm responsible for my sisters, so I'm not ready for . . ." She'd almost said *a relationship*.

But all he'd asked about was one date. Was it even a date? He'd said just the two of them. That had to mean a date, didn't it? Or maybe he'd only meant as friends, and she'd misconstrued it. But if they'd be alone together . . .

Her thoughts chased one another in a convoluted circle. But they kept coming back to the letter writer. If she could still write to him . . .

She shook her head. That wouldn't be right.

Jeremiah must have thought she was saying *neh* to him again. A deep sadness entered his eyes, and he started to turn away.

"Wait. I didn't mean I don't want to spend time with you."

He didn't face her. "If you and your sisters would like to go on the sleigh ride tonight, I can pick you *all* up in the van at seven."

"I'm sure the whole family would like that. I'll ask the girls."

After they returned, the idea received resounding cheers from Maleah, a happy grin from Rose, and a nod from Lilliane.

"I'll see everyone at seven, then." His back stiff, Jeremiah rotated his chair to face the line of customers forming by his checkout.

"Aren't you coming for supper first?" Maleah asked.

Jeremiah didn't answer, and Keturah assumed he needed

to hear the invitation from her—if he even wanted to come for a meal after she'd wounded him. Still, she had to ask.

"You're welcome to eat with us first at six. We always like having you."

"*Jah*, we do," Maleah chimed in.

"I'll be there." His raspy voice communicated his hurt.

The rest of the afternoon, he kept his chair angled so she couldn't see his face, and he'd lost his usual jovial friendliness toward the customers and her. Keturah hadn't realized how much she appreciated his smiles and his company until they were gone.

He left with a subdued goodbye and barely lifted his hand in a wave when she called after him, "See you tonight."

Keturah's heart ached for him, and he stayed on her mind as she and her sisters headed home. She asked Lilliane and Rose to fix supper, while she went to her room. As she always did now when she faced a problem, she sat at the desk and pulled out paper and a pen.

Without hesitation, she started the letter and poured out her concerns:

Have you ever cared for someone but been torn because you have feelings for someone else? That's the situation I'm in right now, and I don't know what to do.

Keturah didn't want to admit she'd fallen for her *Friend.* Well, not exactly fallen, since she hadn't met him, but they had a deep connection. He'd become more than a friend. He served as a confidant, a mentor, a lifeline. He'd helped her during the most difficult time of her life.

But Jeremiah had been there for her too. He'd cheered her, taken over the bookkeeping, smoothed over the troubles with Lilliane, and brought more fun into their lives.

How did you choose between two men you cared about? If she said *jah* to Jeremiah, she wouldn't feel right keeping this correspondence going. She should be sharing these things with the man she was dating if they were to have a future together.

But she couldn't go out with Jeremiah. Not when she so longed to hear back from *A Friend Who Cares*.

By the time Jeremiah showed up for supper, he'd spent an hour in prayer, struggling to accept Keturah's answer. He tried to bury his feelings for her, but that proved impossible. If friendship was all she could offer him, he'd accept that. It might slash him to ribbons inside, but spending time around her was better than never seeing her again.

"You okay?" Darryl asked as he drove Jeremiah to Keturah's house.

"I guess."

"You don't sound too sure. Anything I can help with?"

"Not really."

"Sometimes it helps to share burdens."

Jeremiah's heartbreak remained too new, too fresh. "Maybe later. Thanks for asking, though."

When he exited the van, he headed to the porch as if to an execution. The front door flew open, and Maleah appeared, her grin sunshine-bright.

Jeremiah pasted on an answering smile.

Behind her, Lilliane warned, "Don't go out in the snow."

"I can't help it. I'm excited to see Jeremiah." But she withdrew her stockinged foot before she set it on the light dusting of snow on the walkway. Instead, she backed up and pulled the door open wider.

Eating dinner with Keturah proved agonizing. He hadn't realized how far his fantasies about her had gone. He imagined her sitting in the empty space at his left . . . as his wife. Luckily, Maleah, who sat on his right, kept up a constant conversation that covered his daydreaming.

And Maleah claimed the space beside him in the sleigh too. With Snickers on his other side, he couldn't sit by Keturah. Instead, she squeezed in next to Maleah, so he didn't even have the pleasure of staring at her in the seat in front of him. He could only sneak occasional peeks. And he couldn't talk to her over Maleah's excited babbling.

Maybe that was just as well. It thwarted his plan to confess the truth. Right now, he couldn't bring himself to tell her. Not when the stars twinkling overhead reminded him of his romantic hopes. Not when his dreams had been crushed and his heart scraped raw. Not when the snow from the gliding runners sprayed his face, chilling it to match his frozen heart.

Chapter Twenty-Four

If Jeremiah had been hurt before, reading the first paragraph of Keturah's latest letter ripped open the wounds.

Have you ever cared for someone but been torn because you have feelings for someone else? That's the situation I'm in right now . . .

She cared for two different men. At first, his pulse quickened with the hope that she considered him one of those two men, but after reading her words a dozen times, he decided he was only fooling himself. She'd been so quick to turn him down.

As he'd suspected, she had a boyfriend. A girl as lovely and sweet as Keturah must have many men lined up who were as eager to date her as he was. And she'd made it clear he had no chance of getting into that line.

But she did hold out hope at the end of the letter. Not for Jeremiah, but for the anonymous letter writer. She wanted to meet him in person. In a previous letter, she'd mentioned she'd like to meet him someday. This letter asked to make that a reality.

*If you're willing, I'd really like to meet you in
person. I work at the pretzel stand at the Green
Valley Farmer's Market. Business has been a bit
slower over the past few days, so I could plan to
take a lunch or dinner break to meet you, if that
works for you. If so, just let me know.*

Jeremiah would be happy to meet her any day or
time—if circumstances were different. But no matter
what, he needed to do this. The time had come to reveal
the truth.

She'd already broken his heart once. After she discovered his deception, she'd probably not want to have anything more to do with him.

If he chose this Saturday, Rose and Maleah would be
working, and Olivia had off from college and planned to
come in. Keturah should be able to get away for a late
lunch.

He pulled out his stationery and answered before fears
or doubts could derail him. Instead of his usual long letter,
he scribbled a quick note and sealed it.

"Come on, Snickers, let's go for a walk."

Jeremiah bundled up against the cold and headed several blocks to the post office.

"We might be seeing a lot more lonely days after this,
girl," he said to Snickers as he lifted the envelope up to
the slot.

He hesitated a moment, then slid his letter into the
opening, sealing his fate.

* * *

Keturah's heart pattered as she spotted the corner of a yellow envelope peeking out among the newspapers and circulars in the mailbox. She slipped it out, pressed it against her chest, and drew in a long breath.

At last, his answer had arrived. It had only been two long days, but it seemed more like months as she anticipated his answer. Would he agree to meet? Or would he prefer to stay anonymous?

Her toes and fingers stinging from the cold, she hurried inside and dropped the rest of the mail on the hall table. Then, clutching the letter to her chest, she raced up the stairs to her room.

After shutting the door, she sat on her bed and, with trembling fingers, opened the flap. She pulled out the letter but waited a moment before she unfolded it. What would she do if he said *neh*?

Disappointed, she stared at the one brief paragraph, her eyes unfocused. She didn't want to read a rejection. When she finally got up her courage to read the answer, she wanted to jump from the bed and shout *Hallelujah!* He wanted to meet her.

She reread his words.

> *If it works for you, could you meet me by Hartzler's Chicken Barbecue this Saturday at two o'clock? Let's sit at the table closest to the salad end of the stand.*

He must go to the market if he knew it in that much detail. Maybe she'd even seen him or waited on him.

Did it mean anything that he'd chosen the most secluded corner for their meeting?

How would she ever wait until Saturday?

For Jeremiah, the days dragged on, each one slower and more excruciating than the previous one. Each one taking a step closer to a final break with Keturah. How would she react? Would he still have a job? Would she ever speak to him again?

At last, the day he'd been dreading arrived. Anxiety distracted him from his work. He mixed up customers' orders, knocked stacks of bags to the floor, tore bags as he opened them, and dropped two pretzels on the floor instead of into the bag.

Snickers glanced up at him, alert and ready for his usual command.

"*Neh*, those aren't for you." He issued an order to let her know: "Leave it."

Snickers whined. Normally, she picked up whatever he dropped.

As much as he disliked asking for help, he had to ask Keturah to retrieve the pretzels. That was embarrassing enough, but her attitude toward him made it worse. Ever since she'd turned him down over the sleigh ride for two, she'd been overly nice and gentle. The way you treated people you pitied.

"Keturah, I dropped some pretzels."

"It's all right, Jeremiah. Accidents happen."

She hadn't understood what he needed. "I can't reach them, and I don't want Snickers to pick them up."

"Sorry." Her face reddened. "I'll get them." She came

over, bent down, scooped them up, and tossed them into the trash.

"I'm the one who's sorry," he managed to say despite being breathless at her closeness.

"Don't worry about it. We all make mistakes sometimes. Me more than anyone."

What mistakes had she made? He hadn't seen her make any here at work. Did she mean turning him down? His hopes soared, but quickly plummeted.

Maybe she meant making the dough ahead or installing the self-serve checkout. Or, worse yet, maybe she meant giving him the job.

As the minutes ticked down toward two, his nervousness increased, along with his mishaps. Sometimes he stared into space or checked the clock as people gave their orders and had to ask them to repeat their requests more than once. He only hoped nobody opened a bag to find the wrong kind of pretzel.

Was it his imagination, or did Keturah keep fingering the letter in her pocket? She, too, seemed to be glancing at the clock on the wall across from them almost as often as he did.

At ten minutes before two, he undid the holders on his hands and set down the tools. "If it's all right with you, I'd like to take a break now."

A look of dismay crossed Keturah's face, and she appeared about to protest. Then with a tense smile, she said, "Go ahead, Jeremiah. I planned to take a break soon too, but Olivia can take your place." Keturah beckoned to Olivia, and Jeremiah scooted off.

Snickers trotted to keep pace beside him. Jeremiah wanted to have everything ready before Keturah arrived.

First, he paid for a big bucket of chicken and five orders
of fries to take back to the others at the stand. He asked
Gideon to hold it in the warmer until they were ready to
leave.

Jeremiah planned to treat Keturah to lunch when she
arrived, but he had to reserve their table before anyone
else took it. He had no idea how she'd react to his news,
so he'd selected a location that would give Keturah the
most privacy. And deep down, he had another reason—he
wanted her all to himself.

As he dragged a chair away from the table to make
room for his wheelchair, the letter crinkled in his pocket.
He'd poured out his heart in this letter and hoped to give
it to her, even if she chose never to speak to him again.

The closer it got to two, the edgier Keturah became.
She'd gotten so attached to the letter writer, although she
didn't even know his name. He'd reveal that to her today.
At least she hoped he would. She couldn't wait, but what
if he didn't like her when he met her in person? He might
have built up ideas of what she looked like, how she'd act,
and who she was from her letters. Maybe he'd be disappointed.

Keturah couldn't believe Jeremiah had asked to go on
break right before she needed to leave. She didn't want to
deny him time off, but his leaving interfered with her
plans. Ordinarily, he waited until everyone else had taken
their breaks.

With both of them gone, Olivia would be alone at the
counter, and unless she used the self-serve checkout,
credit card customers might get upset, but many of the

regulars avoided the machine, even though it took cash. She hoped Olivia didn't have to deal with irritated customers. It was unlike Jeremiah to leave without thinking of things like that.

"I'll be gone for at least half an hour," she told her sisters.

Lilliane frowned. "Why so long?"

"I'm meeting someone."

Her sister's annoyance turned to suspicion. "Who?"

Keturah smiled to herself. She imagined her sister's reaction if she told the truth. *A stranger. A man whose name I don't know. Someone I've been writing to for months about my deepest secrets.* "A pen pal."

"Since when do you have a pen pal, and why isn't she meeting you here?"

"It's someone who wrote to me after seeing the article in *Die Botschaft* after Mamm and Daed—"

"Oh." Lilliane turned away. "Don't take too long. We don't have Jeremiah to help."

"Maybe you could bring your pen pal back here," Rose suggested, "and you could work and talk at the same time."

Not today. Keturah didn't say that aloud. She wasn't ready to share her pen pal. Not now. Not until she knew for sure how their encounter went. And maybe not even then. Unless they agreed to begin an in-person relationship.

Ach! She'd be late. As she rushed from the stand, she ran a hand over the front of her hair to smooth it back. She checked that her *kapp* stayed pinned in place and brushed flour from the front of her apron. If only she had a moment to run to the restroom to check her appearance. She had no time for that now. She didn't want to miss him.

But when she approached the table, she stopped before she reached it. Her heart sank. Jeremiah sat in the place *A Friend* had suggested for their meeting. What should she do?

She didn't want to hurt his feelings or ask him to leave. Perhaps she could stand near Hartzler's Chicken Barbecue and keep an eye out for any man who headed toward that table and waylay him.

She tried to sneak past Jeremiah, pretending not to see him. The last thing she wanted to do was to cause him any more pain than she already had, but if the letter writer came and found her talking to another man . . .

Keeping an eye on anyone approaching the table, Keturah slipped by Jeremiah, acting as if she were reading the scrolls Hartzler's had hung overhead telling the Christmas story.

"Keturah?" Jeremiah called to her as she passed.

She spun around. "Oh, hello, Jeremiah." She couldn't say, *I didn't see you sitting there*, because she had seen him. And she'd gone out of her way to avoid him.

"Are you, um, waiting for someone?"

How had he guessed? Had she looked obvious? And how did she answer his question? She didn't want to lie. "I'm going to get some chicken."

The indentations between Jeremiah's brows that appeared whenever he was worried grew deeper. "I see."

Keturah slipped into line but angled her body so she could see anyone who approached the table. Luckily, the long line moved slowly. Gideon seemed to be the only one working.

"I'd like a, um . . ." She should have used her time in line to select her purchase. She studied the food displayed in the glass cases. Lots of different salads, which she'd like, but she didn't want to miss her visitor. She swiveled her head to check for him.

"Are you planning to order?" the *Englischer* behind her asked.

"*Jah*, I, um, want"—she cast about for something to order and noticed the pile of chicken legs—"a leg, please."

Gideon returned with her bag, and it dawned on Keturah that she didn't have any money. "I'm so sorry. I forgot my purse."

"No problem." Gideon laughed. "I've done that before. Well, not forgetting my purse, of course. I meant realizing I didn't have money with me."

Keturah forced out a giggle, but it sounded fake. She checked over her shoulder. Nobody who looked like he might be the letter writer seemed to be hanging around the café tables. "I can come back with the payment."

The man behind her huffed.

"Don't worry about it," Gideon said.

"But I need to pay you."

"I'll stop by sometime for a pretzel, and we can call it even."

Keturah wanted to protest, but the huffs behind her grew louder. And, although she kept turning slightly to keep an eye on people heading for the table, she might miss the letter writer. "All right. *Danke*."

She moved away from the order counter and leaned against one of the glass display cases, near enough to reach the condiments and napkins. She took a brown paper napkin from the holder, then thought better of eating the chicken. She didn't want the letter writer's first sight of her to be as she bit into a chicken leg. With her luck, the juices would drip down her chin, and her hands would be greasy.

So while she stood awkwardly pretending to study the interesting salads on display and watch for an approaching man, Jeremiah stayed at the table. It'd been almost half an hour. The letter writer hadn't shown up. Unless she'd missed him by being three minutes late or he'd been put off by Jeremiah sitting at the table.

Or . . . maybe he'd taken one look at her while she'd been standing here and changed his mind. Perhaps he'd even stopped by the pretzel stand and she hadn't known it. Once he'd met her, he'd decided he had no interest in pursuing an in-person relationship. Her spirits plummeted.

"Keturah?" Jeremiah called to her as she passed.

She tried not to let her disappointment show, but with her dispirited wave and the half-hearted lift of her lips, she wasn't successful. She attempted to add friendliness to her tone. "I need to get back to the stand. Talk to you later."

Jeremiah's sad, lopsided smile twisted her gut with guilt. She hadn't meant to hurt him again, but she couldn't talk to anyone right now. She'd been foolish to put so much hope in a pen-pal relationship.

As Keturah brushed by him, her shoulders drooping and a despondent expression on her pretty face, Jeremiah longed to comfort her. But how could he when he'd been the one to cause her unhappiness? She'd evidently been expecting someone other than him.

The shock on her face when she'd seen him sitting at the table had knifed through him. Then, instead of sitting down for their meeting, she'd made a flimsy excuse and scurried into line at the chicken place. She'd been so flustered, she'd flubbed her order. He couldn't help overhearing her say she'd forgotten her money. She obviously hadn't been planning to buy food. She just wanted to avoid him.

He would have offered to pay, but he didn't want to embarrass her or let her know he'd seen through her pretense. She'd already turned him down once. Why had he set himself up for another heartbreak?

So much for his grand plans. They connected so well on paper, but not in person. Jeremiah pounded a fist on the arm of his wheelchair. Why did he have to be so helpless? How could he expect a girl as lovely as Keturah to have any interest in a man who couldn't walk, one who would need help?

She had enough to handle with running a business and caring for her younger sisters. He couldn't ask her to saddle herself with one more person who needed care.

Lord, please help me to accept Your will for my life.

Jeremiah didn't have to like it; he only had to accept it. Submitting to God's will wasn't easy, but it would bring peace. Although the Lord was drawing him to surrender, Jeremiah still held on to the hurt.

Keturah touched the latest letter tucked in her pocket. Usually, the crackle of paper sent peace flooding through her. Now, rather than calming her, the sound agitated her. She almost snatched the message out and crumpled it into a ball so she could toss it into the nearby trash can.

She'd trusted this man and shared some of her deepest

struggles and secrets. She'd poured out her heart. Had his caring been a sham?

Never again would she write to him.

Despite her resolve, when she returned home after work, she sat at the desk and drew out a piece of stationery. For close to an hour, she agonized. Send a letter? Or break it off by not responding?

Not responding would be the easy way out. Although even that wouldn't be easy. But something deep inside Keturah made her want to give him one more chance. If an accident or illness had prevented him from coming, then cutting him off would be cruel and unfair.

She clicked the pen open and closed several times. Should she write? Or shouldn't she?

She at least owed him a chance to explain.

Dear Friend Who Cares,

To be honest, I've been excited about meeting you in person for weeks now, ever since I first mentioned it. Today, when you didn't show up, I . . .

How could she describe the jumble of feelings coursing through her? And did she want to be that honest? Especially if he'd decided not to pursue their friendship.

. . . was disappointed. I'd really been looking forward to talking to you. Your letters have meant so much to me, but if you'd rather not write or visit, I understand.

Or did she? Not really. They'd been so close. Or perhaps in her loneliness, she'd only imagined it.

I hope you'll write back at least one more time
to let me know whether or not you want to keep
in touch.

> *Your friend,*
> *Keturah*

Maybe they weren't friends anymore, but it was too late. She'd already written it, and she wasn't about to rewrite the whole letter. It had taken her more than an hour to get these words down on paper.

She folded the letter and slipped it into an envelope. Tomorrow, if she still had the courage, she'd drop it into a mailbox. And then she'd wait for her answer.

If the mail wasn't delayed, she'd hear back in two days or so. She'd always looked forward to his letters. This time, though, she almost dreaded his reply.

Chapter Twenty-Five

Jeremiah had never before been so grateful for a Saturday to end. Usually, he missed not being around Keturah for the two days until the market opened again on Tuesday. Not this time.

She'd been so surprised to see him sitting there. But she'd made it clear she didn't want to spend time with him. She'd run away so quickly after she'd discovered he'd been the one writing the letters. Maybe he should have spoken up and tried to work things out, but what could he say?

He'd waited for a while before trailing her back to the stand. He didn't want her sisters to guess he and Keturah took breaks at the same time for a reason. And he needed time to regain enough composure to face everyone.

Other people needed their breaks, though, so he called Snickers out from under the table, picked up his order from Hartzler's, and trudged back to the stand.

"*Danke, danke, danke!*" Maleah jumped up and down when he entered with the bucket of chicken.

"Maleah!" Lilliane clamped a hand on Maleah's shoulder to curb her sister's exuberance. "Jeremiah may have bought that meal for himself, not you."

"Oh." The young girl's face crumpled.

Jeremiah hated to inflict even temporary disappointment on anyone after what he'd just been through. "Don't worry, Maleah. I have plenty in here for you." He held up a bag of fries. "This is yours."

"See, I told you." She flashed a triumphant look at Lilliane and dashed over to grab her fries. She stuffed several into her mouth at once.

Lilliane followed her. "You should at least thank Jeremiah before you gobble those down."

"I already did." The mouthful of fries garbled Maleah's words. "I said it three times."

With a sigh in her sister's direction, Lilliane accepted the fries Jeremiah extended. "I'm sorry for her rudeness, Jeremiah. *Danke*, but we should be treating you this time."

Maleah swallowed, and her hand stopped in midair before inserting more fries. "You could come for supper again tonight."

"Not this weekend." Jeremiah regretted his bluntness when hurt flickered in her eyes. "Maybe some other time." But inside, his conscience called him out for the lie. He'd never be coming for supper again. Not ever.

That seemed to pacify Maleah. "I hope it's soon." She reached into the bucket he'd opened and chose a chicken leg. "You want some chicken?" she called to Keturah.

"I already had some." Her back rigid, Keturah avoided looking in their direction, adding another wound to those she'd already inflicted.

He pasted a smile on his face and forced down one piece of chicken. In their excitement and chatter, the girls didn't notice his preoccupation. "I'd better get back up front." Keturah couldn't wait on the long line of customers alone.

Lilliane wiped the grease from her fingers. "And we should be working too." She put the remaining chicken in the refrigerator.

As Jeremiah headed to his spot, his mind replayed Keturah's reaction to seeing him at the table—her dismay, her avoidance, her escape. But he still wanted to apologize and give her his letter.

He turned toward her. "I have something—"

She motioned toward the lines in front of the stand. "Can it wait until business slows down?"

Because she looked so tense and upset, he dropped the subject. After the stand closed, she went out of her way to avoid him. Her message couldn't have been clearer.

On the way home in the van, Darryl had asked, "What's wrong, man? You look like someone smacked into you with a ten-ton truck and then backed up and ran over you again."

A perfect description of how Jeremiah felt. Squashed. All the life—and hope—squeezed out of him.

He prayed to accept the situation, but sadness swamped him.

Darryl canceled his Saturday evening plans with Olivia to keep Jeremiah company and tried to cheer him up. As much as Jeremiah appreciated it, nothing could erase the images of Keturah's shocked face seared into his soul.

Late Monday afternoon, Darryl drove Jeremiah home from his therapy appointments. "You still down? I thought you'd be on top of the world. I heard you walked several steps today."

"*Jah.*" He had, but for the past two months, his incentive

had been Keturah. He had pictured the surprise and pleasure on her face as he walked toward her. Now, though, that would never happen.

"You don't sound too thrilled."

"I'm tired." He'd been sapped of energy both physically and mentally.

"I know something that might perk you up. I'll be right back." Darryl dropped Jeremiah at the house and then parked the van.

As Jeremiah headed inside, Darryl took off down the street.

A short while later, Darryl came bounding into the apartment. "I stopped by the post office. Maybe this'll help you feel better." He held up a pink envelope.

Jeremiah's stomach curdled. When he didn't reach for the letter, Darryl set it on the desk beside the open copy of *Die Botschaft* Jeremiah had been perusing to distract himself. With a curt *danke*, Jeremiah turned his attention back to the newspaper.

Darryl backed up to the doorway, but studied Jeremiah with concern. "You okay?"

Ashamed of the way he'd treated his friend, Jeremiah met Darryl's gaze. "I didn't mean to take my bad mood out on you. I'm struggling to deal with something that upset me."

"I'm happy to listen if it'll help. That's what friends are for."

"I know. Thanks for that. I'm not ready to talk about it yet."

"Well, when you are, I'm here. Meantime, I'll be praying."

"I can use plenty of prayers."

"You got it." Darryl slipped from the room.

Ignoring the pull to open the letter, Jeremiah continued his search for articles about families who'd experienced losses. But a pink envelope with dainty handwriting floated before his eyes, blocking his vision.

With an exasperated sigh, he picked it up. Previously, he'd eagerly opened every letter. This one could only bring him pain.

Had she sent this before or after their planned meeting? He checked the postmark. Too blurry to read.

If she'd sent it prior to their meeting, it might be filled with her usual anecdotes, questions, and news—peeks into her personality and her soul. That would slash him more deeply than a curtly worded accusation or dismissal.

He opened it warily and began to read. Then he went back and reread every word, trying to process the truth.

He stopped at *when you didn't show up*. He'd been so worried about revealing himself after her last letter, he'd arrived early and sat exactly where he'd told her he'd be. Yet, Keturah hadn't connected him to the letter writer.

So she hadn't rejected him. Trying to view it through her eyes, he'd been sitting at the table where she'd expected to see someone else. No wonder she'd decided not to join him.

And she admitted she'd been eager to see him. But she meant the letter writer, not *him*, the man who worked with her at the pretzel stand. She'd already turned that man down once. And Keturah's expression when she'd spotted him at the table instead of the person she'd expected to meet made it clear her enthusiasm to connect with the letter writer didn't match her lackluster feelings for him.

She'd asked him to write back. This time, though, they needed to have the conversation face-to-face. Once he told her the truth, would she ever forgive him? Or would everything be over for good?

Keturah needed to do something about the situation with Jeremiah. He'd been so helpful and kind. No matter how disappointed she'd been on Saturday, she shouldn't have taken it out on him. She must have hurt him badly, because every time she glanced sideways at him, he refused to meet her eyes. Somehow, she had to get their working relationship back on friendly terms.

But when he came in early on Tuesday, looking grim, he didn't give her a chance to make amends.

"We need to talk."

She'd never heard him speak so abruptly. She agreed they needed to talk, but not now. They had a buggy to unpack and pretzels to prep. "What about at lunchtime?"

"Now would be better. I promise it won't take long."

Keturah hesitated.

"I'd like to do it somewhere we won't be disturbed." Jeremiah appeared agitated and nervous. "Could we go over to the café tables?"

That was the last place she wanted to go.

"Please?"

She couldn't resist the pleading look in Jeremiah's eyes. Besides, she needed to apologize to him and see if they could get on a better footing. "Let me tell Lilliane."

Her sister's lips thinned at Keturah's request that she oversee the unloading and baking.

"I won't be long, but Jeremiah wants to talk to me."

Lilliane surprised Keturah with a smile. "All right."

Jeremiah seemed to have softened Lilliane's prickly temperament. He had a gift for that. Maybe she could start by telling him how much they all appreciated him.

Snickers walked between them as they headed for the tables. Usually, the dog walked on Jeremiah's right, but it almost seemed as if he intended Snickers as a buffer between them.

She must have hurt him more deeply than she realized. He didn't even want to walk beside her.

He headed for the one table she wanted to avoid. "No one will bother us here." He dragged a chair aside so he faced the same direction he had the day the letter writer didn't show up. Snickers lay under the table.

Keturah had no choice but to sink into the chair across from him at the small table for two. She tried not to grimace. But maybe this was a good place to apologize for ignoring him the other day.

"Jeremiah, I'm sorry for hurting your feelings the other day, but I, um . . ."

"You were waiting to meet someone."

"*Jah*, I was. But he didn't show up and that's why—"

"But he did show up."

Confused, she stared at him. "How do you know who I was waiting for? I didn't see him." She'd watched everyone coming in.

"He sat right where he told you he would."

She shook her head. "He said he'd be at this table, but you were sitting here." When he met her eyes, she gasped. "You? But it can't be."

Jeremiah reached into his pocket and pulled out a yellow envelope. He pushed it across the table to her.

"*Neh*, it can't be." But the letter bore the familiar scrawl, the handwriting that always touched her heart.

"But, but you . . ." She choked back a sob. "You lied to me?" She shoved back her chair. The Jeremiah she'd trusted and the letter writer she'd trusted. They'd both betrayed her. *Neh*, only one had. The two of them were the same person. A person she could never trust again.

Jeremiah wanted to reach out and take her hand. He wanted to smooth her horrified expression. He wanted to comfort her, but all he could say was a heartfelt, "I'm sorry." Two words inadequate to take away the distress he'd caused.

"I trusted you." She covered her face with her hands.

"I know, and I'm sorry." But *sorry* couldn't bandage any wounds. "I guess you won't want me working at the stand anymore."

She lowered her hands and faced him, teardrops sparkling on her lashes. "You're right."

He extended the yellow envelope, and she backed up a step. "Please take it," he begged. He wanted her to understand he hadn't meant to hurt her and that he'd never tell anyone what she'd told him.

"I don't want it."

"Please, Keturah."

She reached for it with two fingers and held it as if it were a filthy rag. Maybe she'd take it back to the stand and toss it in the trash. That's what he deserved for deceiving her.

As she walked away, "We Wish You a Merry Christmas" played in the background, adding to Jeremiah's pain. His Christmas would be far from merry.

Somehow, Keturah made it through the day. When her sisters asked where Jeremiah was, she said, "He had to go."

"Jeremiah wouldn't leave us unless he was sick," Maleah declared.

Lilliane's forehead crinkled into her usual worried expression. "I hope he'll be better soon."

So did Keturah. But how did you get better from lying and leading someone along? The first day she'd met Jeremiah, she'd had doubts about letting a stranger into their stand. Now more than ever, she understood her father's reasoning. Maybe he, too, had been burned by someone he trusted.

When they got home, Keturah rushed upstairs and crumpled the yellow envelope into a ball. After she pitched it into the trash, she threw herself on the bed. Her whole world had been turned upside down again. Her parents' death had destroyed her, but Jeremiah's revelation had blindsided her. Betrayed by two men she'd trusted. *Neh*, not two. Only one.

She struggled to bring them both together in her mind. Jeremiah's character had remained consistent at work and in the letters. He'd always been loving and caring. That hadn't changed. Only one thing didn't fit—he'd been a liar.

And not only him, but *A Friend* had kept up that dishonesty.

How could they—no, he—do this to her?

She yanked the letters from the drawer where she'd hidden them. Her first instinct was to rip them to shreds. But she wanted to see if *A Friend* had left clues. Clues she should have discovered. Clues to his real identity. Clues to his deception.

As she read over each one, her eyes misted. His caring shone through on every page. It seemed so genuine. His words still touched her, but she refused to give in to her emotions. Anger welled in her. How long had he been duping her?

She tried to put the letters on the timeline of her relationship with Jeremiah. Knowing they were the same person, she could trace the first meeting to the day Jeremiah had offered to take her place in the stand. He'd already written to her by then, and he'd heard back from her. He'd come to buy a pretzel. But had he come to check her out? Or to introduce himself?

But why had he concealed his identity from the beginning, before he'd ever met her? Had he spied on her before sending the letter?

Neh, she would have noticed him. Handsome men in wheelchairs didn't frequent the pretzel stand. Although if he hadn't come to the stand and had only observed her from a distance, she might not have noticed.

Curiosity propelled her to the wastebasket. She plucked out the envelope and did her best to smooth it flat before pulling out the crinkled letter. Then she hesitated. Did she really want to read this?

Dear Keturah,

*I never meant to hurt you. When I first wrote to
you, I didn't want to burden you with sending a
response, so I sent the letter anonymously. After you
posted in the newspaper asking me to contact you,
I wrestled with telling you the truth.*

*I regret that pride led me to give you a previous
address because I didn't want to admit I was in
rehab. I didn't want pity.*

She could understand that. But once he started working
in the stand, she knew about his wheelchair and rehab. He
had no excuse after that.

Jah, it would have been awkward. She might have been
embarrassed, but at that point, she'd mainly written about
her grief and questions that bothered her. But the later letters? Her face burned. She'd confessed a lot of personal
details, and all the while, he'd worked beside her, pretending he didn't know.

She couldn't forgive him for tricking her like that.

Her cheeks and her temper burning, she lowered her
head and read the next sections.

By giving in to hochmut, *I started a snowball of
lies rolling downhill, growing larger and larger as
it went. I have no excuse for what I did, and I'm
ashamed about deceiving you.*

*At first, I thought we'd have one conversation
by letter, and it would be over and forgotten.
Instead, our letters turned into the most wonderful
connection I ever had in my life. I debated telling*

you who I was, but, selfishly, I didn't want our
letters to end.

Neither did she. Those letters had been her lifeline.
But now that she knew the truth, even *A Friend*'s—*neh*,
Jeremiah's—promises rang hollow.

Your secrets are safe with me. I will never tell
anyone the things you shared. I've always been
your friend—in person and in the letters—and my
deepest regret is destroying your trust.

Although he'd misled her, Keturah believed he
wouldn't reveal the contents of their letters to anyone.
That was the least of her worries. She pictured Jeremiah
working beside her, knowing every private thought she'd
spilled into the letters.

Another thought struck her. What had she written about
Jeremiah to *A Friend*? She'd praised him. And described
things Jeremiah had done. How could he have let her keep
writing things like that about him? She would have been
too ashamed to read compliments about herself.

He'd owned up to his pride in the letter. Maybe that
hochmut ran deeper than he'd admitted. Yet, that conflicted
with the Jeremiah who worked with her. He'd always
come across as humble. And he put other people's needs
first. Which was the real Jeremiah?

As she reviewed the other topics she'd written about,
she groaned. In all the incidents she'd mentioned about
Jeremiah, had she indicated her interest? She hadn't admitted her feelings outright, but anyone who knew her as
well as the letter writer did could read between the lines.

Was that why Jeremiah had asked her to go on a sleigh ride alone?

After his invitation, she'd written about being torn over her feelings for two different men. He must have figured out she meant him. How could she ever face him again?

She wouldn't have to. He wasn't coming back to work. *Thank heavens*. But even as she thought it, part of her missed him. And she'd also miss the letters.

A few weeks ago, she'd been unable to decide between two men she cared about. Then she discovered they were one and the same. Now she had neither.

Rose tapped on the door. "Supper's ready. Are you coming down?"

"Not tonight. I feel sick." *Sick* hardly described the awful churning inside her stomach, not to mention her heart and her mind.

"Do you want me to get you something?"

"*Neh*, I just want to rest." But that would be impossible.

How would she get through this long weekend? And what would she tell her sisters when Jeremiah didn't show up on Tuesday? Even worse, how was she going to get through work—not to mention life—without him?

Chapter Twenty-Six

Keturah shut herself in her room for the next two days. She barely ate the broth Rose brought up to her. She reread the letters and wrestled with her feelings of anger and betrayal.

Late Monday night, as she recounted all the ways Jeremiah had hurt her, God spoke to her heart.

Isn't anger as much of a sin as lying? And what is causing your anger?

Ashamed, Keturah examined her own heart. Her anger stemmed from embarrassment. And the source of her embarrassment was pride. The very sin she railed against in Jeremiah's actions.

Matthew 7:3 came to mind: *And why beholdest thou the mote that is in thy brother's eye, but considerest not the beam that is in thine own eye?*

She had no right to accuse Jeremiah of *hochmut* when she had the same fault. After all, why had she told Jeremiah not to return to the stand? Because of embarrassment. Although they needed his help, she'd let her pride stand in the way.

But she still didn't want to face him. It upset her that

he'd read all her private thoughts and feelings. And she didn't know how to deal with the resentment bubbling up inside.

Don't you? her soul whispered.

Was God testing her again to see if she'd learned her lesson about forgiveness? If so, she had failed.

On Tuesday morning, Darryl woke Jeremiah early, as he usually did. Jeremiah groaned and rolled away from the hand shaking his shoulder. He'd tossed and turned all night, and he'd only just fallen asleep.

"What's wrong? You're always awake and raring to go."

An overwhelming sense of shame lay like a dead weight in Jeremiah's stomach, and grief constricted his throat. He couldn't answer, so he just shook his head.

"You're sick?" Darryl placed a hand on Jeremiah's forehead. "You don't have a temperature. Your stomach? Something you ate, maybe?"

Jeremiah didn't want to tell another lie. He'd already told enough. As he had every waking minute since he'd given the letter to Keturah, he begged for God's forgiveness for his *hochmut*, his selfishness, and his deceit.

"*Neh,*" he choked out. "I, well, Keturah asked me not to come back to the market." *Not that I blame her.*

"What? I thought you were doing a good job."

"It wasn't because of my work. I, um, did something to hurt her. Very badly."

"That's what had you depressed all weekend?"

"*Jah.*"

Darryl leaned forward as if expecting to hear more. "Want to talk about it now?"

Not really. Jeremiah tussled with his pride. He didn't want to confess how he'd made a fool of himself. But Darryl's compassionate expression invited Jeremiah to tell the whole story.

After he finished, Darryl's forehead wrinkled. "So, let me get this straight. You were writing letters to her anonymously, but working beside her all that time?"

Miserable, Jeremiah nodded. "I kept wanting to tell her, but then I thought she might be embarrassed I knew so much about her, so I didn't." He squirmed inside. That wasn't the whole truth. "I did think about her feelings, but I also wanted to avoid admitting what I'd done."

"I'm not trying to make you feel worse, but if that happened to me, I'd probably be furious."

"I know. I don't blame her."

"And that's why the pink envelope didn't cheer you up on Saturday. Sorry I gave it to you."

"You did the right thing." In some ways, the letter had made him feel better about some things and worse about others. But nothing could compare to the pain of knowing he'd never see Keturah again. Or be able to write her any letters.

After wrestling with her conscience and praying all night, Keturah woke, groggy and tired. She forced one foot after another, but all morning, she felt as if she were slogging through sludge, her feet bogged down by muddy slime.

Things only got worse when she reached the market.

"Where's Jeremiah?" Maleah looked around for him. "I have to leave for school soon, and he isn't here yet."

"He won't be coming in." *Not today. Not any day.*

"I want to tell him something."

So do I. But she might not ever get a chance to do that.

"Maleah," Rose said gently, "if he's sick, we should be praying for him instead of worrying about ourselves."

Maleah bowed her head and mumbled, "Dear God, please make Jeremiah better really quickly. Bring him back to us, please, because I want to talk to him."

Although she should point out her sister's selfishness, Keturah turned her back, because she wanted to say the same prayer. She busied herself with counting money and tried not to notice the big empty space beside her.

"You shouldn't want Jeremiah to get better for your sake, but for his," Rose gently corrected Maleah.

Rose's words chastened Keturah as well as Maleah.

Once the market opened, Keturah regretted not having Jeremiah. On Saturday, she'd been too upset with him to notice his absence. In fact, she'd been relieved. But today, every time she turned to catch his eye or bask in his smile, she faced a vacant spot. She hadn't realized how often she'd relied on him for support.

If only she hadn't been so hasty on Saturday, he'd be here to handle this rush of customers. Olivia came up to help her, but as sweet as she was, she couldn't take Jeremiah's place.

During a brief letup in the lines, Keturah breathed out a sigh, partly of relief and partly of longing. Ordinarily, she'd talk to Jeremiah. Not seeing him there made her lonely.

Mrs. Vandenberg hobbled up to the counter. "Do you have a minute to talk?"

After asking Olivia to handle the orders, Keturah went to the side of the stand to talk to Mrs. Vandenberg.

Mrs. Vandenberg glanced around with a puzzled look on her face. "Where's Jeremiah? I'd hoped to talk to him as well."

Keturah bit her lip. "He—he's not working here anymore."

"What?" Mrs. Vandenberg took a wobbly step backward.

Keturah prayed she wouldn't fall. Mrs. Vandenberg pressed one veined and wrinkled hand to her heart.

"But why?"

Keturah hung her head and traced circles on the countertop. "We had, um, a disagreement."

"Well, we'll need to work that out immediately. Actually, it'll have to be handled before tomorrow. I've arranged for some publicity for the stand and for this rehab project." She listed slightly to one side as she lifted her cane to point at the self-serve machine.

Keturah's heart was as shaky as Mrs. Vandenberg's balance. When the elderly woman returned to leaning on her cane, Keturah exhaled softly.

"They'll also be doing a story about the Christmas Extravaganza on Thursday, but tomorrow's appointment will be with you and Jeremiah."

Me and Jeremiah. That was no longer a possibility.

"Alyssa McDonald, a reporter with the *Central Pennsylvania Star*, will be here with Jake Davis, a photographer who will take pictures of the stand. I did remind them about your aversion to being photographed, so they plan to interview you and Jeremiah."

An interview? Keturah's throat tightened. The idea of answering a stranger's questions and having her answers broadcast to everyone in the area made her want to draw back into a protective shell. If what had happened with Jeremiah had been embarrassing, this would be a hundred times worse.

Without giving Keturah time to protest, Mrs. Vandenberg rattled on. "Now, about Jeremiah . . . The best thing to do is ask his forgiveness."

In the wee hours of the morning, Keturah had already come to that conclusion. But doing it proved daunting and impossible. She never expected to see Jeremiah again. Mrs. Vandenberg had just removed that excuse. But how could Keturah face him and admit why his betrayal had cut her so deeply?

When Darryl returned after dropping Rose and Maleah at the market, he knocked on Jeremiah's door and then peeked in.

"Rose and Maleah were upset you weren't working at the market today, and they said to tell you they're praying for you to feel better soon."

Keturah must not have told them what had happened.— Although he truly wasn't feeling well, so she hadn't lied.

Darryl glanced at his watch. "We should leave soon if you're going to make it to your evening therapy appointments on time. Or do you want me to cancel for today?"

Jeremiah debated. All he wanted to do was stay in bed and wallow in his sorrow. But he'd set a goal for himself. He wanted to walk by Christmas. His original reason—to surprise Keturah—no longer existed. Still, he should meet that goal for himself, not for someone else.

"All right. Let's go."

Not long after they got in the van, Jeremiah's phone rang. The social worker at the rehab center had suggested he keep a cell phone with him in case he ran into problems when he was alone. Right now, he wished he'd never agreed. He'd rather not talk to anyone. He let it ring.

"You going to get that thing?"

Jeremiah didn't want to distract Darryl when he was driving. Reluctantly, he answered.

Mrs. Vandenberg's cheery voice came over the line. "I have a wonderful opportunity for publicity for the pretzel stand. Would you be willing to do an interview with the *Central Pennsylvania Star* tomorrow?"

The *Star* was the area's largest newspaper. They wanted to talk to him? "Wouldn't it be better for Keturah to do it?"

"They'll be interviewing her. But we're talking about the partnership with the rehab center, so I need you too."

It would be torture to be around Keturah even for an hour, yet he owed Mrs. Vandenberg so much. "Could I do my part of the interview at a different time?" After all, Keturah wouldn't want to see him either.

"I can arrange that, but what's going on with you and Keturah? She's so downcast, and when I asked her why you weren't working, she said the two of you had a disagreement. Right before I left, she mumbled something about pride. I don't think she intended me to hear that."

So, she had read his letter. He'd prayed she would. After she took the envelope, she looked as if she'd rather burn it.

A long silence ensued, and Jeremiah realized Mrs. Vandenberg was waiting for an answer. "I hurt Keturah, and now she's upset with me."

"That's odd. I didn't get that impression at all. She seemed to be referring to herself."

As much as Mrs. Vandenberg could read people's minds, she'd definitely made a mistake this time.

"*Neh*, Keturah didn't do anything wrong. It was all my fault."

"Have you asked for forgiveness?"

"Not exactly." He'd given Keturah the letter to explain why he hadn't told her the truth, and he'd apologized for hurting her. And he'd assured her he'd never divulge her secrets. But he hadn't specifically asked her to forgive him.

"I'd suggest doing that." Mrs. Vandenberg's brisk tone made it seem as if asking for Keturah's forgiveness would magically heal their broken relationship.

As much as Jeremiah wanted to hear Keturah say she forgave him, he couldn't put her in that awkward position. If he asked her, she'd do what the Bible commanded and forgive him, but would her heart be in it?

"You'll do the interview tomorrow?"

"Of course. As long as I can come at a different time than Keturah."

"If that's what you really want."

He didn't, but he'd do it for Keturah's sake. "It would be best."

"Why don't you come at eight? I expect the interview will last an hour at the most, which will give you plenty of time before your Wednesday therapy sessions."

Mrs. Vandenberg kept track of his schedule? How did she have time to do that? She must have dozens or even hundreds of projects she supervised.

"I told Keturah to come at eight, but I'll ask her to

come at nine fifteen. The cameraman can use the time in between to take photos of the stand."

"I'll be there."

Darryl gazed at him curiously when he hung up. "I recognized Mrs. Vandenberg's voice. Did I hear her say you'll be doing an interview with the *Star*? You'll be famous."

That's the last thing Jeremiah needed or wanted. In addition to fame being against everything he was raised to believe about being humble, this interview meant he'd have to reveal his rehab status to the world. He hadn't even been able to face telling Keturah the truth when he'd written that second letter. Now he'd have the whole Central Pennsylvania area pitying him.

To avoid thinking about it, he threw himself into therapy that evening.

"Wow, Jeremiah, you're really exerting yourself today," his therapist marveled.

Sweat dripped down Jeremiah's face and stung his eyes, but he was determined to conquer this. As much as he'd hoped the painful process of learning to walk again would keep his mind off Keturah, it didn't work. Instead, each agonizing step became another step away from her.

Chapter Twenty-Seven

Jeremiah woke on Wednesday morning, his stomach twisted into a ball of dread. How intrusive would the reporter be? Would she ask about the accident? Would she pry into his injuries? He didn't want to talk about any of that.

If only he hadn't agreed to do this. But how could he turn down Mrs. Vandenberg? And this would help the pretzel business. He couldn't refuse.

He tried to calm down by telling himself they'd only be talking about the stand, the cash machine, and how he coped with the job. He'd try to keep the focus on Mrs. Vandenberg's idea of using the stand to help rehab patients.

After knocking, Darryl stuck his head in the door. "You awake and ready to start a wonderful day?"

"I guess."

Darryl stopped and stared at Jeremiah. "That doesn't sound like you."

"I have to do the newspaper interview today." Surely Darryl hadn't forgotten that fact. He'd been nattering about it nonstop since Mrs. Vandenberg called yesterday.

"Yeah, I know! Aren't you lucky?" He hurried over to the bed.

"Not really. I'm nervous."

"I've found when I'm nervous, the best thing to do is to concentrate on the other person. I try to think about what I can do to help them. It takes the focus off me."

How had this nineteen-year-old become so wise?

"You're right. I'll try that." But inside, Jeremiah's stomach wouldn't let him relax. Darryl's advice worked for him because he was open, honest, and outgoing. Actually, Jeremiah had been too. Before the accident.

"Well, let's get you looking good for the interview." Darryl, in his usual upbeat manner, hummed a hymn as he helped Jeremiah shave and dress.

As they finished each task, Jeremiah's tension increased. The clock ticked closer to eight. Why did the hands inch along whenever he couldn't wait to do something, yet today they whirled faster and faster?

When Darryl finished, he stepped back and smiled. "You look great. Good enough for a picture." He imitated looking through a camera. "Smile."

Jeremiah started to protest, and Darryl laughed. "I know. No photos. I was just teasing. And I wanted to erase your glum expression."

Was his anxiety that obvious? Jeremiah attempted a smile.

Darryl shook his head. "You're gonna have to do better than that. Maybe you could think about God's grace and all the blessings He's given you."

Although Darryl had been trying to help, his words

pierced Jeremiah. How could he be grateful for God's goodness when he stayed focused on all he'd lost?

"We'd better leave." Darryl headed for the door. "I'll bring the van around, and I'll be praying your interview goes well."

"*Danke.*" Jeremiah moved to the desk, planted his elbows on it, and dropped his head into his hands.

Dear Lord, please guide my words and thoughts today. Help me—

A horn honked outside. Time to go.

Fresh snow had fallen during the night, but the path to the street had been shoveled. Jeremiah tried to appreciate the clean sidewalk and pristine snowbanks, but his heart wasn't in it. Between his break with Keturah and the pending interview, he could barely slog out to the van.

After Darryl opened the door and Snickers helped pull Jeremiah's chair up the ramp, Darryl tried again to lift Jeremiah's spirits. "I hope you have fun. This is so exciting."

Not for me. Jeremiah's breakfast sloshed in his stomach. He managed an unenthusiastic *jah*, which dimmed some of Darryl's enthusiasm. Guilt over puncturing his friend's enthusiasm jagged at Jeremiah's conscience.

"Sorry. It's just nerves." He tried not to think about it. But so many questions tumbled through his mind. When did privacy take precedence over truth? Did you have to tell everyone all of your inner thoughts? Why was it so nerve-racking to be honest about inner thoughts and feelings?

That question brought Keturah to mind. She must have felt this exposed after discovering the truth about him being the letter writer. If only he'd spared her that pain by being honest from the start.

When Darryl pulled into the farmer's market parking

lot, a redhead stood outside, shivering in a down coat, while a man snapped pictures of the exterior of the market, including all its Christmas decorations. The redhead motioned for the photographer to join her as Jeremiah rolled toward them.

Mrs. Vandenberg's car pulled in next to them, and she emerged with a bright smile for everyone. "Good morning, Jeremiah." Her greeting contained a bracing note of encouragement.

Had she sensed his hesitation? She always read people so well, she must have.

She performed the introductions. "Meet Alyssa McDonald, a reporter from the *Central Pennsylvania Star*, and Jake Davis, the photographer."

Alyssa thrust out her hand, and Jeremiah forced himself to shake it. He did the same with the photographer. He hoped his clammy hands and weak grip didn't reveal his nervousness.

The reporter's wide, toothy smile would make a good ad for toothpaste. Her infectious smile was the kind he couldn't help but return. Something inside Jeremiah relaxed. The *I-care-about-you* expression in her eyes signaled she wouldn't try to hurt him. He prayed that was true.

"I'll leave you three alone." Mrs. Vandenberg studied Jeremiah as if wondering whether he'd be all right. "You already have my comments for the article. Keturah should be here at nine fifteen. I'll stop back around eleven to lock up."

Jake hurried to open the door and let Jeremiah go in first. He'd never been inside when the cavernous building was empty. Despite the lights glowing overhead, the deserted stands creeped Jeremiah out. Although they'd all been decorated, with their lights out and people missing, they lost their luster. Much like his life with Keturah had gone.

Alyssa stopped and stared. "I can't wait to see this tomorrow with everything lit up. It'll be beautiful. Isn't it cheerful and Christmassy?"

Jeremiah nodded to be polite. The word *Christmas* made him ache inside. *Neh,* that shouldn't be. It meant the birth of Christ, and how could that make him sad? He'd been focusing too much on earthly things, like his plans for surprising Keturah.

Beside him, Alyssa kept nattering away. "The Christmas Extravaganza article will come out in Friday's Entertainment section so people will know about all the exciting Saturday events."

Until yesterday, Jeremiah had been too busy working to pay attention to the schedule, but Gina had announced over the loudspeaker that Santa would be arriving in a sleigh. Jeremiah winced. The sleigh reminded him of his rejection by Keturah. Now she'd also rejected him as the letter writer.

The reporter interrupted his gloomy memories. "Mrs. Vandenberg suggested we use the tables and chairs for the interview. I guess there's a food court in here?"

"Sort of." Jeremiah gestured toward Hartzler's Chicken Barbecue. "They have a few tables over there." The last place he wanted to go today.

"Can you point out the pretzel stand for Jake? He can take pictures while we talk." Alyssa's gleaming smile reappeared.

Breathing a sigh of relief that he wouldn't have to fend off requests for photos, Jeremiah gave Jake directions.

Alyssa huddled into her coat. "I guess it's chilly in here without all the people."

Jeremiah had never thought about it, but with the ovens going and people rushing around, he'd never noticed the chill. They probably cut back the heat on days the market was closed.

"How long have you worked here?" Alyssa flipped open her notebook and pulled out a pen.

"I started in October."

"It must be fun to work here."

It had been, but now . . . He couldn't tell the reporter that. "Most of the time the market's so busy, there's no time to think about it."

Alyssa started by discussing Snickers, who lay under the table by his feet. Very gradually she eased him into deeper, more personal topics, like his rehab and the adaptations he used at the stand. From there, she moved into his accident and his mother's death.

She'd really done her research, and she was such a pro, he barely noticed how she'd led him to spill details of his life he rarely shared with anyone. Until she hit him with a zinger.

"So, your mother died on the same day as Keturah's parents? Is that how you two connected?"

Jeremiah froze. "What?" *That couldn't be right, could it?*

"You didn't know?"

His mind rushed back to the *Die Botschaft* article. The author had submitted it a few weeks after the accident as an update on the four orphaned girls. She'd mentioned their parents had died the previous month. Back then, Jeremiah had noted that Keturah's parents had died in the same month as Mamm, but he'd never realized it had happened on the same day. He'd been focused on Keturah's fresh grief and that the girls had been orphaned. He'd written to other people who'd experienced a loss around then, and he'd never assumed they'd been connected to his accident.

"I'm guessing from your silence and puzzled expression you had no idea."

"*Neh*, I didn't."

"Are you all right? You look really pale. We can talk about something else."

Worry niggled at his brain. Accidents in Amish country happened more frequently than they should, but how likely was it that two accidents occurred on the same day unless . . .

When he didn't answer, Alyssa's tone turned gentle. "Why don't we talk about the market job again for a while?"

That topic wouldn't be any easier, but Alyssa didn't realize Jeremiah didn't work here anymore. He should explain that, but then she'd ask why.

Alyssa went back to the adaptations and Jeremiah's feelings as he'd moved from the rehab center to working here. Those questions he could answer honestly, but he couldn't wait for the interview to end. The chaos in the back of his mind wouldn't let him rest. He needed to unearth the truth.

Leaning across the table, he interrupted Alyssa's interview wrap-up. "Please can you not print the part about our parents dying on the same day?" He disliked the pleading note in his voice, but he had to stop her from raising questions in Keturah's mind—at least until he checked out his suspicions.

"Why? It's an interesting fact that will intrigue readers."

Exactly what he was afraid of. If Keturah read it, wouldn't she try to find out more about that day? And she'd discover . . .

Alyssa still waited for an answer.

What can I tell her?

He could explain and come clean about the truth. But then she'd probably print it. If what he suspected actually had happened, Keturah might never speak to him again.

"Bringing up the details might be painful for all four of the girls." Jeremiah *rutsched* in his chair. The statement itself might be true, but he'd used it as a smoke screen.

A troubled expression on her face, Alyssa tapped her fingertips on the table. "I don't like upsetting people, Jeremiah, but my job is to give people the facts. If I skipped that important point, my editor would be furious, and my readers wouldn't trust me."

"I see." That left him with a dilemma. Ordinarily, Keturah wouldn't read the *Star*, so she'd never know what Alyssa wrote. This time, though, she'd check out the interview.

His mind raced. He had to find out the truth.

"When will the paper come out?"

"We'll be printing this interview in the Sunday Lifestyle section."

"Could you not mention my *mamm*'s death to Keturah? She doesn't know, and I want to tell her myself before she reads it in the paper."

Alyssa's forehead wrinkled. "I planned to include both of your reactions. I can't make that promise."

That left only one choice: to tell Keturah his suspicions. If he did it before she talked to Alyssa, it might make Keturah anxious and spoil her interview. But if he waited, Alyssa would give Keturah the news. And Keturah might assume he'd also hidden this from her.

Chapter Twenty-Eight

Too keyed up to wait, Keturah arrived at the market long before her scheduled interview time. Concern about talking to the reporter wasn't the only thing that was making her nervous. She hoped to find time to speak with Jeremiah. She needed to be honest with him. That wouldn't be easy.

Keturah swallowed hard when she spotted him at one of the tables talking with a vivacious redhead. He seemed mesmerized by the *Englischer*, and they were chatting away. The reporter said something, and Jeremiah laughed. She'd never thought of the possibility he might be attracted to another woman.

Was he with the church? If so, she had nothing to worry about. If not . . .

What was she doing? She planned to be honest with Jeremiah and let him know how she felt about him writing the letters and about sharing so much personal information with him. And what she'd learned about herself because of his deception. But that didn't mean she wanted to have a relationship. Still, she couldn't tamp down the attraction she'd been trying hard to ignore.

She leaned against a pillar that semi-concealed her, but then she stepped away, because if Jeremiah spotted her skulking back there, she'd look as if she were trying to spy. So far, he hadn't looked her way. He seemed totally absorbed in the interview—and the reporter.

By observing the changes in his face as he answered questions, Keturah could guess his emotions. She hadn't realized how closely she'd observed every nuance of his expressions as they worked together.

Then the reporter said something, and Jeremiah jolted back in his chair as if he'd been shot. Keturah tried to identify his reaction. Shock and desperation. What had the reporter asked to cause that?

He leaned forward as if begging, pleading. Did the reporter plan to print something he didn't want publicized?

After what Keturah had been through with the letters, she sympathized. And her deepest feelings hadn't been revealed in the public. Whatever he hoped to keep secret, she hoped the reporter complied.

Jeremiah glanced up, and their eyes met. A sickish expression crossed his face. Keturah's stomach sank. Had he revealed their letter writing? Or, worse yet, told the reporter something personal about her?

He wheeled abruptly away from the reporter. Keturah stood frozen in place. Did she want to intercept him as she'd planned? Or would it be better to let him go out of the building and out of her life?

"Wait," Alyssa called after him. "Before you go, Jeremiah, would you be willing to pose for a few pictures with Keturah?"

Neh! "We don't—" Keturah's voice squeaked. She swallowed hard to loosen her throat muscles.

Jeremiah turned to face the reporter and answered before Keturah could control her words. "We don't believe in photographs."

"I know," Alyssa said. "I thought maybe you could pose with your backs to the camera."

Jeremiah turned back to Keturah. The protectiveness in his eyes revealed he wanted her permission to accept the request. If she shook her head, would he defend her?

Keturah hesitated. Daed would never have allowed her to do this. He wasn't around to stop her, but going against his rules always seemed wrong. Even more, Keturah worried about Lilliane's reaction. Her sister had become the conscience in the family.

"If you don't want to do it," Jeremiah said, "then I won't either." He turned to Alyssa. "I'm sorry, but we can't participate."

He'd stood up for her. Keturah shot him a relieved smile.

He looked startled, and she regretted giving him a contradictory message. She lowered her eyes.

"Aww . . ." Alyssa sounded downcast. "Readers will be disappointed to see an empty stand. I promise we won't show your faces. Please?" She put her hands together in supplication. "Pretty please?"

Despite her conscience telling her otherwise, Keturah wanted to do the photograph. For a completely wrong reason—she wanted a picture with her and Jeremiah in it.

Even more than disobeying Daed's rules. Even more than upsetting Lilliane. Even more than not giving in to pride, Keturah longed to do this. Guilt warned her not to agree.

Jeremiah studied her face. Could he read her struggle?

She hoped he wouldn't guess the reason she'd changed her mind. With a pleading look, she said, "Would you mind?"

His brow creased, and she regretted asking him. Would he refuse?

After a minute, his forehead smoothed out. "I'm willing to do it, if you are."

His answer dropped the huge stone of guilt from her conscience. Keturah almost said *neh*, but the desire to have a picture of him, even from the back, to remember him once he'd left, pushed her to agree.

She turned to Alyssa. "We'll do it." Keturah ignored the warning of the small voice inside and focused on the reporter's beaming face.

"Thank you, thank you! I know this is a lot to ask of you." Joy flowed from Alyssa, partially erasing Keturah's worries. She rushed ahead of them to the stand. "Jake, they've agreed to a few shots."

Keturah's heart sank as they posed Jeremiah at the warmer. Jake directed him to open the warmer to take out a pretzel.

"You have any pretzels we can use as props?" he asked.

Keturah headed for the new refrigerators. "I have a few leftovers from yesterday. We break them up to use as samples."

She unwrapped the pretzels, shoved the wrappings back into the refrigerator, and shut the door. When she reached the warmer, she had to stretch past Jeremiah. His face red, he backed up a little as she hung pretzels on the rack.

Behind them, the photographer directed Jeremiah back into position. Keturah scrambled out of the way. Once Jake finished with Jeremiah, he turned his attention to her.

"Could you take one of those pretzel trays from the shelves there?" He pointed to the racks in the glass-fronted refrigerator.

She followed his instructions to put the tray on a work-table, stand with her back to the camera, and move to one side so the tray showed. Then he had her pick up a pretzel and hold it out as if she were about to drop it in the pot where they boiled water.

"If you angle your body a little more to the right, your face won't show." Jake waited as she moved. "There, that's perfect." The camera clicked several times.

The photographer rearranged their angles for several more shots. Keturah's arm ached from staying frozen in place. She could only imagine how Jeremiah must feel. He'd held his position even longer than she had.

"Okay, that's good," Jake called. "I got a few shots that might work."

"Whew." Jeremiah set down the tool he used to lift out pretzels.

"Sorry, buddy," Jake said. "I'd like to get a few more pictures with you in them. Mrs. Vandenberg mentioned you have a unique way to open bags. I promise to only shoot your hands."

Jeremiah stretched his hands and rubbed them against each other briskly. Then he picked up the tool he used for the bags.

Jake leaned over the counter to watch. "Pretty nifty trick. Very impressive. If you flip open a few more, I'll snap some pictures."

Keturah admired Jeremiah's smooth but tricky maneuvers and his calmness as Jake zeroed in for closeups. Her hands would have been shaking under such scrutiny, but Jeremiah flipped every bag up perfectly. She wondered if he even needed the tools anymore. He seemed to have gained so much dexterity.

She'd been so busy waiting on customers, she hadn't noticed his improvements. And seeing him in his usual place made her miss his help. She had to talk to him, but with her heart and mind a mass of contradictions, no words came when Jeremiah wheeled around to face her.

"Keturah, I need to tell you something." His voice, low and urgent, revealed deep distress.

She nodded, glad he'd initiated the conversation, but she worried about him.

Alyssa breezed over and glanced at the clock. "Oh, no. The photos took longer than I thought. Keturah, can we get started with your part of the interview? We need to be at the Clinic for Special Children for another interview in a little over an hour."

Mutely, Keturah apologized with her eyes and signaled to Jeremiah to wait.

He must have gotten her message, because he nodded.

Keturah followed Alyssa to the table where she'd interviewed Jeremiah, her mind on him rather than the reporter. What had disturbed him? Except for the day he'd confessed to being the letter writer, she'd never seen him without a calm, peaceful expression or a happy smile.

Seeing him so upset added to the nerves zinging in her stomach. She still cringed about having exposed her private thoughts in letters to Jeremiah. Now she'd be talking about herself to a reporter who'd share their conversation with everyone in Central Pennsylvania. Keturah barely heard Alyssa's first few questions and had to have them repeated.

Although Alyssa likely intended her introductory questions to relax Keturah, they only increased her tension. She couldn't remember when Jeremiah had started working at the stand. It seemed he'd always been a part of the business—and her life.

"Jeremiah said October."

"That's right," Keturah seized on his answer. He'd surely know.

But when Alyssa pressed her for further details on their first meeting, Keturah withheld the story of him volunteering to help the day Maleah ran off to the bathroom. She didn't want to reveal anything that personal. Had Jeremiah told Alyssa about that afternoon?

"The only thing I remember is being impressed at how hard Jeremiah worked and how clever he was at coming up with ways to get around any challenges he had. That still amazes me."

"I can imagine." Alyssa waved in the direction of the stand. "Watching him flip open those bags was remarkable. I'm not sure I could do that even if I had weeks of practice."

Keturah pictured Jeremiah's first few days of stabbing holes in bags and knocking bags onto the floor. She wasn't about to tell Alyssa that.

After a few more general questions, Alyssa stunned Keturah with her next question. "I wondered if you and Jeremiah had connected over losing your parents in the same accident. Jeremiah didn't seem to know about it, but did you?"

The same accident? Was that why he'd written to her? If so, why hadn't he ever mentioned it? Had Jeremiah told them when his mother had died?

Keturah tried to recall that conversation. He'd told them his *daed* had died when he was six. But *neh*, when he'd talked about his *mamm* telling him pretzels should remind him of praying hands, he'd only said she was gone.

She'd even asked the letter writer if he'd experienced tragedy because he understood her emotions so well. He'd never answered.

Before she'd learned of Jeremiah's deception, she would have guessed he'd done it to keep the focus off himself and on her grief. This revelation added more doubts. How truthful had the letter writer been?

Jah, the letter writer was Jeremiah, but often, writing letters enabled people to be more open and honest. At least, it had been that way for her. But had the letters also contained lies? At that thought, something inside her broke.

"Keturah?" Alyssa had cocked her head to one side, waiting for an answer.

"I'm sorry. I don't remember the question." It had something to do with the date of Jeremiah's *mamm*'s and her parents' deaths.

"I didn't mean to upset you. Jeremiah also seemed distressed by it." Alyssa repeated the question about her parents and Jeremiah's mother being in the same accident.

"*Neh*, I didn't know that." But did he?

"So, how did you meet?"

Keturah didn't have time to think about the accident. She needed to keep her mind on the interview, but each question Alyssa asked contained a barb. How did she answer this one?

"Jeremiah came to the stand to buy a pretzel." Although

Keturah's response was accurate, had she sidestepped the truth?

The corners of Alyssa's perpetually smiling mouth drooped. Evidently, she had been expecting a more romantic or interesting meeting. "And how did he end up working for you?"

"Mrs. Vandenberg brought him to meet me a few days later. She asked about adapting the stand for him, and I agreed. I needed help in the stand, so this seemed to be God's answer to prayer."

Alyssa's face lit up. "Yes, God can work miracles. I've had some miraculous changes in my life since I turned my life over to the Lord. His plans for our lives are wonderful."

Keturah should agree, but at the moment, God's plan for her life seemed to be enduring sorrow.

"I'm sorry. I didn't mean to sound uncaring, especially not so soon after you've lost your parents. I'm sure going through such an agonizing time can make you question God."

"But *all things work together for good*," Keturah intoned, her heart not quite in tune with her words. Perhaps later, she'd look back and see the truth of it. At the moment, she struggled to believe.

Even worse, that verse brought back all the comfort she'd felt when she'd read it in the letter—Jeremiah's letter. And pain flooded through her.

Alyssa's chirpy voice interrupted Keturah's dark memories. "I've been finding that even negative things do end up being blessings when I focus on yielding to God's will."

Over the past several days, Keturah had wrestled with surrendering her hurt to the Lord, but part of her still wanted to prod and poke at her wounds, to justify her anger and resentment. She needed to talk to Jeremiah to start resolving those issues.

Chapter Twenty-Nine

Jeremiah sat off to one side, where he could observe Keturah. He could tell the exact second Alyssa brought up the date of his *mamm*'s death. Would Keturah believe he didn't know? And what if he discovered her parents had been on the van trip? He'd be responsible . . .

His anxiety had reached a fever pitch by the time Alyssa stood, ending the interview. With a friendly wave in his direction, she and Jake departed.

Keturah didn't move from the table. She kept her head bowed. Was she praying?

Reluctant to disturb her, Jeremiah approached her slowly.

When she lifted her head, her eyes glimmered with tears. "I'm glad you stayed. I need to talk to you. I've spent a lot of time praying about this and—"

"Wait. Before you say anything else, there's something I need to confess. I don't want you to think I hid something else from you. Alyssa must have told you about my *mamm* dying—"

"In the same accident as my parents." Keturah finished his sentence.

The same accident? His worst fears had been confirmed. *Dear God, give me the courage to tell the rest of the truth.*

"I killed your parents," he blurted out.

A puzzled frown crossed Keturah's forehead. "A drunk driver smashed into the van."

Suddenly, the whole nightmare washed over him. Metal crumpling. Glass shattering. Screams that went on and on.

"Jeremiah?" Keturah leaned toward him, her eyes worried.

He shook himself back to the present. He'd been about to tell her something. Something important. Something his mind refused to process.

"Are you all right?"

The anxiety on Keturah's face made him long to comfort her. But first, she had to know the truth. All the fragments of memory rearranged themselves into an accusation pointing directly at him. "If it weren't for me, your parents would still be alive. I arranged that trip."

Keturah squeezed her eyes shut and lowered her head. When she spoke, her voice was barely audible. "Don't blame yourself. It was God's will."

Jeremiah had railed against God's will after he'd become aware enough to understand the extent of his injuries. And again when he'd learned his beloved *mamm* had died. After he'd surrendered and released his anger, the Lord had given him peace. But now . . .

This time, he blamed himself rather than God. If he hadn't pursued his selfish wish, his *mamm* and Keturah's parents would be here. He forced words through his constricted throat. "For years, I'd dreamed about seeing the Pennsylvania Grand Canyon."

"So did my *daed*. He wanted to see one of the wonders God created."

"And he didn't get to do that." They hadn't made it to their destination. Jeremiah's selfish wish had cut short many lives.

"You were in the accident too, weren't you?" She looked as sick as he felt.

"*Jah*, and I wasn't conscious enough at first to find out who else had been . . ." Those horrible days in the hospital flooded back, and he battled against the darkness. He didn't want to get stuck in the past. "Once I started to recover, I should have checked."

"It seems like you had enough to do. I'm sure it wasn't easy."

"It wasn't, but I should have made time." If he had, he would have found out about Keturah's parents. Would he have done things differently if he'd known?

"But you took time to help others." Keturah wished she could say something else to wipe the guilty expression from his face. Even when he'd been in terrible pain, he'd spent time writing to her. And he'd jumped in and offered to help at the stand when he couldn't even do the job.

"I should have done more." Jeremiah set his elbows on the table and lowered his head into his hands. "Maybe some of the others have children or need assistance."

"A politician gave everyone money." Keturah had only recently learned about the money the man had deposited in her parents' account.

"But I could have helped in other ways."

"You did what you could at the time. You need to forgive yourself."

And speaking of forgiveness . . . Keturah took a deep breath. "The reason I asked you to stay is because of the letters . . ."

Jeremiah raised his head, his face a mask of anguish. "I wish I could go back and do it all differently. I wouldn't let pride get in the way."

"That's what I wanted to talk about—pride."

Jeremiah nodded and stared down at the table. Before he could apologize again, Keturah cut him off.

"My pride, not yours."

He lifted startled eyes, but Keturah couldn't hold his gaze. Not while she discussed this.

"After you told me you were the letter writer, I was upset and angry."

"I don't blame you for being furious. As Alyssa probed for my secrets today, I didn't want them splashed across the pages of a newspaper. It made me regret what I did to you even more."

Keturah needed to get this conversation back on track. She had a confession to make—several, in fact. "And I regret what I did to you."

"You didn't do anything to me."

"*Jah*, I did. I lied when I let you think I didn't want you to work at the stand anymore."

"I can come back?"

"We all need you, and"—she ducked her head—"I've missed you."

"I've missed you too." Jeremiah's voice was husky.

"But that's not the only thing I wanted to say. God

showed me that my anger came from embarrassment and pride."

Jeremiah started to speak, but Keturah held up her hand to stop him. She had to finish everything she intended to tell him.

She bit her lip. "No wonder God and the church warn us about *hochmut*. Pride keeps us silent when we should speak. It makes us pretend we're someone we're not. And it causes us to hide the truth."

"*Jah*, I did all of that. I'm so sorry, Keturah. I know I don't deserve it, but will you forgive me?"

She did, but she wanted him to understand she'd not been blameless. "You know how I fought forgiving my *daed*? I've spent the past few days struggling with forgiving you."

Jeremiah hung on her every word. The pleading in his eyes made her realize she hadn't answered his question.

"*Jah*, I forgive you."

Jeremiah expelled a long, relieved sigh.

"If you'll forgive me."

"Of course, but you haven't done anything wrong."

And now Keturah had to admit her own cover-up. She didn't want to keep any secrets from Jeremiah. Could she do this?

She focused on her nervous fingers pleating her apron as she forced out her words. "What upset me most about discovering you were the letter writer is my fear that I exposed my deepest feelings."

"It's all right. I went through many of the same doubts and questions."

"That's not the part that bothered me. You were a wonderful *gut* help with all of that." Keturah *rutsched* in her chair. "What embarrassed me most was the letter where I'd written about, um, caring for someone but being torn because—"

"You had feelings for someone else." Jeremiah finished her sentence in a monotone.

"*Jah*, I couldn't believe you'd read my thoughts about you." *Not just thoughts. Deepest feelings.*

Jeremiah drew in a sharp breath. "You wrote that about me?"

"*Jah*. I couldn't go out with you because I didn't want to give up writing the secrets of my heart to someone else."

"You mean the two men you were torn between were me and the letter writer? There's no one else?"

"*Neh*, there never has been." She forced herself to look up and meet Jeremiah's gaze. Her heartbeat accelerated at the excitement dancing in his eyes.

"So then"—he reached out to cover her hand with his—"can I ask you to go on another sleigh ride? Just the two of us?"

Keturah had only one answer for that question this time. A strong and sure *jah*.

Jeremiah's heart ricocheted hard against his chest, battering his ribs. He couldn't believe it. Keturah liked him in both of his roles. All the intimacy of their letters could now be added to their friendship—and a possible future relationship.

The market door banged open, and Mrs. Vandenberg tottered in.

Belatedly, Jeremiah realized he was still holding Keturah's hand. After a quick, gentle squeeze, he let go.

"Well, it doesn't look as if you two need an intervention." Mrs. Vandenberg appeared disappointed for a second, then she smiled. "I'm glad the newspaper interview did the trick."

Had she set that up to get them back together? Jeremiah had heard gossip that Mrs. Vandenberg enjoyed playing matchmaker.

After all she'd done for them, she deserved to have some pleasure.

Keturah beamed. "You'll be happy to know Jeremiah will be back at work tomorrow. And, yes, we both forgave each other." She frowned. "Well, I forgave Jeremiah. I'm not sure he forgave me."

"There's nothing to forgive." He tried to convey his answer with his eyes. *Love keeps no record of wrongs.*

"That's terrific. I'll have to pass along this news to Alys—" Mrs. Vandenberg tilted forward so eagerly, she almost toppled over.

Jeremiah reached out an arm to steady her.

"Thank you, young man, but I'd rather see those strong muscles where they belong—wrapped around your future wife's shoulders."

Had she read his mind again?

Keturah's cheeks pinkened, quickening his pulse.

Mrs. Vandenberg gave him a pointed look as if suggesting he should follow her instructions.

He cleared his throat. "We don't believe in doing things like that."

As he spoke, Keturah's cheeks flushed brighter.

"What a pity." Mrs. Vandenberg shook her head. "Well,

if you can bear to take your eyes off Keturah for a second, I'd like to lock up the building."

Now it was Jeremiah's turn for burning cheeks.

A few days later, Mrs. Vandenberg's influence and matchmaking talents again became evident.

After a starry Saturday night snuggled beside Keturah, both of them wrapped in blankets as falling snow kissed their cheeks, Jeremiah dragged himself away from his sweet dreams of her on Sunday morning when a sharp *rat-a-tat-tat* bounced against his bedroom door.

Darryl peeked into the room with a grin on his face. He pulled a newspaper from behind his back. "Look who made the first page of the *Star*'s Lifestyle section."

The headline jumped out at Jeremiah: *Tragedy Births a Christmas Miracle.* A large pink heart tied with a Christmas bow encircled a picture of him and Keturah from the back. He held out his hand, eager to see the pictures up close. Not of him, but of Keturah.

Then he skimmed the story. With great skill, Alyssa had woven their joint tragedy into a God-ordained meeting that resulted in hope, healing, and love. She'd also intertwined the story of Christ's birth into his and Keturah's trials and triumphs.

Alyssa had quoted Mrs. Vandenberg about Keturah and him finding true love. Now that he was confident Keturah shared his feelings, he didn't mind if the whole world knew.

Chapter Thirty

The next few weeks flew by as Keturah spent as much time with Jeremiah as possible after work, often with her sisters. On rare occasions, they managed to sneak off alone.

With snow on the ground and pine perfuming the air, they enjoyed the season, but Keturah still hadn't fulfilled her resolution to make Christmas special for her sisters.

"I wanted to make a special gift for each of them," she confided in Jeremiah. "But I haven't had a chance."

"Maybe I'm taking up too much of your time," he teased.

"*Neh.*" Every minute she spent with him was precious.

"Why don't we go downtown to shop?" With a twinkle in his eye, he added, "Since you're getting gifts, it can be just the two of us."

"Perfect."

As she and Jeremiah headed home with books for her sisters, they took the long way around so they could admire the lights and decorations. Once they reached the farmlands, only a few houses had candles in the windows.

Keturah breathed in the peaceful atmosphere as they

pulled into her driveway. "The bright lights were pretty, but I like God's lights better." She pointed to the stars overhead.

"I do too." But Jeremiah seemed to be staring at her instead of the sky. "I also enjoy looking at starlit eyes."

Her cheeks heated, and her whole body tingled under his gaze. Breathless, she asked, "You're coming caroling with our church group tomorrow night, aren't you?"

"I can't wait."

Neither could she.

Caroling with Jeremiah on Christmas Eve proved to be magical. The cold, crisp air invigorated her—or maybe part of it was Jeremiah's presence. And Keturah's heart soared as her soprano notes blended with his bass. She'd never felt so in tune with anyone before. She couldn't help dreaming of a future together.

Maleah kept wriggling between them, though.

Lilliane leaned over and whispered to her little sister, "Why don't you stand on Jeremiah's other side?"

"I can't. Snickers is in the way."

"Here." Jeremiah jiggled the leash to move Snickers forward and make a spot for Maleah.

Now Keturah could move closer to Jeremiah. She kept one mittened hand on his chair arm. Although he shouldn't, a few times as they hung back from the group, he gave her hand a quick squeeze.

As everyone headed off afterward, Keturah invited him back to the house for hot chocolate.

With a secret smile, he asked, "Will we get any time alone?"

"I'll do my best."

By the time they returned, everyone was shivering. Keturah sent Maleah up to take a warm bath and get ready for bed. Then Lilliane and Rose went into the kitchen while Jeremiah kindled a fire. Keturah lit the candles on the pine-draped mantel and savored this brief time alone with him. They thawed their hands and toes over the flames, and Snickers curled up near the hearth.

Soon, her sisters returned with mugs of hot chocolate and plates of Christmas cookies. The steamy, chocolatey liquid, the smoke drifting from the hearth, the bite of cinnamon on her tongue, and Jeremiah's nearness filled Keturah with contentment.

Only one thing was missing—their parents. More than anything, she wished Mamm could be here to meet Jeremiah. Her eyes stung.

As if sensing her distress, Jeremiah's fingers, warm and comforting, closed over her hand. His sympathetic gaze met hers. He must be missing his *mamm* too.

Nostalgic for Christmases past, they all stared into the flames until Maleah pranced downstairs in her nightgown, her damp hair hanging loose.

"Yummy." She reached for the cookies.

"Let me fix your hair." Reluctantly, Keturah let go of Jeremiah's hand and, with rapid, practiced moves, tamed her sister's unruly hair into a neat braid that hung to the middle of her back.

"I love Christmas! Don't you, Jeremiah?" Maleah danced in a circle. "It's my favorite time of year." Her braid flew in the air as she twirled.

Keturah dove for the hot chocolate tray before Maleah knocked it off the table.

"Stop!" Jeremiah thundered. "Don't move!" His words cracked through the air, freezing everyone in place.

Keturah gripped the tray, her eyes on his contorted face as he stared at Maleah. Inside, she shriveled. A replay of Daed's temper. The old sickness welled up.

He kept his eyes fixed on her sister. "Don't move an inch," he commanded.

Maleah, eyes wide with horror, trembled. Keturah's defensiveness, her protectiveness kicked in.

Jeremiah raced his wheelchair toward Maleah, who stood like a statue, arms still outstretched. Keturah barreled after him. She grabbed for the handles to pull him away.

"*Neh!*" he yelled. He jerked away from her.

She grabbed again and held fast, throwing all her body weight back to keep him in place. She didn't know what had gotten into him, but she had to stop him. She'd never let him hurt Maleah.

Suddenly, he lurched from the chair. Keturah had been pulling so hard, the empty wheelchair slammed backward, smashed against her, and knocked her over. She hit the floor hard.

She had to get to her sister before he did. But he stood and tottered forward. How long had he been able to walk? Had he been faking all this time?

He staggered past Maleah and reached toward the mantel. With one hand he supported himself against it, and with the other, he gently untangled the end of her braid from the candleholder.

Keturah's breath hissed out.

If Maleah had moved, she'd have pulled the candle down on her.

Adrenaline still coursing through her veins, Keturah couldn't stop shaking. "I'm so sorry, Jeremiah." Her voice came out as a whimper.

Jeremiah didn't answer. Still supporting himself on the mantel, he tucked Maleah's braid over her shoulder.

The tenderness and caring in that gesture melted Keturah's heart.

"It's all right now," he soothed, although his breath still hitched in his chest from the near-accident. And from standing so suddenly.

Her face a mask of dread, Maleah stared at him looming over her. Then she collapsed onto the floor in hysterics. Curling into a ball, she rocked back and forth.

Jeremiah lowered himself to the floor beside her. He landed heavily. He had no idea how he'd get up again, but he had to comfort Maleah.

Cradling her in his arms, he whispered, "I didn't mean to scare you."

Across the room, Keturah winced and pulled herself to her feet. Had he knocked her over with his wheelchair? He hadn't meant to do that either.

Sobs shook Maleah's body, and he pulled her closer.

"You . . . yelled . . . at me," she gasped out between cries.

"I didn't want you to get hurt. If you'd moved forward, your braid would have pulled the candle down on you."

Keturah knelt beside them and smoothed a few loose strands of Maleah's hair back from her face. "You're all right now. Jeremiah saved you."

"I thought"—Maleah broke into fresh wailing—"I thought . . . you were Daed."

Keturah shivered. If only Jeremiah could wrap an arm around her too and pull her close. The story she'd told him in the letter flashed through his mind. Their father's temper. How she'd challenged him. Like she'd done here.

He turned to her with an admiring smile. "You're fierce when you're defending your sister. Remind me never to get in your way when Maleah's hurt."

"I really am sorry. I didn't notice her braid."

"You were too focused on chasing me." He'd meant to tease her, but as soon as he said it, he realized that could be taken two ways. His cheeks heated, and he hoped she couldn't tell in the candlelit room.

Most likely she could, because her cheeks darkened, and she pressed her hands against them. "I thought you were going to hurt Maleah. I had to stop you."

"You did that for sure."

"But you walked." She stared at him in wonder. "How long have you been doing that?"

Was that a hint of suspicion in her tone?

"A few weeks, but I'm still not steady on my feet. I can't go far."

"You reached Maleah."

Maleah peeped up at him and sniffled. "I thought you were going to hit me."

"*Ach*, Maleah, I'd never do that. And I promise never to yell at you again either."

"You do?"

He nodded.

"Except if it's an emergency," Lilliane said behind them.

Jeremiah twisted around to face her. She sat on the

couch, her hands bunching her apron. Rose stood in the doorway with a fist pressed against her lips.

Jeremiah wished he could go back and undo his harsh words, but he'd had no other way to reach Maleah in time. "I didn't mean to frighten everyone."

"You did, though," came Lilliane's blunt reply. "But you had to," she conceded.

"Will you all forgive me?"

Keturah stood and brushed down her skirt and apron. "There's nothing to forgive. As Lilliane said, you did what you had to do, and we're all grateful to you for saving Maleah. When I think of what could have happened . . ." She shuddered.

Maleah threw her arms around his neck and hugged him. "*Danke*, Jeremiah."

It had been so long since he'd been hugged. Mamm hadn't been much of a hugger, but the day of the trip, she'd pulled him into a hug and told him she loved him. Had she somehow sensed it would be their last day together?

His throat constricted, and his eyes burned. He couldn't believe he'd be spending Christmas without her, but Maleah would be missing both her parents. So would Keturah, Lilliane, and Rose. If only he had some way to ease their grief.

Maleah pulled back so she could look up at him. "Will you come for Christmas tomorrow?"

He'd been planning to stop by to drop off presents and maybe talk to Keturah. For the past two weeks, he'd been planning what to say.

"*Jah*," Rose and Lilliane chorused.

Only one person hadn't spoken. Keturah. He had to check with her first.

She stood staring down at him, her eyes wet with tears. "You're always welcome."

Lilliane took one look at the two of them and shepherded her sisters from the room. "Time for bed, everyone."

As the footsteps faded up the stairs, he and Keturah were alone at last. She sank onto the floor beside him.

"*Danke* for your quick reaction. You saved Maleah. I'm still shaking." She held out a trembling hand.

Jeremiah wrapped his hands around both of her small, soft ones. He'd intended to comfort her, but he hadn't counted on his reaction. Could she hear his heart hammering out of control? He let go of her hands.

"Oh, Jeremiah." She gazed at him as if he were a hero.

His heart leapt. Maybe she'd be ready to hear what he planned to say.

"You gave Maleah something I always dreamed of—a hug to comfort me when I cried."

He longed to do that now, but he clutched at his suspenders to keep from reaching for her. He determined that if she said *jah*, he'd always hold her whenever she cried. And plenty of other times too.

"Daed didn't believe in coddling us, and he didn't want us to cry. You're so good for Maleah." She ducked her head and peeped up at him shyly from beneath her lashes. "You're good for all of us."

Was this the opening he'd been waiting for?

"And all of you have been good for me too." He hesitated a moment, then added softly, "Especially you."

A slow smile spread across her face, and she stared up at him, starry-eyed.

All the words he'd rehearsed fled. All he wanted to do was sweep her into his arms, but he restrained himself. "I have something to ask you," he stammered.

"The answer is *jah*."

"You don't know the question."

Her expression softened. "I'll always say *jah* to you."

"But . . . but . . ." It couldn't be this easy. Not after he'd agonized for days. Not after he'd practiced what he'd say for hours on end. Not after spending all last evening writing a letter. His first love letter.

He reached into his pocket and handed it to her.

She took it and pressed it to her heart. "I've missed your letters." Firelight illuminated her beautiful face as she opened and read it. Then she lifted damp eyes to his face.

"My answer's still the same. *Jah*, you may court me."

Jeremiah wanted to ask her something much bigger, but this was the first step to his greater dream. He intended to be walking when he asked that next question.

His heart filled with happiness, he pulled her into a hug. With a contented sigh, she rested her head against his shoulder, sending a thrill through him. And he vowed to keep up the letter-writing tradition for the rest of their lives together.

Epilogue

Three years later . . .

Under a mantel draped with evergreens, flames blazed bright. With Snickers curled beside him, Jeremiah sat on the floor, his arms outstretched. Keturah stood several feet away, holding their year-old daughter's hand.

"Walk to Daed." Keturah let go, and Beth toddled a few steps before tumbling into his arms.

"Very good, Bethie." Jeremiah hugged her, then smiled at her adorable mother. He'd give her a hug later. He hadn't forgotten the promise he'd made to himself to hold her whenever he could. And he'd make sure their daughter never lacked cuddling.

Keturah held out her arms. "Let Bethie walk back to me."

Jeremiah set Beth on her feet and supported her until she had her balance. "Go to your *mamm*."

His daughter took several unsteady steps and almost fell. Keturah reached out to catch her.

"Beth walks like me," Jeremiah observed.

"She does not."

"You're right. She does a better job."

"Oh, you." Cradling Beth, Keturah scooted over next to him and leaned her head against his arm. "You barely limp when you're tired. You've come so far."

"I'm grateful to God for that." And for the lessons he'd learned along the way. God had shown Jeremiah that He could use any situation for His glory. Even though he might never recover completely, Jeremiah had surrendered his future to the Lord, confident he could trust God's will in all things.

"I'm thankful too." Keturah cuddled closer. "I've always loved you. And I always will. No matter what."

Keturah's unconditional love had taught Jeremiah to accept himself and to be thankful in all circumstances. They'd weathered a lot of hardships together, but God had been there every step of the way.

Still cradling his precious daughter, who'd been their special Christmas gift last year, he leaned over and kissed Keturah's forehead. His whole being swelled with gratitude for all God had given him.

He and Keturah both missed their parents, especially around the holidays. If only his mother could meet Bethie. Mamm would adore her. Jeremiah swallowed the huge lump in his throat.

"I wish Mamm were here. She loved babies."

Jeremiah marveled at how often the two of them mirrored each other's thoughts. "I was thinking the same thing about my *mamm*."

Keturah breathed out a sigh. "I should be grateful for what I have. God has given us so much."

He certainly had.

Beth reached up, grabbed Jeremiah's beard, and tugged.

"Ouch." Jeremiah gently disentangled her hand. "If you

keep pulling on my beard, you might make me look like a bachelor."

"*Neh*, you'd better not." Keturah fake frowned—not at Bethie, but at him. "If she rips out even one hair, you save it. I'll glue it back on. I don't want anyone to think you're single."

Jeremiah laughed. "You look as stern as you did that day I yelled at Maleah."

Keturah tried to hide her smile but ended up bursting into giggles. "I still can't believe I did that."

"What's so funny?" Maleah stood in the doorway.

"Remember when I grabbed Jeremiah's wheelchair to stop him from hurting you?"

"Jeremiah's never, ever hurt me." Maleah sounded indignant.

"I mean that's what I thought he was going to do. He was only trying to rescue you from that candle."

Ever since that Christmas, Keturah only set out battery-powered candles. They didn't look quite as pretty, but they were safer.

"I remember that." At ten, she looked as if she wanted to forget she'd been that young.

The scent of turkey wafted into the room, and Keturah rose. "I need to baste the turkey."

"Let me help you." Jeremiah pushed up with one hand, slightly overbalanced by Bethie.

Maleah rushed over. She held out her arms for Beth, who giggled and went to her aunt. "I'll take her into the kitchen and get her a snack."

The front door banged open, and two people stomped their boots on the mat.

"Is that you, Lilliane?"

"*Jah*, and Michael."

Lilliane and Michael had started courting a few months ago, and the change it had made to her disposition was remarkable. The young couple poked their heads into the living room, both of them grinning from ear to ear.

"We'll go help in the kitchen."

"*Danke.* Jeremiah and I will be coming soon."

"It's going to be a crowded kitchen," Jeremiah whispered as he drew Keturah to him. "Maybe we can have a little *alone* time first."

"I'd like that." She gave him a secretive smile and slid a hand into her pocket. Paper crinkled. Keturah always kept his most recent letter close. She tied the rest with ribbon and saved them in her top dresser drawer. Even the very first ones he'd sent her.

He'd kept his vow and still wrote love letters to her at least once a week. He loved watching his wife shed a tear or two over each one.

Four Christmases together, and each one was sweeter than the one before. "God sent His most special gift on Christmas, His only Son. And then He gave me you, the love of my life."

"And Bethie."

"*Jah*, and Bethie." Jeremiah's soul overflowed with gratitude as Keturah snuggled against his chest and lifted her face for his kiss. He held his darling wife close and let his lips express all the tenderness and thankfulness in his heart for her and for all of the many blessings they shared.